D0059704

New York Times and *USA TODAY* bestselling author **Heather Graham** has written more than two hundred novels. She is pleased to have been published in over twenty-five languages, with sixty million books in print. Heather is a proud recipient of the Silver Bullet from Thriller Writers and was awarded the prestigious Thriller Master Award in 2016. She is also a recipient of Lifetime Achievement Awards from RWA and *The Strand*, and is the founder of The Slush Pile Players, an author band and theatrical group. An avid scuba diver, ballroom dancer and mother of five, she still enjoys her South Florida home, but also loves to travel. Heather is grateful every day for a career she loves so very much.

For more information, check out her website, theoriginalheathergraham.com, or find Heather on Facebook.

Delores Fossen, a *USA TODAY* bestselling author, has sold over seventy-five novels, with millions of copies of her books in print worldwide. She's received a Booksellers' Best Award and an RT Reviewers' Choice Best Book Award. She was also a finalist for a prestigious RITA® Award. You can contact the author through her website at www.deloresfossen.com.

New York Times **Bestselling Author**

HEATHER GRAHAM

THE LAST NOEL

**HARLEQUIN
BESTSELLING
AUTHOR
COLLECTION**

**HARLEQUIN®
BESTSELLING
AUTHOR
COLLECTION**

Recycling programs
for this product may
not exist in your area.

ISBN-13: 978-1-335-40624-8

The Last Noel
First published in 2007. This edition published in 2021.
Copyright © 2007 by Heather Graham Pozzessere

Secret Surrogate
First published in 2006. This edition published in 2021.
Copyright © 2006 by Delores Fossen

This edition published by arrangement with Harlequin Books S.A.

For questions and comments about the quality of this book, please contact us at CustomerService@Harlequin.com.

Harlequin Enterprises ULC
22 Adelaide St. West, 40th Floor
Toronto, Ontario M5H 4E3, Canada
www.Harlequin.com

Printed in Lithuania

MIX
Paper from
responsible sources
FSC® C021394

CONTENTS

THE LAST NOEL
Heather Graham

With much love and best wishes for some wonderful people who are like Christmas gifts all year long:

Aaron Priest, Lucy Childs, Adam Wilson,
Dianne Moggy, Margaret Marbury,
Loriana Sacilotto, Donna Hayes, Craig Swinwood,
Alex Osuszek, K.O., Marleah and all the folks in PR
and art, and very especially for an incredible woman
who can also spell—Leslie Wainger.

Prologue

"But...this is *Christmas Eve!*"

The old man, frail and almost skeletally thin, stared at them in disbelief. His voice was tremulous, and he seemed to shake like a delicate, wind-blown leaf.

"You're right. It *is* Christmas Eve, old-timer, and you're not supposed to be here," Scooter said.

Craig found that he couldn't speak. This wasn't supposed to happen. There shouldn't have been anyone here. When he'd hooked up with Scooter Blane, the man had been all but invisible. He and his partner, Quintin Lark, were becoming heroes in a certain stratum of underworld society for their long string of extremely profitable robberies. But no one had ever gotten hurt. Ever.

But they only hit places that were empty.

Like this place should have been today.

There had been rumors, though. Rumors that the pair could be ruthless when they chose. But rumors were just rumors. Crooks needed them, went out of their way to create them, because they lived and died for them.

Killed for them?

But the real word on the street was that the pair were experts at slipping in and slipping out. Hitting fast, disappearing.

As far as Craig had been aware, they had never hurt anyone or even, thanks to careful planning, come across anyone still working during one of their heists.

He had discovered when he threw in with them that Scooter was frighteningly savvy with electronics. He'd seen that demonstrated when they arrived tonight and Scooter had broken the alarm code in a matter of seconds, unlocking the door as if they were being invited right in by an invisible host.

And now...

Now he was discovering that Scooter was equally adept with firearms.

Like the Smith & Wesson .48 special he suddenly pulled.

"But I *am* here. And I'm not letting you destroy my livelihood," the old man said now, despite the gun in Scooter's hand.

Craig was pretty sure that the octogenarian's name had to be Hudson. The sign on the small shop in the valley advertised it as Hudson & Son, Fine Art, Antiques, Memorabilia and Jewelry.

It was the jewelry and antiques they'd come for. Scooter and Quintin were becoming infamous all through the Northeast for knocking off a long string of jewelry and antique stores. They went for family establishments—the type not found in malls. The kind in small towns, where the biggest crimes tended to be speeding or graffiti. They struck, then disappeared, and the insurance agencies were the ones to pay. Easy in, easy out, and no one got hurt, except in the wallet.

Craig had never heard of Scooter or Quintin using a gun.

Then again, he'd never heard of them ripping off a place where someone had remained behind after hours.

But there was a first time for everything. Here, in a little hick town in Massachusetts, they had found the place where someone was still around.

Craig felt ill.

He knew the pair were successful because of Scooter's talent with electronics, which ensured that they were never caught on videotape. No witness could ever describe their faces, because there never were any witnesses. In short, they had never been seen.

Until now.

"Scooter, it's Christmas. Let's just get the hell out of here," Craig said.

Scooter looked at him, shaking his head as he scooped up jewelry and threw it into a bag. "No, sorry, I don't think so. Even if I wanted to, and I don't, I don't think Quintin's ready to go."

That was all too obvious, Craig thought, looking over at the other man. Already Craig had figured out that, while Scooter talked as if he called the shots, it was Quintin who really ran the operation. And Quintin wasn't all that fond of Craig, so he knew he had to be careful.

"There's got to be a safe, so open it, pops," Quintin was saying now.

"Sir, please," Craig said politely to Mr. Hudson, silently begging the old man to back down and do as he was told. "Open the safe."

"No."

"I'll shoot you, you old fart, and don't think I won't," Scooter told him.

"Do it," the old man said.

"Come on, guys. There's a storm coming in, and we need to get the hell out of here before it does," Craig said. "Why don't we just leave the old guy alone and get out of here?"

"Told you that the kid was a mistake," Quintin said disgustedly to Scooter. Quintin was a big man, but not fat. He was pure muscle, with small dark eyes, a bald head and the shoulders of an orangutan. He was oddly fanatic in his dress. He liked to be neat, and he was fond of designer clothing. He was in his forties, and despite his occupation, he was quite capable of speaking and appearing like a gentleman.

Scooter was just the opposite: thin as a rail. He had a wiry strength, though. Sandy hair worn a little too long, and eyes that were so pale a blue they were almost colorless. Scooter was somewhere in his midthirties, and Craig was becoming more and more convinced that he had some kind of learning disability. He often sounded totally vicious, but at other times his voice held the awe of a child, and he was sometimes slow.

Craig was the youngest of their trio and the newcomer. He wondered just how odd he looked, joined up with the two of them. At twenty-five, he considered himself in good shape, but, of course, the life he'd chosen demanded that he be fit. Bitterness at the past had made him work hard. He was blue-eyed and blond, like the boy next door. Quintin had liked that about him. What Quintin didn't like about him, Craig had never quite figured out.

As they all stood there, at something of an impasse, the store was suddenly cast into pitch-darkness as a loud crack announced the splitting of a nearby power pole.

"Nobody move," Scooter snapped.

A backup generator kicked in almost immediately, and they were bathed in a soft, slightly reddish light. In those few seconds, though, the old man had tried to hit the alarm. Craig could read the truth in his eyes and in the nervous energy that made him shake just slightly. Scooter saw it, too.

"You stupid old fool," Scooter said softly.

"The power was out," Craig said quickly. "The alarm was dead."

"I don't give a damn," Scooter said. "Open the safe. Now!"

But old man Hudson seemed totally indifferent to his own impending doom. He even smiled. "I don't care if you shoot me."

"Just open the safe, sir. What can possibly be in there that's worth your life?" Craig asked.

Quintin looked at him contemptuously.

"Look, you old fool," Quintin said to Hudson, "He won't just shoot you, he'll make you hurt. He'll shoot your kneecaps, and then he'll shoot your teeny-weeny little pecker. Now open the safe!"

"You must have insurance," Craig pointed out reasonably. He was stunned at Quintin's viciousness. Not that he knew the man well. This was actually his first real job with Scooter and Quintin. Before, he had been trying to pass muster. When he'd been taken along tonight, he'd thought he'd been cleared. And he had been—by Scooter. But Quintin was hard.

And Quintin didn't like him. Didn't trust him.

Craig knew they'd worked with another guy before, who hadn't been arrested, and hadn't been found dead. He had just disappeared. And that was how Craig had gotten in.

Well, he'd wanted in, and he'd gotten what he wanted,

Craig thought, and swore silently to himself. This wasn't the way it should have gone. And now he was going to have to do something about that.

Scooter still looked ready to shoot. The situation was rapidly turning violent.

Craig reached nonchalantly behind his back for the Glock he carried tucked into his waistband. Before he could produce it, Quintin slammed him on the shoulder. "You've got no bullets, buddy," he said softly.

Craig frowned fiercely, staring at him.

Quintin stared back, dark eyes cool and assessing. "Were you planning to shoot the old man—or one of us?" he asked. "I took away your bullets, *friend*."

"Why'd you do that?" Scooter demanded.

"Didn't you hear me? I don't trust him not to shoot one of us," Quintin said, then turned back to Hudson. "Come on, asshole. It's now or never."

"*You're* the asshole, Quintin," Craig said. Damn it, he thought. What was he going to do without any bullets?

Finally the old man turned and started turning the dial on the safe. As soon as it opened, he stepped away, staring off into the distance, as if none of it meant anything to him anymore.

Craig felt a sudden deep, overwhelming surge of sadness. What the hell was this old man doing alone on Christmas Eve? Where was the son listed on the sign? Where was the rest of his family?

Was this really the sum of life? Men wanted sons. Sons wanted the keys to the car. *Sure, Dad,* the son said. *I'll help with the business.* And then he found something else that interested him more and was gone, until one day Dad was old. And alone.

"Bag it up," Scooter demanded, pointing to the bills and jewelry in the safe. "Bag it all up."

"You know you're not going anywhere, right?" the old man asked calmly.

"Wrong, pops. We're going straight to New York City. Hiding in plain sight," Scooter said happily.

Craig felt his stomach drop. Scooter had just told the old man their plans, not to mention that Hudson had seen their faces. Craig could practically see the death warrant in his mind.

"A nor'easter is coming in," the old man said, sounding so casual. "Hasn't been one this bad in years, I can tell you."

The weather *was* turning; Craig could feel it. The storm that should have gone north of them had veered south instead, he thought, then went back to wondering why Hudson was at work and alone on Christmas Eve.

"Right. Like I'm afraid of a little snow." Scooter sniffed.

Did the old man have a cell phone? Craig wondered. He had lied before. He was certain the man had hit his alarm already, but there were no sirens drawing near, no sign of help.

Now, with no indication of panic or hurry, the man started filling the bag Scooter handed him with bills and jewelry.

"We got it all. Let's go," Craig said.

"*You* go," Quintin said. "Get in the driver's seat and wait for us. And don't fuck up."

"Let's all get the hell out of here," Craig said. "Come on. You've got what you came for."

"Wuss." Quintin sniffed. "Or worse."

"What do you mean, worse?" Scooter asked.

"Cop."

"I'm no cop. I just don't want to do life over a couple of

lousy bracelets," Craig said, but he felt a bead of sweat on his upper lip. Quintin was one scary SOB. His eyes were like glass. No emotion, empathy or remorse lay anywhere behind that stare.

"The old guy's seen our faces, and thanks to Scooter—" he shot the man a scathing glance "—he knows where we're going," Quintin said.

"And he's probably legally blind and totally deaf," Craig argued.

"I'm not taking that chance," Quintin said harshly.

"And I'm not going to be party to murder," Craig said and turned to appeal to the other man. "Scooter, you're an idiot if you listen to this thug," he said. "We'll all get locked away forever for murder, and I'm not as old as you guys. I don't want to spend the next fifty years without a woman."

Quintin started to laugh. "Don't worry about it, kid. They lock up people like Martha Stewart. Killers, hell, they get to walk away free. Crazy, isn't it?"

"Craig…we gotta do what Quintin says," Scooter insisted.

"Even if what he says is stupid?" Craig asked.

"Fuck you," Quintin said, casually pulling out a gun. "Keep talking like that and you won't have to worry about jail."

Craig assessed his situation. No question it was dire. He was probably in the best shape of his life, and he was the youngest of the three of them. In a fair fight, he could probably take out Quintin, no matter that the man was an ape. But there were two of them. And it wasn't going to be a fair fight. Because they had guns. With bullets.

There would never be a fair fight with Quintin.

He turned to plead with Scooter again, but he was too late. Quintin, moving faster than Craig would have thought possible for a man his size, cracked Craig on the head with the butt of his gun.

Craig literally saw stars, and then the world went black.

As he sank to the ground, he heard the deafening sound of an explosion.

The blast of a gun...

He'd screwed up.

What a great, last thought to have—and on Christmas Eve.

As he sank into unconsciousness, he was certain he could hear the familiar refrain of a Christmas carol.

Oh, tidings of comfort and joy.

Chapter 1

The stereo was on, playing songs of Christmas cheer. Skyler O'Boyle took a moment to listen to a woman with a high, clear voice who was singing, "Sleigh bells ring, are you lis'nin'…"

Then, even over the music and from her place in the kitchen, she heard the yelling.

"I said hold it. Hold the tree!"

Skyler winced.

Christmas. Home for the holidays, merry, merry, ho, ho, ho, family love, world peace.

In her family? Yeah, right.

The expected answer came, and the voice was just as loud. "I *am* holding it," her eldest son insisted.

"Straight, dammit, Frazier. Hold it straight," her husband, David, snapped irritably.

In her mind's eye, Skyler could see them, David on the floor, trying to wedge the tree into the stand, and Frazier, standing, trying to hold the tree straight. That was what happened when you decided "home for the holidays" meant everyone gathering in the old family house out in the country. It meant throwing everything together at the last possible moment, because everyone had to juggle their school and work schedules with their holiday vacation.

"The frigging needles are poking my eyes. This is the best I can do," Frazier complained in what sounded suspiciously like a growl.

His tone was sure to aggravate his father, she thought.

Some people got Christmas cheer; she got David and Frazier fighting over the tree.

Where the hell had the spirit of the season gone, at least in her family? Actually, if she wanted to get philosophical, where had the spirit of the season gone in a large part of the known world? There were no real Norman Rockwell paintings. People walked by the Salvation Army volunteers without a glance; it seemed as if the only reason anyone put money in the kettle was that they were burdened by so much change that it was actually too heavy for comfort. Then they beat each other up over the latest electronic toy to hit the market.

"It's nowhere near straight," David roared.

"Put up your own fucking tree, then," Frazier shouted.

"Son of a bitch…" David swore.

"…walkin' in a winter wonderland."

Please, God, Skyler prayed silently, *don't let my husband and my son come to blows on Christmas Eve.*

"Hey, Kat, you there?"

Great, Skyler thought. Now David was getting their daughter involved.

"Yeah, Dad, I'm here. But I can't hold that tree any

straighter. And I hope Brenda didn't hear you two yell-ing," Kat said.

Skyler headed out toward the living room, ready to head off a major family disaster, and paused just out of sight in the hall.

Had she been wrong? Should she have told her son he shouldn't bring Brenda home for the holidays? He'd turned twenty-two. He could have told her that he wasn't coming home, in that case, and was going to spend the holidays with Brenda's family. And then she would have been with-out her first-born child. Of course, that was going to hap-pen somewhere along the line anyway; that was life. With the kids getting older, it was already hard to get the entire family together.

"Oh, so now I have to worry—in my own house—about offending the girl who came here to sleep with my son?" David complained.

David wasn't a bad man, Skyler thought. He wasn't even a bad father. But he had different ideas about what was proper and what wasn't. They had been children them-selves, really, when they had gotten married. She had been eighteen, and he had been nineteen. But even as desper-ately in love as they had been, there was no way either of them could have told their parents that they were going to live together.

Current mores might be much wiser, she reflected. Most of *her* generation seemed to be divorced.

"What century are you living in, Dad?" Frazier de-manded. Apparently his train of thought was running alongside hers. "There's nothing wrong with Brenda stay-ing in my room. It's not as if we don't sleep together back at school. You should trust my judgment. And don't go getting all 'I'm so respectable, this girl better be golden.' We're not exactly royalty, Dad. We own a bar," he finished dryly.

"We own a pub, a fine family place," David snapped back irritably. "And what's that supposed to mean, anyway? That pub is paying for college for both you and your sister."

"I'm just saying that some people wouldn't consider owning a bar the height of morality."

"Morality?" David exploded. "We've never once been cited for underage drinking, and we're known across the country for bringing the best in Celtic music to the States."

"Dad, it's all right," Kat said soothingly. "And you… shut the hell up," she said, and elbowed her brother in the ribs. "Both of you—play nice."

Skyler held her breath as Frazier walked away and headed upstairs, probably to make sure his girlfriend hadn't heard her name evoked in the family fight.

It was probably best. Her husband and son were always at each other's throats, it seemed, while Kat was the family peacemaker, who could ease the toughest situation. She'd gone through her own period of teenage rebellion on the way to becoming an adult, and getting along with her had been hell for a while. But that was over, and now Kat was like Skyler's miracle of optimism, beautiful and sweet. A dove of peace.

She wanted to think that she was a dove of peace herself, but she wasn't and she knew it.

She was just a chicken. A chicken who hated harsh tones and the sounds of disagreement. Sometimes she was even a lying chicken, for the sake of keeping the peace.

But this was Christmas. She had to say something to David. He really shouldn't be using that tone—not here, not now and not with Frazier.

Frazier just… He just wasn't a child anymore. He didn't

always act like an adult, but that didn't make him a child. David was far too quick to judge and to judge harshly, while she was too quick to let anything go, all for the sake of peace. There had been hundreds of times through the years when she should have stepped in, put her foot down. She'd failed. So how could she blame others now for doing what she'd always allowed them to do?

At last she stepped out of the shadows of the hallway and looked at the tree. "It's lovely," she said.

"It's crooked," David told her, his mouth set in a hard line.

"It's fine," she insisted softly.

"That's what I say, Mom," Kat said. She was twenty-two, as well, their second-born child and Frazier's twin. She walked over to Skyler and set an arm around her mother's shoulders. "I'll get going on the lights."

"*I'll* get the lights up," David said. "You can take it from there."

Skyler looked at her daughter. Kat could still show her temper on occasion, but she could stand against her father with less friction than Frazier. Maybe the problem with David and Frazier was a testosterone thing, like in a pride of lions. There was only room for one alpha male.

But this was Christmas. Couldn't they all get along? At least on Christmas Eve and Christmas Day? Other people counted their blessings; shouldn't they do the same? They had three beautiful, healthy children: Jamie, their youngest son, was sixteen, and then there were the twins. None of them had ever been in serious trouble—just that one prank of Jamie's, and that should be enough for anyone, shouldn't it?

"Mom," Kat said, "I'll decorate. Anyone who wants to can just pitch in."

David was already struggling with the lights, but he paused to look at Skyler for a moment. He still had the powerful look of a young man. His hair was thick and dark, with just a few strands of what she privately felt were a very *dignified* gray. She had been the one to pass on the rich red hair to her children, but the emerald-gold eyes that were so bewitching on Kat had come from her father.

Where have the years gone? she wondered, looking at him. He was still a good-looking and interesting man, but it was easy to forget that sometimes. And sometimes it was easy to wonder if being married wasn't more a habit than a commitment of the heart.

Skyler winced. She loved her family. Desperately.

Too desperately?

David cursed beneath his breath, then exploded. "They can put a man on the moon, but they can't invent Christmas lights that don't tangle and make you check every freaking bulb."

"Dad, they do make lights where the whole string doesn't go if one bulb is blown. Our lights are just old," Kat explained patiently.

Skyler looked at her daughter, feeling a rush of emotion that threatened to become tears. She loved her children equally, but at this moment Kat seemed exceptionally precious. She was stunning, of course, with her long auburn hair. Tall and slim—though, like many young women, she was convinced she needed to take off ten pounds. Those eyes like gold-flecked emeralds. And she had an amazing head on her shoulders.

"Yeah, well…if we stayed in Boston and *prepared* for Christmas…" David muttered.

Not fair, she thought. He was the one who had found this place years ago and he'd fallen in love with it first. Once upon a time, they had come here often. The kids had loved to leave the city and drive the two hours out to the country. They never left the state, but they went from the sea to the mountains. And everyone loved it.

She realized why she had wanted to come here so badly. It was a way to keep her family around her. It was a way to make sure that if her son and his father got into a fight over the Christmas turkey, Frazier couldn't just get up and drive off to a friend's house. Was it wrong to cling so desperately to her children and her dream of family?

"Mom, need any help in the kitchen?" Kat asked. It was clearly going to be a while until the lights were up and she could start on the ornaments.

Skyler shook her head. "Actually, I'm fine. Everything is more or less ready. We're going traditional Irish tonight—corned beef, bacon, cabbage and potatoes, and it's all in one pot. We can eat soon. Tomorrow we'll have turkey."

"Want me to set the table while Dad argues with the lights?" Kat asked.

Skyler grinned. "See if you can help him argue with the lights, and I'll set the table. We'll just eat in the kitchen, where it's warm and cozy."

Kat smiled at her mother.

Skyler couldn't have asked for a better daughter, she thought as she made her way back to the kitchen. They shared clothes and confidences, and she had learned not to worry every time her daughter drove away.

With her daughter here…

Skyler felt as if there were a chance for a Norman Rockwell Christmas after all.

Frazier came running down the stairs, followed by Brenda. They were an attractive couple, she had to admit. He was so tall, muscled without being bulky, with hair a deeper shade of red than his sister's. And he, too, had his father's eyes. Next to him, Brenda was tiny, delicate. And blond.

"Way too perfect," Kat had told her mother teasingly, since she'd met Brenda first.

"You might want to turn on the TV and check the weather update," Frazier said.

"That storm is getting worse," Brenda added shyly.

"Really?" Skyler said, offering Brenda what she hoped was a welcoming smile. Not only was Brenda tiny and blond, her brilliant blue eyes made her look like a true little snow princess. Skyler had been relieved to learn that she was twenty-one. When she'd first met the young woman, she'd been terrified that Frazier had fallen for a teenager, but Brenda simply looked young because she was so petite. She tended to be shy, but she certainly seemed very sweet.

Okay, it would be nice if she talked a bit more to someone in the house other than Frazier, but really, what wasn't to like about her?

David was too entangled in the lights to find the remote. Skyler saw it on a chair and flicked the TV on. A serious-looking anchorman was delivering a warning.

"We're looking at major power outages, and despite the fact that it's Christmas Eve, because the weather is already turning vicious, we suggest that anyone who may have medical or other difficulties in the event of a power loss get to a hospital or a shelter now. And everyone should be prepared, with candles and flashlights within reach."

"Ah-ha!" David cried, and they all turned to stare at him. He shrugged weakly. "Sorry. I untangled the lights."

"Let's get 'em up, and then let's eat," Skyler suggested cheerfully. "With luck we can finish before the power blows, and if it does, we can play Scrabble by candlelight or something."

"Wretched weather," Kat muttered, her attention turning back to the television. "Mom, Dad, why didn't we buy a house on a Caribbean island?"

"We couldn't afford a house on a Caribbean island," David said, but he sounded a lot more cheerful than he had earlier. He hesitated, then said, "Frazier, will you grab that end?"

Frazier hesitated, as well, before saying, "Sure, Dad."

"Good. You two deal with the lights, and I'll get the food on the table," Skyler said.

"Let's get Mister Sixteen and Rebellious down here, too, huh?" Kat said. "He can give us a hand."

"Good idea, and would you get Uncle Paddy, too?"

There was a short silence after she spoke. Perhaps she'd even imagined it, she thought.

David wasn't thrilled about her uncle being there, she knew, and she was suddenly thankful that they'd both been born the children of Irish immigrants. He would never expect her to actually turn away a relative, even if he felt that Paddy was a drunk who deserved whatever he was suffering now. Which wasn't really fair, she thought, but David was entitled to his opinion.

Often enough, Uncle Paddy was the real Irish entertainment at the pub. In his own way, of course.

Kat sprang to life, dispelling whatever awkwardness there might have been. She grinned and ran halfway up the stairs, then called, "Jamie! Jamie O'Boyle! Get your delinquent ass down here on the double. Uncle Paddy…dinner."

"I could have yelled myself," Skyler said.

"But you'd never have used such poetic language," Kat said, and even David laughed.

* * *

The first thing Craig realized when he came to was that his head was killing him.

Quintin packed one hell of a wallop.

He didn't know how long he'd been out, didn't know how far they had come. All he knew was that even from where he lay, tossed into the backseat of their stolen vehicle, when he first cracked his eyes open it looked like the whole world had turned white.

Impossible.

He closed his eyes again, waited a long moment, then reopened them. The world was still white. It was snow, and not just snow, but fiercely blowing snow. Hell. It was a nor'easter and a mean one. A blizzard.

He ached all over and wondered if anything in his body was broken.

And what about the old man they had robbed?

His stomach tightened painfully when he caught sight of a familiar stand of trees and realized he knew exactly where they were. For a moment, memories filled his mind and drove away the pain, and then every muscle in his body tensed in an effort at self-preservation, as the car suddenly spun and came to a violent halt in a snowdrift.

"Asshole!" Quintin shouted from the front seat.

"You're the asshole," Scooter returned savagely. "You try driving in this shit."

"Doesn't matter now. We're stuck. We'll have to get out and walk."

"We're in the middle of nowhere!" Scooter protested.

"No, we're not. There's a house right up there," Quintin snapped, pointing. "I can see the lights in the windows."

"What? We're going to drop in for Christmas dinner?" Scooter demanded angrily.

"It's still Christmas Eve," Quintin said. "The season of peace and goodwill toward men."

"Fine. We're going to crash somebody's Christmas *Eve* dinner?" Scooter asked, sounding doubtful, even disbelieving, and thoroughly uneasy.

"That's exactly what we're going to do," Quintin said.

Craig's head was still in agony. Despite that, he felt a terrible sense of dread. Inwardly, he cringed, his mind screaming.

He knew that house. He had dropped by often in a different time.

In a different life.

He remembered it so well: set on a little hill, a beautiful house, comfortable and warm, a place where a family—a real family—gathered and cooked and celebrated the holidays.

How could they have settled on that house? How could the fates be that unfair? It wasn't even right on the road, for God's sake; they should never even have known it was there as they drove past in the storm.

"We've got to get away from here. Far away," Scooter argued.

Good thought, Craig approved silently.

"Far away?" Quintin mocked. "You're out of your mind. Just how far do you think we can get in this weather, without a car—seeing as someone drove ours into a snowdrift? We need a place to stay. Are you insane? Can't you see? We're not going to get anywhere tonight."

Scooter was silent for a moment, then said, "We shouldn't see people tonight."

"Don't you mean people shouldn't see us?" Quintin asked. He laughed. "Like it will make a difference. Whatever we have to do, we'll do."

In the back, eyes shut again as he pretended he was still unconscious, Craig shuddered inwardly and considered his options. Depending on how he looked at things, they went from few to nonexistent.

Sorrow ripped through him at the thought of the old man they had left behind, followed by a fresh onslaught of dread.

He prayed in silence, trying desperately to think of a way out and cursing fate for his present situation.

How the hell had he ended up here? And tonight of all nights?

"Ah, me poor bones," Uncle Paddy moaned when Kat went up to repeat the news that dinner was ready, although he looked quite comfortable, reclining against a stack of pillows on the very nice daybed that sat near the radiator in the guest room. He had been happily watching television, and he'd apparently gotten her mother to bring him up some tea and cookies earlier. She suspected he hadn't been in a speck of pain until she'd knocked briefly and opened the door to his room.

She stared at him, then set her hands on her hips and slipped into an echo of his accent. "Your old bones are just fine, Uncle Patrick. It's no sympathy you'll be getting tonight."

Her uncle looked at her indignantly—a look he'd mastered, she thought.

"A few drops of whiskey would be makin' 'em a whole lot better, me fine lass."

"Maybe later."

"I've got to be getting down the stairs," he said.

"Uncle Paddy, even I know it's easier to get down a flight of stairs *before* taking a shot of whiskey," Jamie said from behind Kat, making her start in surprise. So her little brother had finally left the haven of his room, she thought. He was only sixteen, but already a good three inches taller than she was. He even had an inch on Frazier these days. He was thin, with a lean, intelligent face. He worried that he didn't look tough enough, but he wasn't exactly planning to be a boxer. He was a musician, something that came easily enough in their family. He loved his guitar, and when he played a violin, grown men had been known to weep.

It occurred to her that she hadn't spent a lot of time with him in the last year, and this was a time in his life when he could use some sane guidance from his older siblings. She remembered being sixteen all too well.

The opposite sex. Peer pressure. Drugs. Cigarettes.

Once, she'd thought of him almost as her own baby. Even though there were only six years between them, she'd been old enough to help out when he'd been born. Then again, they hadn't grown up in the usual household. Their home was by Boston Common, the pub closer to the wharf, and they'd all spent plenty of time in that pub. When she'd been a teenager, her friends had enjoyed the mistaken belief that she could supply liquor for whatever party they were planning.

She could still remember the pressure, and the pain of finding out that some of her so-called friends lost all interest in her when she wouldn't go along with their illegal plans. It wasn't until she'd had her heart seriously broken her first year of college that she'd learned to depend on herself for her own happiness. That she could be depressed and work in her parents' pub all her life or she could create her own dreams.

Age and experience. She had both, she decided, at the grand age of twenty-two.

She smiled at how self-righteous she sounded in her own mind. Well, maybe she was, but she knew she was never going to make the mistakes her parents had made. She wasn't going to live her life entirely for others. Oh, she meant to have children. And it looked as if Uncle Paddy was around to stay. But she was never going to torture herself over her husband's temper or the bickering that went on around her.

To hell with them all; that would be her motto. God could sort them out later.

But, for the moment, she realized, she was concerned about Jamie—and the fact he had been so quick to lock himself away. What had he been up to?

She knew, despite her mother's determination to keep certain situations private between herself and a particular child, that Jamie had gotten himself into some minor trouble up here last year. Luckily for him, a sheriff's deputy had just come to the house and commented on how easily calls could be traced these days.

"You're behaving, right?" she said to him now.

He'd been in his room since they'd gotten there. Of course, he'd made no secret of the fact that he thought she and Frazier should deal with their father on holidays, seeing as the two of them got to escape back to college after a few days, while he had to deal with his parents on a daily basis.

Jamie just grinned and nodded toward Uncle Paddy, who had taken offense at Jamie's last comment and was staring at his youngest nephew with his head held high in indignation.

"At my age, a bit of whiskey is medicinal," he announced.

"Yeah, whatever," Jamie said irreverently. "But the whiskey is downstairs. So grab your cane, and we'll be your escort."

Kat grinned. Maybe this Christmas would be okay after all, despite its somewhat rocky start.

"Come on, Uncle Paddy. You're not that old, so move it," Jamie said.

"There is simply no respect for seniors in this house," Paddy said. "The abuse your poor wee mother takes…" He shook his head.

"My mother is neither poor nor wee," Kat retorted. "Now come on. It's Christmas, and we're going to have fun and be happy."

"Yes, dammit. Whether we like it or not," Jamie agreed.

Kat reached for Paddy's arm. With a groan, he rose. "Ah, me old bones."

"Your old palate can have a wee dram the minute we get you down the stairs," Jamie assured him.

Paddy arched a brow. "Are ye joinin' me then, lad?"

"Sure, it's Christmas."

"Ye're not of an age."

"Like you were?" Jamie said, rolling his eyes.

"This is America."

"So?" Jamie said. "My parents run a bar. It's not like I haven't had a shot now and then."

Paddy let out an oath. Kat knew what it was because she'd been told as a child never to learn Gaelic from Uncle Paddy. Luckily, not many people spoke Gaelic, so they seldom knew what he was saying when he was out and about and swearing at the world.

Now he waved a hand at them and headed for the stairs under his own power. "The young. No respect," he muttered, then raised his cane and shook it at them.

They both laughed and followed him downstairs.

Skyler had all but the last of the food on the table when Uncle Paddy entered the kitchen and headed straight for the liquor cabinet.

"Your beer's on the table," she said, her tone slightly sharp. She realized that she was looking over her shoulder, hoping that David hadn't seen Paddy heading straight for the whiskey.

"I'll take a beer, too," Jamie said cheerfully, coming in behind Paddy.

"Jamie…" she said warningly.

"It's better than the hard stuff, right?" Jamie asked.

"Actually, I think a beer and a shot have about the same alcohol content," Kat said, following her brother into the kitchen.

"What, now our son is heading straight for the liquor, too?" David demanded harshly from behind Kat.

His words tightened the knot of tension already forming between Skyler's shoulder blades as she remembered the "incident" with Jamie.

"Jeez, Dad, would you lighten up?" Jamie demanded.

"Great. I knew we should have gone to your family," Frazier murmured to Brenda, as they walked into the middle of the argument.

Take control, Skyler told herself angrily. All your life, you let things go, trying to maintain the peace. Now for once in your life, do something. "David, Jamie, please," she said. "It's Christmas Eve."

"We own a bar," Jamie said. "What's the big deal?"

"Stop it, Jamie. Stop it now," she said firmly, wondering why family gatherings had to be such a nightmare.

"Pub," David corrected irritably. "And that's no reason for my kids to be drunks, too."

"Ye'd be referring to me, eh?" Paddy demanded.

Take control, Skyler ordered herself. And finally spoke up. "Uncle Paddy, you have a drinking problem, and you know it. Jamie, you may have a beer. One." She stared at her husband. "I'd rather he drink with us than away from us, if he's going to drink. And he *is* going to drink. So...sit down. Kat, Frazier, Brenda, what would *you* like to drink?"

"Just water for me," Brenda said hurriedly.

Of course someone so slim and tiny wouldn't consume a liquid with calories, Skyler thought. Then again, at least the girl had answered on her own. She had been so quiet since her arrival.

She was shy. Not like this group.

"Frazier, what will you have?"

"I'll have a beer—if Dad doesn't think it will turn me into an alcoholic."

David stared at his older son, still irritated.

"Don't be silly. Your father knows that you don't abuse alcohol."

"Yeah. Not like some of those old boozehounds at the pub," Frazier said.

"Boozehounds? Those fine fellows put food on your plate," Paddy said.

"Including the ones who fall off their bar stools?" Frazier asked.

"We don't serve drunks," David snapped.

"Dad's right," Kat said, grinning, "We reserve the right not to serve people who are falling off the bar stools."

"Even when they're our relatives," Jamie chimed in.

"Jamie..." Skyler cautioned with a sigh. So much for taking control. David was clearly taking every word seriously, which did not bode well for a pleasant meal.

"Mom, what would *you* like to drink?" Kat asked.

Skyler hesitated, shaking her head. "Hell. Just give me the whole bottle of whiskey."

To her amazement, there was silence.

Then laughter.

Even David's lips twitched.

"Come on, guys, let's all behave," Kat said. "We're driving Mom to drink."

"Let's eat," Skyler said with forced cheer. "Sit down already."

"You want us anywhere in particular?" Kat asked, walking up behind her mother and hugging her.

"In a chair at the table, that's all," she said, and gave her daughter a little squeeze in return.

"We're short a place setting," Kat noted.

"No, we're not."

"Yes, we are. Count," Kat said.

"There are six place settings, and five of us and... Brenda and Paddy," Skyler said. "I'm sorry. I'll get another plate."

"I'll go find a chair," Kat said. "I think there's an extra in the den."

"I'm so sorry, guys," Skyler said as Kat hurried out.

"That's okay, Mom. You can't count, but we love you anyway," Frazier teased, smiling at her.

She smiled back. "And Dad?"

His smiled wavered for a moment. "We love Dad, too, of course. Although I think he can count."

"Cute," Skyler said. "Brenda, please sit down and just ignore my family."

Uncle Paddy was staring at her questioningly, and Brenda looked acutely uncomfortable. How the hell had she miscounted? She just hadn't been thinking clearly. She'd been too busy listening in on other people's conversations. Worrying.

She didn't want arguing. She wanted peace and the whole Norman Rockwell picture.

"I'm sorry for intruding on your family Christmas—" Brenda began.

"Don't be silly, you're not intruding in the least, and we're delighted to have you. I'm just getting absentminded in my old age," Skyler said.

"It's all those years in a bar," Frazier teased.

"Pub," David said.

"Beer fumes," Jamie put in.

David groaned exaggeratedly. "All right, enough with the pub and the beer. Brenda, you are entirely welcome here. Please sit down."

"Please," Skyler echoed. "Jamie likes to say that I have adult attention deficiency disorder. Personally, I think it comes from my children," she explained, staring firmly from one of her sons to the other. "Let's all sit and enjoy our dinner."

Suddenly the doorbell rang.

Skyler looked at her husband, who looked back at her, his eyebrows arching questioningly. "You have more company coming?" he asked. His tone, at least, was light. "Someone's long-lost relative? Stray friend?"

She glared at him fiercely. "No."

"Why would anyone be traveling in this weather?" Brenda mused.

So she did speak without being spoken to, Skyler thought, then wanted to kick herself for the unkind thought. But the girl was so quiet most of the time. Probably, her family didn't fight all the time, and she just felt uncomfortable, intimidated.

"Someone might have had an accident, Dad," Frazier suggested.

"If someone is hurt or stranded, of course they can come in," Skyler said quickly.

"What idiot would be out in this weather?" David asked.

The bell sounded again.

"We could just answer the blasted thing and find out what's going on," Paddy said.

"I'll get it," Jamie said.

"No. I'll get it," David said firmly. "You all just sit."

But no one sat.

David led, Skyler close behind him, everyone else behind her. The swinging door that separated the kitchen from the dining room, which sat to the one side of the entry, thumped as one person after another pushed it on the way through.

The bell rang again.

"Hurry, someone might be freezing out there," Skyler said.

And yet, even as she spoke, she felt a strange sense of unease.

Somehow Norman Rockwell seemed to be slipping away.

And she—who took in any stray puppy, who always helped the down and out, animal or human—didn't want David to open the door.

Chapter 2

The chair in the den lost a leg the minute Kat picked it up. She let out a groan of frustration and tried to put it back on.

It would go back on, but it wouldn't stay, because a crucial screw seemed to be missing. She looked around, getting down on hands and knees to see if it had rolled into a corner somewhere. No luck.

No problem. There was a chair at the desk up in her room, and she knew it was fine, because she had been sitting in it earlier while she was online.

She was upstairs when she heard the doorbell ring. Curious, she walked to the window and looked out. She saw a car stuck nose-first in a snowdrift, barely off the road, down where the slope of their yard began.

The bell rang again, and two men backed out from beneath the porch roof and stared up at the house. Strangers. She could barely see them; the wind was really blowing the snow around, and they were bundled up in coats, scarves and hats, but something about their movement made her think that they were in their thirties—late twenties to forty, tops, at any rate.

She frowned, watching as they moved back out of sight and the bell rang for a third time.

Not at all sure why, she didn't grab the chair and run down the stairs. Instead, she found herself walking quietly out to the landing, where she stood in the shadows, looking and listening.

"We know it's Christmas Eve," one man was saying.

"And we're so sorry," said the second.

"But we ran off the road and we need help," said the first.

"A dog shouldn't be out on a night like this," said the second.

"We were just about to sit down to dinner." Her father's voice, and he sounded suspicious. Good.

"Dinner," the first man repeated.

Peering carefully over the banister, still strangely unwilling to give herself away, Kat tried to get a look at the men. One was bulky and well-dressed, and shorter than her father and Frazier by a few inches; since they were about six-one to Jamie's six-two, that made the stranger about six feet even.

The other man, the one who had spoken first, was leaner. He had the look of…a sidekick? Odd thought, but that was exactly the word that occurred to her. He needed a haircut, and his coat was missing several buttons. Even his knit cap looked as if it had seen better days.

When the heavier man took off his hat, he was bald— clean-shaven bald. He had thick dark brows, and eyes that were set too close together.

Beady eyes, Kat thought, then chided herself for watching too much *C.S.I.*

"Good heavens, come in and get out of the cold," her mother told the pair.

Her mother would have taken in Genghis Khan, Kat thought, although she didn't sound entirely happy about extra guests at the moment. Maybe because it was Christmas Eve, she decided. But really, what choice was there? The two men could hardly go anywhere else.

But what the hell were they doing out to begin with? Maybe they didn't live here near the mountains, but anyone who lived anywhere in New England knew how treacherous the weather could become in a matter of hours, and the TV and radio stations had been talking nonstop about this storm for two days before it even got here. It had been touch and go whether the family even made it up here in time.

"Thank you, ma'am, and bless you," the tall man said, holding out his hand. "I'm William Blane, but folks call me Scooter. And this is my associate, Mr. Quintin Lark."

"How do you do, and I, too, thank you," the stocky man said.

Her father looked at her mother and smiled in solidarity. At that moment, despite the bickering that never seemed to stop, she was reminded of how much she loved her parents. And that she was proud of them. Her father worked hard, doing everything around the pub. He lugged boxes and kept the books, but he could pick up a fiddle or a keyboard and sit in with a band, and he was always willing to pitch in and wash glasses. He managed the kitchen, the bar and the inventory.

And her mother… Her mother had raised three children, working all the while. Like Kat's dad, her mom could sit in with the band. She had a clear soprano and a gift for the piano. She served drinks and meals, tended bar and always picked up a broom and a dust rag when needed.

Her mother was the key element that truly turned the place from a bar into a pub, Kat decided. She *listened.* She knew their customers. She knew that Mrs. O'Malley's cat had produced five kittens and that those kittens were as important to Mrs. O'Malley as Mr. Browne's new grandson was to him. She knew old man Adair had gotten part of a mortar shell in his calf during the war—World War II, that was—and that as stubborn and sturdy as the old fellow might appear, his leg ached on an hourly basis. Her mother cared about people, perhaps too much. And in her pursuit of constant cheer, she had often sacrificed the truth.

Even now, she was frowning sympathetically. "You say you had an accident? Where? What happened?"

"We didn't listen to the weather report, I'm afraid," Quintin said.

"We were listening to a CD, instead of the news," Scooter said. "We ran off the road just at the edge of your property. I wasn't even sure we'd make it this far."

"Not to worry," Skyler said. "We have plenty of food. Come on into the kitchen."

"I'll just get some more chairs," David said.

"Wasn't—" Jamie began.

"No," Skyler said firmly, staring at Jamie. "No...we'll be fine in the kitchen. We just need more chairs."

Kat's jaw dropped. Her mother—her *mother*—was suspicious.

And pretending that she wasn't in the house.

"Right," her father said. "Two more chairs. Jamie, take Quintin and, uh, Scooter into the kitchen. Get them a drink."

"A shot of whiskey," Skyler said. "You both need a good shot of whiskey. Just to warm up." She sounded nervous,

Kat thought, though no one who didn't know her would notice.

"Whiskey sounds great," Scooter said.

"Let's all go into the kitchen," Quintin added, and Kat thought she heard something ominous in his voice.

"I've got to get more chairs," David said.

"No," Scooter said softly.

It should have been a perfect holiday tableau: a family opening their doors to stranded travelers on a cold and stormy Christmas Eve.

But something just wasn't right. It was as if the picture was out of focus.

Everyone just stood there awkwardly. And then, subtly, Quintin's face changed.

Kat could see the way he smiled. It was a slow smile. A scary smile.

"We need to stay together. All of us," Quintin told them.

Kat felt as if she were staring down at a scene in a play, and someone had forgotten a line.

What in God's name had tipped everyone off? How had her mother, the soul of trust, figured out—and so quickly— that there was something unsavory about their uninvited guests?

And how had the creep, Quintin, realized that her parents were suspicious?

"This is my house," David said. "We're happy to keep you from freezing to death, but you'll behave by my rules in my house."

"Can't, sorry," Scooter said. He actually looked a little sad.

"Oh? Come on now, we were just about to have dinner, so let's all honor the spirit of the holiday and sit down together."

Good acting job, Dad, Kat cheered silently, then realized that it hadn't made any difference.

Quintin was staring at her mother. "What made you become so mistrustful? Surely you're not a detective, but...a psychiatrist, perhaps? No matter. Yes, this is your house. But I'm the one with a gun. In fact, my friend Scooter has a gun, too. Neither one of us wants to hurt you, but we're outnumbered. Thankfully, you seem to be a nice family. A smart family. So I'm sure you'll see the wisdom of behaving when I tell you that if any one of you gets out of line... Mom here gets it. So the rest of you might be able to take us, but you'd go through the rest of your neat little suburban lives without a mom. So we all stay together," he said softly. "Can't take any chances. After all, you might have a gun of your own squirreled away somewhere," he said, turning to her father.

"Bullshit!"

Her father was a big man—in good shape, as well. He lunged at Quintin, and her brothers, bless them, followed his lead. But Quintin was fast. He pulled his gun before her father got to him.

"Stop now, or Mom is dead!" Quintin roared.

The sound of a bullet blasting ripped through the night, followed by the shattering of glass exploding into a thousand pieces, as Scooter took out a lamp.

"Nobody move," Quintin said.

Everybody stood still, as ordered. Brenda started to cry.

"Shut up!" Quinton said.

Frazier put his arm around Brenda, drawing her close to him.

Uncle Paddy seemed the least disturbed of all of them. He seemed to be assessing the invaders with remarkably sober eyes.

"No more heroics," Quintin said. "We've given you one chance. Next time, someone dies. Because I'm not going to prison again, ever. I'd rather die first. And if I'm going to die, I'll happily take someone with me. Understand?"

Her poor father, Kat thought. She had never seen him in so much agony. His whole family was threatened, and he was powerless.

A sense of panic seized Kat, like a wave of cold that washed over her and left her trembling. For a moment the world went black. She fell back against the wall in an effort to remain vertical as she fought the nausea that seemed to grip her stomach with an icy, merciless hand.

She inhaled deeply and tried to think. Despite their threats, she didn't know if the pair had ever actually murdered anyone. They were probably thieves. On the other hand...

They were armed. And they had introduced themselves, she realized with a further wave of nausea. That could only mean that whether they'd killed before or not, they weren't planning to leave any witnesses. She shuddered, fear threatening to consume her. She only hoped they hadn't realized just how much danger they were in.

She fought it. She was the only hope her family had.

"All right, folks, if we're all calm, we can get through this. I want your cell phones. Now," Quintin said.

Jamie and Frazier reached into their pockets. As Jamie handed his over, he said, "There's no service out here now, anyway. We're lucky to stand on the roof and get service even when there isn't a storm."

"You never know. Come on, come on, the rest of the cell phones," Quintin said.

David immediately produced his from his pocket.

"Mine's in my purse," Brenda squeaked.

"And where would that be?"

"Right there—the table by the door," Frazier said.

"Get it," Quintin ordered him.

"How about you, Mom? Where's yours?"

"Don't you call her *Mom*," Jamie warned.

"Jamie…" David said.

"My name is Skyler," her mother told the men.

"Fine. Skyler, where's your phone?"

"In the kitchen, charging," she said.

"And yours, pops?" Quintin asked Paddy as Frazier handed over Brenda's phone.

"I wouldn't be havin' one of those new-fangled things," Uncle Paddy said.

"Everyone in the entire world has a cell phone," Quintin said.

"I'd not be the entire world," Paddy said.

"Watch it, old man," Quintin warned.

"He really doesn't have a cell phone," Frazier interjected.

Quintin eyed him long and hard. "You're a big kid. Feisty, I imagine, like your dad. Don't go playing Superman. I do mean it. You do, and someone will die."

"He's not going to be Superman," Skyler said quickly. "None of us will, okay?"

"Just remember this. I will not go back to prison," Quintin said.

"Let's eat," Scooter said cheerfully, and actually gave her father a friendly punch on the shoulder. "So how is the missus in the kitchen? Is she a good cook?"

"It's all right, David," Skyler said softly, when he started tensing. She stared at him, her eyes pleading.

David managed to choke out an answer. "She's a wonderful cook. And you obviously mean what you say, so don't worry. We'll cooperate in every way."

"Bastards," Uncle Paddy suddenly hissed, thumping his cane for emphasis.

"Paddy, quit banging your cane and shut up," her mother snapped. "We'll have no one dying here tonight. Jamie and Frazier, Scooter can accompany you to the family room. Just grab the bar stools—I'll be happy to sit on one."

"Me, too," Brenda chimed in, the tear tracks drying on her cheeks.

"Quintin, you can join the rest of us in the kitchen."

Her mother had somehow taken control. Amazing, Kat marveled.

Quintin laughed. "Yes, ma'am. We seem to have ourselves an Irish matriarch here, Scooter. There's no one fiercer. And she's a fine cook, we're told. Good thing, because I'm starving. And freezing."

"There are sweaters in the hall closet, right over there," Skyler said, pointing. "Take off your coats. I don't want you sitting at my table in those filthy coats."

Mom, be careful! They'll shoot you for sure, Kat thought, her heart sinking.

But Quintin only laughed again. "All right. You," he said, indicating Brenda, "get the sweaters, so we can all have dinner."

He stared at Brenda, who was staring back at him like a doe caught in the headlights of a speeding car.

"Hop to it!" Quintin said, and Brenda did.

"What about Crai—" Scooter began, doffing his coat and accepting one of David's old sweaters.

"Later," Quintin said.

"But it's freezing out," Scooter said.

"Later, after dinner."

"But—"

"What happens, happens," Quintin said.

What the hell are they talking about? Kat wondered. *Who or what is "Crai"?*

"We'll put your coats in the mudroom," Skyler said, and Kat could see that her mother was trembling as she picked up Scooter's discarded coat and tossed it into the small tiled mudroom off one side of the foyer where they were standing.

"I'll hang mine, if you don't mind," Quintin said, suiting his actions to the words. "Now let's go. I'm starving."

He looked up suddenly, and Kat instantly backed even farther into the shadows, her heart thundering. Had he seen her? Apparently not, because he set his hand on Skyler's shoulder and repeated, "Let's go."

"Get your hands off her," David said.

Quintin seemed surprised, but he only smiled. "Just remember, everyone on good behavior. Everyone. We keep close together, like a good family, and no one gets hurt."

They left the entry hall and moved into the kitchen, and Kat was left alone with her roiling thoughts.

She felt frozen, paralyzed, but she knew she had to get past that. Her mother had kept them from knowing she was in the house for a reason: so she could save the family.

Or so she could live when the invaders massacred the rest of the family.

No. That wasn't going to happen. She would find a way to make sure of it.

She prayed silently for strength. What the hell should she do? How was she supposed to get help in the middle of a blizzard?

She couldn't wait until the weather calmed down, because Quintin and Scooter were waiting for the same thing. Then they would no doubt steal one of the family's cars and get back on the road.

And before they went on the road…

They would kill her entire family. They hadn't hidden their faces. They had blithely offered their names. Of course, they might have made up the names they had given, but she didn't think so. The most likely scenario was that they would have dinner, savor the warmth of the house and then kill her entire family.

She turned and hurried silently down the hall to her room. She tried her cell first, but she wasn't at all surprised to discover she had no service. She hesitated, then quickly tried the landline. But either the wires were down or their unwelcome visitors had cut the lines.

Think, she commanded herself. There had to be something she could do.

She could run, but where?

Oh God, it was all up to her. And she was in a panic, failing…

She drew a deep breath.

She could not—would not—fail.

She must be in a state of delayed shock, Skyler decided. She should be paralyzed, either entirely mute or screaming, but instead she was talking, moving, almost normally. They all were, thanks to that basic instinct for survival that kicked in no matter how dire the circumstances.

The singer on the CD that had gone on playing in the background moved on to "O Holy Night." She had wanted peace so badly before but now…

Now she just wanted everyone to live.

"What the hell is that stuff?" Scooter asked, staring at one of the serving dishes.

"Bacon and cabbage, to go with the corned beef," David

said sharply. Bless him, he was actually bristling at the insult to her cooking, despite the circumstances.

"Don't look like bacon," Scooter said.

"It's more like Canadian bacon," Frazier said. "It's the Irish tradition to have bacon with the cabbage."

"Cabbage is worse than bacon," Scooter said, wrinkling his nose.

"Taste it. All the flavors mix together. It's good," Skyler heard herself say as if she were coaxing a five-year-old. "Brenda, would you pass the potatoes, please?"

She could do this. They all could. It was the only way to stay alive. Because if they didn't stay calm and pull this off...

At least, she prayed, Kat would survive.

As Scooter reluctantly accepted the bowl of cabbage, Skyler dared a glance at David. His jaw was locked, a pulse ticking at his throat. His eyes touched hers, and they were filled with humiliation. He had failed to protect his family. He wanted to do something.

She shook her head. *No.*

"Hey, you're right. This shit is good," Scooter said.

"My mother does not put *shit* on the table." Jamie bridled.

There was silence for a moment; then Scooter grinned. "Sorry. It's just that...been a while since I've eaten a family dinner." He set his fork down suddenly. "I can't do this."

"You can't do what?" Skyler demanded, her heart racing. He couldn't sit and eat with them when he planned to shoot them all in a few hours?

"Leave it," Quintin said.

"Come on," Scooter protested. "The kid could be dead."

Quintin frowned, then swore in exasperation. "The kid could be a cop."

"No, he's not," Scooter insisted.

"What kid?" Skyler demanded, feeling as if she were about to explode, as if she were choking and stars would burst in front of her eyes before the total darkness of death descended.

Surely they couldn't mean Kat?

"What kid?" David breathed.

Quintin waved his fork dismissively. "Nothing for you to worry about, buddy."

Skyler was surprised to see David lean forward intensely. "Haven't you guys ever been in a blizzard before? If you left someone out there in this, he'll die. A few years ago, one poor old woman died *after* the storm. She froze to death just trying to get her mail."

Scooter looked at Quintin. "The kid is no cop," he insisted. "I don't want anyone to die if I can help it." Then, as if realizing that he was sounding too soft, he added, "But don't any of you forget we've got guns, and we'll use 'em if we have to."

"Mom first," Quintin reminded them very softly, and Skyler lifted her head to stare at him. He laughed suddenly. "Look at the little lioness. You think it would be worse if I threatened one of the children. For you, yes. But for the kids here... You think they'd want to go on living, knowing they got you killed?"

"Ah, it's all clear to me now," Paddy said suddenly.

"What's clear, you old Mick?" Quintin demanded.

"Why, that you were abandoned by y'er blessed mother," Paddy said.

"I wasn't abandoned," Quintin snapped back. "The drunken bitch died. Maybe you should watch it, Mick. You could be next."

"Speaking of abandoning people..." Skyler cut in. "Have you abandoned someone outside?"

Quintin grinned. "You *want* us to bring in our buddy and put the odds even more in our favor?"

There was no way she could hide the confusion that filled her when she added that thought to the mix.

"That's all right. You're good people," Quintin said surprisingly.

"I want to get the kid," Scooter said stubbornly.

"The food will get cold," Quintin said. "And how do you propose we get him?"

"Those two get him out of the car and carry him in," Scooter said, indicating David and Frazier. "You sit here with your gun trained on Mom and they won't make trouble."

"The wind is blowing like a son of a bitch," Paddy noted.

"So it is," Quintin said. "Go get coated up."

The blow to his head had been bad. Craig groaned, shivering, his teeth chattering. He tried to open his eyes again.

Somehow he managed to sit up so he could get a look at where they were, and his heart sank.

Oh God. He'd hoped it was just the blizzard and the pain confusing him, making him see the familiar where it didn't exist, but he hadn't been confused. What he'd seen was all too real.

This was Kat's family's country home, the one she always joked was out in the boondocks, where people still knew one another and where they cared.

Kat.

With her music and her laughter. He could remember far too vividly the times they had come up here for weekends when her family was away, the nights they had spent cuddling on the couch, watching old movies, unable to keep their hands off each other.

Casablanca rolled across his mind. He could hear Humphrey Bogart saying, "Of all the gin joints, in all the towns, in all the world, she had to walk into mine."

Except that Kat O'Boyle hadn't just walked into his life.

He had plowed into hers.

Maybe it wasn't the house, he thought, and looked again.

Nope, it was. Painted white and black with detailed Victorian gingerbreading. The porch, the sloping yard... This was the house, all right.

Maybe they weren't here. But he knew they were. He could see lights in the windows, and in the living room, a Christmas tree strung with colorful lights.

What the hell was the matter with these people? They lived in Boston. Why hadn't they bought a vacation home somewhere warm? Anywhere but here.

Maybe, he hoped against hope, Kat wasn't there.

No, Kat never missed Christmas with her family.

He closed his eyes, wishing he couldn't see the house. When he opened them, he thought about getting out of the car, then decided to give it another second, even though the backseat now seemed as cold as the middle of an iceberg.

Even if something had happened and Kat wasn't here, her family was inside. He'd never met them, but he felt as if he knew them. Her father, set in his ways. Her twin brother, Frazier, whom he'd at least seen when Kat pointed him out once across campus. Her little brother, Jamie. He'd wanted to meet her family. Even when she had complained about them, it had been with love.

Her parents were just so old-school, she had told him once. They had both been born in the States, but their parents had come over from Ireland, and sometimes it felt as if they had only recently come over themselves. Her father thought Mexican food was weird and sushi would kill her one day. She'd once suggested they hire a country singer at the pub, and her mother had looked at her as if she'd betrayed the nation.

They fought too much, Kat had said, even admitted that they probably should have gotten a divorce.

No, he'd told her. It was great when people believed so strongly in marriage that they made it work no matter what. He'd never told her about the way his parents had gotten divorced. They hadn't meant to hurt him, of course. They were decent people who'd gotten so caught up in their own pain that he had gotten lost in the shuffle. And then, when time had passed and some of the wounds had healed...

Then everything had really gone to hell.

He closed his eyes again, and when he opened them...

There was a face looking in the window at him.

Kat's face.

He blinked to banish the hallucination. Then he heard the door open and realized she was real.

"Craig?" she murmured incredulously. "Craig Devon?"

"Kat?" He couldn't see clearly, couldn't think clearly, but he knew he had to shake it off.

"Oh my God! What are you doing here? Did they kidnap you or—"

She broke off, staring at him. He steeled himself, feeling his heart freeze and then shatter into little pieces.

"I heard you were in jail," she said. Her voice had gone as cold as the snow around them.

Jail? He felt like laughing. She didn't know the half of what had happened.

His choice, of course. The turns his life had taken

weren't the kind a man longed to share with the woman he loved. The woman he longed to have love him in return.

Kat.

So impossible.

Of all the gin joints, in all the towns, in all the world…

Damn, his head hurt and his tongue was thick, but he needed to speak and speak fast. "What are you doing out here?" he asked her. "Those bastards in your house—"

"I know," she said coldly.

"So how did you get out—"

"They don't know about me," she said.

The world seemed to steady around him. He could see her in the moonlight that glowed softly through the snow. The red fire of her hair was like a silk frame around her face, and though there wasn't enough illumination for him to really see her eyes, he knew them well. Technically speaking, they were hazel, but the word wasn't enough to describe the reality. They were green, and they were gold. Sometimes they were the sun, sometimes like emeralds. But tonight they were filled with disappointment, even revulsion.

"They didn't kidnap you, did they?" she asked.

He struggled to sit. "No. But, Kat—"

He broke off when he heard a sound, and turned to look as the door to the house opened. Scooter was there with two men. Craig squinted. Kat's older brother and her father, he had to assume. "Kat." He found the strength to grip her shoulders. "Someone's coming—one of them. So if they really don't know about you, you need to get the hell out of here. Do you understand me? Disappear."

"You're one of them."

"No…not exactly. One of them hit me and—"

"One of them hit you?" she interrupted skeptically.

"Yes, and left me out here. Now get the hell out of here!"

The men were coming down the walk. She could see them now, Scooter, her father and Frazier.

"Craig, if you're with them…"

"Please, Kat, I don't know what they'll do. Go for help."

"Go for help?" she inquired. "I barely made it to the car in this wind. See the way they're all hunched over against it? Where am I going to go, Craig? How the hell am I going to get help?"

Snowdrifts were everywhere. They were going to see her footprints, he thought, as the wind picked up, howling. Maybe the snow was blowing around enough to hide her footprints.

He roused and took hold of her shoulders again. He could see her eyes. Gold and emerald. His stomach lurched. She'd been the first really good thing in his life, and he had screwed it up. "I'm begging you to get out of here and find help before Scooter sees you."

"There is no help, Craig."

"Then hide somewhere."

"Hide?" she asked indignantly. "They have my family. I can't just run away and hide. Do you have a gun? If you have one, give it to me, damn it."

"Kat, I don't have a gun."

"But you were with them."

"Kat, I'm begging you, go!"

"Are you with them or not?"

"Kat, I…"

His head throbbed with pain and humiliation at the look in her eyes. If they caught her… Lord, if they caught her… He opened his eyes and looked up.

She was gone, vanished into the snow.

He prayed for the snow to fall faster, the wind to blow harder, to cover all traces of her escape.

Scooter and the others had nearly reached the car. The door she'd used was still open, and her prints were still obvious. With a desperate burst of strength, he dragged himself out of the car and let himself collapse into the snow, thrashing to cover her tracks, his thoughts tormenting him.

Once upon a time, he had lived in a different world. He'd been in love with a gorgeous redheaded coed. They'd saved money by eating in and watching old movies on television.

Bogie.

Bergman.

Casablanca.

Of all the gin joints, in all the towns, in all the world...

Run, Kat, run.

Chapter 3

Everyone left in the kitchen stared at Quintin except for Uncle Paddy, who continued to eat without even looking up. "Ye've outdone yerself, lass," he told Skyler. "This is delicious. Isn't it—Quintin? That's yer name, right?"

Quintin had been staring back at Skyler and Jamie, but now he turned his attention to Paddy. "Yes, it's very good," he said.

"Thank you," Skyler said. Ridiculous. She was thanking a killer for complimenting her cooking. But they had to get through this somehow, and if being polite was what it would take, then she would be as polite as if she'd been valedictorian of a finishing school.

"You spend a lot of time cooking?" Quintin asked.

"Not really," Skyler told him, and without thinking, started to rise. He tensed. "Sorry. I just thought I'd have a beer," she said.

"I'll have one while you're up," Quintin said.

"Hell, I'll be joinin' that party," Paddy said.

Even Brenda spoke up. "Mrs. O'Boyle, I'd love a beer, too."

"I'll just grab a six-pack," Skyler said. Poor Brenda. The girl was probably wishing herself miles and miles away right now.

She could have been with her own family. In fact, Frazier could have been with them, as well.

She was the reason they were here instead. She had subtly tried to make him feel guilty for even considering spending Christmas somewhere else. *But, Frazier, you really should come while we still have the house. You know we'll probably get rid of it soon, since there's no sense keeping it now that you kids don't really enjoy it anymore. Just this year...*

Just this year. So Frazier was here with her, along with Brenda, and now they might well die with her.

Stop thinking that way, she commanded herself, but she couldn't help it. Could these men really let them live? They seemed ruthless enough to have killed already. And if you were going to go to prison for life, hell, what difference did it make just how many murders you were being punished for?

"I take it there will be dessert?" Quintin said, almost as if he were a real guest.

"Blueberry pie, apple pie, chocolate-chip cookies," Skyler said.

"Wow."

"My parents own a pub," Jamie said.

"So blueberry pie is Irish?" Quintin asked.

"It's universal, I think," she told him.

"What about pumpkin? I thought that was traditional," Quintin said.

"That's Thanksgiving," Jamie protested.

"We can have pumpkin pie for dinner tomorrow, if you like," Skyler told him.

"Sure, I like pumpkin." He frowned. "So where is this pub of yours?"

"Boston," she said.

Quintin started laughing. "You live in Boston, and this is your vacation home?"

"Hey, we could use some help over here!" Scooter shouted from the front door, interrupting the conversation.

They all leaped up and went rushing out. Between them, Frazier and David were supporting a semiconscious man, his eyes closed, his legs barely moving as they walked. The mysterious not-a-cop, Skyler assumed.

This man clearly wasn't like Quintin or Scooter, hardened and with an edge. This man was younger. Not much older than Frazier and Kat, she realized.

And he was hurt. A trickle of dried blood marred his forehead and matted his hair. Light hair. His eyelashes fluttered as he looked up at her, and for a moment his eyes went very wide, as if he knew her. As if he somehow recognized her. Which was ridiculous, she thought, because she'd never seen him before in her life.

A pained smile tugged at his lips; then his eyes closed again and his head dropped. The only reason he was still vertical, she realized, was because her husband and son were supporting him.

He looked as if he'd fallen face-first into the snow somewhere along the way, and he was tall, even slumped between her husband and son. He looked to be about their height, and except for his present exhaustion, in excellent condition, like an athlete rather than a thief.

Really? she mocked herself. And just what did thieves usually look like?

Like the other two men. Hard, dangerous, cold—and soulless.

"Set him down on the sofa," she said.

As soon as they did so, she knelt down beside him and carefully probed the wound on his head. He cried out involuntarily, his eyes—dark blue, she saw in the light—fluttering open again.

"Hey," Scooter protested. "Don't hurt him."

"Like it makes any difference," Quintin muttered.

"I'm just trying to see how badly he's hurt," Skyler said. "I think he may have a concussion." She looked from Quintin to Scooter. "He should never have been out in that car. You could have killed him."

Her words were met with silence.

Maybe they—or one of them, anyway, she thought, remembering Quintin's cavalier attitude toward bringing him in—*had* been trying to kill him. Or else had taken the attitude that if he died, he died.

"Told you," Scooter said.

"He deserved what he got," Quintin snapped.

Deserved…

So who had cracked him in the head? Someone they had accosted earlier tonight?

Or Quintin?

"Jamie, can you get the first aid kit, please? It's up in my bathroom."

She heard a click and looked up quickly. Quintin had clicked off the safety on his gun, and his finger was on the trigger.

"I'll just get the kit. I swear it," Jamie said, staring at Quintin.

"Please," Skyler said softly. "This man is your *friend*," she added, hoping it was the truth.

"I'll go with him," Scooter said.

"Make it fast," Quintin said. "There's still a meal on the table. And dessert."

As she listened to Jamie's and Scooter's footsteps on the stairs, Skyler realized everyone else was clustered around her. Frazier had his arm protectively around Brenda's shoulders, but his eyes were on Quintin and the gun. Uncle Paddy was standing silent, leaning on his cane. David stood as tense as strung piano wire, watching her.

The torment in his eyes was terrible to see. Worse than her fear that she would be shot. Almost as bad as her fear that her entire family would be massacred if they made a wrong move.

Or even if they didn't.

As soon as Jamie came back with the first aid kit, she found the antiseptic and bathed the cut, happy to have something to concentrate on other than her fears. He stared at her steadily the entire time.

She almost fell over when Brenda stepped forward. "I can see if there's any kind of fracture, Mrs. O'Boyle. I'm pre-med."

"That would be great, thanks," Skyler murmured, trying to hide her shock, though she did remember Frazier saying Brenda was brilliant.

"Just a concussion," Brenda said with surprising confidence a minute later. "I'm sure he'll be all right."

Skyler and Brenda looked at one another. Even Skyler knew he shouldn't be lying down on her couch. He should be in a hospital. But that wasn't going to happen. He was going to have to make it—or not—on his own.

Craig Devon.

She couldn't believe it.

Kat's mind raced. She'd made it around to the back of the

house, where at least she could flatten herself against the house and get some shelter from the ripping wind. But despite the slight relief, she felt as cold inside as she did on the outside.

Craig Devon was somehow connected with the monsters who'd invaded her house.

She remembered—so clearly—the first time she'd seen him. It had been her first year of college and Craig had been just about the most gorgeous human being she'd ever encountered. It had been one of those storybook things: she'd noticed him across a crowded room, and then he had noticed her back.

Looking back—as she often had after their breakup—she realized there had been something not quite right from the start. She had been madly in love with him, so much so that she'd avoided introducing him to her twin, because she hadn't wanted Frazier going all brotherly and protective on her. She woke up each morning longing to stay in bed with Craig. She remembered all the times they'd laughed about some incident or other within her family. She'd told him all about her parents and her brothers; she'd talked about the pub and Uncle Paddy, about how much she missed her grandparents. She'd admitted hating their accent when she was a kid, because it marked them as strange, different from her friends' families, then growing up and missing them so much because they had held such a wealth of knowledge about a different time and a different place. She had been an open book.

He hadn't even been a short story.

Had he always been a criminal? she wondered now. Where had he and those monsters come from to wind up plowed into a snowbank in front of her family's country house? Had he…

Killed anyone?

She refused to believe it.

But there was no denying that he was somehow connected to the two men holding her family hostage.

She thought back to the way they had broken up. Their relationship had seemed so full of promise. He hadn't been a music major, like she was, but he had joined her and some of her bandmates often enough. He could play a guitar as well as many a weekend would-be rock star. His major had been international law, and he was a senior who'd made dean's list every semester. He'd seemed to be the type of guy who would go off and solve at least a few of the world's problems. He'd been popular and worked in the gym, helping the disabled students. He'd been...wonderful.

She recalled how sometimes, when they'd been studying, she would look up to see him watching her. He didn't move; he just watched her with the warmest expression in his eyes. Sometimes he would smile, then go back to studying. Other times he would drop his book, never taking his eyes off her. A slow, mischievous smile would curve his lips, and then the look in his eyes would become passionate. They were both young, after all.

Before Craig, her sexual experience had been limited to three awkward occasions with Pete Barrows, her high school flame. With Craig, she'd learned what it was all about. The excitement. The climax. The longing created by the look in someone's eyes, a scent, a word, a touch. He was gentle, forceful, exciting. Being with him was never awkward, but always incredible, frequently filled with laughter.

She remembered one occasion, lying naked, waiting for her heart to slow and her breath to come naturally, when he had suddenly turned to her and asked, "Hey, do you know what they rated that new pirate movie?"

"What?"

"Arr," he'd said, and they'd both laughed.

"My God, that's a horrible joke," she'd told him, but she'd forgiven him immediately when he'd pulled her into his arms and they'd made love all over again.

Her life had been perfect. She was getting good grades, having a wonderful time, and she was madly in love.

Until, out of the clear blue, he'd told her that he was changing his life, that he didn't really love her, that he was leaving right after he graduated.

She had been stunned. She'd spent a week drinking and crying, and nearly flunked out. She'd gone to his gradua-tion, hoping… But he hadn't even shown up.

She'd been mean to her parents and ignored her broth-ers. She'd spent what now seemed like half her lifetime wallowing in self-pity. But finally she'd pulled herself to-gether, refusing to allow herself to self-destruct over a guy who had turned out to be a jerk.

And now…here he was again. She could barely believe it.

He had just…walked out. On her, on his life. And why? To become a criminal?

Had he just woken up one morning thinking, *Wow, it would be great to befriend the dregs of society and start robbing people, maybe kill a few?*

She realized suddenly that if she stayed where she was much longer she was going to start suffering from hypo-thermia, even though she'd put on the warmest clothes in her bedroom. She had to move. She was pretty certain she could slip back into the house through the basement win-dow—the same way she had left.

Numb, she made her way to the back door—which squeaked, which was why she hadn't dared to use it—and slipped back through the window. She made a mental note to tell her father that a robber could easily break in that way, then laughed at herself, given that they'd let robbers—or worse—in through the front door tonight.

She shivered and hugged herself, trying to both warm her body and thaw her mind, and looked around in the dim light filtering in from the stone stairway leading down from the pantry.

The basement had seemed full of promise when she first headed down. She'd been certain there would be something down there that she could use as a weapon. The yardman was always leaving his tools behind.

But not this time. The basement offered nothing but the Ping-Pong table, paddles and balls. It was swept clean. There wasn't even a broom.

But, if she'd found something, what good would it have done? There were two of them. Or three, if Craig regained a semblance of strength.

No! her mind raged. Craig knew this was her family. He would never hurt her, and he would never hurt them. Or would he? What the hell did she know about him anymore? She hadn't seen him since he had coldly broken things off and walked away.

Had he become a dope addict? Was that what had changed his life? He hadn't looked like he was on anything out there in the car. He had just looked injured. Had one of the others hurt him? Or had he been injured while attacking an earlier victim?

She crept up the stone stairs that led to the pantry and the servants' stairway in the back of the house.

They didn't have any servants, of course, but the house had been built back when there was huge money in Western Massachusetts. The size and isolation of the place—and the cost of heating it—had been the reasons her family had gotten such a good deal on the house years ago.

She had hoped to escape to the neighbors' house for help, but her nearest neighbors were at least half a mile away. In the storm, she wasn't sure that she could find her way through the forest between the properties, but if she went by the road it would be more like two miles, and she knew she couldn't last that long in this weather.

And she wasn't even sure the Morrisons would be there or that she could get in. Artie Morrison had told her father that he was buying a condo in Boca where he could head for winter, now that he and his wife were retired and the kids had moved away.

After that, the next closest place was the jewelry and antique shop, and that was certainly closed for the holiday. Mr. Hudson was sick. He had cancer. Her mother had told her sadly that he was going to L.A. for the holidays, and that sometime during January, he and Ethan, his son, would come back together and close up for good, transferring what remained of the stock out to California, where Ethan and his wife now lived. After that...

Another human being was at least five miles away.

There was no hope of driving the cars; they were in the garage and the snow had already blocked the door. She'd had high hopes for the invaders' car, which was how she'd come to discover Craig in the first place. But even if he hadn't been in it, even if she hadn't been stunned into shock, she couldn't have driven it anywhere. Its nosedive into a snowbank had left the hood accordioned. That car was going nowhere.

Obviously they intended to steal a car when the snow cleared. A car no one would need—because they wouldn't leave anyone alive....

Stop, she commanded herself. She didn't know who these men were. Maybe they were so confident of their ability to get away that they didn't care if anyone knew their names. Yes, they carried guns, but that didn't mean they would use them.

But they might. There was one dead lamp upstairs to prove it.

At least it was just a lamp. At least the scrawny bastard who called himself Scooter hadn't shot a member of her family. Yet.

Breathe, she told herself. *Breathe. Think.*

All right, so she couldn't get help because she couldn't get anywhere alive. And dead, she would do them no good at all. But she wasn't doing anyone any good hovering in the basement, either.

If only her father kept a gun.

But he didn't.

He'd never even kept a gun at the pub, joking that he and her mother might shoot each other. But the truth was, he didn't believe in guns. He didn't like them. He had always been afraid that if you drew a gun and didn't kill your enemy immediately, that gun might be taken away and turned on you or another innocent. Besides, the pub was a stone's throw from a police station.

So there was no prayer of finding a gun in the house, but how did you combat a gun without a gun of your own?

There had to be a way.

She moved carefully up to the pantry, then stood dead still, listening. Voices didn't filter back this far with any clarity, but she could tell they were all in the living room, and she could hear the man named Scooter speaking, followed by her mother. After a minute her ears became attuned to the acoustics, and she began to make out parts of their sentences.

"You took a nasty blow…head," her mother said. "I cleaned…have quite a cut there…your hairline. You…careful not to sleep for a while."

"He's all right. Dinner…getting cold," Scooter complained.

"You're the one…had…out for him," Quintin snapped.

"I could…frozen…death!"

That was Craig's voice. And he had snapped back at Quintin, apparently comfortable enough with the other man to show his anger. Her heart sank. He *was* with them.

"Let's…back to the kitchen," Quintin said.

"I need…first aid kit away," Jamie said.

"Leave it," Quintin told him.

"What should…do with him?" Scooter asked.

Him? Kat frowned, then realized with relief that he had to be talking about Craig.

"He…stay…stare…tree for a while," Quintin said.

Kat heard shuffling and people talking over each other, presumably getting Craig settled in the living room, followed by the sounds of everyone else returning to the kitchen. Without a plan—or a weapon—she knew it was time to retreat. She used the sound of their approach to cover her own escape back up the servants' stairs to the second floor.

David O'Boyle sat at his own table, completely powerless, in a fury, feeling beyond humiliation or help. He was trying with everything in him to keep his mouth shut. He was praying with the same words over and over again: God, help. Oh, God, help. God, help. Help….

He had met his wife's eyes so many times, had seen the plea in them. There was nothing they could do that wouldn't get them killed except play this game.

Great game.

Scuzzy criminals who were probably cold-blooded murderers were sitting at the dinner table. *His* dinner table.

They were complimenting the food, drinking his liquor, making conversation as if they belonged there.

How the hell was he supposed to keep from throwing himself at one of them, even if it meant taking a bullet? But he couldn't take the risk that the other one would shoot Skyler or one of the kids. God help him, if there was just one of them... But there were two.

No, now there were three.

Of course, one was prone and possibly passed out in the living room, so at the moment, he didn't count. And he was younger, maybe not as bloodthirsty. Or maybe more so.

Hell.

He looked over at Paddy.

Fuck the old bird. He was chatting away with their vicious guests as if they were long-lost comrades from Dublin, filling their glasses again and again with whiskey, and saying the same things over and over, as if he had Alzheimer's.

Filling their glasses...

Was he hoping to get them drunk?

Maybe so, and it wasn't such a bad idea, now that he thought about it. Hell, it was better than anything he'd come up with.

No heroics. Quintin had sworn that he would kill Skyler, and David had the feeling that he'd do it.

"So when did you leave Ireland, old man?" Quintin asked, accepting another shot of Skyler's best single malt.

"The summer of sixty-four," Paddy said. "I'd had it with the violence." He winked at the table. "The minute I got to the States, I decided to be a Buddhist."

"Uncle Paddy, you're not a Buddhist," Jamie said.

"He's an alcoholic. That's his religion," Frazier told Quintin and Scooter. But there was no malice in his words. He was almost smiling as he looked at his uncle.

"'Tis true. I do worship a fine single malt," Paddy admitted.

"So then you opened a pub?" Scooter asked.

"No, sir, I did not. My sainted and now dearly departed sister and her husband opened the pub. I merely worked in it."

"He thought he was the social liaison," David heard himself say. But there was no malice in his voice, either.

I'm sorry I ridiculed you and wanted you out of my house, David thought. He was sorry that he'd argued with Frazier about the tree, too. He was sorry that he had so often been quick to find fault with all his children.

He stared across the table at Frazier. They might all end up dying in the hours to come. But not all of them, because he wouldn't let that happen. When the time came...

When would that time be?

He didn't know, but when it did, he would throw himself on one of the men and hope the others would overpower the second man left behind. And that someone would live.

But it wouldn't come to that for a while. Not while the wind and snow continued to rage. Not while the invaders were still being fed. Not while his family continued to entertain them.

David wanted to tell Brenda that she was welcome in his house, that he was glad she and Frazier made each other happy.

But he didn't want to draw attention to the women in his house. For all he knew, Quintin and Scooter could be rapists as well as killers. In fact, he was afraid that the only reason nothing like that had happened was because Quintin wanted two guns available at a moment's notice.

He went back to trying futilely to think of a way.

She came down the stairs in silence, a vengeful fire goddess with the red of her hair blazing against the white parka she'd found in her parents' closet.

Craig felt an instant rush of panic and looked toward the kitchen. There was no sign of anyone returning to the living room, but Quintin and Scooter knew nothing about Kat, and he was desperate for it to stay that way.

"What the hell are you doing?" he mouthed as she walked toward him.

"What the hell are *you* doing?" she mouthed in return.

"Listen—" he whispered when she was close enough to hear him.

"No, you listen. If you let them harm a single hair on the head of any one of my family, you are a dead man, do you understand?"

"I told you to get the hell out of here," he said.

He tried to sit up, but though the room swam, he resisted the temptation to go under again. She touched his face, and her fingers were soft and cool.

"You're burning up," she said, stepping back.

"Get out of here," he told her.

"I need to know—from your lips—that you're with them."

"You don't understand." He broke off when he heard a chair scrape against the kitchen floor. They could be heading back. "Get out of here, Kat, now."

She had heard it, too, but she paused, staring at him in a way that made his insides curl. "Do you have a gun, too? Are you going to shoot someone?"

"I had a gun.... Quintin took the bullets."

"So you *are* with them," she said in disgust.

"No."

Another chair scraped back.

"Get out of here," he told her again.

That time she listened and silently disappeared back up the stairs just as Quintin came into the room.

"You're sitting up. Feeling better?" Quintin asked.

"Yeah. No thanks to you, you asshole."

"Careful. You're the asshole, and I can make you a dead asshole real easy. In fact, I *should* shoot you. That would guarantee good behavior out of this family."

"Great. Why?" Craig demanded, making sure to keep his eyes on Quintin. Not to let them wander. Kat was on the landing, he was certain. Listening. Watching, perhaps.

"Why?" Quintin demanded, as if surprised.

"Yeah. Why bother with them?" Craig asked.

"I like the food. The comfort. The warmth of the house. Hell, I even like the feeling of having a family for Christmas."

"Glad to hear it."

"What else is there to do? There's no way to go anywhere in this storm, so tonight, we're all just one big happy family," Quintin said.

"The storm will stop eventually. What then?"

"And then we leave. I may let you live then, and I may not," Quintin said.

"What about them?" Craig demanded, lowering his voice.

Quintin smiled. "What about them?"

"What happens to them?"

Quintin shrugged. "Well, tomorrow is Christmas. Not a good day for anyone to die."

"And then?" Craig persisted.

"Then," Quintin said very softly, "it won't be Christmas anymore."

Chapter 4

"I said, no more," Scooter muttered irritably.

"What?" Paddy demanded, waving the whiskey bottle in the air. "No more? This is the best, I tell ye, my good man."

"I said enough," Scooter said.

David was afraid that the man was really losing his temper. Although Scooter liked to talk big, Quintin was definitely the boss of the two. But Quintin was in control of himself, while Scooter was like a loose cannon.

"Scooter," he said.

The man looked at him in surprise, perhaps because David had spoken to him by name. "What?"

"He...uh...it's Alzheimer's."

Scooter frowned; then his eyes widened. "You mean the old fart's going senile."

"Yeah."

"What?" Paddy demanded indignantly. But it had been his ploy all along. A good ploy? David didn't know. But all of them were acting, and Paddy's act was as good as any other. He lowered his head for a moment.

"Nothing," David said.

"He's not crazy, he's just a drunk," Jamie said.

"A drunk going crazy," Frazier told his brother.

"I'm not drunk yet—unfortunately," Paddy complained.

"Close enough," David said, though he didn't really think Paddy was close at all. After years of pickling his brain, the old man could hold a prodigious amount of liquor.

"Everybody be nice," Skyler commanded, rising and picking up her plate. "Frazier, hand me that platter, please."

"What are you doing?" David asked.

"The dishes, obviously," she said.

Do the dishes matter when we all might be dead soon? David wondered.

He didn't ask the question aloud. As he rose to help clear the table, Quintin returned to the kitchen, along with the newest arrival.

The guy still looked a little green, but he offered what looked like a genuine smile. "I'm a little late. Mind if I grab something?"

Skyler turned to him with a smile. "Of course not. What would you like?"

That was Skyler through and through, David thought: making sure a crook didn't go hungry. They couldn't even get rid of rats at the pub in the normal way; they had to go out and buy the humane traps, then set the rodents free out in the country. Even when the rats were bigger than the alley cats that continually hung out looking for scraps.

"Are you feeling better?" Skyler asked the newcomer.

He shrugged. "I feel hungry. I think the smells coming from the kitchen gave me strength."

Just what they needed: to give the guy strength. "Sit. I'll

get you a plate," David said. What else was there to do? At least this one was polite.

"Who plays the piano?" Quintin asked.

"Everyone in the family," David replied curtly.

"Do you all sit around the piano and sing Christmas carols?" Scooter demanded, laughing.

"Yes," Skyler informed him icily.

"Christmas carols, huh?" Quintin said thoughtfully. "That might be…interesting. It's not like we want to watch the news."

Ice trickled along David's spine. They didn't want to watch the news. Why not? What were the men afraid he and his family would learn about them if they were to watch the news? Or would anyone even know anything yet, with the storm at full fury?

"Christmas carols sound great," Craig said. He looked at Jamie. "Is the piano your favorite instrument now? Or is that guitar I saw in the living room yours?"

Jamie shrugged. "The guitar's mine, but I like them both."

Now? David thought. The man had said "now." As if he knew Jamie. But that was impossible…wasn't it?

"Frazier can play the piano way better than me," Jamie went on.

"Except for my dad," Frazier said. "Not to mention my mom. She's the one who usually plays at Christmas."

"She loves Christmas," Jamie supplied.

"Christmas carols, turkey…a warm house," Scooter said, almost talking to himself.

"So everyone in the family is a musician," Quintin said, frowning as he glanced at Scooter.

"Comes from owning the pub," David explained. "We didn't have a lot of money when we took it over from Skyler's parents. We couldn't afford to hire a band, so we made our own music." He looked at his wife and smiled, suddenly remembering the years gone by. Lean times, hard times, but they'd made do. Skyler had heard the old Irish songs all her life, and her light, melodic voice more than did them justice. His sons had grown up liking harder, Celtic-tinged rock. Frazier's favorite band was Black 47, and he often headed down to New York to hear them.

Suddenly David realized that Quintin was studying him with something like envy. "I wanted to play the guitar," the man said, sounding natural for the first time all night. "I sucked. Took after my mother, who couldn't carry a tune in a bucket."

"What about your father?"

Quintin shrugged. "Never knew him—never even knew who he was."

"I could teach you a few chords," Jamie volunteered.

"Yeah? Well, we'll see," Quintin said, reverting to form.

"Let's hear some carols," Scooter said.

"Music," Paddy said. "'Tis an Irish tradition, that it is. Along with a good whiskey. Drinking fine whiskey, now there's a talent that can be learned quick."

"We're going to sing Christmas carols, Uncle Paddy," Frazier said.

"You all go ahead," Skyler told them. "I'll finish up the dishes."

"We'll all stay together," Quintin said firmly.

"Fine. Then let me finish the dishes," she insisted.

"What difference do the dishes make?" Quintin asked softly, something ominous in his tone.

But Skyler spun around. "I was under the impression that you wanted a turkey tomorrow. If you want a turkey tomorrow, I have to clean up in here tonight. That's how you run a good business. You keep up."

David was stunned at the way she was standing up to Quintin. Skyler was an enigma. She always had been. She hated controversy, and most of the time she was the sweetest human being in the world, but every so often… When it came to the right way to do things, she could definitely stick to her guns.

"Fine. Everyone, up and help out," Quintin said.

Scooter wanted Christmas, David thought, and Quintin wanted turkey, which meant that, at least for now, they had time….

David maneuvered to stand next to his wife at the sink. As she rinsed the dishes and he set them into the dishwasher, he had a moment to whisper to her. "I *will* do something," he swore.

"No."

"Skyler…"

"Don't make them angry."

"Skyler…"

"They plan to kill us before they leave. I know that. But wait, please. It's only Christmas Eve, and it's still snowing. We have time."

"Time for what?"

"I don't know. But…it's Christmas."

Right, Christmas, with its tidings of comfort and joy. Only a few hours ago he had been irritable because Paddy was there, because Frazier had brought home a girl, because Jamie was holed up in his room, because they couldn't get the tree to stand straight. Now…he just wanted them all to be alive to celebrate New Year's Eve.

She stared at him with clear, level eyes. She was praying for a miracle, he realized. And who was he to deny her? Hell, he wasn't in any hurry to die.

"Help may be out there," she whispered, and left it at that. They both knew that Kat was still…somewhere.

"Sure," he said, and began to hum "Silent Night" to take his mind off the situation.

The next thing he knew, something hard was sticking into his back. It took him only a second to realize that it was the cold nose of Quintin's gun.

"Quit whispering," Quintin said coldly.

David turned around despite the gun and stared at Quintin. "What the hell do you think we could be saying that's such a big deal?" he demanded.

Quintin thought that over, then shrugged. "Are you done in here yet?" he asked Skyler.

"Just let me wipe the table and start the dishwasher," she said. "While we still have power."

"You have a generator. I saw it." Scooter pointed from across the room.

"Yes, we have a generator. And enough gas to keep us going for about twelve hours," David told him.

"I'd hate to waste gas doing the dishes," Skyler said. "We'll probably need it to cook with tomorrow."

"Time to head out to the living room. Everyone. All together," Quintin said, still holding the gun.

Brenda made a little noise, not so much a sob as an involuntary sigh.

"Don't cry," Quintin said. "I bet you can be plenty tough when you need to."

Frazier, pulling Brenda close, stared at him.

Quintin grinned. He had the power. He knew it, and he liked it. So far, he was just playing with them, but if he went after Frazier's girl…what would his son do? What would *he* do?

Together, they went out to the living room. Frazier, silent, his eyes on the invaders, sat at one end of the sofa, holding Brenda against him. Her eyes were wide, luminous with unshed tears. Jamie perched on a chair nearby, staying close to his brother. Skyler took the piano bench. Craig sat at the other end of the sofa, keeping his distance from his cohorts, who chose the armchairs near the fireplace. The better to keep an eye on the captives, David thought, or because Craig wasn't really one of them? He remembered Quintin's accusation that Craig was a cop, and he wondered.

"There are no ornaments on this tree," Scooter complained.

"We hadn't gotten to it yet," David said.

"You have ornaments, though. Right?" Scooter wanted to know.

"Of course we have ornaments," David said wearily.

"Where are they?" Scooter asked.

"In the attic. We hadn't brought them down yet," David explained.

Scooter looked at Quintin. "We need ornaments."

Quintin glowered with aggravation. "All right. Scooter, you take Dad up there and he can get the ornaments."

"They're heavy boxes," David said. "And there are a lot of them. I'll need help."

"You—go with your father," Quintin said, pointing at Jamie.

"Sure," Jamie said, but he hesitated.

"What now?" Quintin demanded.

"Frazier and Dad always bring down the boxes. My si— my mother and I pick out which ornaments go on the tree first. It's tradition," Jamie said stubbornly.

"You people and your friggin' traditions! Fine. You—" Quintin said, pointing at Frazier. "Go with your father."

Brenda clung harder to Frazier, wide-eyed and terrified.

"Brenda," Skyler coaxingly said, walking over to her. "Come over to the piano with me. We'll find some sheet music, okay?"

Brenda nodded, tried to smile and got up to join Skyler.

"I think the ornaments can wait for just a minute," Quintin said suddenly. "I want to hear something on the piano."

They all went still. David was suddenly aware of the ferocity of the wind outside the safety of the house.

Where was his daughter? Had she gone for help? Was she lying dead in the snow somewhere?

No. Kat was smart. She would know that she couldn't make it for help in this weather. Know that she would have to stay hidden, that eventually she would have to listen as they shot down her family.

Don't think that way, he told himself. *Believe.*

Believe in what? God? Miracles? One of his mother's sayings suddenly came back to him. *God helps those who help themselves.* And he *would* help himself and his family, by God. When the time was right.

Whenever the hell that was.

"Someone play the friggin' piano," Quintin snapped.

Skyler sat down, taking Brenda's hand and inviting the girl to sit next to her on the bench. She trailed her fingers over the keys, and David knew she was thinking about what to play.

She started singing "We Wish You a Merry Christmas," and David thought again that this was beyond bizarre, his family and the men who would probably kill them sitting around the piano on Christmas Eve.

To David's amazement, Jamie walked over to the piano

and started singing, too. Then Frazier joined in, followed by Brenda, and David realized that somewhere along the way he'd started singing himself.

And so had Scooter.

The house was warm, everyone was full after dinner, the music was good, and this felt ridiculously like a warm family scene.

When Skyler finished the first song, she went into "O Little Town of Bethlehem." From there, she sang about the little drummer boy, letting Jamie take the lead. Uncle Paddy backed him up with his fine Irish tenor.

When the song ended, Craig clapped, Scooter followed suit, and even Quintin smiled.

"We should get the ornaments now," Scooter said eagerly. "And she should keep playing," he announced, pointing at Skyler.

"All right," Quintin said.

Skyler immediately started playing a rousing rendition of "Rudolph, the Red-Nosed Reindeer."

Tears were streaming unnoticed down Kat's face as she sat on the second-floor landing, listening, paying attention to every word, every nuance of tone.

She knew she couldn't leave. She wouldn't make it even a quarter-mile, much less the distance she would need to go. She had to wait for the weather to subside. The problem was, that was when the killers would be ready to leave, too, and before they did...

She was also afraid to leave. Afraid something terrible would happen if she did.

She was her family's only hope for survival, and she didn't know what to do, so she listened to the music and let her mind wander, hoping her subconscious would provide an answer while the rest of her mind was distracted.

Christmas carols were a family staple at the holidays. They could argue among themselves until they were ready to tear each other's hair out, but the fighting stopped when it was time to gather around the piano.

She felt a surge of fury. Those *monsters* were gathered around *her* piano in *her* home, threatening *her* family as her mother played the piano.

She was still in her parka, afraid to get caught without it, though she had unzipped it because the house was warm.

Warm and cozy, smelling deliciously of dinner and the bayberry candles her mother had set out. It always amazed her. They came here so infrequently and stayed so briefly, but this place had become a true holiday home for them. In a matter of hours they always managed to get their act together, despite all the bickering.

She felt a lump in her throat, a rolling in her stomach. Craig Devon—the tall, blond, muscular Mr. Gorgeous she had once loved—was down there with her family. The family he knew so much about because she had told him so much about them, while he'd told her nothing about himself.

Because, despite his boy-next-door looks, he was nothing but a criminal.

How had he gone from being a man filled with promise to what he was now? As she stared down at him, her nausea threatened to spill over. She remembered reading about a rash of heists conducted by thieves who hit small jewelry and antique shops throughout the Northeast, mainly in rural areas and mostly at night. And Hudson's, she thought now, was so close to this house. Police had warned that the thieves might be armed and very dangerous. One article had said police were searching for the killer or killers of a night watchman at a bank, who had been found dead near one of the jewelry stores, although they felt it was an unrelated incident. But what if it had been related after all?

If these men had killed before, they would certainly be willing to kill again.

If...

Maybe they hadn't killed the night watchman.

Right. There was a heist, and there was a dead man, but some passing maniac had done it.

That had been in New Hampshire. *Live free or die.* Apparently they had taken the state motto to heart.

She shifted slightly, gritting her teeth, and tried hard to remember any other details. As she moved, she felt her worthless phone in her pocket. She pulled it out, thinking that it couldn't hurt to see if she could get a signal.

She swore silently at the no-signal message, then stared in disbelief when the phone flickered for a moment and went dead. As she stared at the traitorous cell, she heard the music stop and people start talking about going up to the attic.

She scrambled to her feet, knowing that, whatever she was going to do, she had to move fast.

"Ready?" Scooter asked David.

"Sure," David said. "Frazier, let's go get those boxes down."

"Wait a minute," Quintin said. "What else is up in that attic?"

Skyler stopped playing and turned to answer him. "We don't have a gun up there, if that's what you're afraid of," she said flatly.

Quintin actually grinned, shaking his head. "Bleeding-heart liberal, huh? Guns don't kill, buddy. People kill," he said.

"Thanks. I'll remember that," David told him.

"You don't hunt, I take it?" Quintin said.

"No, I don't hunt."

Quintin shrugged, as if David were only half a man.

"Some men don't need to hunt," Skyler said, staring at Quintin. "They don't need guns."

Quintin laughed. "Well, right now, I've got the gun, and that makes me the man to watch, doesn't it?"

"Skyler..." David said soothingly.

"I've got the gun, and if I want 'em, I've got the cute little blonde, your wife and your sons," Quintin said to David. "And that makes me feel very important."

"Let's get the ornaments, Frazier," David said tightly.

"Scooter, watch them," Quintin warned.

"Quit acting like I'm a damn idiot," Scooter snapped.

"You're not an idiot, you're like a fucking little kid, wanting to decorate the Christmas tree," Quintin retorted.

"Hey!" Craig spoke up. "Cut it out, you two. Quintin, the tree and the music are nice."

"Why the hell not have Christmas?" Scooter demanded.

Quintin narrowed his eyes. "Fine, let's have Christmas." He turned to David. "Just don't do anything stupid up there and make me shoot your wife. Or even Blondie over there."

Brenda gasped.

"Oh, shut up," Quintin commanded.

"It's all right," Skyler said, putting her arm around the girl as they sat on the bench.

"I'm just going to get the ornaments," David said. "That's all."

Scooter had his gun out, and he used it to gesture toward the stairs. "I'll be right behind you guys," he said. His tone was pleasant and yet somehow disturbing.

David headed for the stairs, walking heavily. If Kat was

still in the house, listening, watching, she needed to be warned.

Don't do anything foolish, Kat, he prayed silently. You have to live.

He heard his son behind him, and Scooter behind Frazier. When they reached the upstairs hall, he pulled down the ladder to the attic and started up.

"No tricks," Scooter warned.

"No tricks," he promised wearily.

He couldn't think of a trick that could save them. Not now. Not when Quintin was holding a gun on the rest of his family.

A thought raced through his mind. What if they could disarm Scooter? At least Frazier might have a chance to live.

And he would know his life had been at the cost of his family and the woman he loved.

"Don't get too close to your father, kid. Let him hand you the boxes," Scooter said.

"I have to stand at least on the second rung to reach," Frazier told him.

"Yeah, yeah, all right. Hurry up," Scooter said nervously.

So Scooter was the nervous type, David thought. Maybe if they learned more about the three men, it could be useful.

He grabbed one of the ornament boxes and turned to hand it to Frazier. His son's eyes met his, and David realized that for once, his son was looking to him for a lead.

He offered a smile and tried to fill it with the assurance that they would get out of this somehow.

Frazier nodded, and David found himself mentally listing his sons' strengths. Jamie was young and thin, but tall, strong and perceptive. Frazier was always at odds with him, but he was strong, bright and a creative thinker. They might not have any options right now, he thought, but the time might come, if they could just stay alive until then.

Stay alive—and pray their captors would make a mistake.

There were three of them now, including Craig, the injured one. But was he as much of a danger as the others? Hard to tell. Just how injured was he, anyway? He would bear further watching. He was with the criminals, but there was definite tension there. Maybe that was the answer: playing them against each other.

"Should Frazier take that one on down?" David asked.

"What do you mean? You planning something?" Scooter asked suspiciously.

David almost laughed. "I wish I had a plan. Should he take that box downstairs now, then come back so I can hand him the next one? Or do we all walk downstairs and back up again with every box?" he asked.

Scooter scowled, then turned to Frazier. "Take that one down and get right back up here. And you," he said, indicating David with the nose of the gun. "Don't make a move until the kid is back up here. Any tricks, kid," he said, returning his attention to Frazier, "and I put a hole through your old man's chest."

"Unfortunately, I don't have any tricks," Frazier said.

David knew when Frazier reached the living room with his box. Both he and Scooter could hear Quintin's explosion.

"Scooter!"

"What the fuck?" Scooter demanded, going to the rail.

"You let the kid walk down here alone!" Quintin raged.

"I have a gun on his dad, and you have a gun on his mother and his girlfriend," Scooter said. "He's just bringing the box down and coming right back up."

David could hear Quintin muttering. Scooter stared back

at him, and he had to prevent himself from smiling. "Quintin really runs you on a tight rope, huh?" he asked.

"Quintin doesn't run me."

"Sure he does."

"Shut up. We work together. No one runs me."

"Sure. Whatever you say."

"Here comes the kid. He's back. Get another box, and then get down from there. You're done."

"Sure." David stepped up into the attic again. Frazier was back on the second rung below him, ready to take the next box of ornaments. David reached for the box and just barely kept himself from gasping aloud.

Kat was there.

She was three feet away, shoving the box silently over to him with one hand and putting a finger to her lips in the age-old signal to keep silent. "I can't get away," she breathed so quietly that he could barely hear her. "And my phone is dead."

He nodded to let her know he understood, then mouthed the words, "Charger in my top bedside drawer."

"I love you," she whispered, and his heart soared.

"I love you, too."

"What the hell's taking so long?" Scooter demanded.

"Nothing. I'm just getting a grip on it," he said. He stared at his daughter for a long moment, then smiled with encouragement and breathed, "Be careful."

She nodded and slipped into the shadows as he climbed down and handed the box to Frazier.

"That's it, all right?" David said, using irritation to cover his relief at knowing Kat was still alive.

"Yeah, yeah." Scooter waved the gun. "Go on, both of you, downstairs. Listen. Your old lady is playing 'Deck the Halls,' so let's go deck 'em."

Chapter 5

It was insane, Skyler thought. There they were, all gathered around the old piano, just like the quintessential Christmas family. But in reality it was the most terrifying situation she'd ever known. Despite that, as if trying could somehow make it real, she found herself racking her mind for the most cheerful Christmas carols possible. "Frosty the Snowman," anything with a bit of a lilt. Meanwhile, Jamie chose ornaments and handed them out. Brenda had somehow found her courage and was helping. The room was cozy and smelled of the bayberry candles she loved, along with the faint scent of dinner.

It couldn't have looked more like Christmas, at least as long as she ignored Craig, who was sitting on the sofa, watching and still looking a little green around the gills.

Her panic had subsided, hovering in the background and only rearing its ugly head occasionally, when she let herself think about what was really going on.

Suddenly her attention was caught by a loud laugh. It was Scooter, who seemed to have the time of his life, helping to decorate the tree.

"These are great ornaments," he said to Jamie. "Are they Irish?"

"No, just from Macy's," Jamie told him.

"And this one?" he asked, holding up a red tear-shaped glass ornament.

"That's an old one," Frazier told him. "From my grandparents, right, Mom?"

"Yes. It's part of a set my parents brought over from Ireland," Skyler said between songs. She took a moment to look over at Quintin, who was listening without expression. What the hell was going on in that man's mind? she wondered, then tried to figure out just how many more Christmas carols she knew.

She started to sing "What Child Is This?" the Christmas version of "Greensleeves." When she dared a look at Quintin, his eyes were almost closed, and he seemed strangely at peace.

"Do you know any Irish carols?" Quintin asked when she'd finished.

"Does a bear shit in the woods?" Jamie demanded. "Sorry, Mom."

She shrugged. She'd heard the word before. Sad enough to say, she'd probably used it herself, even in front of her children.

"Do you want to hear more Christmas music," she asked Quintin, "or just music in general? Jamie could get his guitar." She looked at Frazier. "And we could do with a violin."

"Yeah," Quintin said. "Yeah, that would be nice."

They all stared at him.

"The boys' instruments are upstairs in their bedrooms," Skyler said.

"Go with them, and keep the gun on them," Quintin told Scooter.

"Why?" Scooter demanded. "The kids know if they do anything, Mom gets it right between the eyes."

In the end, Skyler thought with a moment's panic, Mom will get it between the eyes anyway. David and I need to just throw ourselves on top of these guys and hope the kids can...

No, not yet. They had all night. The storm was still freezing everything in their little world. There was time.

"Go with them," Quintin insisted to Scooter.

Suddenly Craig spoke up. "I can do it."

Quintin looked at him, a strange, twisted grimace on his face. "But you're not armed, are you?"

"Scooter can give me his gun. You don't need two of them down here."

"I don't think so," Quintin said, staring at Craig.

Craig shrugged, as if it made no difference to him. "Whatever."

Scooter let out a sound of aggravation. "Next time, you do it," he told Quintin.

"Just get going," Quintin said flatly.

Scooter stared at Jamie and Frazier. "Come on."

To Skyler's surprise, Quintin looked from David to her after the others left and said, "This is really nice, this whole family thing, the music." Without warning, his eyes hardened. "So don't go ruining my good mood, okay?" He turned to Brenda then. "What about you? You play an instrument? Or do you just sit around looking pretty?"

Skyler put an arm around the girl. "Brenda is pre-med."

"She's going to be a doctor?" Quintin started to laugh.

"What's wrong with that?" Brenda asked him, surprising Skyler by speaking up so firmly.

"Are you tall enough to reach the operating table?" Quintin asked.

"She's not just tall enough, she's smart enough," Skyler snapped.

"Why don't you leave them alone?" David asked, his tone low, his words spoken with a tremendous dignity that squeezed Skyler's heart.

"I could," Quintin mused. "But I don't want to. And hey… I've got the gun."

Skyler rose and, hands on her hips, stared at the man who was destroying her family. "Brenda is at the top of her class. One day, when you've been shot and there's a bullet lodged in your brain, she could be the doctor operating on you. She plans on making something of herself. That's more than what some people here can say."

David stood, and she knew she had frightened him, that he was afraid Quintin would retaliate violently.

"Sit down, both of you," Quintin said patiently. "I'm just an old chauvinist—sorry. The kid is smart? Good for her. Are you and the boy engaged, then?" he asked Brenda.

"No," she said.

Quintin turned to David. "And you don't mind them shacking up in your house?"

David stared back at Quintin. "Yes, I mind. But I love my son, and I respect Brenda."

"Still, it's not like it was when you were a kid, huh?" Quintin said.

"No," David agreed flatly. "Times change."

"That they do," Quintin said, and though his voice was quiet, there was menace in his tone. "That they do."

* * *

Kat, who'd been watching from the second-floor balcony, leaped up lightly and fled as soon as she saw Scooter and her brothers coming up the stairs.

She raced to her room, grabbed the phone from the charger and leaned against the closed door, her heart racing as she tried to listen to what was going on.

While she listened, she punched buttons frantically and tried to send out a 911 text message, but whether or not it got through, she didn't know.

Not that it mattered. Until the storm abated, no one could get here anyway, she thought, then went back to eavesdropping.

"Come on, come on," Scooter said, as he ushered the two boys along the hall. "He just has to have his damn music, so let's just get the damn fiddle and be done with it."

"You have something against violins?" Frazier asked belligerently.

"Calm down and don't be a jerk. You're just like Dad," Jamie accused him.

"I'm not like Dad!" Frazier denied heatedly.

"Oh yeah? You get pissed off every time someone is late. But then you're late to everything, and you say it's because you think everyone else will be late."

"Who are you to talk? Ever since you got that car, you never even show up for family occasions half the time."

"That's because I'm stuck with them *all* the time," Jamie reminded him.

"Because you're sixteen," Frazier told him.

"At least you're a twin. You always had Kat around. I have to deal with Mom and Dad all alone."

"You have a twin?" Scooter asked Frazier suspiciously. "Where?"

Against the wall, Kat sucked in a breath and held it.

"She escaped," Frazier said quickly.

"Escaped?" Scooter echoed.

"Escaped the family this Christmas. Which is exactly what I should have done," Frazier said quickly.

Their voices faded as they walked farther down the hall. When she could tell from their footsteps that they were outside Frazier's room, Kat dared to open her door and peek around the jamb. Her brothers were looking her way, and their eyes grew big when they spotted her. She shook her head in warning, and they nodded almost imperceptibly.

She held up her phone and mimed dialing, hoped they understood, then mouthed, "I love you," and slipped back inside her room, shutting the door carefully. A moment later she heard them coming back down the hallway.

Suddenly the phone clutched in her hand let out a beep. She froze.

"What was that?" Scooter demanded, and she realized he was right outside her door.

"What?" Jamie asked.

"That noise," Scooter said.

"What noise?" Frazier demanded, sounding impatient. "This is an old house. It creaks and groans all the time."

"It wasn't any fucking old-house sound," Scooter snapped. " It was a beep. Now come back here and open that door."

Frazier did his best to stall. "That door?"

"What are you, stupid? Yes, *that* door. Open it."

Kat could hear their voices, even though she had dived into her closet and hidden as best she could behind the clothes, scrunching into a corner and pulling an old comforter over herself.

"Get in there," Scooter snapped to Jamie and Frazier.

Her heart pounding, afraid her every breath was a thunderous gasp, Kat cowered as far back as she could go and listened.

"Don't you two pull anything," Scooter warned.

"What are we going to pull?" Jamie demanded.

Kat heard a thump and realized Scooter had gotten on his knees to look under the bed.

"What the hell do you think you're going to find?" Frazier demanded.

"Whose room is this?" Scooter asked, ignoring Frazier's question.

"My sister's," Jamie said. "When she bothers to show up."

"But she didn't show up?" Scooter asked.

"Have you seen her?" Frazier asked in return, sounding aggravated by the question.

"She's in love," Jamie said. "She went away with her boyfriend."

"Yeah?" Scooter said, doubt still evident in his voice.

"Will you hurry up and look wherever you're going to look?" Frazier queried impatiently. "Your crazy friend is down there with my family and my girlfriend, and he's going to start thinking something's wrong if we don't get back."

"Open that closet door," Scooter said.

Jamie snorted derisively. "Why? You think the bogeyman is in there?" he asked.

"Do it!" Scooter yelled. He sounded tense and on the edge of hysteria.

The door opened.

"Nothing here," Jamie said impatiently, although he had to know she was there.

She heard footsteps on the floorboards outside her refuge. Scooter?

"I heard something," Scooter snapped.

"I bet I know what it was," Jamie said. "You must've heard one of the smoke detectors. The battery's probably going or something."

"A smoke detector?" Scooter said doubtfully.

"Yeah, look. There's one right there. On the ceiling."

"I dunno," Scooter said. "Make it beep again, kid."

"I don't know how to make it beep," Jamie argued.

"Then figure it out," Scooter said. "Figure it out."

Quintin rose, his gun in his hand.

David stayed seated and did his best to remain calm, but the other man had a firm grip on his weapon, and it was clear that he knew how to use it. He'd used it before, David was certain. There was something in the man's eyes. A coldness. A complete lack of conscience.

He liked to be amused. Entertained. And right now they were entertaining him. He didn't want to think what would happen when that stopped.

Quintin was starting to look nervous, David realized. The others had been upstairs for what felt like a long time.

Maybe Craig had picked up on the same thing, because he suddenly said, "Quintin, you want me to go see what's going on?"

Quintin flashed him an impatient glance. "No."

"What the hell do you think I'm going to do? I'm half-dead and I don't have a weapon. I'll just go up and see if Scooter needs help."

"Go to the foot of the stairs," Quintin said, "and just yell for him."

Craig nodded and got up. "Yeah, sure. Hey, Scooter!" he yelled when he'd reached the stairway. "What's going on?"

"He's being a jerk!" Jamie shouted from above.

David felt his stomach lurch. *Please, Jamie, for the love of God, watch your mouth. We're playing a dangerous game.*

"Hey!" Scooter objected angrily.

Craig glanced at Quintin, frowning.

Jamie appeared on the landing. "He thinks I can make the smoke detector beep again," he called down.

A beep? David thought. *They'd heard a beep? It had to be Kat's phone.* He didn't know whether to feel hopeful or even more terrified.

"Hey, Scooter, get back down here," Craig called.

He was gripping the banister to stay upright, David realized. He didn't look well, but he was basically fit, and he was still on his feet, despite being hurt and then left out in the car.

Scooter had defended Craig, David mused. And Quintin didn't trust him. He filed that information away for later.

Scooter appeared at the top of the stairway, the boys in front of him, and looked down. "Do smoke detectors beep?" he asked Quintin.

"Of course they beep," David answered. He hoped he had just the right note of impatience in his tone.

"Do they?" Quintin asked him.

David frowned, hoping he was a decent actor. His pulse was pounding, and he realized that Quintin might not have to kill him, because he felt ready to have a heart attack all on his own. "A smoke detector beeps when you need to replace the battery," he said.

"Then why isn't it still beeping?" Scooter asked loudly.

"Because the battery beeps slowly at first, to warn you," David answered.

"Did you look around up there?" Quintin demanded.

"Of course," Scooter said.

"And?"

"I didn't find anything."

"Then get back down here."

"All right. One more minute."

David swallowed hard. Was Kat about to be discovered? And that beep…

Had her phone *worked?*

Knowing he had to do something, David got up and started to walk toward the stairs.

"Where the hell are you going?" Quintin demanded.

"Upstairs."

Quintin shook his head. "You stay right here."

"Look, I know what the problem is. I can show Scooter, so you two don't have to be worried about anything going on."

"I'll go," Craig said.

"What? Are all you people deaf or just stupid? I said you stay here," Quintin snapped.

David forced himself to sit back down calmly, then looked over at Skyler. She looked scared, her eyes too wide as they met his. He hoped Quintin wouldn't notice and re-alize something was going on.

She must have realized the danger, too, because she looked away and trailed her fingers over the piano keys. "Come on, guys, hurry up," she called. "It's time for Irish music."

"Oh, Danny boy, the pipes, the pipes are calling…" Uncle Paddy began.

* * *

Scooter was prowling around the room again. Kat could hear him from her hiding place in the closet.

"Please, come on," Jamie begged, real fear in his voice. "Didn't you hear him? Your friend is starting to sound dangerous."

"Starting?" Scooter said distractedly. "He always sounds dangerous. He is dangerous."

"So let's get down there."

"I'm telling you, I heard something beep."

"What? You think we have a bomb?" Frazier demanded.

"I think something's…not right," Scooter said.

"Please," Jamie begged. "Can we just go back downstairs?"

Kat willed herself to be perfectly still. She prayed her heartbeat wasn't as loud as it sounded to her own ears.

The floorboards creaked as Scooter kept walking around her room. It felt like forever, though it was certainly only seconds, before the closet door was flung open once again and he started pushing the hangers around.

Any second now, he would find her, and then they would all be dead.

Kat could almost feel him as he reached for the comforter on top of her. She felt the pressure as his fingers closed around it, and then she heard a scream as the entire house was pitched into darkness.

The power had gone out at last.

Chapter 6

"Hell of a night," Deputy Sergeant Sheila Polanski said, rubbing her hands together in a vain attempt to warm them.

The power at the sheriff's office had gone out long ago. They had switched over to their emergency generator smoothly enough, but since everything was run at taxpayer expense, the emergency generators didn't allow for much heat.

And they called it *Tax*achusetts.

Hell, she called her beloved home state Taxachusetts herself, but even so, the state budget didn't kick in much to supply heat for this particular sheriff's office out in the country. They were small and located in an area where there was seldom trouble, so they were expected to run on a shoestring.

There was only one person answering to her tonight: Tim Graystone. Tim had managed to pull the Christmas Eve gig by being their newcomer. Young and raw, only on the job for a month. And honestly, it wasn't as if his inexperience mattered. This area was sparsely populated and too far east to share the crimes that faced their neighbors in ski country, where an abundance of tourists made an appealing target for theft. And they were too far west to run into the troubles that Springfield, with its larger population, had to deal with.

Then again, Sheila had learned in her twenty years of duty, anything could happen. Three years ago, Barry Higgins, as mild mannered as they came under most circumstances, drank too much and shot up the civic center, killing his own minister in the process. In '95, Arthur Duggan had murdered his wife. That had been sad, but bound to happen. The best minds and hearts in social services had tried to get her to swear out a warrant against her husband, not to mention leave him. They'd told her over and over again that he would kill her one day, and finally he had.

But those were the only two violent crimes that had ever come their way. So even though they were a skeleton crew, it didn't seem likely that young Tim would have much to deal with tonight. The phone and electric lines were down, and the storm continued to rage. There wasn't much for them to do other than sit around and bitch about the weather.

Tim grinned. He was a good-looking fellow, just turned twenty-seven. Despite a hitch in the service, he'd gone through the academy and college before joining the force here, reporting to Sheriff Edward Ford. All told, there were only twelve officers working the county, six by day and six by night, though the schedule didn't mean much, because they were always subbing for one another. Edward, as the boss and the only duly elected official, usually stepped up to the plate and took Christmas Eve duty, but he had just remarried and the new Mrs. Ford, though forty, had decided to procreate. So Edward and his bride were already checked into one of the many offshoots of U Mass Medical, awaiting the new little Ford.

As a result, Sheila was working with Tim tonight. He was working here because, after his time in the service, he had come home to find his father dying of heart disease, leaving his mother alone to raise his much younger sister. He'd decided to stick around to guide her through the teenage years and throw some financial support his mother's way. Sheila didn't warm to just anyone, but Tim, she liked.

If she'd ever been able to have kids, she would have wanted one like him. But she hadn't been able to, and her husband had left her because of it.

She sat down, though she had been pacing back and forth to keep warm. Tim might have been living in warmer climes for the last few years, but he didn't seem to feel the cold. He was seated at a desk, his fingers laced behind his head and his feet propped up.

"Met any women up here yet?" she teased.

He shrugged. "A few. How about you?"

"How about me what?" Sheila asked.

"When are you going to get remarried?"

"Tim, look at me. I'm sixty-two years old, and I look like a mop. Bone thin, and my hair's gray and frizzy."

"You've got great blue eyes," he said, then leveled a finger at her. "And we're off at six. You can sleep for a few hours, then drag your butt out of bed and come on over. My mom's an expert with a turkey."

"Maybe. You don't have a bunch of old geezers coming over to try to fix me up with, do you?"

"No—and I'm not asking you to find anyone for me, either. Just a nice Christmas dinner."

She shrugged.

"You're coming?"

"Sure," she said, then jumped as Tim dropped his feet to the floor with a thump and sat up straight to stare at the computer screen.

"What is it?" she demanded.

"Look at that," he said.

Their emergency phone lines went straight to the computers once the power went down and the generators kicked in, though it was a makeshift system that only let them receive calls, not respond or call out. Now they both stared at the screen, which registered a text message sent from a cell phone.

Help. Emergency. 225 Elm.

"Two-two-five Elm," Tim said.

"The O'Boyle place. They always come up from Boston for the holidays. This had better not be another damn prank like the one their kid pulled last year."

Tim looked at her. "I suppose there's no chance we can—"

"Wait to check it out? No such luck. Bundle up, buddy. Duty calls."

"Okay," Tim said, masking his reluctance. "But how the hell are we going to get way out there?"

Suddenly the computer pinged and another message came through. The voice was tinny through the cheap speakers, but the worry in Ethan Hudson's voice was clear as he asked them to check on his father, who had stayed late at his shop and never made it home.

"Poor guy probably plowed into a snowbank," Sheila said. "Somehow, we've got to get out there. At least they're both in the same direction."

* * *

There was silence after the scream, a silence so complete and acute that Kat could almost taste it, like something metallic in the air.

This was it. The opportunity they needed.

And her brothers took it. She heard Scooter cry out as someone grabbed him, then long moments ticked past, punctuated by grunts and shuffling.

Then the generator kicked in.

She realized that what had seemed like forever had in reality been only a matter of seconds, and she cursed the generator they had begged their father to buy, though she had no idea whether the outcome would have been the same without it.

She was still in the closet when the dim light from the hallway showed her Scooter on the floor of her bedroom, Frazier straddling him and Jamie sitting on his feet.

There was a bruise darkening on Frazier's face, but Scooter looked the worse for wear, as well, with a bloody lip. And his gun was on the floor.

Jamie made a dive for the gun, reaching it before Scooter could reclaim it.

"Hold it on him, Jamie...." Frazier cautioned.

Jamie held it. Pale as a ghost, he held it.

Frazier got quickly to his feet. Scooter, wary, stayed where he was, nervously eyeing the gun. "You don't even know how to shoot that thing, boy," he said.

"Aim and pull the trigger, that's what I'm thinking," Jamie said.

By then Frazier was next to him. "Give it over, Jamie."

Jamie passed the gun to his brother without a word.

"Get up," Frazier ordered, flipping off the safety. "Slowly. I don't want to kill you."

"No? Why not?" Scooter asked calmly.

Too calmly, Kat thought. Didn't he care if he lived or died? Shouldn't his survival instinct kick in?

"We're going downstairs, slowly, calmly, with you in front of me. And no tricks," Frazier said.

"Okay," Scooter said, and started walking toward the door.

Kat was planning to scramble out of the closet, but Frazier shook his head in warning as he passed, so she stayed silent and watched them leave the room before she crept free of her hiding place.

She was immediately grateful for her brother's caution when a second scream sounded, followed by the explosive thunder of a shot.

The darkness, sudden and total, took Skyler by surprise. She screamed and leaped to her feet before freezing, terrified that if she moved, she would crash into something. Then she gasped, hearing movement—thudding and scuffling—from upstairs.

Without warning, the lights came back on as the generator kicked in.

Under cover of darkness, while she had been frozen in fear, everyone else had shifted. Paddy had his cane raised, ready to strike viciously. The problem was, he had misjudged people's positions and was about to hit her. She screamed again, at the same time realizing that David had made a leap for Quintin.

But Craig was between them. Defending Quintin from David? Or…

Sweet Lord, had he been about to attack Quintin himself?

There was no time to ponder the question. The sound of her scream had barely faded when the air was split by the deafening report of Quintin's gun. He struck out viciously with his other hand, sending Craig crashing back on the couch as David cried out hoarsely.

Then Quintin raised his gun and leveled it on Skyler, nothing but ice in his eyes.

"Mom, get back to the piano. Old man, back in your chair. The rest of you…sit. If I fire again, it will be directly at you, not into the air. And I don't miss."

He whirled on Craig. "You are one sorry son of a bitch," he said. "Maybe," he mused, "I should just finish you off, because you're worthless."

David spoke before Quintin could fire. "Good idea. Shoot him. He stopped me from reaching you," he said in a strange mocking tone.

Quintin was still for a moment. Then he lowered his gun. "All right, Craig," he said. "Maybe you're of some use after all. But remember, I'm always watching you."

In a split second, he was at Skyler's side, and she felt the cold, hard nose of his gun pressed to her ribs.

"Scooter, get your sorry ass down here!" Quintin yelled.

"The kid has a gun on me!" Scooter shouted.

"And I have one pressed into his mother's ribs." A nasty smile twisted his features. "I've killed before, kid. And I haven't got a hell of a lot to lose. Shoot Scooter or try to shoot me, and your mom's dead. Give the gun back to Scooter, then get back down here."

"No, Frazier!" Skyler cried. "Shoot them both!" Then she cried out in fear as David instinctively moved to protect her.

Quintin moved like lightning. The nose of the gun never shifted from her side as Quintin lashed out and caught

David off guard, sending him flying so hard against the wall that she could have sworn she heard the crack of his skull before he slumped to the floor.

"Dad!" Frazier shouted in anguish as he and Jamie pushed Scooter in front of them into the living room.

"He's not dead, kid, but your mother is about to be," Quintin said.

"No, please," Frazier begged, and set the gun down on the ground. Scooter immediately turned around and retrieved the weapon, then slugged Frazier in the jaw, hard.

Her son staggered back, and she jerked free from Quintin's hold, heedless of whether he shot her or not. "Don't you touch my son!" she shrieked as she flew at Scooter, who backed off in shock. Then she turned to Quintin, and the look she gave him dared him to stop her as she walked over to her husband. "David?"

He groaned softly.

"I'll get him up," Craig volunteered, and hurried over to help. Her husband wasn't a small man, and Craig wasn't at full strength, but he managed to lift David and carry him to the sofa, then lay him out where he had been himself not all that long ago.

"Okay, okay, very sweet," Quintin said. "Now let's everybody get it together here. Stay calm. Collected. Cool. I think we need something hot to drink. Maybe a little Irish coffee will put us all back on an even keel."

Skyler swallowed, and tried hard not to think about how badly hurt her husband might be. "Fine," she said and started for the kitchen.

"No, no, no. You're too dangerous. You just proved that against stupid over there," Quintin said.

"Hey!" Scooter complained.

"You let a couple of kids overpower you," Quintin told him. "How smart was that?"

Scooter flushed and looked furious—as if he might try to deck one of the kids again, Skyler thought, and noticed that Frazier was still rubbing his jaw.

"We'll all go to the kitchen," Quintin said.

"What about my husband?" Skyler asked worriedly.

Quintin stared at David, who still hadn't regained consciousness.

"I'll watch him," Craig said to Quintin. "I saved your ass, and like you keep saying, you've got the gun. What the hell am I going to do out here with a half dea—with an unconscious guy?"

"Fine. The rest of you, let's go," Quintin said.

The room still smelled like gunpowder from the shot he had fired, Skyler thought as she turned and started for the kitchen. "Come on, kids. And, Jamie, don't even ask. You're getting cocoa. You, too, Uncle Paddy."

Kat stood silently on the landing again, shaking.

What the hell had just happened? Her brothers had bested Scooter. The confrontation should have gone their way, but instead...

That bastard Quintin! She found herself furious that Massachusetts didn't have a death penalty. She would have liked to slip a noose around the man's neck herself.

She swallowed, her thoughts racing. *What now?*

They had all gone into the kitchen, so her mother could make Irish coffee—except for her father and Craig, who were still in the living room.

Craig...

She tried to harden her heart as she crept close enough to the banister to see. His hair was too long, and his face looked thinner. Too thin, as if the last three years had been rough on him. If so, he'd deserved it.

How had he gone from being Mr. Perfect to Scuzz of the Year?

He was talking to her father, she realized. She strained to hear, but she couldn't make out what he was saying. What she *could* tell was that her father had regained consciousness, because he was saying something back.

Craig rose and started toward the kitchen.

"Hey," her father said hoarsely, quietly.

"Yeah?" Craig asked, pausing.

"Thank you," David O'Boyle said softly.

Thank you?

Why was her father saying thank-you to one of the men who'd invaded their house?

Craig went toward the kitchen. "What the hell are you doing?" Quintin demanded as he pushed open the swinging door.

"He's starting to come around. I'm going to get some ice for his head," Craig said, and then the rest of the conversation was lost as the door swung shut behind him.

Kat hesitated. Everyone except her father was in the kitchen, she realized. How long would they stay there?

Suddenly she didn't care.

She flew silently down the stairs and raced to her father's side.

"Dad?" she whispered.

"Baby, get away from here."

"But, Dad, I'm afraid for you."

"I'm all right, honey. I had hoped you'd gotten far away by now," he said, his tone hopeless.

He had hoped she wouldn't die with the rest of them, she thought.

"I… It's a blizzard, Dad."

He smiled sadly. "I know. Get back upstairs."

"Dad, I texted the cops and I think it went through," she said. "So hang in there, okay?"

"We're hanging."

They both heard the sound of someone pushing against the swinging door to the kitchen.

"Go!"

"I'm gone!"

She flew back up the stairs to her previous vantage point and watched as Craig walked over to her father with a bag of ice in his hand.

How? she wondered again. How did you go from bad jokes and the world's most charming smile to…this?

Did you hear about the three guys who headed out for a good time one night? Two of them walked into a bar.

Yeah?

And one didn't.

I don't get it.

He ducked.

They'd both laughed, and then she was in his arms, and she could still remember the way his fingers had felt, moving over her bare flesh….

Quintin seemed to be relishing his Irish coffee. "Delicious," he told Skyler, and he grinned, as if he were a welcome guest in her home and not a monster holding a gun on her family.

"Glad you like it," she said dryly. "May I please go to my husband now?"

"He's okay. The kid's taking care of him. The kid has a heart," he said, and it wasn't a compliment.

"And that's a bad thing?" she said.

"It'll get him killed," Scooter said curtly. He was seated at the table and had gulped down his own drink, all the while continuing to eye her two sons bitterly.

"Would you like another?" she asked Quintin.

"You trying to get me drunk?" he asked.

"On Irish coffee?" she inquired.

Quintin shrugged. "Sure. Make me another."

As she rose, she asked, "Would you open the door and ask your friend how my husband is doing."

"Scooter, do it," Quintin said.

"I'm not your slave," Scooter protested.

"No, you're just the idiot who almost got us killed," Quintin said pointedly.

Scooter flashed them all an angry look but rose. "I'll have another one, too," he said.

"Of course," Skyler agreed, deciding it might be a good thing to mollify Scooter at the moment. Quintin was more dangerous, but, cornered, Scooter could be very bad, she was certain. "And thank you," she added.

"Sure." He opened the kitchen door. "Hey, Craig," he called.

"Yeah?"

"How's O'Boyle?"

"He's conscious, and he seems okay."

Skyler tried not to show just how relieved she felt as she fixed more drinks.

"Can I have another hot chocolate, Mom?" Jamie asked.

"May I," she corrected.

"You can have as many as you want," Jamie answered pertly. "You're the mom."

"Jamie…"

"Yeah, yeah, *may* I? Please?"

"Of course."

She turned around. "Anybody else?"

"Indeed, I'd be pleased to accept another," Paddy said.

"Me, too, thanks," Frazier said.

Brenda was just staring ahead, seemingly lost in her own world again, after her earlier bravery. Then, to Skyler's astonishment, the younger woman blinked, looked at Frazier as if to take strength from him, and stood up. "May I go out and check on Mr. O'Boyle? I *am* planning a career in medicine, as you know."

Quintin leaned back, looking genuinely amused.

"Yeah, that's right. But you know what? I haven't got any degree, and I can tell you this. He took a thunk on the head, but he's going to be all right. He may have a headache for a while, though."

"I'll just see how he's doing," Brenda said, and started for the door.

"Wait just a minute," Scooter protested.

"Let her go," Quintin said.

"You're the one who keeps saying—" Scooter began.

"She's two inches high, O'Boyle is still dizzy and Craig is out there," Quintin said.

Scooter stood, taking the first drink from Skyler's hand. "I'm going out there, too," he told Quintin. "You and I are the ones with the guns. Besides, you never know." He glared at Jamie. "It's the innocent-looking ones who cause all the trouble."

Jamie looked at Quintin after Scooter left the room and shrugged. "Hey, it's not my fault he was an idiot."

Quintin leaned forward. "No, it wasn't your fault. But you act up again and I shoot your mom. And that would be a pity since we all want a good turkey dinner tomorrow, don't we?"

Skyler set his cup down before him, then returned to the

counter, got the other cups and placed them before Paddy and her boys.

She realized that Paddy was staring at Quintin, assessing him. Just as he had been doing ever since their house—and their lives—had been seized.

"I'm going to see how David is," she said in a tone that brooked no interference.

Quintin lifted his cup to her. "Go on. Then we'll see about sleeping arrangements for the night."

"What?"

"You'll need some sleep to cook that turkey tomorrow," Quintin said cheerfully. "We'll need blankets and pillows if we're all going to camp in the living room."

She stared at him blankly, and he started to laugh. "Did you think the family was going to go up to their nice warm beds tonight? Please, Mrs. O'Boyle. We're all going to stay together. Just like one big happy family." He smiled as if he'd just thought of something. "And I never did get my Irish music. That will go well with my drink, don't you agree?" He rose then, still grinning. "Irish music and a slumber party. What a perfect Christmas Eve."

Chapter 7

"It's dying down some, thank God," Sheila told Tim as they surveyed the department's snowmobiles, which were half buried, despite being parked under a carport behind the station. "Let's start digging."

One big happy family, having what amounted to a pajama party on Christmas Eve, Craig thought, looking at the sham festivities going on around him.

Quintin was crazy, he decided. Psychotic. The man was actually enjoying this. He was playing with these people, making them enact some sick mockery of what the night should be, letting them hope that if they did just as they were told, he would let them live. But he wouldn't. As soon as he was ready to leave, he would kill them.

But what the hell else was there to do but play along and pray that the moment would come when at least some of them could be saved?

He was amazed that he hadn't given himself away when the lights had gone out. He couldn't believe Quintin had believed he'd tried to save him, not attack him.

David O'Boyle had stood up for him. And he'd done it just right.

Why?

He'd never met the O'Boyles. His relationship with Kat hadn't gotten that far before everything went to hell. And yet her father seemed to have figured out that he had no intention of killing them, that he even planned to help them—when the time was right.

Somehow they had to wrest both guns away before blood was shed. But for the moment…

Kat, at least, was still safe—somewhere. He had to pray she would remain so.

God, he loved her. Still. He hadn't seen her in nearly three years, but she hadn't changed, at least not on the outside. But inside… Inside, she was stronger. There didn't seem to be a naive bone left in her body. Or a trusting one.

He had done that to her.

"Bravo," Quintin said as the O'Boyles finished a rendition of "Silent Night" that belonged on CD.

Craig happened to look up then, and he saw her. Kat was on the second-floor landing, looking down, tears in her eyes.

Eyes that met his briefly before she realized she had given herself away and disappeared.

"Hey, what are you looking at?" Quintin demanded.

Craig turned to Quintin and said calmly, "Nothing. Just wondering where the bathroom is."

"My jaw is killing me," Frazier said flatly. "Can I quit for a while?"

"Why don't we play a game?" Jamie suggested.

"A game?" Quintin said, and again there was that awful edge amusement in his voice. *Yes, entertain me.*

The sick thing was, Craig knew they had probably all lived so long precisely because they entertained him. And, of course, because they were snowed in and Quintin wanted turkey tomorrow.

"A game," Craig said. "Like…?"

"Trivial Pursuit. We can be on teams," Jamie said.

"No more going upstairs to get things," Quintin said.

"It's under the coffee table," Skyler said.

"All right, get it out," Quintin agreed.

Craig dared to glance upstairs again, and he silently whispered a prayer of thanks when Kat was nowhere to be seen.

The storm wasn't over, but it had definitely eased up.

Kat certainly had done lots of thinking. There were ways to fight, it was true. The problem was that Quintin had been telling the truth. The next time they fought, someone was going to die.

She stood in the basement by the window, reflecting on her chances of getting out and finding help.

There really wasn't anything to think about. She might die of exposure if she went out there, but she had to give it a try, because they didn't stand a chance if she kept hiding out here. Quintin's strength—along with the two guns, of course—was that he didn't care if his cohorts died, while her family would fight to the death for each other.

Imagine that. Dysfunctional as they were, they would always be there for each other when the chips were down. Besides, weren't all families dysfunctional?

She gave herself a shake.

There was only one way to win. And that was to take down Quintin.

Craig would never hurt them. He might have gone the wrong way. He might be scum. But she just couldn't believe he would hurt her family.

Who was she kidding? He hadn't loved her. He'd made that clear.

Something had gone wrong with Craig, terribly wrong. But no matter how wrong it had gone, she couldn't believe he would kill her or anyone in her family. She couldn't let herself believe it, because if she did, she would lose her courage, and then they would all be doomed.

But there was still Scooter. He might be weaker than Quintin in every way, but he still had a gun, which meant he was dangerous.

She hesitated, afraid. Terrified that any move she made would be the wrong one.

Then she squared her shoulders. There was only one way for her entire family to survive. Both men had to be disarmed. And for that to happen, she had to somehow reach the sheriff's office and pray someone was there.

If she was caught...

She was dead.

And she didn't want to die.

But if she just stayed here and waited and just cowered as her family was massacred...

She wouldn't want to live.

She wrapped her scarf more tightly around her neck and pushed up the window.

David looked over at Skyler and forced himself to smile reassuringly at her.

What a joke, he thought. He was supposed to be the man

of the house, the protector of his family. Well, he'd been one hell of a failure, hadn't he?

But his wife wasn't looking at him as if that was the case. Strange and bitter, but true. They'd been at odds getting ready for Christmas. She'd complained for years about how hard it was to pull everything together when they went away to celebrate, so this year, he'd been ready to give in and stay in Boston, but she'd wanted to come here.

To keep the family together, she'd said. The kids might have come around for dinner otherwise, but someone would have shown up late or left early. There would have been bitching. Arguments. And by five or six, everyone would have been gone. Even Jamie, who always wanted to spend more time with his friends than his family these days.

But could you really hold a family together by force? And did the kids really want to be here? Did he and Skyler really even know each other after all these years of constantly being at odds?

And yet...

Skyler was staring at him as she hadn't in a very long time. There was so much caring and concern in her eyes. And more. A message, as if she were trying to tell him it had been a good run, and that she loved him...whatever might come.

He tried to make his eyes say something, too. He tried to tell her that they *would* survive this.

And he knew there was something else, something they both agreed on: their children were going to survive, no matter what it took.

And they both knew that Kat was still there, a hidden asset against these men.

He returned his attention to the game, trying to hide his

true feelings about this insane parody of family life Quintin was making them play out.

Suddenly Quintin was on his feet. "I hear something," he said, tension in every line of his body.

"Yeah, us," Craig said, frowning.

"No. Outside," Quintin said. "Somebody's out there."

The wind was still blowing, the snow still falling, but damned if Tim hadn't gotten the snowmobiles dug out and ready to go.

Sheila, so bundled up that she doubted she would even recognize herself, took her seat, gunned the motor and took off. Tim followed right behind.

There were abandoned cars along the road. They checked every one, glad not to find anyone frozen inside. They kept going—up a hill and across the valley—as a full moon struggled to shed its glow through the dark clouds hiding the night sky. Finally Sheila saw a shadow rising up beside the road and knew immediately what it was.

An old building that had stood there as long as she could remember, with a sign on it reading Hudson & Son, Fine Art, Antiques, Memorabilia and Jewelry.

"Hey," she shouted to Tim over her radio. "There's the Hudsons' store."

"Let's go."

He was off his snowmobile and on his way to the door before she was.

She followed him, her nose freezing, so cold that she was afraid it was frostbitten. She couldn't help but wonder what she would look like if she had to have the tip of her nose cut off. It wouldn't be a pretty sight.

When they reached the old building, the snow was piled high against the door, but that didn't seem to daunt Tim in the least. He ran back to his snowmobile in a flash, then came back with the snow shovel he had loaded on the back.

"Good thinking, kid," she complimented him, then examined their surroundings while he started to dig. What she saw made her blood run cold.

"Look," she said, pointing toward the rear of the old structure.

They both paused in silence. Lionel Hudson's huge old Cadillac was still parked and collecting snow beside the building.

"He's in there," Sheila said.

Tim redoubled his efforts to clear the door. As soon as the drift was out of the way, he tried the door. Unlocked. Struggling against wind, he pulled it open.

They both drew their weapons, tense, staring at one another for a long moment, and then Sheila nodded. She had a feeling their guns wouldn't be necessary. Whatever evil had visited here, it was already gone.

Even so, they entered carefully, making all the right moves.

They were greeted by darkness and silence. Tim drew out his flashlight and sent the beam skidding around the shop.

"Lionel?" Sheila asked into the void.

There was no reply.

Sheila turned on her own flashlight and walked around the counter. There was no sign of Lionel.

Tim headed toward the back of the store. Suddenly Sheila heard him gasp.

"Sheila?"

"Tim?"

She joined him and heard her knees creak as she crouched down beside him.

"It's blood, Sheila," he said.

Her heart flip-flopped. "Do you think they might have taken him hostage?" Tim asked.

She shook her head.

"Where is he, then?"

She stared at him for a long moment, then rose. She ran back outside, suddenly heedless of the dark and wind and pelting snow. She plowed her way through until she reached the old Cadillac.

"Sheila, stop," Tim said, racing up behind her.

"But—"

"There's blood on the snow," he said quietly. "I'll look."

"I've been a deputy for most my life," she told him. "I've seen it all."

"He was a friend of yours."

Was.

She swallowed.

"Help me," she said to Tim.

Together they dug away the snow with their hands and struggled with the door to the Cadillac. As soon as they got it open, she directed the beam of her flashlight into the backseat.

"Oh God," Tim breathed.

Chapter 8

Quintin told Scooter to keep everyone together, then walked toward the front door and opened it. A blast of cold hit them like a ton of bricks.

"Quintin, what the hell?" Scooter complained.

"I heard something," Quintin said.

"It must have been the wind," Frazier said. "Blowing stuff around."

Quintin flashed him an angry glance, then returned to staring into the night.

There wasn't much to see. The snow was too thick.

David cleared his throat. "If you want the generator to work all night and through…through dinner tomorrow, you can't overwork it. You don't want the heat giving out, do you?" he asked rationally.

But Quintin wasn't even listening to him. "Someone's out there," he said.

Quintin turned suddenly and aimed his gun at the group. "Craig, Scooter, get your coats on."

"Come on, Quintin, you've gotta be joking," Scooter complained.

"I'm dead serious," Quintin said, nodding meaningfully at Skyler.

"What do I care if you shoot her?" Scooter grumbled.

"What'll you care, doing life in prison?" Quintin said. "Anyway, Mr. Softie there will care."

Swearing, Scooter headed for the closet. Craig followed suit. As he buttoned his coat, he turned to Quintin and asked, "What the hell are we looking for?"

"Someone is out there," Quintin said.

"How the hell could anyone be out there? They'd be frozen by now," David pointed out reasonably.

Quintin stared at him coldly, then turned to Skyler. "Mom, come over here. Now."

David tensed as if he were about to move.

"I told you, I'll shoot her next time," Quintin said very softly.

"Just chill, everyone. It's fine," Skyler said, walking over to Quintin. He pulled her against his side and slipped an arm around her. It wasn't an affectionate gesture. He held her with the muzzle of the gun pointed to her cheek.

"Get out there," Quintin said coldly. "And if either one of you tries to pull anything, just remember that Mom here will end up with half her head blown away. Got it?"

Craig followed Scooter to the door, figuring Scooter still had a gun.

"Lookit all this damn snow. What the hell are we supposed to do?" Scooter muttered to him.

Craig shrugged. "Plow our way through it," he returned, his heart thundering. Kat had to be out here. But the snow was so deep, there would be no way to hide the trail she'd be making through the deep, white blanket that surrounded the house. And if Scooter found her... "Look, we'll just stay out here long enough to make Quintin think we really searched. Hell, Scooter, David was right. No one could survive out here."

He thought they were making their way down the front walk to the road, but it was difficult to tell. The wind was still high and flakes were still falling, and that combined with the depth of the snow on the ground made it almost impossible to tell where they were.

"Listen!" Scooter said suddenly.

"To what?"

"A motor."

"You hear a motor?" Craig said. He tried to make his tone incredulous, but he could hear it, too.

It wasn't coming from anywhere near the house, though. It was distant, the sound carrying unnaturally because of the wind.

"What the hell do you think it is?" Scooter demanded tensely.

Craig shrugged. "It's nowhere near here," he finally said, as if he'd only just managed to hear it.

"You sure?" Scooter stared at him.

Scooter had been the one to want him in the group, he reminded himself. Unlike Quintin, Scooter trusted him, and he could use that to his advantage.

"Scooter, listen," he said calmly. "It's probably just a fire engine or an ambulance or something. No one is coming to this house. There's no reason for them to."

"There's the car," Scooter said.

"Buried now. No one can see it."

Scooter stood there, staring at the moon as it tried to

peek down through the heavy cloud cover. Snowflakes fell on his gaunt face and stuck to his eyelashes. After a moment he smiled. "I don't want trouble tonight," he said.

"I know. It's warm and comfortable in there. And the food's good."

"I like having Christmas," Scooter said. "I never had Christmas when I was a kid. I never knew who my dad was. And my mom…she drank. And then there were the men. She'd rather buy a gift for any asshole she thought might marry her than for her own kid." He looked at Craig. "None of her men ever stayed around, though, so she drank herself to death. And there was never Christmas until I made my own. First year after the old lady was dead, I hit up one of those department-store places. I stole a tree and all kinds of ornaments. But I got caught, and I was old enough to do real time. Haven't had Christmas since then. What about you, kid?"

"Me?"

"Did you even know who your dad was?"

"Oh, yeah. I knew who he was."

"And your mother?"

Craig shrugged, looking away. "She died young."

"She drink herself to death?"

"No."

"Then—"

Craig swung around. "Look, I want to have Christmas, too. I want turkey tomorrow—hell, I think even old Quintin wants turkey tomorrow. We've just got to keep things calm and him on an even keel. We can't have him going all ballistic every time he hears a noise."

"Yeah, yeah, but…what the hell is it about you that he doesn't like?" Scooter demanded, staring at him.

"Damned if I know," Craig told him, shrugging, but inside he felt sick.

I wanted to stop him from killing the old man, he thought. And maybe Quintin *hadn't* killed him. Maybe…

Quintin *had* killed him. He knew it. He had failed. God, he had failed.

He couldn't fail now. Somehow he had to find a way to disarm both men, to get them going after each other instead of the O'Boyles.

Scooter spun around. "Hey, I hear something! Over there."

Scooter started plowing his way through the snow, his gun out. Swearing softly in dismay, Craig followed.

He saw the trail leading away from the basement window through the snow and his heart sank.

Kat.

He forced his own path through the snow, somehow getting ahead of Scooter even though the other man had started off first, and then, even over the sound of the storm he heard her. Heard her desperate breath as she tried to run through the mammoth buildup of snow.

Then he heard the explosion of a bullet, followed by the soft sucking sound as it shot through the snow and into the wet ground.

"Stop!" he shouted to Scooter.

"There's someone. There *is* someone!"

Another bullet ripped through the night.

"Stop shooting!" he shouted to Scooter. "You're going to kill me."

He had to reach Kat first. He redoubled his effort, but she was young and fit.

And she was running for her life.

He ran harder, barely grimacing when his ankle caught and twisted in a rut beneath the snow.

Kat let out a gasp as another bullet exploded, far too close.

"Scooter, you idiot, stop!" Craig raged.

She was directly in front of him. He jumped for all he was worth, catching her by the shoulders. Together, they flew facedown into the snow. She screamed and fought but he was stronger than she was.

He turned her over, and shock filled her eyes when she recognized him.

"Stop fighting, please," he implored in a whisper.

"You could have let me go!"

"Don't you understand? He would have shot you. I had to take you down or else he would have killed you," he told her softly.

For a moment, she was still, eyes staring into his. Then she spat at him.

He swallowed hard. He could hear Scooter coming up behind them and knew he had to talk fast. "For the love of God, for your life, for the lives of your family, you don't know me. You've never seen me before. And quit fighting."

She stared at him. Green eyes like gems in the strange light, snow falling delicately on her cheeks. And all across the snow, the deep red flow of her hair.

Just like blood. Blood on the snow.

"Bastard!" she hissed.

He swallowed and nodded, and then Scooter was there and there was no more time to talk.

"I guess Quintin isn't such an idiot after all, huh?" Scooter demanded. "Lookee, lookee. What have we got here?" He hunkered down, grinning at Kat.

Craig didn't like the look of his grin. He liked it even less when Scooter reached out to touch her cheek.

Once again, Kat spat.

"Why you—" Scooter began. He was going to hit her.

Craig caught his hand.

Scooter stared at him, mistrust dawning in his eyes.

"No...it's Christmas, remember? Come on, Scooter, let's just make it through the night."

Apparently that made sense to Scooter, who nodded. "No more of that, girlie," he said. "Christmas or no Christmas, I *will* slug you next time." He stood. "Let's get her inside and let Quintin figure out what to do with her."

Craig nodded, trying to help Kat to her feet. She wasn't particularly cooperative.

"What the hell is going on out there?" Quintin yelled from the house.

"We got a girl!" Scooter cried out. "A wild one. The older kid's got a twin, and I think this is her."

"Tell the wild one to come along nice and quiet or Mom gets it."

Craig saw Kat's shoulders slump. Saw the utter despair and desolation darkening the emerald beauty of her eyes.

"Let's go," he said curtly.

Inwardly, he trembled and wondered how they would manage to get through the night, if there had been truth, a premonition, in that vision of her hair spread out...

Like blood on the snow.

Lionel Hudson was dead from a single bullet between the eyes.

Sheila kept feeling the sting of tears against her eyelids. Lionel had lived his years as a good man, a fair man, always ready to help others. And now he was dead.

Executed.

She raged against the idea. She didn't even feel the snow against her cheeks or the bite of the cold through her clothing.

Tim laid an arm around her shoulders. "Sheila."

"Yeah?"

"You said he had cancer."

"Yeah."

He inhaled deeply. "I've seen people die of cancer. It can be slow and painful."

She looked at him, enraged. "So this is better?"

"I'm just telling you that he's beyond pain now."

She swallowed, shaking her head. Beyond all pain. A bitter wave of anguish seized her, and she almost laughed out loud.

"Sheila."

"Yeah?"

"Whoever did this is still out there."

She nodded, still feeling numb.

"Sheila, that other message came from just a few miles from here. Right?"

She nodded.

"I think that's where our killer is."

Again, she nodded. "We need some major help here. Like a swat team from Springfield."

"We don't have help. We have you, and we have me."

"Tim, if the man who killed Lionel—"

"I'd say it was two men. Maybe even three. The way he was dragged out here…don't think one man could have done it."

"Okay, so if these men are in the O'Boyle place…we have to be careful. They've already killed once. They'll kill again without a thought."

Tim nodded. "Maybe…" He looked away.

She frowned, her knees threatening to buckle. "Maybe they're already dead," she said, finishing the thought he couldn't voice.

He shrugged unhappily, not meeting her eyes.

"All right. We've got to get over there as fast as we can."

"And then…?"

"We'll figure that out when we get there."

Quintin was furious, and Craig had never felt more afraid in his entire life.

When they reached the house, Quintin stared at Kat in fury, but he didn't touch her. Instead, he backhanded David with a vengeance. Skyler screamed in protest, but she'd already raced forward to grab her daughter.

The others started to move.

Oh God, this was it, Craig thought. The bullets and the blood would start now.

"Wait!" he cried, stepping forward.

But David was just as set against a bloodbath. "Stop, everyone…everyone just calm down. Please!"

"You knew she was out there!" Quintin raged, looking at David first, then swinging around to stare accusingly at the rest of the family. "You all did."

Frazier replied, his tone like ice, "We thought she was dead already. In the storm," he said flatly.

Quintin, waving his gun wildly, paced the foyer. "You know, I tried. I really tried. But you people don't learn. I'm going to have to kill one of you."

"No!" Skyler screamed.

"Come on, Quintin, if you kill anyone, we can't have Christmas," Craig said.

"Quintin," Scooter seconded quickly. "Calm down.

We've got the girl. And even if we hadn't gotten her, where the hell could she have gone in this? Come on, no real harm done."

He actually smiled at Kat, as if she might be grateful. As if she might actually like him for buying time. Craig forced himself to keep still.

"You're all a pack of liars!" Quintin accused, and aimed the gun at David. "Liars."

Craig looked around, afraid someone would make a move and bring down hell. The tension in the room was palpable. "Please, Quintin," he said. "We caught the girl."

"Craig got her," Scooter said.

Quintin glanced at Craig, who stared back expression-lessly.

"Please," Skyler murmured, and walked toward Quintin. "I swear to you, Kat is our only other child. No one knows you're here. And you're an intelligent man. You can't blame us for wanting to hide her."

"And she didn't try to attack us or anything," Craig said. "She was just trying to run away."

There was silence.

Still explosive.

Tension still so thick in the air it could be cut by a knife.

If Quintin started shooting, what should he do? Craig wondered. Throw himself on the man and pray he could disarm him before getting killed, and that someone else could overpower Scooter before too many of the others died, as well?

"I need a drink," Paddy announced firmly into the si-lence.

"Yes," Skyler said, white as the snow, her features stretched more tightly than the wires of her piano. "Please, let's all calm down. It's late. But we…we've actually had a good day. We had a nice meal, music, a fun game. We...we have Christmas tomorrow. The snow will stop, the roads will clear, and you can escape. For now...let's have a drink."

Paddy turned and started for the kitchen.

"Hey, Mick!" Quintin thundered.

Paddy turned to him, arching a brow.

"No one goes anywhere alone."

Ignoring Quintin, the old man turned away and started walking again.

Craig caught Paddy's eyes. It was an act, he realized. The old man was terrified and playing for time.

"A drink sounds good to me, Quintin," Craig said. "I think I've still got a fever, and it was freezing out there. I need something to warm me up."

"All right. A drink," Quintin said after a long moment. "But we tie up the father first."

David's jaw tightened, but he didn't move.

"Where's there some rope in this place?" Quintin said, turning to Frazier.

"Dad, have we got any rope anywhere?"

"What kind of criminals forget rope?" Jamie muttered, sounding every inch the quintessential sulky teen.

Scooter actually laughed. Quintin cast him a venomous glare.

"You have my wife, my daughter, my sons, an innocent girl who's here as a guest and my wife's uncle. What do you think I'm going to do?" David demanded, sounding not just exhausted, but beaten.

Craig caught David O'Boyle looking at him with what seemed to be mistrust.

Well, as Scooter had said, he'd been the one to bring Kat down. That was important. Quintin had to believe in him, even if it meant that David might not.

"Everybody into the kitchen," Quintin said. "Even you, Dad. Fuck!" He swore with no apology. "There's got to be rope around here somewhere. We're not settling down for a warm winter's night until we find some rope."

Skyler didn't appear to be ready to let her daughter go, Craig noticed. She was still arm in arm with Kat as they went through the swinging door to the kitchen. "Give me this parka—it's soaked," she told her daughter.

As if a soaked parka mattered when there were men with guns in the house, he thought dryly.

But Kat slipped off the parka. "Mom, can you make me a hot toddy?"

"Yes, certainly. We don't want you catching your death of cold."

Her words hung strangely in the air.

Skyler, still white and stricken, turned to the stove. Craig watched her face as she picked up the kettle, moved the few feet to the sink and started to fill it. He could actually see her thought process. He knew she was longing to bring the water to a full boil and throw it in his face.

He decided to keep his distance.

"There was no chair for you when we got here, so I guess you weren't invited to the family dinner, huh?" Scooter asked Kat. "Why not? Were you bad?" His tone had an awkward flirty note to it that Craig found alarming.

"We miscounted," Jamie said.

"See? You miscounted, and we don't have rope. Everyone screws up," Scooter said.

"We didn't screw up," Quintin said. "We just didn't expect to be part of a group for so long."

It was a warning. They all knew it.

Quintin's mood was teetering at the edge of madness, Craig thought. The arrival of Kat O'Boyle had shaken him.

"It was cold out there. I would love a hot toddy, too, please," Craig said, to cut the tension.

The glance Skyler shot him was not forgiving.

Good God, couldn't anyone see? If he hadn't tackled her, Scooter would have killed her.

Or maybe they did see. Maybe they couldn't help but put up a wall against anyone who wasn't one of them.

"Hey, it's eleven forty-five," Scooter said. "Christmas in fifteen minutes."

"Kat…are you hurt?" Brenda asked softly.

"No, I'm fine, thanks, Brenda. Just cold."

"Brenda is great at Trivial Pursuit," Jamie said out of nowhere.

No, not out of nowhere, Craig realized. The kid was trying to diffuse the tension and get back to where they had been before Kat was discovered, when things had been calmer, easier.

"I'm not surprised. She's a straight-A student, right?" Kat said, smiling at Brenda and glancing toward her brother.

"I can't even hum 'Yankee Doodle,' though," Brenda said.

The petite little blonde was gaining in the strength department. She had looked shell-shocked for so long. Now…

She might actually be one of the calmest members of the group.

"Mrs. O'Boyle, would you mind bringing out some of those cookies you made earlier?" Brenda asked.

Quintin stepped forward. "Everyone sit."

"It's difficult to make drinks and get cookies if I'm sitting down," Skyler said.

"Don't be a wiseass," Quintin said, but the tension in him seemed to have eased down a notch. "You do the drinks."

"How about I get the cookies?" Kat suggested.

Quintin scowled at her. "You shouldn't be allowed to have any."

"But…you wouldn't expect me to be stupid, would you?" Kat asked him. "I'm sure if it had been you, you would have hidden, too."

He stared at her, then nodded. "Yeah, and I'd have gotten away, too. Now forget the cookies and everybody sit."

They sat at the table, as ordered, and Skyler started handing out the toddies.

"Don't forget me," Jamie said.

His mother paused.

"Go ahead and give him one. Maybe he can get some sleep before…before Santa comes," David said dryly.

"Presents!" Scooter said excitedly, then looked oddly at Quintin. "Except we don't really live here."

"We always have extra presents," Skyler said.

Scooter grinned, and everyone started to drink, the tension easing into the background under an onslaught of hot whiskey.

And then the doorbell rang, and as quickly as that, the tension was back.

Chapter 9

Skyler barely held back a scream.

Kat could see her mother's struggle and pleaded silently, No, Mom, no! Don't scream. It will be a bloodbath.

Quintin jumped up as if he were on springs, his gun at the ready and aimed at each of them in turn. He stared at David. "Who the hell is that?"

"I don't know," David said.

"Like you didn't know your daughter was running around outside, right?"

"I swear to God," David said quietly. "I don't know who it is. No one else was invited over, and it's ridiculously late. We should just ignore it."

"Right. Ignore it," Craig agreed.

Quintin shook his head. "It's the cops."

"Yeah, the cops," Scooter echoed, frowning.

Quintin turned to glare accusingly at Kat. "What did you do?" he demanded.

"Nothing."

"What did you do?" he repeated.

"What could I have done?" she asked. She desperately tried to keep her eyes level with his, to keep her voice low and soothing. "Quintin, haven't you noticed? The phones are all down."

"What do you think we are?" David asked. "Magicians? This is a small town. Everyone knows we come up here for Christmas. It's probably just someone wanting to make sure we weathered the storm all right."

"I'm telling you, it's the cops," Quintin said, still looking at Kat.

"If it is, they're probably just checking on all the houses they can reach," Kat said, staring back at Quintin with complete innocence. "The office is just a few miles down the road. They'll have seen our lights." Her heart was racing. What if the officers barged in, saying they'd gotten her message? What if they walked in with their guns cocked?

The bell rang again, ratcheting up the tension. She swallowed, turning slightly and praying she wouldn't give herself away. Because they were right. It had to be the cops at the door. And when they came in...

She looked over at her mother, knowing that any call from this address was already suspect, thanks to Jamie and that prank he'd pulled.

Which was going to be worse? Cops thinking they were pulling another prank and coming in unprepared, or taking it seriously and walking in ready to shoot?

Maybe neither. Maybe there was a God.

There had to be a way to tell them they were under siege.

Quintin pointed at Skyler. "You. Over here by me. Scooter, you and Craig take the family and answer the door. Except for you, kid." He pointed at Jamie. "You stay in here, too. The rest of you, greet them and get rid of them. If you don't, I'll kill your mom and your brother. And if you cause any trouble out there, the cops will die, too."

"It might not be the cops," Frazier said.

"Yeah? Well, whoever it is, get rid of them."

The bell rang for a third time, and Quintin looked even edgier than before.

"Scooter…you and Craig can be brothers. Craig…you're the daughter's boyfriend. I'm warning you all, my finger's twitching. I'm going to be sorry if Mom here doesn't make it to Christmas, but I swear, I *will* kill her *and* the boy if anyone makes a wrong move out there. Do you all understand?" Quintin demanded.

"They'll break the door down if they have to ring that bell any longer," Craig pointed out quietly.

"Go!" Quintin ordered.

David led the family out to the foyer to answer the door. Kat followed, aware that Craig was right behind her, painfully aware that Quintin was holding Jamie and her mother at gunpoint in the kitchen.

As Kat watched, her father looked out the peephole. Her entire throat felt constricted. She prayed that the police wouldn't come barging in, demanding to know who had sent out a plea for help.

Maybe it hadn't gotten through and this really was just a courtesy call because of the storm.

"Well?" Scooter demanded from behind Brenda, who was gripping Frazier's hand tightly.

"It *is* the cops," David said.

"Open the door. And no tricks. If you betray me, your wife dies, your kid dies, and I'll take down your daughter first, you got it?" Scooter said.

David reached for the door.

"And quit looking like scared rabbits, all of you!" Scooter demanded. "Act naturally."

David nodded and opened the door.

There were two of them outside. They were in their county uniforms, under deep blue, heavy, hooded coats, and they were wearing clunky boots because of the snow. Kat knew the woman, Sergeant Sheila Polanski. She'd first met her when she'd been a very young child. The young man—tall, fit, friendly looking, not really handsome but with a nice smile—was a stranger.

Don't say anything about a text message, she begged in silence. Don't even look at us curiously, please.

To her amazement, they were both smiling. Shivering, but smiling.

Maybe her text really hadn't gotten through.

"Sheila, my God, how are you?" David said. "What are you doing out here on Christmas Eve?"

"Just checking that everyone's okay. Mind if we come in?" Sheila asked, stepping forward without waiting for an answer or an invitation.

With no other option, David led their two visitors into the living room. "David, this is Tim Graystone. He just started working with us a few months back."

"How do you do," Tim said, shaking David's hand.

"Tim," Sheila said, casually sweeping out a hand, "this is Frazier O'Boyle, his twin, Kat, their great-uncle, Patrick—and how are you, Paddy, you old coot?" she demanded.

"Fine, me darlin', fine," Paddy said, giving Sheila a hug.

"How's the hip?"

"Healin' fine, lass, healin' just fine," Paddy replied.

"And let's see," Sheila continued. "I'm sorry, David. I can't introduce your guests, because I can't say that I know them."

"Sheila, Tim, I'd like you to meet my son's girlfriend, Brenda, and this is… Craig," David said.

Craig slipped an arm around Kat, and it was all she could do not to jump clear out of her skin. She managed to keep her smile in place.

"I'm with Kat," Craig said, then nodded in Scooter's direction. "This is my brother. We call him Scooter."

"A big Christmas welcome to you all," Sheila said.

"So, Sheila, what's it like out there? Storm letting up? Everyone okay?"

Kat was amazed that her father managed to speak so casually, but then, she was equally amazed she could stand there herself, smiling as if nothing were wrong, while all the time pure panic was racing helter-skelter through her veins.

"Power's down everywhere," Sheila told him.

"So we decided we'd just check in on people, make sure no one is freezing or sick and can't get to a hospital," Tim said.

He seemed like a nice guy, Kat thought, and prayed that he wouldn't die tonight. He'd sounded so convincing, too. Could it be true that they really had just happened by?

"Where's the missus?" Sheila asked David.

"Skyler? Oh, she tired out a while ago. She's in bed," David said.

"Well, since I doubt I'll see her tomorrow, you give her my Christmas regards," Sheila said.

"Sure thing."

"What about your youngest?" Sheila asked.

"Jamie? He went to bed a while ago, too."

"A teenager in bed?" Sheila said skeptically, but she was grinning.

"He believes in Santa," Kat joked quickly, just in case Sheila was going to push the issue.

"A teenager who still believes in Santa?" Tim asked politely.

Craig squeezed Kat a little too tightly to him and said, "No, what Jamie actually believes in is the prospect of presents."

"Yeah," David said. "He knows there's a new computer under the tree for him. He was ready as hell to go to bed so he can get up and claim it at the crack of dawn."

"Waking us all up with him," Frazier groaned.

"We can't sleep late?" Craig asked Kat.

She forced herself to look up with a lover's smile— something she found it all too easy to do. "No, darling, I'm afraid we can't. It's Christmas."

"Ah, young love," Paddy murmured. "Much like what we share, Sheila, me love."

Sheila just laughed, shaking her head.

"I've half a mind to move up here full-time and make an honest woman of ye," Paddy said to her.

Sheila looked from Scooter to Craig, shaking her head. "He's quite the character, isn't he?" She smiled.

"You two don't look much alike," Tim said thoughtfully, inclining his head from Craig to Scooter.

"We're half brothers," Craig said.

Everything seemed to be going okay, Kat thought, wondering what she could possibly have expected when she sent that text. Quintin had Jamie and her mother hostage, and with Scooter and Craig hovering, there was no way to get information to Sheila and Tim. Now all she wanted was for them to say goodbye and get out, to save themselves.

"I hate to intrude, but…have you got some coffee going

by any chance?" Tim asked. "It's freezing out there, and we could really stand to warm up."

Kat prayed that the silence that seemed to last an eon was really only a few seconds. "Coffee?" she breathed.

"Have a seat. I'll throw on a pot," David said.

"Tim," Sheila chastised. "We can't inconvenience the O'Boyles like that."

"It's no problem," Kat said. "I'll put the coffee on, Dad." She extricated herself from Craig's arm. "Be right back."

"Please," Craig said softly.

Please...what? she wondered, and knew, as she headed toward the kitchen, that he was watching her go.

In her mind, she could see the look in his eyes, see him looking at her as he had once done. What was it? Why was he here? Had he really saved her from being shot? Was he the world's best actor? And if he was, who was he playing, her family—or his supposed cohorts?

She pushed open the door to the kitchen, terrified of what she might find. Jamie and her mother were sitting side by side at the table, Quintin standing behind her mother with the nose of his gun pressed against her temple.

Kat's heart lurched. His finger did indeed look to be twitching, just as he'd said.

"It's going fine," she said softly to him. "The young cop just wants a cup of coffee."

Quintin frowned fiercely. Kat watched his trigger finger, almost afraid to swallow.

"Look, they think Mom and Jamie are in bed. They'll be gone as soon as they get their coffee. It will be fine," she whispered quickly.

The gun moved away from her mother's head for a moment as he indicated the counter. "Do it."

Skyler stared at her daughter, her hazel eyes wide but steady.

Kat turned and quickly prepared the coffee, then reached under the counter.

"What the hell are you doing?" Quintin demanded in a heated growl.

"Getting a tray. For cups, and cream and sugar," Kat said, noticing that her mother and Jamie had both hands on the table. As she watched, Skyler took her son's hand and gently squeezed it.

The swinging door opened slightly. "Sweetheart," Craig said, "how's that coffee coming?"

"Almost ready," she said, thanking God that her mother had one of the new pots that made a full pot in sixty seconds.

"I'll take a cup, too, babe," he said.

"Anyone else?" she asked.

"Yeah, your dad."

The exchange sounded so casual, so easy, she thought. "Okay. It's coming."

"Do you need help?"

"No, thanks. I'll be right out."

She tried not to shake as she got the creamer and the sugar bowl and set them on the tray. She could feel Quintin's eyes on her as she poured four cups of coffee. Done, she turned to look at him again.

The gun was once again pressed against her mother's temple.

Skyler managed to smile at her, then Kat hurried out, her back pushing against the swinging door to open it. She had barely reached the living room before Craig was there to take the tray from her. His eyes met hers, and for a moment, she dared to believe.

But...

Even if he was on their side, what could he do? He didn't have a gun, which meant Quintin would shoot at least one of them before he could be stopped.

Craig set the tray on the coffee table. Brenda was cuddled up on Frazier's lap in one of the big armchairs. Her father was seated in the other, while Uncle Paddy had chosen the love seat. He was rolling his cane between his hands, and when his eyes touched hers, they were grave. Then Sheila spoke to him, and he quickly laughed. The show was on, she thought.

Tim and Sheila were on the sofa. Scooter was standing by the fireplace, one elbow resting on the mantel. She could see the bulge of his gun tucked into his waistband beneath his flannel shirt.

Couldn't the cops see it, too?

But Sheila wasn't even looking at Scooter. "I've been telling Tim how talented all you kids are," she said. "Would you play something for him, Kat?"

Kat saw that Craig had taken a seat beside Sheila on the sofa. He seemed very calm. Of course he was. He was one of *them,* after all. Or was he? And what the hell was going on in the kitchen now? Was Quintin hearing this? How could she possibly play the piano? Why didn't Craig or Scooter say something to stop this farce?

"My mom is the one who can really play," Kat said.

"You're good, too, Kat. How about just one song while we finish our coffee?" Sheila suggested.

Frazier lifted Brenda off his lap and joined Kat at the piano. "Let's do our public servants a Christmas Eve kindness and give them some music with their coffee," he said. "I'll sing backup."

"No, you sing lead, and I'll take the harmony," Kat said. "Sure."

Her twin's eyes met hers, and she knew that he was trying to look reassuring, strong. As if help were an actual possibility.

She stared back at him, her smile sad. They both knew that Quintin and the others were counting on them to play it out until the end, and that they were all going to die.

But we'll pretend until the bitter end, she thought, and looked around the room as she started to play.

Scooter looked almost misty-eyed, as he stared at them from his place by the mantel. Her father's fingers were clenching the arms of his chair. Craig was leaning toward Sheila, looking as if he'd just finished saying something. And Sheila…

Sheila didn't seem to be paying any attention to the music. She was watching Scooter with a thoughtful look on her face, as if she were weighing whatever Craig had just said.

Despite herself, Kat felt hope begin to bloom in her heart.

She turned back to the piano, and she and Frazier launched into a song. When they finished, their audience broke into applause. Tim even gave them a standing ovation. "Sheila, you were right. They're great."

"Thanks very much," Frazier said, then walked back to rejoin Brenda in the armchair.

"Well, I guess we'd better be going back out into the cold," Sheila said with a sigh. She and Tim both rose and started toward the door.

Craig walked casually over to Kat and slipped an arm around her waist. She swallowed. She couldn't pull away without revealing the pretense behind their relationship, much less turn on him and demand to know the truth.

For the moment she needed to focus on being grateful that he could play his part so well. She needed to thank God that her text message, which had once seemed to be their only hope, hadn't gone through. She needed to just keep playing her part so Sheila and Tim would leave.

Before they all wound up dead.

Craig led her to the door, where everyone was congregating to say goodbye.

"Have you checked on the other families in the area?" Frazier asked.

Was there a slight hesitation before they answered? Kat wondered. A moment when the two officers looked at each other almost conspiratorially?

"We checked in on everyone we could get to. I was a bit worried about Mrs. Auffen—she's eighty, you know. But she was fine. Everyone in this area has a generator," Sheila said.

"I've trying to convince Sheila that we can go back to the office and warm up while we wait for the morning crew," Tim said.

"If they make it in," Sheila said skeptically. "I have a feeling we'll be on till afternoon," she said to Tim, who just shrugged.

"Well, good night, folks. And thanks for the coffee, and the entertainment," Sheila said.

"Yeah, thank you, guys," Tim said. "It was nice to meet you."

"Good night. Take care," David said.

"Drive safe," Craig added.

The two cops were almost out the door. Any second they would be in the clear, Kat thought, and she could rush back into the kitchen and see if her mother was all right.

"Hey, wait," Scooter said suddenly, his voice low, sounding like a growl deep in his throat.

Chapter 10

Craig's heart froze in his chest. They were in the clear, dammit. The cops were leaving. And they knew. *They knew.* He'd managed to whisper a few words to Sergeant Polanski, and she had nodded her understanding. They were safe, at least for now, and the cops would come back when they could do something. It was a miracle.

Or so it had seemed. But now…just when they were leaving, Scooter was stopping them. What the hell was going on?

"Wait," Scooter repeated.

"What?" Craig asked, knowing he must sound almost desperate, as he stared at Scooter.

"We're forgetting something," Scooter explained. His narrow face seemed to broaden with his sudden smile. "It's Christmas!" Scooter exclaimed. "It's Christmas Day. Merry Christmas!"

Craig thought his sigh of relief was almost as loud as the

blizzard that was still raging, although with a little less vehemence than before, just outside the open door.

But Scooter was still grinning, apparently unaware of anything besides his own joy in the holiday. "Come on, everybody. Wish each other Merry Christmas."

"Right. Merry Christmas," David gasped in what was clearly relief.

"Merry Christmas, Bren," Frazier said, then smiled down at his tiny girlfriend and lightly kissed her lips.

"Merry Christmas, Dad," Kat said, and turned to her father.

Of course, Craig told himself, trying to tamp down what he knew was an irrational sense of disappointment.

"Sheila, me love." Paddy laughed, and hugged the deputy.

"Merry Christmas, bro," Scooter said, and shot Craig a warning look before hugging him.

Brother? Craig thought. Oh, no. Not in any way. But he couldn't allow himself to show his revulsion—his horror at how this night was turning out.

He'd known all along that Quintin and Scooter were thieves, he just hadn't realized how much could be stolen. Not just property, but sanity. Love. Christmas spirit.

Lives.

He drew away from Scooter, trying to maintain a cheerful expression as he watched the others. They had gone from Christmas Eve to Christmas Day, a time to offer love and the olive branch of peace to family and friends.

Under Scooter's encouraging eye, Kat gave her brother a hug. Then Paddy and Brenda and even Tim and Sheila.

And then him.

He tried. He tried so hard with his eyes, to explain everything he had never been able to tell her. To somehow make her understand that he'd never intended to be here tonight, to bring danger to her family's door. That he hadn't shared the truth before because the truth had been too painful, and because, at the time, he'd believed that even if she knew the truth, she couldn't—wouldn't—love him.

He lifted her chin and said softly, "Merry Christmas, Kat. And many, many more," he added, even more softly, then lightly kissed her lips.

And she didn't pull away.

She stared hard at him when he finally lifted his head. She'd always had the most beautiful eyes. Irish eyes, green cat eyes to fit her name.

Sheila cleared her throat. "We'd really better go. The best to you all. Good night."

"Merry Christmas," Tim said.

And then, finally, the door closed behind them, and Craig was able to let out a silent sigh of relief at last. The cops were gone. It was Christmas Day. And he'd already witnessed a miracle.

No one here had died, and finally they had hope.

"They're gone," Craig announced, pushing his way through the swinging door. "They're gone, Quintin, and the O'Boyles played it just like pros."

The sound of the opening door had made Skyler jump. Actually, any movement made her jump. And that wasn't particularly smart, because every time she started, she felt the touch of the gun. One of these times she would startle Quintin, and without even thinking, he would pull the trigger.

"I probably should have killed them," Quintin said thoughtfully, almost as if he weren't still standing behind her, his words casual—as if he didn't still have a gun pressed against her temple.

"Quintin, no," Craig argued. "You don't want to kill cops. It makes other cops crazy. They've been here, and now they're gone, and they're not suspicious of anything. Think about it. It's the best thing that could have happened."

"Yeah, maybe," Quintin said, but there was no conviction in his voice.

Skyler didn't like the other man's tone. He sounded more on edge than ever.

"Quintin, I'm telling you the truth," Craig said.

Skyler didn't like the curl of Quintin's lips. The man was sneering. Quintin didn't like Craig, really didn't like Craig. And Quintin was the one who called the shots.

While Craig…

Scooter had boasted that the man had been the one to catch Kat. Maybe so, but just looking at him, and then at Kat, she was certain there was more to the story. Something was going on between the two of them. It was as if they knew each other. Certainly they were close enough in age for it to be a possibility, but Frazier didn't seem to know him.

And what the hell difference did it make whether he and Kat knew each other or not?

A lot. Because things might come to a point when the only thing that mattered was whether Craig was with them…or against them.

Scooter came barging through the swinging door, herding the rest of the family in front of them. "It's Christmas," he said happily. "Merry Christmas, Quintin!"

"Merry Christmas, Scooter," Quintin said, but he didn't move. At Skyler's side, neither did Jamie. It felt as if a week had gone by, as if the three of them had been frozen there forever.

She squeezed her son's hand. *Giving false encouragement?* she taunted herself. But maybe it wasn't false.

And wasn't it a parent's job to teach hope against all odds?

She dared to turn her head away from the muzzle of the gun and face her son. "Well, we made it through another crisis," she said, and forced a smile. She released his hand and looked up at Quintin. "May I turn the coffeepot off?"

"Yeah, go ahead."

She rose, and David ignored their captors and strode straight over to her, then slipped his arms around her, turning her to face him. She frowned slightly, wondering how the cops had come and gone without noticing that both Frazier and David had darkening bruises on their faces.

"Merry Christmas, Skyler," David said, and he kissed her.

She kissed him back, forgetting for a few seconds that they had an audience and pouring all her love for him and her relief that they had made it this far and were still alive into the kiss.

"Get a room," Frazier teased.

"We have a room," David said, grinning slightly and not looking away from his wife.

"Yeah, they have a room, they're just not going to be using it tonight," Quintin said.

"But would it be okay to get some sleep?" Jamie asked.

"Sure. Anyone who wants to can drift off right in the living room," Quintin said.

"I could never sleep," Skyler said with conviction.

"How about you just try to rest?" David suggested.

"You'd better rest. You have to cook that turkey in the morning," Scooter said.

Skyler nodded, suddenly exhausted. "All right, I'll try."

"Not until I've had me chance to say Merry Christmas

to me niece," Paddy announced. He walked over to her and hugged her, taking the chance to whisper, "Sheila knows."

She hugged him more tightly, adrenaline racing through her. Was he crazy? Was he just trying to give her hope?

Or could it be true?

As Paddy pulled away, she lowered her eyes to hide the light of hope, choosing to believe what he'd said was true—that the cops knew—and realizing that everything had to be played out meticulously.

Or else someone would die.

Sheila didn't want to go far from the O'Boyle house, but it was freezing and the snow was still flying and their snowmobiles didn't offer any protection against the storm. She also knew they had to carefully weigh every possible course of action and that they wouldn't think clearly if they were freezing.

Her small Colonial house was closer to the O'Boyle residence than the office was, so she led the way there to make plans. Since they had no way of communicating to anyone from the office, anyway, it didn't make much sense to go all that way back.

"I know that guy's face," Tim told Sheila, rubbing his hands in front of the fire she had quickly stoked. "The youngest one."

"From where?"

"I don't know. But I've seen him."

Sheila was doubtful. "On a most-wanted list?" she asked skeptically. "I sure don't know who he is. That's not the kind of face you forget. But he managed to talk to me. Smooth as silk. He told me there were two armed men, the one we saw and another one in the kitchen with Mrs. O'Boyle and Jamie, and he'd kill them if we acted suspicious in any way. He said we had to find a way to take them both down."

Tim glanced at her. "He said all that?"

"Right in the middle of an Irish lullaby," she said flatly.

"Well, we thought our guys might be in there," he said.

She produced a piece of paper. "He was definitely telling the truth. Paddy Murphy slipped this into my pocket."

Tim took the note from her. It was crumpled, since Paddy had wadded it into a tiny ball before slipping it into her pocket when he hugged her.

"'Two men with guns. Must be taken together. Will kill if threatened. Be careful,'" Tim read aloud. He looked at her. "Clever old geezer," he said.

"Thank God we went in carefully," she said. "But what do we do? Try to get hold of the state police somehow? If we go at them with enough guns…"

"No," Tim said.

She looked at him.

"Sheila, Lionel Hudson is already dead. They killed him. It won't make any difference to them if they have to kill again. If we go up against them in force, the first thing they'll do is kill that family just to get them out of the way."

They were both silent, thinking.

"He had it right, that guy Craig," Sheila said. "Scooter, or whatever his real name is, and the guy in the kitchen have to be taken down together."

"The question is, how?" Tim said, turning away from the fire to pace. "We can come up with some excuse and go back over there."

"Sure. And then we're up against the same thing we were before, only this time we know it. One of them will hole up somewhere with a couple of the O'Boyles, and he'll kill them if we make a move. They'll do it—even if they're going to die themselves—because they don't intend to go down alone."

"Oh God," Tim said suddenly.

"What?"

"They're going to figure out pretty soon that not only have we figured out who they are, but that we've seen their faces. If they want to get away clean, they'll need to kill us, too."

"Tim, we have to go at this logically and reasonably," Sheila said.

"What about negotiations, then?" he asked.

"They won't negotiate, I'm sure of it," Sheila said. "But we won't give in, either. And we'll have help," Sheila said.

He looked at her questioningly.

"The family," she said. "They're not armed, and they're scared as hell, but I promise you, they'll fight to the death for one another."

He nodded. "Good point."

"And I don't know who the hell that Craig kid is, but he'll help us, too. He's not one of them."

"Maybe he was just trying to sucker you in," Tim warned.

"No, he was being honest. I'd swear to it," Sheila said.

"Here's the thing. I'm armed, you're armed, and the killers are armed. There's not going to be a chance for any warning shots. We have to take them both out."

"Easier said than done," Sheila replied.

"We just have to get back in that house."

"Ring the doorbell again?" Sheila said. "I don't think so."

"Of course not. We have to get in without being seen."

The house remained comfortably warm, despite the bitter cold outside. Thanks to the generator, the lights on the tree continued to blink their message of Christmas cheer. But the living room was silent.

Quintin had dragged one of the big upholstered chairs over to block the front door and was on guard, a watchful eye on the living room, his gun resting comfortably in his lap. Scooter was in the other armchair, asleep, his gun tucked in his waistband, where no one could steal it without waking him.

Uncle Paddy had the love seat, Kat's parents were on the couch, and everyone else had blankets right on the floor. Kat was all too aware of Craig lying right up against her, even though there was no longer any need to keep up the pretense of being a couple.

Time ticked by. Kat watched the clock. Nearly one o'clock.

One-thirty.

She had to believe in a miracle. Had to believe that what Uncle Paddy had whispered to her under cover of a goodnight hug was true—Sheila and Tim would be back, and would have the good sense not to come in with guns blazing. Because if they did?

Quintin would take out half her family before he died.

Her mother was curled against her father, and Mom's eyes were actually closed. If she could ignore the circumstances, they made a nice picture. She so seldom saw them this comfortable with each other anymore.

She shifted, trying to get more comfortable, and Quintin's hand tightened on his gun. He eyed her for a long time without saying anything, so she closed her eyes and pretended to rest.

A moment later, she barely withheld a scream when Craig threw an arm across her in his sleep and pulled her closer. She gritted her teeth, ready to push him away, and then she realized that he wasn't asleep at all. His eyes were open, and he was staring at her intently, meaningfully. "Keep it together," he whispered. "They're coming back. And they know what's going on."

Her eyes widened. "How do you know that?"

"I told them."

She was silent for a very long time. "I wish I believed you."

For a second, he wore a pained expression. "I wish you did, too," he said. And then it was as if something fell over his eyes. A curtain. As if...

As if he wouldn't allow himself to care.

"Quiet down, all of you!" Scooter snapped, waking up suddenly, apparently under the impression that something was going on.

He must have been dreaming, Kat thought, and looked at the clock.

Two o'clock.

She couldn't believe it, but despite her fear and the disconcerting presence of Craig beside her, her eyelids were starting to droop. She was exhausted.

Her mother and father appeared to be sleeping. Frazier's eyes were closed. Jamie hadn't moved.

She looked across the room. Uncle Paddy's eyes were only half closed. His lips twitched, and he gave her a thumbs-up sign.

She tried to smile in return.

In the end, after going over and over the possibilities, Sheila and Tim decided that trying to slip into the house in the middle of the night would be a mistake.

It seemed most likely—though not, they thought with grave concern, certain—that if it came to a massacre, it wouldn't be until night fell on Christmas Day. Sheila had lived in the area her whole life, and she could second-guess the wind and read the snowfall. This storm wasn't going to slack off enough to allow the killers to escape for hours, at least.

With his military training, Tim was the expert in subterfuge, and in his opinion, given that there were only two of them, trying to enter the house in the dead of night, when at least one of the killers would be alert and on guard but the family would most likely be asleep and too disoriented to help in their own rescue, would be a grave mistake.

They decided to make their move just before daybreak. They would take the snowmobiles as far as they could without risking being heard, then walk the rest of the way. Their plan was to reach the house with darkness as a cover, but not to attempt a break-in until the inhabitants were actually rising.

"I think we're crazy," Sheila said.

"No, you think *I'm* crazy," Tim said with a smile.

"Whatever," Sheila said dryly.

"Are you ready?" he asked.

"Hell, no. So let's go over it one more time."

Tim frowned. "I just wish I could remember where I've seen that Craig guy before." He paused in concentration. "Maybe not actually him…maybe just a picture of him."

"And you're absolutely certain it wasn't the ten-most-wanted list?"

Tim shook his head. "I'm certain. Anyway, you said the guy is trying to help us."

"Yeah."

"But what if…?"

"What if it's all a lie? What if he's trying to trick us?" Sheila asked him.

Tim didn't answer.

* * *

Kat couldn't remember how the hours had passed, or just what time it was when she finally drifted off.

When she awoke, she was wrapped in Craig's arms. And he wasn't sleeping anymore, either.

His fingers were gently stroking her hair. She turned and caught his eyes, and for a second she froze, just watching him. There was so much pain in his gaze.

Then a shield slipped over his gaze and he shifted uncomfortably. "Sorry," he murmured.

Was that for the sake of Quintin and Scooter? Because she had the impression he wasn't really sorry at all, that for a moment he had been living in the past, remembering a time when they had so often fallen asleep together, then woken up in each other's arms.

She closed her eyes in anguish. For just a moment, she had been living in the past, as well.

It was coming up on first light, she realized, the darkness not as thick as it had been. Everyone else was waking up, too, she saw.

"I see people are finally up," Quintin said. "Good. Because I'd like some coffee."

"Coffee, sure," Skyler said.

"I'll make it, Mom," Kat said, getting to her feet.

And away from Craig.

She stretched, one eye on Quintin, who looked wideawake. She wondered if he'd stayed up all night.

"Scooter, you awake?" Quintin asked.

"Yeah."

"Good. You keep an eye on the happy family, and I'll go watch our little escape artist make the coffee."

"Wait," Skyler said.

Quintin turned to look at her.

"Bathroom break," Skyler said, "And don't tell me you're coming in with me, because you'll have to shoot me right now."

"That can be arranged," Quintin said, his eyes narrowed dangerously.

"Hey," David snapped. "Just do what you did last night. Let everyone have a minute's privacy. It's not like we don't all need the same thing."

Quintin didn't look happy, Kat thought, but he must have decided that the alternative was worse, because he let everyone line up and take a turn in the downstairs bathroom. As for him, he must have a bladder the size of a football, she thought. He hadn't gone all night, and it didn't seem that he had to go now.

Or maybe…

Maybe his faith in Scooter was so small that he didn't dare disappear, even for a moment.

"You. Make the coffee and get something on for breakfast," he said to Skyler.

"Don't talk to my wife that way," David said, then added, "Please."

"All right. Please, Mrs. O'Boyle, coffee and breakfast."

"Since you asked so nicely…" Skyler murmured sarcastically.

"I'll help my mother," Jamie offered.

"I can set the table," Brenda said.

"Sure. Scooter. You watch them. Craig, you get in here, too. You," he said, pointing a finger at Kat. "Come with me."

"Wait a minute," her father said, frowning.

"Calm down, Dad," Quintin said. "I just want to ask the girl a few questions, that's all."

"Where are you going with her?"

"I just want to open the door and see the weather," Quintin said.

Frazier spoke up warily. "I can give you a weather report. The weather sucks."

"The snow's not going to stop until tonight," Paddy said. Quintin looked at him skeptically. "I can tell, man. I can feel it in me hip. The weather won't be letting up for hours, till darkness, I say."

Quintin gave him a strange look. Kat wondered if he knew they were all aware they would only live as long as the roads were impassable.

As soon as everyone else had gone into the kitchen, Quintin turned to Kat. "Open the front door," he told her, gesturing with his gun.

She shrugged and walked ahead of him across the foyer and did as he'd commanded.

The snow was still coming down, but the house had gotten so warm that the blast of cold air actually felt good for a moment.

"Step outside," Quintin told her.

Swallowing hard, all too aware that he was standing behind her, a gun to her back, did so.

"Turn around."

Did he mean to shoot her in the face, so she could see death coming?

Slowly, she turned around, her mind racing.

"Who is Craig?" he demanded, following her out into the snow and closing the door behind him.

"What?" she gasped, astonished.

"You know him," he said.

"I know he's a filthy bastard who's broken into my house and threatened my family," she said.

She was stunned when he lashed out, striking her hard across the cheek. "I want the truth," he announced.

"I just said—"

"The truth. Or I'll knock your front teeth out next," he said.

He couldn't let it happen, Craig thought. If Quintin had Kat outside, he wanted something, and he would hurt her to get it.

He tried to act nonchalant in front of the family and Scooter, but he knew her parents and the rest of her family were going just as insane as he was, knowing she was outside with Quintin.

David broke first and started toward the kitchen door.

"Get back here!" Scooter shouted. "Don't make me shoot you."

"Everybody calm down," Craig said. "Stay cool. I'll go out and see what's going on, okay?"

"Craig," Scooter said with a frown. "Didn't Quintin say—"

"Yeah, but you don't want to have a riot before the turkey, right?" he demanded.

He didn't wait for Scooter to answer. He turned around and headed out, praying that Scooter wouldn't do something stupid.

The minute he opened the front door, he saw that Kat's cheek was bright red. That bastard had hit her! It was all he could do not to behave like a suicidal idiot and attack Quintin right then and there.

"What's going on?" he asked as casually as he could.

"I didn't ask you to come out here," Quintin said.

"I thought you'd want to know her dad is getting antsy and I'm worried that he's going to do something stupid."

Quintin stared at him, then sneered and shrugged. "I was just telling Miss O'Boyle here that she needed to tell me where she knows you from. Now. Before I take out her teeth."

Craig's jaw nearly dropped.

"But now that you're here, you can tell me. Or I *will* shove her teeth down her throat. Maybe break her nose in the process."

Craig stared at him as incredulously as he could. "What the hell are you talking about?" he asked.

Quintin had turned to face him, momentarily taking his attention off Kat, and Craig was suddenly glad as hell, because he could see something behind one of the snowbanks.

Something blue.

Cop blue. Sheriff's-department blue.

"Quit screwing around. I'll shoot you faster than you can exhale if you cross me," Quintin said.

Craig dared to hesitate before responding. The snowbanks didn't provide much cover, and whoever was out there was trying to get around to the back of the house. He had to keep Quintin's attention on him until their rescuer was safely out of sight. "We knew each other in school," he finally said, figuring the truth—or at least a piece of it—was the best defense.

"Ages ago," Kat said.

"We went to the same college, Quintin, and that's that," he said.

Thankfully, Quintin was still staring at him, frowning. "College?"

"College," Kat repeated firmly.

"You've got a college degree, pretty boy?" Quintin demanded. "You telling me that's where Scooter found you? Like I'd believe that."

"He doesn't have a degree. He dropped out," Kat said.

"But you knew each other there," Quintin said, his skepticism clear in his tone.

"We just told you that," Craig said. The cops were safely out of sight. Of course, if Quintin went for a walk right now, he would see the prints in the snow, but there was no reason for Quintin to go for a walk.

He had to play it cool, but he also had to get Quintin back in the house and give the cops time to find the door or window or whatever it was that Kat had used to slip out last night. Then they could hide in the house, listening, until the right time came for them to make their move.

"Who else do you know in there?" Quintin demanded.

"No one," Craig said.

"Never met her folks?"

"Why would I have met them?" Craig asked impatiently.

"She never brought you home?"

"We had a few classes together. We didn't date," Kat said, staring straight at Quintin.

"We need to go back in," Craig said. "I'm worried about what Scooter might do if her parents start freaking."

"Fine. But remember this. I'm not interested in women and true love. If you cause trouble, I'll kill you. If you try to stand up for this broad, Craig, I'll kill you. Got it?"

How he longed to put his fist through Quintin's face.

"I haven't caused any trouble," Kat said.

"Oh, yeah?" Quintin squinted, assessing her long and hard. "No trouble? What do you call trying to escape last night?" He stared at her assessingly for a long time, then at Craig, and finally at the sky.

"Quintin," Craig said, trying not to let the edge of fear snaking through him show in the tone of his voice. "Quintin, what are you doing? Come on. Don't rile everyone up by making them think…by making them worry about something that isn't even happening. Let's go back in. Before Scooter does something stupid."

"Please?" Kat said.

"Right," Quintin said at last. "It's Christmas Day. Time to make the turkey, huh?"

"My mother will make a great breakfast first," Kat said. She was losing it. Craig could hear it in her voice. "If we get in there now!"

"You don't call the shots, little girl. But…" Quintin paused, let the silence draw out menacingly, then smiled. "By all means, let's go in." He swept out an arm, and she walked into the house first, followed by Craig.

And then by Quintin.

Chapter 11

Skyler thought it was amazing she hadn't burned the bacon into charcoal or ruined the French toast. She had never felt such terror. Blood, bone, muscle…her entire system was flooded with it, and she was shaking so badly she could barely stand. But she had to keep moving.

That monster had taken her daughter.

She was afraid David would explode. Frazier looked like a powder keg ready to blow. Even Jamie looked as if he was going to go through the roof.

Only Paddy was managing to remain calm. "David, pour the coffee and bring me a cup, will ye? Me legs botherin' me more than a mite."

David tried. He poured the coffee. But, glancing his way, Skyler was afraid that one of the cups was going to shatter in his hands.

"Skyler, lass, that smells good enough to tempt the fairies, so it does," Paddy said. "Now, turkey, turkey is a fine meal. But I'm as happy meself with the likes of your French toast, though why they call it *French* toast makes no sense to me, no sense at all."

"I have no idea, Uncle Paddy," Skyler replied, wondering how on earth he could sound so calm and what he was up to.

"Who knows and who cares?" Frazier said, his eyes on his father.

Skyler was afraid that the glances being exchanged between father and son indicated that they were ready to attempt another go against Scooter. She had to find a way to stop them before they invited disaster.

Scooter was perched on one of the stools at the counter, his gun out, the safety off. She knew David and Frazier were both willing to die for Kat, but she didn't want that to happen, and if they moved now, it almost certainly would.

And then Kat, out there with Quintin, would certainly die, as well.

What about Craig? she wondered. Were his cohorts planning on killing him, too, when they didn't need him anymore?

But just when she thought hope was gone, Kat came striding into the kitchen, Craig and Quintin behind her.

"Smells good in here," Quintin said pleasantly, as if he weren't still holding a gun.

She couldn't quite manage a thanks, not at that moment. "It's the bacon and coffee, I imagine."

"I'll take a coffee," Quintin said.

"I'll get it," Craig offered quickly. As he poured, he smiled at Skyler.

"What the hell?" Quintin growled. "You said you never met her before."

"And I haven't. Can't a man smile at a pretty woman? What the hell is your problem, Quintin?" Craig demanded.

"Have *you* ever met him before?" Quintin said to David.

"Where the hell would I have met him?"

"You?" Quintin spun around to stare at Frazier, who shook his head.

"Oh, for the love of God," Craig said to Quintin. "I went to the same college as Kat. We had a few classes together." He turned to the others. "Now Quintin here thinks I'm conspiring with you. That I managed to wreck the car in front of your house." He turned back to Quintin and eyed the other man challengingly. "Damned difficult, since *I was knocked out* when it happened," he said, glaring.

"You went to college with Kat?" Skyler said, ignoring the last part of his speech.

"Yes," he said, then, eager to change the subject to something less fraught with pitfalls, asked, "Hey, is that French toast?"

"It is, and if you want to get that serving platter, the first batch is ready to go," Skyler said.

"Forget that," Quintin said as Craig reached for the platter. "Where's my damn coffee?"

"Hell, you distracted me," Craig told him.

"I'll get the coffee," Brenda chirped, rising and picking up the cup Craig had left on the counter.

"You!" Quintin said suddenly, pointing at her. "Did you ever see this guy before?"

Brenda handed him the coffee, which he took with his left hand, his right still brandishing the gun.

"I told you, I'm pre-med," Brenda said. "Not Crime 101."

Quintin enjoyed that. He actually laughed.

French toast, bacon, coffee, juice, butter and syrup all went on the table. Skyler didn't sit but instead started making another batch of French toast.

Every once in a while, she froze briefly as it hit her again that they were actually sitting and eating at her table—horrible men, men who were probably killers—and she was serving them while they sat calmly beside her children.

It was unbearable.

But it had to be borne.

"So when are you putting the turkey on?" Quintin asked.

She hesitated, then turned to face him. "Soon, so I can make sure it's fully cooked before the generator starts to run out of gas. Actually, we should probably start trying to conserve a little now, so we can be sure of having light and heat tonight."

"We could turn off more lights, turn down the heat," Frazier said.

"No," Quintin said.

And there it was. Unspoken but clear.

Quintin didn't care if they lost power later. He wouldn't be here.

And they wouldn't need it.

Uncle Paddy suddenly spoke up, breaking the chilly silence that had settled over the room after Quintin's comment. "It's Christmas. Let's open the gifts."

"Yeah, let's open the gifts," Scooter said. "No, wait. Why should I care about presents? It's not like I'm getting any."

"I told you, we always have extra gifts," Skyler said.

"What? A fruitcake?" Scooter demanded sulkily.

Skyler actually laughed, shaking her head. "No, *nice* gifts."

"Don't you have to be good all year for Santa to bring gifts?" Quintin asked. "I think Scooter has been really naughty, don't you?"

Is he actually making a joke? Skyler wondered.

"Ignore him. I love getting presents," Scooter said.

"So where are these gifts?" Quintin asked.

"Normally, they'd already be under the tree," Skyler said.

"But this isn't 'normally,' is it?" Quintin said meaningfully.

"Most of them are in my room."

"And our rooms," Frazier said.

"We can all go upstairs, then," Skyler said.

"No. Scooter, you're in the kitchen with Mom," Quintin said. "Blondie, you stay here, too, and help with the cleanup."

"I can help in the kitchen, too," Kat said.

"Not you," Quintin told her.

"But—"

"Not you."

"Where am I this time, Quintin?" Craig asked.

"With me."

"You still don't trust me," Craig said.

"Smart guy for a college dropout," Quintin said. "Let's go."

As they left the kitchen, Brenda started bringing plates over to the sink. "Thank you for breakfast, Mrs. O'Boyle," she said politely. "It was delicious."

Skyler almost broke out in laughter at the insanity of the situation, but she managed not to. "Thank you, Brenda. I'm glad you enjoyed it."

"Yup, that was great," Scooter said and he was smiling at her, almost like a kid.

A kid with a gun pointed right at her.

"Thanks," she answered, feeling she had to say something or risk his mood turning ugly.

"Are you going to get the turkey ready?" he asked excitedly.

"As soon as this is all picked up," she said.

With Brenda helping her, the work went quickly. While

Brenda was getting out the special Christmas dishes with the trumpeting angels on them, Skyler realized she couldn't stuff anything more into the garbage bag.

She tied it shut, then started for the basement door without thinking. She caught herself quickly, hesitated, then said, "Scooter?"

"Yeah?"

"Is it all right if I dump the garbage in the basement?"

He frowned. "Quintin'll be mad if I—"

"All I have to do is open the door and toss it down, just so it's out of the way and won't stink up the kitchen."

He looked at Brenda, who was getting out more dishes, her back to him. "Yeah, sure go ahead."

Skyler nodded and walked across to the pantry, then past the servants' stairway. She could hear voices from upstairs.

"It's just a big box," Jamie was saying. "Honest, it's not dangerous."

"All right, all right," Quintin growled.

"If you want Scooter to open those extra gifts my wife was talking about, you're going to have to let me open that closet door," David said.

Shaking her head, feeling the sting of tears in her eyes, Skyler pulled open the basement door and almost screamed aloud, stunned to see two faces looking up at her. As it was, it felt as if her heart came to a dead halt in her chest.

Help had arrived.

Sheila Polanski and a young man she hadn't seen before. He had to be the deputy Sheila had brought with her the night before. They were standing at the bottom of the stairs; they had clearly been listening to what was going on upstairs.

Sheila brought her fingers to her lips, and Skyler knew. They were waiting. Waiting for the right time.

"Hey, what's taking you so long?" Scooter asked accusingly.

"I'm not taking so long," she protested, looking in his direction and tossing the garbage bag down the stairs. She didn't dare look, but she was sure the two deputies were quick enough to dodge it.

She was trembling so hard that she was afraid Scooter would notice. She didn't dare look at him. Instead, she headed straight for the refrigerator and opened the door.

She nearly jumped when she felt Scooter right behind her, and she turned, gulping.

"What the hell is the matter with you?" he demanded.

"You scared the hell out of me," she told him.

"Sorry," he said, and grinned, then glanced over at Brenda, who had turned, wide-eyed. "She's getting out the turkey," he said happily.

"Right. Where do these little plates go, Mrs. O'Boyle?"

"You can leave them on the counter until we set up for dinner," Skyler said.

"Where's the stuffing?" Scooter asked, looking deeper into the refrigerator.

"I make it separately."

"Why?"

"Because I don't put it in the turkey. Bread crumbs suck up moisture, and I want the turkey moist."

"Good thinking," he said approvingly, beaming at her.

She glanced past him toward the pantry. The door to the basement was ajar, and Sheila was visible just behind it. Scooter's back was to the door, thank God, but Quintin...

Quintin was upstairs, with her family. And a gun.

She dropped the turkey, and Scooter stooped to pick it up. She took advantage of the second when his attention was distracted to shake her head vigorously. She could hear the group coming back down the stairs and knew the time wasn't right. The right time would be when they were all together. When both men were preoccupied and could be taken at once.

Scooter handed her the turkey and looked around, as if he thought he should have seen something, but hadn't.

"What's going on?" he asked suspiciously.

Just then the door to the kitchen opened and the rest of the family trailed back in, Quintin last, his gun in his hand.

"Presents are under the tree," Jamie said.

"And I found you the best present ever," Kat said, going over to embrace her mother.

"The cops are here," Skyler whispered while they were hugging.

"No way. *I* got her the best present," Jamie said.

"Any present from my children is always the best present," Skyler said, and she turned to hug him, too.

Frazier laughed. "Hey, maybe *I* got her the best present."

Looking across the room then, Skyler saw Scooter's expression. It was deeply sad, and she read in his eyes that he intended to kill them all. Or at least that Quintin did and Scooter wasn't going to stop him.

But not until they'd had turkey.

"I'm not sure how brilliant this is," Sheila whispered, shivering as she hovered close to Tim in the basement.

"Hey, we're in, aren't we?" Tim said.

"Yeah, we're in, but…we're still in the same situation. How the hell are we going to get in position to take out both men at once without one of them shooting one of the O'Boyles?"

"Patience," he said.

Very little light filtered into the basement, just a little

daylight coming through the grimy window, so Tim's face was in a shadow. And it was difficult, from down here, to hear what was going on above. If Skyler O'Boyle hadn't been alone coming to the door, they would have been caught. Neither of them had realized she was there until it was almost too late. They'd only made it back down in the nick of time.

"Patience is great. But when and how?" she murmured.

"Over turkey?" he asked.

She exhaled. "Oh God, Tim, we can't fuck this up. It'll be a bloodbath if we do."

"Clean shots," he said. "Scooter and Quintin."

"Over the turkey," she said.

"The turkey isn't going to care," he murmured, and then he frowned, listening intently.

The turkey had just gone into the oven, and he could tell from the footsteps that everyone had gone into the living room.

"Oh, wow!" Jamie cried delightedly, staring raptly from his gift to his parents, then back to the package he had just unwrapped. "You found it," he said incredulously.

Skyler, sitting in one of the upholstered chairs, smiled. "Your father found it."

"Kat, open yours," Skyler said.

"Why does she get to go next?" Scooter asked.

Kat turned to him. "We go by age. Jamie is the youngest. Then me."

"Aren't you and your brother twins?" Quintin asked.

"We are, but I was born first," Frazier said.

"So...what? You're five seconds older?" Quintin scoffed.

"Ten minutes, to be exact," Frazier said. "Besides, Kat is impatient. I'm not."

"You are so," she teased him.

"You're right. I *am* impatient. So open your box so we can get to mine."

"When do I get to open mine?" Scooter demanded.

"After Frazier. You're older than he is," Skyler said.

Scooter sighed.

"Actually, Kat and I should both go after Brenda," Frazier said.

"Hey," Scooter protested.

"It's how we do Christmas," Kat said calmly.

"All right," Scooter said with a sigh.

He had a gun and could have demanded the right to open his present next, Skyler knew. But he didn't. Scooter really wanted this Christmas. A real Christmas. A family Christmas. Even if he intended to massacre her whole family after dinner.

Skyler almost smiled. He and Quintin didn't know about the cops in the basement.

"I can actually wait," Brenda said.

"Open your package," Scooter ordered.

"It's from the whole family," Skyler pointed out.

"Mom, do you mind if she opens the one from me first?" Frazier asked.

"Of course not," Skyler said.

And then she knew. Before Brenda even opened the box and squealed, she knew. It was an engagement ring.

Frazier hadn't even told them!

Maybe he had meant to. Maybe he hadn't had the chance. She caught his eyes and read the apology in them, and she knew he *had* meant to tell them, perhaps even ask for their blessing.

"Oh, Frazier," Brenda breathed.

"Will you marry me, Brenda?" Frazier asked softly.

"Yes, oh, yes," she said, and kissed him.

"Get a room, would you?" Jamie moaned.

Blushing, Brenda sat back. "Behave, almost brother-in-law," she said.

Skyler could hear her older son swallow. Frazier didn't know that help was waiting just downstairs and that they might survive. It had been extremely important to him that Brenda know he had gotten her the ring.

Because the wedding might never come to pass.

"That's a beauty," Scooter said, stepping closer to examine the ring.

Skyler noticed Craig watching the older man uneasily. Almost as if he were afraid Scooter was going to wrench the ring away from Brenda there and then. "All right," she said quickly. "I need to baste the turkey soon, so we should keep going, but, Brenda, Frazier, congratulations."

"Let's move on now," Scooter ordered. "Kat, open your present."

"I'm sorry, but I'm not sure your father and I managed to top Frazier's present to Brenda," Skyler warned her daughter. She was trying not to watch Craig, because Craig was still watching Scooter.

And Scooter was watching the ring.

Skyler felt a sudden knot in the pit of her stomach. They were probably jewel thieves. Which meant that they would definitely be stealing Brenda's ring. And the only reason they weren't stealing it right now was because they intended to wait.

Until after the turkey.

"My boots!" Kat cried delightedly, opening the box. She had seen this particular pair of knee-high, fur-lined boots in a boutique window over the post-Thanksgiving weekend, when she'd been out shopping with her mother. They'd been hugely expensive, so she had just sighed and walked away. But she had coveted them, and Skyler had seen that and gone back for them later.

"Well, they're bigger than the ring," Jamie said.

"Fine. They're great. Frazier, open your gift now. Do it," Scooter commanded.

"Is it all right if he opens his from me?" Brenda shyly asked Skyler.

"Of course," Skyler said, wondering if Brenda had bought Frazier a ring, as well.

But it wasn't a ring. It was a medallion. A beautiful, simple St. Christopher's medal in gold.

Once again, Scooter jumped out of his seat to admire it. And once again, when Skyler looked at Craig, she saw the tension in his features.

"Brenda…it's beautiful," Frazier told her.

"You two have great taste," Scooter noted. "Now me!"

"I think Craig is younger than you are," Skyler said firmly.

Scooter frowned. "You have a gift for him, too?"

"We don't always know who might stop by around the holidays," David said. "Skyler likes to be prepared."

"It's okay," Craig said. "I don't need anything. Let Scooter open his present."

Skyler followed his eyes and registered the way Quintin was just sitting and watching everything, his gun at the ready.

"No, you have a present, and you *are* younger than I am, so open it," Scooter commanded.

"Scooter…" Craig protested.

"It's Christmas, and we have to do Christmas right," Scooter said.

Such hopeful words, Skyler thought, and today, knowing what was to come, also so ominous.

Craig opened the box Skyler quickly handed him.

"This is perfect," he murmured, pulling out a deep blue cashmere scarf. "Absolutely beautiful. Thank you."

He looked at Skyler, and she smiled at him. She longed to say that she knew he wasn't with the monsters holding her family hostage. And then she felt a tightening in her stomach again. There were cops in the basement, cops who undoubtedly thought he was one of the criminals. Cops who, if they managed to save her family, might well kill him.

She looked away to hide her thoughts. She couldn't afford to care. Her family had to come first. And it was still far from certain that her entire family would survive what was to come.

What did she know, anyway? He had come here with the other two. He was one of them. Just the one...

With a conscience.

But she noticed that her daughter was looking at him, as well. And for a moment Kat looked as if she were going to cry.

How well had she known him? Skyler wondered.

"My turn!" Scooter insisted.

"Yes, Scooter, it's your turn," David said patiently.

"Which box is mine?" he demanded.

"This one," Paddy said, pushing a box toward Scooter with his cane.

Scooter didn't tear into the paper. He picked up the box and held it, studied it, as if awed by the wrapping alone.

"Great bow," he said. "Pretty paper."

"I wrapped it," Kat said.

He glanced at her with a quick smile. "Wow."

"Open the damn thing, Scooter," Quintin said.

"I'm getting to it. I'm getting to it."

He still didn't rip into the box. He carefully, painstakingly, removed the bow, the ribbon and then the tape. He folded the ribbon and the paper, and set them carefully aside, as if they were a part of the gift. Then he opened the box.

He stared at the contents, then looked up at Skyler. "Cranium," he breathed, almost in awe.

"You seem to like games," she said.

"It's great. It's the coolest Christmas present I've ever gotten." He hesitated, frowning, as if trying hard to remember. "It might be the only Christmas present I've ever gotten."

"Look underneath," Skyler said.

He did, and his eyes widened in wonder. "Trivial Pursuit," he said happily. "Quintin, look, two games."

"Great."

"Mom, it's over to you now," Kat said.

"We need to wait," she said, as she stood and walked in the direction of the kitchen. "I have to baste the turkey." She spoke more loudly than necessary, hoping the cops could hear her and would get back downstairs, if they'd come upstairs to listen better. She had no intention of accidentally betraying the blessed deputies who intended to rescue them. "If I don't baste that turkey, it will dry out, and you don't want a dry turkey, do you, Quintin?"

"That will be my present. The turkey," Quintin said pleasantly.

"I'd like a soda," Jamie said.

"I need water," Kat added.

"Should we all go into the kitchen?" Skyler asked Quintin calmly.

Quintin shook his head. "Scooter, take Mom into the kitchen. And watch her closely. Mrs. O'Boyle, when you come back, bring the kids something to drink."

Skyler shrugged. "All right."

What was it about Quintin? Did he know? Why did he insist on keeping them all split up?

Scooter followed her into the kitchen. On her way over to the oven, she noticed that the dishes Brenda had stacked on the counter had been moved slightly, as if someone had leaned against the edge and bumped them.

She tried to act normal as she opened the oven and tended to the turkey, but her heart was thundering. She wanted—needed—to get back over to the basement door, but she didn't have another trash bag to get rid of. And if she walked that way for no good reason, Scooter would no doubt follow her to see what she was up to.

"Mmm-mmm!" Scooter said.

She jumped. He was right next to her.

"Can't wait," he said, sounding just like a kid.

She was suddenly certain that she didn't need to open the basement door. They weren't down there anymore. So where the hell were they?

Chapter 12

"Scooter!" Quintin shouted, then stared around the room impatiently. "How long does it take to baste a turkey?"

"I imagine Skyler's started the rest of the food," David said stiffly.

"We can all go in and see, if you want," Craig suggested.

"You can go to the door and find out what's going on," Quintin told him.

"Sure," Craig said. *What the hell kind of radar does Quintin have?* he wondered. The cops would need to get Quintin and Scooter together to take them out, which suddenly seemed impossible to manage. But he walked to the swinging door and did exactly as he had been told, just pushing the door inward and calling through, "Mrs. O'Boyle? What's going on?"

To his amazement, Scooter turned to him and announced proudly, "We're cooking."

Craig turned back to Quintin and said, "They're cooking."

"*They're* cooking? Scooter can't cook," Quintin said.

"Mrs. O'Boyle is teaching me," Scooter shouted happily.

Quintin stood. "I don't like this," he said, agitated. "Dad, you and the boys stay there. Uncle Paddy, in the kitchen. Blondie and Miss Troublemaker, you two get in the kitchen, too."

He'd seemed so calm, almost laid-back, when they were opening presents, but now, Craig thought, he was actively disturbed, even anxious.

Maybe worried that Scooter was beginning to like the family too much, that he wouldn't be able to do what was necessary when the time came.

"Where do you want *me,* Quintin?" Craig asked.

"Kitchen." Quintin narrowed his eyes. "I trust you about as much as I trust your redheaded girlfriend."

"I'm not his girlfriend," Kat said, her voice hard.

"You're a girl, and you were his friend," Quintin said impatiently. Craig swallowed, every muscle in his body seeming to clench, as Quintin reached for Kat, the gleaming silver nose of his gun aiming for her temple. "Everyone move," he barked.

Craig could see the agony that ripped at David O'Boyle as he watched his daughter being threatened and forced himself to remain in his chair. Meanwhile, Brenda and Paddy rose, ready to obey the order to move into the kitchen.

"Ye don't need to be manhandling me niece," Paddy said with dignity. "We'd know ye meant business without havin' to terrorize the lass."

"Just get in the kitchen," Quintin said.

"Scooter," Quintin snapped, holding the door open so he could see what was happening in both rooms.

"What?"

"Get the hell out here."

"But—"

"Get out here. And be on guard. Keep your safety off and your gun on Dad. Now."

Scowling, Scooter appeared. "Quintin, I was learning how to make candied yams."

"Eating them will have to be enough for you," Quintin said.

"Quintin, you don't have to make a misery out of dinner," Scooter said.

"Just get out here. I'm not going to make a misery out of anything. I just can't figure out how you can keep an eye on Mom if you're making candied yams."

Pouting, Scooter went out to the living room.

Craig walked past Quintin into the kitchen, Paddy and Brenda ahead of him. With an impatient sigh, Paddy took a seat at the table, setting his cane on top of it. Brenda paused by the sink, and Kat, shoved forward by Quintin, walked over to her mother's side.

"You're starting the rest of the food?" Kat asked.

Skyler nodded, looking as if she had just lost a negotiation she thought she should have won. "Yes. I was just putting the brown sugar on the yams. Brenda, would you start the green-bean casserole? It's easy, just the beans, mushroom soup and then the fried onion rings. Everyone loves it. Unless they hate green beans. Or mushrooms. Or onions."

Skyler realized she was chattering on about nothing, just hoping to break the tension. But Brenda nodded and started on the casserole, while Kat took over the yams. Sighing, Skyler opened the oven to baste the turkey again.

Quintin took a seat next to Paddy, and Craig noted unhappily that someone sneaking up from the basement couldn't possibly get a clean shot at Quintin. Nor was he certain that anyone would have tried. He was sure Quintin was keeping everyone split up to make sure at least one O'Boyle would die, no matter what.

"So, Quintin," Craig said.

"What?"

"It's Christmas."

"Tell me something I don't know, college boy."

Craig forced himself to smile. "I was just thinking that we should have a drink to celebrate."

"It's early."

"Not in Ireland," Paddy offered.

"I'd even like a drink," Brenda admitted.

"Well?" Craig asked Quintin.

"What the hell. Go on."

As he stood to walk toward the counter where the liquor was kept, Craig felt Quintin's hostile gaze following him, and he sensed that Quintin was practicing his aim, the 9mm Smith & Wesson pointing right at his back.

That gun could blow a hole the size of a dinner plate right through him, and he suddenly and inconsequentially imagined himself as a cartoon character looking down at a huge hole in his stomach. He wondered vaguely if cartoons were still as violent as they had been when he was a kid.

"What'll it be?" he turned and asked the others.

"Whiskey, neat," Paddy said.

Quintin shrugged. "Same as the old Mick."

Craig poured the drinks, brushing by Kat. He couldn't believe that three years had passed. Three years and a staggering change in his life.

Craig set drinks in front of Paddy and Quintin. He wondered if it would be possible to somehow block Quintin's view of the others, forcing him to move and allow someone a good shot at him. But as he hovered, Quintin looked up at him suspiciously. Besides, he thought, if the two officers were in the house, which he had to believe was true, they weren't going to take a shot until the exact right moment. They wouldn't go for Quintin unless they had a clean shot at Scooter, as well. He moved back to the counter. "Brenda, did you want your whiskey neat, too?"

"Good God, no, you'll have to put something else in it for me," she said.

"Soda?" Craig asked.

"Sure. Cola, lemon-lime, whatever," Brenda said, intent on getting the last of the mushroom soup out of the can.

"You should never mix good whiskey with crap like that," Quintin said. "It'll give you a hell of a hangover. Not that it will matter."

A stunned silence followed his words.

Craig quickly handed Brenda her glass. She took it with shaking fingers, her blue eyes wide with fear.

He couldn't reassure her. Not at the moment. "Skyler, Kat...would you like something?"

Skyler shook her head, staring in at the turkey again.

Kat looked daggers at him. He knew she was wondering what the hell he was doing and letting him know she didn't want anything from him. Ever.

He poured himself a shot and went to sit next to Paddy. "Cheers," he said, and lifted his glass.

Paddy stared at him. *"Slainte,"* he returned.

Craig turned to Quintin. "They've seen us, you know," he said thoughtfully.

"What?"

Craig shook his head. "Those cops who came by last night. They've seen us. So when we leave here, after... whatever, they'll know we were here."

To his amazement, Quintin stared at him and blinked,

and Craig realized that the other man hadn't realized the mistake he had made. He'd been obsessed with having this safe haven. He'd thought he had everything under control. And he hadn't realized what he had done.

Quintin sat perfectly still for a very long time, until finally Craig dared to speak out again. "It doesn't make sense to kill anyone here," he said.

Quintin smiled slowly, and he aimed the Smith & Wesson right at Craig's face. "But they didn't see *me*," he said, and smiled malignantly. "And it won't make any difference to anyone if I kill you."

Would he have done it? Craig didn't know, because Skyler was suddenly right there, and she had clearly reached the end of her rope. "Stop it! I mean it. I have had it with the bickering and the backbiting, and I don't give a damn if it's you two or my own kids. Read my lips. *This is Christmas!* I'm cooking a turkey. And I am sick of the entire world behaving like a pack of two-year-olds. There will be no more fighting around this table, do you understand?"

Quintin was stunned. He just stared at Skyler, who stood over him, her hands on her hips, her eyes flashing.

He didn't shoot Craig, and he didn't shoot Skyler.

And after a moment, he even began to laugh.

Craig could hear Kat's gasp of relief, and he looked over and saw her doubled over, shaking.

He stood. "Kat, are you sure you don't want a drink?"

"I can get it myself," she said, and turned away.

David O'Boyle sat on his chair, in his living room, with his Christmas tree and his sons, and stared at the man who was holding a gun on him.

Scooter seemed to feel he'd been duly chastised. He wasn't joking around, and he wasn't talking about Christmas. He only glanced toward the kitchen now and then, as if he were willing Quintin to come back.

They could all hear the rise and fall of conversation coming from the other room. *What's going on in there?* David wondered. To take his mind off the things he couldn't control, he turned to Scooter and asked, "How long have you worked for Quintin?"

"I don't work for Quintin," Scooter said, frowning.

"Oh?" David said politely. He folded his hands in his lap.

"I don't work for Quintin," Scooter repeated, more vehemently this time.

"Sure. I believe you."

"It's the truth."

"I said I believe you."

"You know, if anyone works for anyone…it was my thing first. My gig."

"Right," David said. "That's one hell of a gun you got there."

Scooter sneered. "What would you know about it?"

"I don't own a gun," David said, "but that doesn't mean I don't know anything about them. I've heard the sales pitches, read about the laws. They always ask what you want a gun for. You know, are you a hunter? Marksman? Do you need it for self-defense? Strange, I never heard anyone claim they had the best gun for holdups and harassing innocent families. And killing, of course, but, hey, that's just an assumption."

A muscle started twitching in Scooter's jaw. "Shut up. Just…shut up. You know, if you'd had a gun, you could have shot me."

"And maybe Quintin would have shot half my family while I was doing that."

Scooter looked down, embarrassed, for a moment. "You

got a nice family," he said when he looked up. "All you have to do is…well, don't try anything, okay?"

"Quintin plans on killing us, no matter what," David said.

"Now that's just not true," Scooter said, but he was a bad liar.

"He who lives by the gun dies by the gun," Jamie said.

Scooter only laughed. "No death penalty in this state," he said. "That's why I moved up here."

"From where?" Frazier asked.

"Louisiana. I went to Florida first, but then I figured a state without the death penalty would be best for me," he said. He sounded pleased with himself, as if he thought he'd been very smart to have figured that out.

"Scooter, has it occurred to you that a cop could shoot you?" David asked.

"Yeah. You're a nice guy, but a cop might not know that," Frazier said.

"I don't give cops a reason to shoot me," Scooter said. "I just hold up places when no one is there. I mean…" His voice trailed away.

"Do you actually know how to shoot, Scooter?" David asked.

"Of course! I shoot beer bottles all the time. Hey, don't you go thinking I'm easy. My aim is good. And this thing can blow a hole in you…well, you saw the lamp."

David felt ill. He thought he had understood everything Scooter *hadn't* said. Scooter had never killed anyone. But Quintin had.

And Quintin was more than willing to do it again.

And no matter what Scooter said, he did what Quintin ordered, which meant that if he had to, Scooter would shoot any one of them to save his own hide.

"Beer bottles and people. Two different things," David said.

"But…" Scooter began, then fell silent.

"What?" David said. Scooter's mood swings were the scariest thing about the man.

Scooter was frowning and looking toward the stairs. "What the hell?"

"What?" David asked, alarmed.

Scooter stared at him. He was nervous, wound up and angry. "How the hell many kids do you have?"

"Three."

"No, really."

"I swear to you, Scooter. I only have three children."

"There was someone on the stairs."

"It must have been a trick of the light," David said, his heart thundering.

Craig had told him, when he'd tried to help him after Quintin had bashed his face half in, that help would be coming. And Craig *had* been sitting next to Sheila last night…. He was afraid to breathe. Were the cops in the house? Was that why Skyler had looked at him strangely earlier?

"I saw something," Scooter insisted.

"A trick of light," David repeated.

"Quintin!" Scooter shouted.

Scooter was going to say something, David realized. And if he did, everything might be lost. He stood and said, "My God…"

"What?" Scooter demanded.

"Smell that turkey."

The kitchen door swung open and Craig appeared. Apparently Quintin was using him as his communications man. "Quintin wants to know what you're shouting about, Scooter."

"Turkey," David said. "It smells absolutely great. We were just wondering how soon dinner would be ready."

Scooter stared at Craig and frowned, as if he were trying to remember his train of thought.

"Scooter, what's up?" Craig asked.

"I don't want to be out here. I want to be in the kitchen," Scooter said.

"I'll tell Quintin," Craig told him.

The swinging door closed.

"I thought you didn't work for Quintin?" David said.

"I don't." He looked as if he were thinking about heading straight for the kitchen, but then he stopped. "I don't work for Quintin," he snapped. "But...we're a team. You know. Teammates!"

"Sure," David said.

"You're wrong. You're all wrong," Scooter told him.

"Whatever you say," David said.

"You have to understand. Quintin...he's my friend. He cares about me. So I have to be his friend. Show him I care about him."

"Friends don't hurt friends," David said.

"Or make them do things that will hurt them in the end," Frazier offered quietly.

"Quintin is my friend," Scooter insisted, his gun hand starting to shake.

"Whatever you say. We believe you," David said reassuringly.

"Smell that turkey," Jamie said encouragingly.

The nervous twitching in Scooter's fingers abated.

"Turkey, potatoes, gravy...and dessert. Lots of dessert, Scooter," Frazier promised.

Kat pretended it took great artistry to put the brown sugar on the yams, then sliced the butter into tiny increments to put on top, anxious to stay in the kitchen with her mother. Besides being constantly terrified, she was now completely confused.

Craig had purposely drawn out the truth they had all been trying to ignore—as if, by keeping quiet, they could keep it from being true. Then he had pointed out a fact that might actually save their lives.

And she…she was continually praying that the cops in the house would shoot Quintin and Scooter.

Was that a horrible thought? Wanting to see someone's brains blown out? Maybe, but after the way the two men had terrorized her family…horrible or not, it was there.

But what the hell was Craig really up to, and whose side was he on?

She had seen what he had done, trying to maneuver Quintin into moving and giving one of the cops a chance to shoot him, if they had split up and the other one had been able to get a bead on Scooter. But Quintin hadn't played along, and nothing had happened.

Had Craig somehow known nothing would happen? Was everything he was doing now just an act? Was he playing both sides against the middle, waiting to see who came out on top before jumping one way or the other? If Quintin and Scooter were able to escape, would he throw in with them and go, too? But if not, would he try to pretend he'd been a good guy the whole time, playing along with the gun-wielding duo just to survive?

Once upon a time she had adored him. She had gotten up every morning wanting to see him. She had done all the little things women did when they first fell passionately in love. Her legs were constantly clean-shaven. She had watched her diet, exercised, angsted over her imperfections, and she had marveled at the amazing fact that he was in love with her, too.

Lust had played a part, too. He had the kind of face that belonged on magazine covers. He was fit without being musclebound, and back in those days he'd sported a healthy tan. She'd watched him in class sometimes, hoping to meet him, then had been almost afraid to believe her luck when she did. They'd talked about spending spring break in the Bahamas, just the two of them. Renting a little cottage on a beach somewhere, diving, snorkeling, swimming, parasailing…making love in the waves, with a cool breeze wafting over them.

And then…

Cold, hard and fast, it had been over.

And, oh God, the heartbreak. To escape her pain, she'd done every stupid thing possible. Stayed out too late, drank too much, slept with the wrong guy just because he was on the football team. She seemed to remember that he'd been able to open beer bottles with his teeth. She wondered vaguely if he still had any.

She might even have gotten into drugs, but when she'd started on the wrong path, Frazier had suddenly thrust himself back into her life, yelling at her and, somehow, as her twin, suffering with her. Growing up, they had argued the way any siblings would, but when it mattered, he'd been there for her. He'd straightened her out.

And her mom… Back then, when she'd been in so much pain after Craig's defection, her mother's every word, her concerned calls, had driven her crazy. But now—now more than ever, with life hanging by a thread—she had to wonder how she had ever been so cruel to someone who loved her so much.

And, of course, there was her father. Jamie. Even Uncle Paddy. They meant everything to her. Surely she couldn't lose them now.

It was suddenly very hard not to burst into tears as she thought about all the family stories and hoped she could remember them all to tell her own children one day, if she ever had any.

If she lived to have any.

Once she and Craig had talked about having kids, lying in each other's arms and musing about the future. He'd believed passionately that children needed a mother and a father, and said that he wanted at least two, because no one should have to be an only child. And he had believed that both parents should have dreams.

So what had happened to his dreams?

"What *are* you doing?"

She nearly jumped a mile, stunned to see that Quintin had walked up without her noticing and was standing next to her.

"Yams. I'm making the yams."

"It looks as if you're trying to paint the Mona Lisa."

"Hey, this is Christmas dinner. It has to be perfect," she said, and looked around. She was alone in the kitchen with Quintin. Where had everyone else gone? And when?

"Get that in the oven," he said. "Let's go."

"Where are we going?" Her heart skipped a beat. She couldn't help it. Quintin scared the hell out of her.

He smiled, as if he knew and enjoyed the fact.

"It's Christmas, baby girl. And there are still gifts to open. Don't you want your mom and dad to get their presents?"

He touched her then, brushed her face with his fingers, and she thought she would scream, or fight or do something terrible that would get her killed, and then everyone else.

The swinging door opened, and Craig came in. A criminal? Or the boy next door?

Whichever, he had arrived at just the right moment. She tried to keep her heart from leaping. She couldn't forgive him now, not even if they were all going to die. Only an idiot forgave the person who had crushed her.

"Hey, Quintin, come on," Craig said impatiently. "Mrs. O'Boyle said we can eat in about an hour after Kat gets the yams in the oven."

Quintin took a step back and aimed the gun at her, then turned to aim it at Craig for a moment. "I call the shots," he reminded them both, then grinned. "The shots—get it?"

Kat turned her back on him and shoved the casserole dish into the oven, in the space left for it right beneath the turkey.

Upstairs, their backs against the wall of the hallway, Sheila hovered with Tim. They had quickly realized, once they were inside, that they weren't going to be able to rush up the basement stairs and shoot the men from the top step, so they'd crept up the back stairs when everyone was in the living room.

"Shit," Tim swore, glancing down the stairs.

"What?" she whispered.

"It's as if they know," Tim said.

"They don't know we're here," Sheila said. "I know that no one saw us come in."

"Maybe when Mrs. O'Boyle opened the door to the basement that Scooter guy sensed something," Tim said thoughtfully.

"It doesn't matter now. We've got to find a position where we can both get a clear shot," Sheila said.

"We'll never get a good chance at both of them."

"They'll have to get careless," she argued.

He nodded, then looked at her. "Sheila, we may have

to…well, in the end, it might be better to take light casualties rather than—"

"No, don't say it," she warned him.

"We're running out of time," he said flatly. "We have to do something."

"Not yet."

"Sheila, can't you hear it?"

She swallowed hard. "You mean the storm."

"It's letting up."

"I know."

"In war, there are casualties."

"This is a house, not a war zone."

"Soldiers have to die sometimes."

"We're the only soldiers in here," she told him. "And we have a little more time. Plus we know the layout of the house now."

"So we're going with my plan then?"

She nodded, and he looked down toward the living room, then lifted his hand.

She slipped by him, hurrying for the landing of the servants' stairway.

Chapter 13

Craig tried desperately not to appear anxious, but he couldn't help wondering what the hell Sheila and Tim were doing and how much longer it was going to be before they made their move. Had they gone upstairs? Were they watching from the landing, as Kat had apparently done earlier?

The two of them had to be upstairs, he decided. And they had better move soon, because time was running out.

But how the hell would they ever get the opportunity when Quintin and Scooter seemed to be more on guard than ever, constantly surrounding themselves with members of the family to shield themselves at all times. But from *what?*

They couldn't know the cops were in the house, could they? He was absolutely certain Quintin hadn't seen the two deputies outside.

Every second was terrible.

Quintin had decided he wanted to hear more music, so Skyler was back at the piano. Scooter was on the bench next to her, protected by her. To reach him, a bullet would have to go through Skyler.

Clearly the tension was wearing on the family, as well. Skyler had played a few Christmas carols and everyone had joined in, but the performance had been lackluster, and now she was just sitting there, looking lost and defeated.

"What's the problem?" Quintin asked.

She shrugged. "I just…"

Suddenly a plaintively beautiful sound filled the air. Frazier, who was sitting on the floor by the tree, had picked up his violin. Skyler smiled, as if her son had given her a surge of energy. Her fingers moved over the keys, and she started to sing what sounded to Craig like an old folk melody. The entire family sang along, and then, to Craig's amazement, Scooter joined in on the last verse.

> The sailor gave to me a rose
> A rose that would ne'er decay
> He gave it so I'd be e'er reminded
> Of the time he stole my thyme away.…

When the song ended, Scooter was staring at Skyler with tears in his eyes. "That's a sad, sad song," he said.

"You're depressing me," Quintin said, irritated. "Sing something else. Something cheerful. Let's have a happy Christmas carol," Quintin said.

"'Frosty the Snowman,'" Scooter insisted.

Then "Rudolph, the Red-Nosed Reindeer." Scooter liked that one, too.

Finally Quintin looked at his watch. "Enough," he said. "Mrs. O'Boyle, time for you to open something. But come over here, where I can see you."

Scooter, too, remained wary, and positioned himself directly behind Skyler. There was no way anyone could get a shot at him from the top of the stairs, Craig realized unhappily. He kept his attention on Scooter and was barely aware when Jamie handed his mother a box.

"Oh my God, I love it!" Skyler exclaimed, drawing his attention back to her. "It's wonderful."

The gift was a gold locket. The chain was thin, the locket itself small, of far less value than the jewelry Frazier and Brenda had exchanged. Value that Quintin and Scooter had assuredly already assessed. In fact, he was surprised Quintin was allowing them to live out their fantasy until after the meal. Did he intend to take that ring off Brenda's bloody fingers once he had shot her? He had to force himself not to look toward the stairway again, afraid of giving the game away.

"I put a picture of your parents inside," Jamie said.

"Oh, Jamie, what a wonderful gift," she told him, tears in her eyes, though she quickly blinked them away. She started to get up to hug her son.

"Sit," Scooter said. He seemed agitated, and he shrugged, as if confused as to why he had spoken out so quickly and vehemently.

Skyler looked at him questioningly.

"Just...just open the rest of your gifts," he said.

Quintin, frowning, looked over at him. "You all right, Scooter?"

"Yeah, sure."

Skyler continued opening her presents. Her gift from Kat was a delicate bracelet of diamond-chipped clovers. Frazier and Brenda gave her a cashmere shawl and a brooch, and Craig found himself getting more and more nervous about all the jewelry, but he didn't get really uneasy until she opened her gift from her husband. He had gotten her a diamond necklace, one with three beautiful and clearly valuable stones.

But as she exclaimed over it and thanked her husband, no one attempted to move.

"Dad, your turn," Frazier said.

As they began again, it seemed to Craig as if the O'Boyles were making a concerted effort to ignore their unwanted guests. The final gift was for Uncle Paddy, ten hot-stone massages.

"Now maybe you'll get through a day without complaining about the pain in your poor aching back," Kat teased him.

They were all laughing. Almost as if, for just a few minutes, they had forgotten what was happening and were having a good time, just like any family at Christmas.

But that time was slipping away. Or rather, being stolen away, Craig thought.

But the cops were in the house, he reminded himself. There were two cops, himself, the family and Brenda.

How would they ever pull it off?

He thought that maybe Scooter was so strange because he was sad and just wanted a family. And the relationship between Quintin and Scooter was sort of familial, in a bizarre way. He glanced at Quintin, who was clearly growing impatient, then was surprised when Scooter suddenly stood up and pulled Skyler to her feet. "That turkey must be cooked by now. Come on, I want my Christmas dinner."

"Scooter, the turkey has to sit for a little while before I can carve it," David said.

"But we'll get it out of the oven *now,* right, Quintin?" Scooter demanded. "I'll take Skyler in, we'll get the turkey out. Now."

"Yes, fine," Quintin said. But he seemed distracted and stood very still for a minute. "Listen," he said softly.

"Listen to what?" Jamie asked.

"The wind," Quintin said.

"I don't hear it," Jamie told him.

Quintin smiled and said softly, "Exactly."

Chapter 14

The turkey was a beautiful golden brown.

Everyone except Quintin and Scooter helped set the table, and then Kat put herself in charge of drinks, which gave her a chance to watch everyone as she went back and forth, filling glasses. Scooter was almost hyper with excitement, and Quintin, watching Scooter, grew visibly edgy.

When it was time to put the turkey on the table, Quintin took her mother's elbow and led her to a chair. "Someone else can carry the turkey. You'll sit next to me. Now."

Skyler shrugged. "Fine. David carves. See that the bird is in front of him."

"I want some skin," Scooter said.

"You can have all the skin you want," David said.

Everything was even tenser, even worse, than it had been, Kat thought, and all because the wind had stopped. The storm was winding down. Soon the plows would be out, and it would be time for Quintin and Scooter—and Craig?—to run. But before they ran...

"I've got the turkey," Kat said, and carried the bird over to the table.

"Let me," Craig told her, and managed to take the heavy platter and set it on the table in front of her father, who, she saw, was trying not to look at the carving knife too longingly.

"Wait," Quintin said. "Put that knife down."

"You have a better suggestion for how to carve a turkey? You want to do it yourself?" David asked Quintin.

Quintin stared at him steadily. "All right, carve. But I'll be watching you."

"First, grace," Skyler announced.

"Hurry up," Quintin told her, his patience visibly fraying.

"Thank you," she said, then bowed her head and spoke. "God is great, God is good, and we thank Him for this food. Through Jesus Christ our Lord, Amen."

No sooner had she finished than Scooter shot up, waving his gun around. "Did you hear it?" he asked.

"Hear what?" Quintin demanded.

"That!"

"What?" Quintin repeated.

"There's someone in this house," Scooter claimed.

Quintin stood, grabbed Skyler by the hair, and dragged her out of her chair and out the door.

David leaped up to follow.

"Stop!" Scooter shouted, and when her father turned around in response and she saw his face pale, Kat suddenly realized that Scooter had his gun aimed right at her.

"Stop it, Scooter," Craig snapped, and to Kat's amazement, he stepped between her and the gun. "Come on, we have to see what's going on."

Before Scooter had time to object, Craig caught him by the arm and pulled him out. In a rush, the family followed them into the living room, where Quintin was holding Skyler in front of him, a human shield, while he looked wildly around, brandishing his gun as if in search of a target.

Kat saw her father start to rush the other man, but Craig caught hold of him. Not hurting him, just stopping him.

"Everybody calm down," Craig pleaded. "Quintin, stop hurting her."

"I'll hurt her, all right. I'll put a bullet right through her head if whoever is up those stairs doesn't come down right this minute."

"Quintin, what the hell's the matter with you?" Craig demanded.

"Scooter isn't the sharpest tool in the shed, but he's like a damned dog," Quintin said. "If he says someone is up there, someone is up there." He raised his voice. "And whoever the hell it is needs to come down here. Now."

He cocked his gun, and the sound seemed louder than any storm.

"Now!" Quintin raged.

Kat held her breath, a rush of terror weakening her knees, threatening to make her pass out.

Her mother...

Quintin...

The gun...

"Get down here now or she's dead, and you will have killed her."

A split second passed. Then, from the second-floor landing, a male voice said, "Stop! Wait!"

Kat gasped in dismay, sucking in air, all hope lost, as

Tim Graystone walked down the stairs, both hands high in the air.

"Throw your gun down," Quintin demanded.

"Let her go first," Tim said. Kat could see that he was trembling, but his expression was determined. And he was alone.

"I should just shoot her and be done with it," Quintin said disgustedly.

"Shoot me instead," Tim pleaded.

"Stop it! Don't shoot anybody," Craig thundered.

Amazingly, everyone in the room turned to stare at him. "Calm down, everyone. Quintin, please, let go of Mrs. O'Boyle. Officer, toss down your weapon. Come on, people."

"Put that gun down slowly," Quintin commanded.

"All right," Tim agreed.

Quintin eased his hold on Skyler as Tim set down his weapon on the floor right in front of Quintin.

"Get it, Scooter," Quintin said.

He didn't suggest that Craig take it, Kat noticed.

"Where's your partner?" Quintin demanded.

"My partner?" Tim said.

"I'm not stupid. Your partner, the woman who came with you last night. She's got to be around here somewhere."

"Oh, Sheila," Tim said.

"Yes, her. She needs to get down here right now."

"She can't. She's checking out a possible emergency," Tim said.

"You're lying."

"I'm not," Tim insisted. "It's just the two of us, and we had to split up."

There was a horrible, staggering moment then, when Quintin struck Tim with his gun. Hard. So hard that the young deputy fell back, crashing into the wall. Then he aimed at Tim. "Where's your partner?"

"Answering a call out by the highway."

Quintin took a step toward him. Aimed at his kneecap. "Where's your partner?" he repeated.

"You can shoot me to death piece by piece," Tim swore. "But I can't change the facts. She's on another call. I had a hunch something was wrong, but she thought I was nuts. Said she wouldn't come back with me because of the kid, not when there might be a real emergency."

"What?" Quintin demanded.

"He's talking about me," Jamie groaned. "I pulled a prank last year, pretended I needed help.... It's my fault."

Craig moved forward, standing between Quintin and the downed man. "Quintin, think about it. Don't you think she'd have come down here by now if she was in the house?"

Quintin stared back at Craig, lifted his gun and aimed at Craig's face.

"Go on, shoot me, then," Craig said impatiently. "That's not going to change the fact that she isn't here. And listen. It's the wind again. The storm hasn't stopped yet."

"It will. Soon," Quintin told him, narrow-eyed.

"We all need to calm down," Craig said quietly, facing Quintin, ignoring the gun only inches from his nose.

Quintin looked around the room. He was rigid and furious. Kat was amazed he hadn't fired yet. "I want him tied up. Tight." He kicked Tim for emphasis.

"We don't have any rope," Scooter said.

"Get that phone cord," Quintin said.

Craig went for the cord, ripping it from the wall.

"Tie him up, and don't fuck with me. Tie him tight," Quintin ordered.

"I won't fuck with you," Craig promised. Kat could

see him looking at Tim with sorrow and a prayer for for-giveness.

Tim seemed to give him a little nod, as if to say, *You gotta do what you gotta do.*

"I want to see how you're tying him," Quintin said. "Scooter, you keep an eye on them."

"I will, Quintin. I've got my gun on them. I'll shoot the suckers, turkey or no turkey, I swear I will."

Quintin watched as Craig bound Tim with his wrists tightly behind his back. When he was done, Quintin started to laugh.

"What the hell…?" Craig said.

"Cuffs. He's a cop. We should've just used cuffs. Oh, well, you did a good job. Now bring him into the kitchen, so we can keep an eye on him while we eat."

No one moved; tension held them as if they were glued in place.

"Move!" Quintin snapped. "Help Craig bring the cop in the kitchen," he added, turning to Frazier.

Frazier stared back at Quintin for a moment, then hur-ried to Tim Graystone's other side, helping to support him.

In the kitchen, they all took their places again, after Craig and Frazier had used an old extension cord to tie Tim Graystone to the banister of the servants' staircase.

"Serve the turkey," Quintin said to David.

David looked at Quintin. "White or dark meat?" he asked, hatred and fury thick in his voice.

"White."

Somehow everyone was served, but nobody made a move, despite the food on their plates.

"Eat," Quintin said.

Skyler took a forkful of turkey, stared at it, then set down her fork. "I can't eat. And I won't."

"You know, I have been a patient man," Quintin said. "But you're going too far."

Skyler leaned forward and met his eyes. "Am I? You're the one who plans to kill us. All of us. You've only waited because...well, I don't know why. Maybe you didn't want the mess while you were hiding here. Maybe so Scooter could have Christmas. Who knows? But all this time you've made us dance like puppets so we can live a little bit longer. You can make us sing, make us open presents, but you can't make anyone enjoy a Christmas dinner. You can't make me swallow when there's a lump in my throat the size of Texas. Not when a good man is hurt and tied to the banister."

"A good man?" Quintin mocked.

"A good man," she repeated.

"And what makes a good man?" Quintin demanded, sneering. "Being a cop? Bull. A good man is one who knows who to trust—and who not to trust. Who can be trusted by those who depend on him."

"And by that definition, Tim Graystone is a good man," Skyler said.

"I care about Scooter. Does that make me good?" he taunted.

"If you want me to think you're a good man, let Tim come sit at the table and have something to eat," Skyler said.

"Don't be ridiculous," Quintin snapped.

"Quintin, you can keep him tied up," David suggested. "But let him come to the table and one of us will feed him."

"Or none of us will be able to eat," Skyler said.

"I don't understand you at all," Brenda said suddenly, startling them all. She smiled and looked at the ring on her finger, then over at Frazier. "Here," she said, taking off the ring and setting it in front of Quintin. "You're thieves, right? I mean, you were going to take it before you left, anyway, right? I don't even want to think about how."

"Brenda…" Frazier said, his voice breaking.

"Frazier, it's all right. Let him take the ring. Quintin, it's just a thing, a symbol, but whether I have it or not, I know Frazier worked hard to buy it." She smiled. "And I know he did it all on his own, because I could see by his parents' faces that they didn't know anything about it. You can take it away, you can even take away our lives, but what Frazier and I feel…what we have…no one can ever take that away. And no matter what happens, I feel sorry for you."

Quintin just stared at her, reduced to speechlessness for a moment, but then he reverted to form and said, "Very nice. Now, everybody, shut up and eat."

Scooter, oblivious to the mood around the table, dug in, delighted with his breast meat covered with the perfectly roasted skin, but nobody else did anything except push the food around on their plates.

"Shit. Get the damn cop, then," Quintin snapped.

Craig got up to go for Tim Graystone, and Quintin sent Scooter to find a chair. It didn't look to Kat as if Craig and Tim exchanged any words as Craig helped him to the table. Skyler stood as they neared the table.

Once Tim was settled, Quintin looked at Kat. "You're still not eating."

"I'm not hungry."

To her surprise, he leaned forward accusingly. "You ungrateful bitch," he told her. He leaned back again, staring around the table. "You all think I'm a monster, don't you? And maybe I am. But it's people like you made me one."

"No," David said. "We all have to take responsibility for what we become."

"Easy for you to say. You have everything."

"I didn't have everything," David said. "My parents were immigrants and worked nonstop all their lives. I started mowing lawns when I was thirteen and dragging ice for a soda fountain when I was sixteen. I've worked my whole life, too."

"No, no, you don't get it," Scooter said.

"Shut up, Scooter," Quintin said.

But Scooter ignored him and went on. "It's not always about money."

"That's a strange comment, comin' from a guncarryin' thief," Paddy put in.

Scooter barely afforded him a glance. "You really don't understand. Quintin's mother, she was a prostitute. She didn't know who his father was. And she couldn't really keep him herself, so he went to a foster home."

"Scooter..." Quintin said warningly.

"Some folks just take in kids because when you take in kids, you get money. It's a lousy thing for a kid to end up there. Really lousy."

"Scooter, I'm going to shoot you in about ten seconds," Quintin threatened.

"Now my mother," Scooter continued. "Hell, she just drank. Drank and beat the tar out of me. By the time I was about fourteen, I'd had a dozen broken bones and I'd had to sit in the bathroom about eighteen million times while she slept with her latest guy. The first time I stole, it was for her. She wanted a bottle of vodka. I never looked back." Scooter waved his fork. "So then I'm seventeen, and I get hauled into court, and they decide they're not going to try me as a juvenile. So I wind up in prison, with a pack of big-ass jerks, and when I get out, guess what? No one wants to hire you when you've been in jail. So I go home to my mother. Then, I don't know what happened. She was drinking and yelling at me and waving the vodka bottle around. I swear to God, she fell. I didn't kill her. The bitch deserved it, but I didn't kill her. Hey, can I have some more gravy, please?"

They were all dead still, just staring at him. Then Kat heard her mother gulp. "Jamie...the gravy. Please."

"I know your life was awful," David said to Scooter. "But you can change it."

Quintin started to laugh. "Fuck you, O'Boyle."

David turned to Quintin. "And you. You think you can blame everything you do the rest of your life on being brought up in a lousy foster home."

Quintin laughed bitterly. "Let me think. Yeah, I do."

"We all make choices in our lives," David said stubbornly.

"Right," Quintin said. "How about you, college boy? What's your story? Make it a good one. Maybe I'll fall for it."

Kat couldn't help it. She stared at Craig, too. *What is your story?* she wondered. *Make it a good one and maybe I'll fall for it, too.*

Craig shrugged. "Mine is easy. Cocaine," he said.

"You aren't a cocaine addict," Kat said, staring at him.

He smiled slowly, ruefully. "No. I didn't mean me." He hesitated. "My dad. He didn't start off that way. Then... I'm not sure what came first, Alice Diaz or the drugs. Anyway, long story short. One day this man came to see me. He told me my dad owed him a lot of money, and he was going to kill him if he didn't get the money. What was I supposed to do? It was my *dad*," Craig said. "It was the drugs that changed things. And I knew he could change back."

"I think you ought to get your violin," Quintin said dryly to Frazier.

"Shh," Scooter said. "This is a good story."

"Go on," Kat told him.

He shrugged. "Well, I was a student with a part-time job. There wasn't any way I could get the kind of money they wanted. They knew that, of course. They had a plan for me. They'd wanted my dad to do it, but he wasn't in shape, so I was the next best thing."

"What was the plan?" Scooter demanded eagerly.

"My father had worked for a security company till he got so drugged-out he lost his job. He'd installed the system for a jewelry store. They got the information from him, then took me with them. I think I was like insurance for them, to make sure my dad wouldn't lie to them. They told him they'd kill me if he didn't tell them how to get past the alarm, and they told me they'd kill *him* if I wouldn't help them. So I did." He hesitated. "Then they shot me. But they didn't do it right, so I lived. But they cleaned the place out and killed the owner. And then they killed my father anyway."

There was silence.

Craig was staring at Kat.

She stared back. *Why didn't you tell me?* she asked silently. *Why didn't you go to the police?* But she knew. She knew when your family was threatened, you were ready to do just about anything. You would kill for them.

And you would die for them.

"Hear, hear!" Paddy said, breaking the silence.

They all stared at him. Either he was drunk, or he was doing a great job of pretending to be, Kat thought.

"Uncle Paddy, you've had enough," Skyler said gently.

"Good God, not nearly enough, me lass," Paddy protested. "A man should be totally drunk before being shot."

"No one is going to shoot anyone," Craig said. Quintin stared at him, arching a brow.

"It doesn't make any sense to shoot anyone," Craig went on, and indicated Tim. "Don't you understand? His partner didn't come with him, but she knew where he was going."

"It's true," Tim agreed.

"It's like I said before, killing these people won't change anything," Craig finished.

"I think we should have dessert now," Quintin said, as if Craig hadn't spoken.

"What?" Craig asked, confused.

"I believe Tim's partner is in this house. I figured we'd go ahead and have dinner, and then I intend to find her. Of course, finding her won't be all that hard. I'm sure she's within earshot right now. But she knows she can't possibly get both of us, so she's not going to try anything. So... dessert."

They all just stared at him.

"Dessert," Quintin repeated. "Now."

Kat felt her heart was sinking.

The police had failed, and the end was coming.

And now...

Craig looked at her, held her gaze and mouthed something she couldn't make out.

She frowned. What was going on? What was he doing?

"May I serve?" Skyler asked.

Quintin grunted.

She looked at him. "Pumpkin or pecan?"

"Pecan for me, with ice cream," Scooter said.

"Craig?" her mother said after serving Scooter.

"Pumpkin," he said.

"Ice cream?"

"No, thank you."

Skyler set a piece of pumpkin pie down in front of Craig. "Looks great, Mrs. O'Boyle," he said casually and picked up his fork, then shouted. "Duck!" as he stabbed his fork into Scooter's hand, pinning it to the table.

The entire family went down, gasping...shouting...screaming.

Above the cacophony, Kat heard the explosion of a gun, and she dared a peek over the table.

Quintin was staring at her...staring... But he didn't raise his gun. Instead, it slipped from his fingers. His head crashed against the table, a hole in the back of it. Blood started to pool over his dessert plate and onto the tabletop.

Scooter was still screaming, a high-pitched and hysterical sound. Though one hand was still pinned to the table by Craig's fork, he had his gun in his other hand and was trying to aim, trying to shoot.

Craig had leaped across the table to throw himself on the man and the gun, but he didn't have to.

Kat heard a horrible snapping sound, and Scooter started screeching at an even higher pitch, his arm dangling at an unnatural angle. Uncle Paddy was standing next to him, his cane in his hand. He had used it to break Scooter's arm. Craig quickly reached over and picked up Scooter's gun. He immediately flipped on the safety and slid the gun into his waistband.

"Oh God," Skyler breathed. "Oh God," she said again, and started to cry.

Despite the confusion, Kat realized that Quintin had been right about one thing: Sheila Polanski had been in the house all along. Now she came running out of the pantry and into the kitchen.

"Is everyone all right?" she asked anxiously.

The question seemed so ridiculous under the circumstances that Kat almost started to laugh. A dead man was bleeding all over the table, and Scooter was still pinned and screaming.

To her horror, Kat did start to laugh.

Then she was hugging Sheila Polanski and her brothers, and someone was untying Tim Graystone, and she was holding Brenda and they were both sobbing. The next thing she knew, she was in her mother's arms, and then her father's.

It seemed as if the hysteria, the mix of laughter and tears and hugging and kissing, went on forever, and the whole time, Sheila's question kept running through her head.

Was everyone all right?

Kat didn't think they would ever be all right again.

Then she saw Craig. Saw him watching her. And she knew that while they might never exactly be all right, they would be better.

Chapter 15

For a while time moved in slow motion, full of sounds and visuals Skyler knew would haunt her forever.

There was the sound of Scooter's screams. There was a look on his face, in his eyes. She had no doubt that he would have killed them if Quintin told him to. He had genuinely longed for and enjoyed his Christmas, but he would have obeyed Quintin without a second thought.

Another image... The remnants of a turkey dinner, gravy boat still on the table...pies out, ice cream melting...

Quintin's head, bleeding onto his plate.

So much confusion, the storm slowing but not gone, and the need—the bone-deep need—to get out of the house before she went mad. Scooter had been tied up, and Brenda saw to his wounds while he continued to howl.

They had to get out, Skyler thought. She knew she couldn't stay in the house that night.

She knew that, as long as she lived, she would never forget the way Quintin had died, never forget the blood flooding out over the table.

And all of her life she would be grateful that the blood had been Quintin's, that, miraculously, her family had all survived.

The wind finally began dying down for good. Sheila or Tim must have managed to get a signal and make a call, because, to her amazement, it wasn't long before they heard movement outside and realized that the state police had arrived and the house was surrounded.

It seemed impossible. As detectives and crime-scene investigators filled her house, all Skyler could think was that it must have been a dream. A nightmare. They had lived those hours so intensely, and then...

So quickly, it all seemed so impossible.

She couldn't mourn Quintin, but she almost felt badly for Scooter. Almost. The threat against her family had been far too terrifying for her to feel anything that resembled forgiveness for him yet, but maybe the time would come.

Skyler *had* feared for Craig when the police got there. She had been ready to testify that, whatever he had done in the past, he wasn't a killer and had in fact been ready to die for her family.

But the police didn't take him away. Instead they started to talk to him as if they knew him, knew all about him.

Tim was the one who explained it all to her. "I knew I had seen his face," he said, grinning. "And I finally remembered. He works with the state. He graduated from the state police academy with one of my buddies. I'd seen him in their graduation photo."

"So...he *was* a cop. All along," Skyler said.

"All along," Tim agreed, amused by her choice of words.

They *were* rather foolish, she thought. He hadn't suddenly become a cop in the midst of everything.

Tim looked at her and took her hands. "I'm sorry we couldn't get to you sooner. I don't know how that guy Scooter knew I was up there."

Skyler shrugged. "He… I don't know. He had an instinct."

"Yeah, well, that almost blew the whole thing. I still don't know why the other guy, Quintin, didn't just shoot me."

"He wanted his turkey dinner," Skyler said.

"Can someone really want a turkey dinner *that* badly?" Tim asked.

"It wasn't the dinner, exactly. Quintin wanted what Scooter wanted, and Scooter wanted… Christmas."

"What an elusive wish," Tim said.

The whole family had to be questioned. Nicely, but still, it seemed to take forever. The punishment for survival was always paperwork, one of the officers joked.

There were even moments of levity, despite the horror of having to relive everything.

At one point Jamie suddenly stopped in the middle of answering a question and asked to be excused to brush his teeth. It was the little things, she thought. They could be so important.

Eventually she saw the body taken from the house on a gurney, zipped into a body bag. Even then, she couldn't bear the thought of going back into the kitchen. She wasn't sure she could ever return to the kitchen.

There were people everywhere. It was early evening when they finally finished asking questions and filling in reports. When they were gone at last, she looked outside and stared at the blanket of fresh white snow, gleaming in the moonlight. From somewhere she could hear a Christmas carol playing.

God rest ye merry gentlemen,
Let nothing you dismay,
Remember Christ our savior was born on Christmas
Day
O, tidings of comfort and joy
Comfort and Joy
O, tidings of comfort and joy.

Warm, strong hands fell on her shoulders, and she turned. David was standing behind her, and he took her in his arms. He started to speak, then stopped.

"It's all right," she said.

"No, it's not," he told her, and smiled awkwardly. "We all... I guess we all start out like Frazier and Brenda. With our hopes and our dreams—swearing to one another that we'll never be like our parents. And then..." He paused, smiling ruefully, shaking his head. "We let things stop us. Small problems become big ones. We see things in different ways, and we assume we can't change, so things fester and grow and...and I was angry that Frazier wouldn't hold the Christmas tree straight. It honestly never occurred to me that he was holding it the best he could."

She looked up at him, searching his eyes. "David...who cares about the Christmas tree right now?"

His smile deepened. "I don't. It isn't anything to do with the Christmas tree. It's life."

She realized she was shaking. "We're alive, David. Our kids are alive," she said.

"And I'm wondering if I deserved to survive," he told her. She gasped.

"Don't misunderstand... I'm grateful. But I keep remembering how strong everyone was, how our kids must have been terrified, but they didn't fall apart. Skyler, *we* survived this. We survived it as a *family*. That's...that's what I didn't deserve."

She touched his face. "But we *are* a family. Not one of us is perfect. No one can be. We have to...we have to just do our best and...stumble along. That's the journey."

"What if we hurt others on our journey?" David said. "When I think about the things I've said, the things I've gotten mad about..."

"David, all we can do is the best that we can, love the best that we can. I'm not suddenly going to become a perfect mother because of today, and you're not going to become the perfect father. But we will be smart enough to know that our lives are a gift, that our children are a gift."

"I do love you."

"I know," she assured him. "Christmas," she murmured. "I always thought it was such a time of promise...."

"And it is," he told her huskily.

"Hey, Dad!" Jamie shouted from upstairs. "Guess what? Tim's mother has a huge house, and Tim just talked to her. He didn't think we'd want to stay here tonight, so she's invited us all over."

David looked up. "That's nice of her, but there are too many of us to—"

"Mrs. Graystone says the more there are the merrier," Sheila said.

"Mom, Dad, please?" Jamie asked.

Skyler looked at David. "I sure as hell don't intend to stay here tonight."

They were all trying hard, Kat knew. Tim's mother, Lydia Graystone, was trying harder than anyone, taking in their entire entourage for a *real* Christmas dinner, on top of her own family and the people she'd already invited over, including Sheila.

Lydia insisted she was happy for the company, and as Kat helped her set up for her turkey dinner—one that she could eat, she was certain, because she was starving now—she thanked her for her generosity.

"It's the least I could do. When Tim told me what happened…" She broke off, shivering. "You have quite an amazing family."

Kat moved to the doorway and leaned against it, looking out into the other room. She had to smile, and not only because her parents looked like newlyweds or because Frazier and Brenda were clearly oblivious to anything but each other. Not even because Tim had a sixteen-year-old sister, Olivia, and she and Jamie seemed to have hit it off as if they were long-lost friends.

But because of Uncle Paddy. Their hero.

He didn't seem to consider himself a hero, but she was certain Craig would have died trying to save them if it hadn't been for Paddy and his cane. But to Paddy, it had simply been something that needed to be done and he'd been there to do it. According to him, life was something you fought for, every immigrant knew that. She smiled, aware of a new appreciation for her uncle and her ancestry that would remain in her heart forever. And Uncle Paddy was smiling at the moment, too, deep in appreciation of Sheila's company.

They had just sat down at the table when the doorbell rang.

There was a collective gasp from her family, and she wasn't surprised when her mother croaked, "Oh God. Don't answer it!"

Tim Graystone set his hand on her mother's shoulder.

"It's okay," he said, and went to see who it was. A minute later, he came back. "Kat?"

"Yes?" She stood, and her heart took flight as she allowed herself to hope.

"An old friend wants to see you," Tim told her, and she knew without being told who it was.

Craig.

She wanted to see him.

She didn't want to see him.

You couldn't go back. She knew that, and knew, too, that she had no real idea what had gone on with him in the last few years, but...

She set her napkin down. "Excuse me," she told the group around the table and fled.

He was waiting for her on the spring porch. Somewhere along the way he had taken a shower and changed clothing, and he was in jeans, boots, a flannel shirt and a heavy wool coat. His hair was sparkling clean, light as straw, soft against his forehead. His eyes were very blue, very deep, serious.

She kept her distance. "I was wondering if we would see you again," she said politely. Oh God, how ridiculous that sounded. She swallowed and tried again. "I'm sorry. I really thought at first that you were with...them. It fit with the way you left school...and there was a rumor at one point that you were in jail."

"Yeah. I started that rumor. It made things easier," he said.

"I'm glad to see you."

"Are you?" he asked, and she wondered if there was a hopeful tone in his voice.

"To thank you for all you did. We're probably all alive because of you."

He lowered his head for a moment, then met her eyes again. "I think we're all alive because of *all* of us," he said.

She shrugged. "Maybe. You might have had a better chance of surviving if it weren't for us, though," she told him.

"Who knows?" he said. "I think Quintin had me pegged from the start. It was the first 'job' I did with them. And I'm pretty sure he knew I wasn't what I pretended to be."

"Still, thank you."

"You're welcome."

He was still looking at her. She shook her head. "You had no right not to tell me the truth."

"That my father was a cocaine freak and loan sharks were going to kill him if I didn't help them rob someone?" he asked softly.

"I loved you. You're not your father. You're not your family."

He looked doubtful. "I think in a way we *are* our families," he said. "You're a lot like both your parents," he said with a smile. "And yes, I remember you used to tell me how they could drive you nuts, but even so, I mean it as a compliment."

"Tonight, I'll take it that way." She paused, then met and held his eyes. "I would have understood you were having problems, you know."

"Your parents owned a bar. My father had gotten into knocking them over."

"I still wish you had believed in me, told me. It would have hurt less."

She was right. He had owed her. But he had been young then, with a young man's sense of pride and shame. And it *had* been a pretty desperate situation, and Kat, being Kat, would have gotten involved. Her life, too, would have been at risk if he hadn't walked away.

But that was all in the past. Who knew what might have happened if they'd taken different forks in the road, made different choices?

"I'm sure you're welcome to have dinner here, too," she told him.

He shook his head uneasily. "I just…needed to see you."

She nodded, looked at him…remembered. And remembering hurt. "We can't go back," she whispered vehemently to herself—but he heard, too.

"No. We can never go back. And, oddly enough… I'm not sure I *would* go back, even if I could. I'd certainly never relive today, but… I'm so sorry I hurt you."

"You did hurt me. You devastated me. But I accept your apology. It's just that…like I said, we can't go back."

He nodded, but he was still staring at her steadily. "We can go forward, though," he said very softly.

She studied him. In the background, she could hear a Christmas carol playing, accompanied by her brother's violin. She had to smile. Unbelievably, she actually felt like laughing. Life was good, so damn good. And she would remember that.

"Come to dinner," she told him.

He hesitated. Inhaled, exhaled.

She offered him her hand. "All you have to do is take a step forward."

He grinned. Accepted her hand. And they walked in to Christmas dinner together.

Epilogue

"It's Christmas Eve," the man said.

The younger Hudson of Hudson & Son looked so much like his father that, for a moment, Craig thought he'd lost his mind.

He hadn't expected the shop to be open. Sheila had told him that before his death, Lionel Hudson had been intending to close the shop and move west to be with his son.

This Hudson wasn't a spring chicken, either. He looked like his father, but at the age of sixtysomething rather than eighty-plus.

"I know. I'm sorry. You're trying to close up. I just saw the sign and…"

Hudson frowned, looking at him. "You're Craig Devon, aren't you?"

Craig was startled. "I—yes." He felt awkward. Guilty. "I'm so sorry about your father."

Hudson nodded, studying him, then offered his hand. "I'm Ethan Hudson. I heard you tried to save my father."

The man was looking at him with such appreciation that Craig felt like a fraud, but he had to say something.

"I didn't know that… I didn't know they would kill anyone. I am so sorry. I should have been more prepared. I—"

"Please," Hudson said, and smiled. "I've heard all about it from Sheila and Tim. You're a good man. I know you would have saved him if you could. I've thought about it a lot, though. He wouldn't have wanted to waste away, to die in agony. Who knows what's for the best?" He shrugged, then grinned. "I remember him with love. That's the important thing."

"I thought the store was closing," Craig said.

"Funny, I thought so, too. But then Dad…died and I came back, and I'm still here. I'm glad, too. I loved this place when I was a kid. I'd sit on my dad's lap when he'd take out his magnifying glass and study a stone. In a way, working here, running this place, I feel like he's still with me." He offered Craig a strange and rueful smile. "Sometimes you learn what really matters, huh? I remember one time, there was a ring a woman wanted to sell. Even I knew the stone wasn't a good stone, but my dad paid her really well for it. And afterward he told me that what's valuable in life isn't things, it's what those things mean to people and what can be made of them." He paused, then said, "Sorry, I guess Christmas Eve is making me nostalgic."

Craig looked away for a moment, then said, a question in the words, "The sign…it still reads Hudson & Son."

"One of my boys moved out here with me, and he works here, too. He's off tonight, though. He has little kids and, well, you know. It's Christmas Eve, he's got a lot to do. I needed to be here alone today, anyway."

"Yeah," Craig said huskily, feeling awkward again. He cleared his throat and looked into the jeweler's cases. "You've got some beautiful pieces here."

"Thank you."

"That solitaire…"

"Are you thinking about getting married?"

Craig looked at him and felt the oddest little tug in his heart. Was he thinking about it? Hell, yeah!

But was *she*?

He was scared. He knew all too well how many things could be stolen. Possessions, of course. Even life. But not the things that mattered in life, not unless you let them be stolen. Morality, love, belief in one's self…these things were forever.

Would she say yes?

He would never know if he didn't take the plunge.

"I'd like to see it," he said firmly. "Although I'm not sure I can afford it on a cop's salary."

"They owe you a big raise, if you ask me," Hudson said.

Craig flashed a smile. "Thanks. But it doesn't actually work that way."

"I can give you a price on that ring you can't refuse," Hudson told him.

"I— No, you don't have to."

"Humor me," Hudson said. "Let's honor my dad. The value isn't in the thing, it's in what you do with the thing, remember?"

"Thanks," Craig told him. "Thanks very much."

Twenty minutes later, Craig drove up the Graystones' driveway, parked and got out of his car. He looked up at the sky and shook his head. This was a very different winter, thank God.

It was evening, but he could see the stars. Millions of them. The air was crisp, and there was snow on the ground. It was a beautiful night.

As he headed up the walkway, he could hear the music.

Someone was playing the piano—Skyler, he was certain. Frazier's violin and David's rich baritone could be heard.

What a year it had been.

They had never gone back. Just forward.

Life was day to day. You laughed, you cried, you got resentful. You were thrilled, furious, jealous...a million different things. It was different, it was the same. Sometimes there was darkness. And sometimes there were special days, special times. Like Christmas.

He heard Paddy's laughter, followed by Sheila's. They had gotten married six months ago, saying they were both far too old to mess around with a long engagement.

The O'Boyles had wound up keeping the house on Elm, even though at first Skyler had wanted to sell it, would even have given it away.

Kat was the one who had said she wasn't going to allow anyone else's evil to steal what had made her happy. Skyler had thought about that for a while, and in the end they had kept the house, though they had completely redone the kitchen.

Even so, they had decided not to have Christmas Eve dinner there and had gratefully accepted Lydia Graystone's invitation.

As Craig headed toward the door, it opened. And there was Kat, fiery hair blazing in the moonlight, her eyes bright with welcome.

"You're late," she announced, but she was all smiles as she ran into his arms.

He started to speak, to tell her about going by the jewelry store on the way, then decided that could come later.

"Merry Christmas," he said simply. "Merry, merry Christmas."

* * * * *

SECRET SURROGATE

Delores Fossen

For Mickey, Stacy, Selena, Scott,
Trent, Miranda and Hunter

Chapter 1

Fall Creek, Texas

Kylie Monroe tightened her grip on the .357 Magnum and kept her index finger on the trigger.

She waited in the dark. Deep in the corner where she hoped the shadows hid her.

Listening.

Praying.

Mercy, was she ever praying.

Maybe those footsteps that she'd heard outside belonged to one of the deputies from the Fall Creek Sheriff's Office. Heck, she was even hoping it was a neighbor who'd dropped by. Fat chance of that, though. Her nearest neighbor was nearly two miles away, and it was close to midnight. Hardly the time for visitors.

Besides, she'd seen no car lights. No sound of an engine. Or any other indication that whoever was out there had neighborly intentions. The footsteps likely belonged to the shadowy figures she'd seen in the woods on the east side of her property.

She made a quick check of the clock on the mantel. Sweet heaven. Where was the deputy? She'd made that 911 call well over a half hour ago.

Of course, it seemed more like an eternity.

Because her legs were trembling, Kylie leaned against the wall of the tiny foyer and tried not to make a sound. That included humming. Several times, she'd caught herself humming a little louder than was probably safe. Of course, maybe no sound was safe right now.

The baby she carried inside her kicked and squirmed as if he or she knew something was terribly wrong. That didn't surprise her. After all, her entire body was tense— every muscle knotted, her breath thin.

It only got worse when she heard another sound that she'd anticipated.

And dreaded.

There was a sharp groan of wood. No doubt from one of the creaky floorboards on the porch. Someone was just outside her door. Mere inches away.

Her heartbeat began to race out of control, but she tried to stay calm. For the sake of the baby. And for her own sake. So she could respond accordingly.

Unfortunately, *respond accordingly* might mean she'd have to use deadly force.

She was a trained law enforcement officer, Kylie reminded herself. Except she hadn't carried a badge or even held a gun for nearly three years. Maybe she wouldn't even remember her firearms' training. But it didn't matter. She would do whatever it took to protect the baby and herself.

"Kylie?" a man called out. "It's me—Lucas Creed."

Oh, mercy.

That didn't do much to steady her heart rate or her breathing.

However, Kylie did lower her gun, and she eased her finger off the trigger. Sheriff Lucas Creed wasn't exactly the threat her body had prepared itself for.

But he was a threat of a totally different kind.

"I didn't hear you drive up," she informed him.

Lucas didn't answer right away, but she thought she heard him mumble something. A not-so-pleased kind of mumbling. One she understood. Because, after all, her comment probably had seemed like some kind of accusation.

"I parked at the end of the road," he responded. "You told the dispatcher you thought there might be trespassers on your property. I looked around. Didn't see anyone."

That was the good news.

The bad news was that Lucas Creed was standing on her porch.

Kylie eased her gun onto the foyer table and inched closer to the door until her ear was pressed right against it. "I asked the dispatcher to send out a deputy." She tried to keep her voice level. Failed miserably. She had to clear her throat and repeat it so that it was more than an incoherent squeaky grumble.

Another pause. A long one. "One of my deputies is transferring a prisoner to Houston. He won't be back till morning. The other's out sick with the flu. I was the only one on call."

Ah. So that explained it. Lucas had no choice but to respond to her 911. That meant he wasn't any happier about this late-night visit than she was. No surprise there.

He despised her.

Worse, he had a reason to despise her.

"You plan to open the door and tell me what this is all about?" Lucas demanded.

That sent her pulse pounding. If she refused to let him in, it would make him suspicious. If she did comply, the same might happen.

And the one thing she didn't want was Lucas getting suspicious.

"You know the drill," he continued, sounding even more impatient. "I have to do a visual check to make sure you're not being held against your will."

Yes. It was standard procedure. Something Lucas wouldn't violate. Even if she was absolutely the last person on Earth he wanted to see.

Kylie glanced down at her stomach. The darkness hid a lot of things but not the second trimester tummy bulge. Almost frantically, she loosened the tie of her flannel robe and fluffed up the fabric. It helped. Well, hopefully it did. Just in case, though, she angled her body behind the door when she opened it.

And she came face-to-face with a man who'd sworn never to see her again.

"Lucas," she said, her throat closing up.

He didn't acknowledge her greeting and didn't make eye contact with her. Instead, he kept a firm grip on his lethal-looking Glock and swept an equally lethal-looking gaze around the yard.

"Is your porch light working?" he asked.

He didn't say it as if it were a request, either. More like procedure. He had to make sure she wasn't injured. Or that someone wasn't lurking behind her, threatening her. To do that, he needed light.

Kylie reached over, hesitantly, and flicked the light

switch on. If she thought it was tough to cope with Lucas in the dark, it was nothing compared to being able to see him.

He was every bit the rough-and-ready Texas cowboy tonight.

Just over six feet tall. Long and lean. Intense and imposing, with a fierce don't-mess-with-me demeanor. He was the kind of man who could stop a heart in mid-beat. Or send one racing.

He seemed to be doing both to her right now.

The past three years had been hard on him. She could see the stress etched on his rugged, naturally tanned face and in the depths of his eyes. Stress that she was responsible for.

Okay. That made her ache. Made her feel guilty. Worse, it made her want to do something to ease what he was going through. She wanted to reach out to him, to tell him how sorry she was. For everything. But Kylie knew Lucas wouldn't appreciate the gesture or the words. And while they might make her feel marginally better, gestures and words wouldn't do anything to help him.

The wind howled, stirring through his slightly-too-long mahogany-brown hair. His firm jaw muscles stirred, too. Moving against each other, as if he were in the middle of a battle about what to say.

Or, more likely, what *not* to say.

"Don't make this any harder than it already is," he mumbled in a rough whisper.

She knew what he meant. He had to come inside, look around. He'd need to put that on the report. Especially *this* report. Lucas wouldn't want anyone to question his procedure or accuse him of cutting corners because of the bad blood between them. But he also wanted to do this as quickly as possible so he could get the heck out of there.

Something she totally understood.

Kylie moved back, still using the door as cover. Lucas didn't say a word. He stepped inside, bringing with him the scents of his well-worn buckskin jacket, the winter frost and the fragrant cedars that he'd no doubt brushed up against to get to her house. His unique scent was there, as well. Something dark and masculine. Something that reminded her that she was a woman.

Oh, no.

That little mental realization shocked her. All right, more than shocked her. It stunned her. Because it had been a long time—years, in fact—since she'd been aware of something like that. This was obviously some by-product of pregnancy hormones. Yes, that had to be it. Because there was no other option. She couldn't be physically attracted to the one man on the planet who would never be attracted to her.

Stupid pregnancy hormones.

They didn't have a clue.

"What happened?" Lucas asked, using his cop's voice to go with the cop's surveillance of her living room and foyer. "Why the 911?"

Kylie quickly tried to gather her thoughts. And not the ones set off by the hormones, either. Those she pushed aside, and she got down to business.

"Around 11:30, I went to the kitchen to get a drink of water." Even though she was trying to hurry this along, she stopped when she heard how shaky her voice was and took a deep breath. This wussiness had to stop. "I looked out the window and saw two men dressed in dark clothes in the woods out near that cluster of hackberries."

He nodded. "I saw the fresh tracks. Could be hunters."

"Could be." And that's what Kylie desperately wanted to believe. That the men were deer or rabbit hunters who'd accidentally strayed onto her property. Nothing more. "But they weren't carrying flashlights, or if they were, they didn't have them turned on."

Lucas made a throaty sound of contemplation and walked across the living room. His scarred boots echoed softly on the hardwood floor. "It's a full moon. Maybe they didn't need flashlights."

"Maybe, but they weren't carrying hunting rifles, and they ducked out of sight when they spotted me at the window."

While he no doubt processed that, Lucas looked around. At the rough stone fireplace. At her seriously outdated furniture. And at her spartan computer desk tucked between two corner windows. He flexed his eyebrows when he noticed an old-fashioned turntable and the stack of equally old-fashioned Bob Dylan vinyl albums.

Lucas gave a you-still-listen-to-that? grunt and walked on through to the kitchen.

Kylie gave a corresponding yeah-I-do grumble and followed him. She hunched her shoulders, hoping he wouldn't turn that scrutinizing gaze on her.

"Any idea who the two men might have been?" With his back to her, Lucas bracketed his hands on the multicolored mosaic-tiled counter near the sink, leaned closer to the window and stared out into the darkness. The gesture looked effortless. Casual, even. But she knew differently. Lucas Creed was a dedicated, thorough lawman. He was examining every inch of the woods.

And every word of her account.

"No. I don't know." Kylie shook her head. "I mean, not really. But I had an, uh, appointment in San Antonio late this afternoon. Then, I did some shopping at the mall on the Riverwalk. It was already well past nine o'clock before I started the drive back home, and I thought someone might have followed me. Dark blue car. Nondescript. There was dirt or something on the license plate so I couldn't see it, but I'm pretty sure there were two men inside."

Sheesh. No being a wuss that time. But her story did have a tinge of paranoia to it. His deep male sound of reflection made her think that Lucas might feel the same way. Hopefully, he didn't believe this was some kind of ploy for attention. If she'd been the sort to seek attention—and she wasn't—she wouldn't have been seeking it from him.

"Have you gotten any suspicious phone calls lately?" he asked, moving from the sink to the back door.

"No." She wouldn't tell him about the eerie feeling, though, that something just wasn't right. While she trusted her instincts and intuition, she didn't think Lucas would. He was a man who required proof and facts, and she was seriously short of those.

He turned on the back porch light. While keeping his Glock ready and aimed in his right hand, he opened the door slightly, and eased out a few inches so he could take a look outside. The badge clipped to the waist of his well-worn jeans scraped against the wooden jamb. "You think this might be connected to one of the articles you wrote?"

That improved her posture. Kylie automatically stiffened, and her back went ramrod straight. She hadn't realized that he knew she was a journalist. But then, why wouldn't he? She had a degree in journalism and had worked briefly for a San Antonio newspaper before becoming a deputy. She hadn't exactly kept that a secret.

Unlike other things in her life.

For the past three years since she'd resigned as Lucas's deputy, she'd yet to step foot inside the city limits of Fall Creek, the town she'd once called home. Instead, she'd moved to the tiny country house where her late grand-

mother had raised her. Added to that self-imposed isolation, she'd been making trips into San Antonio for anything
from groceries to doctor's appointments. That minimized
her chances of running into Lucas. And it'd worked. She
hadn't seen him.

Until tonight.

"The last article I wrote did cause some waves," Kylie
admitted.

"Yeah." And Lucas let that simple acknowledgment hum
between them for several long moments. "The one about
illegal and unethical surrogacy activity."

So, he'd read it. Or at least he was familiar with it. Maybe
he was also familiar with the fact that she'd alluded to a
powerful San Antonio attorney, Isaac Dupont, and the surrogacy clinic director, Kendrick Windham, who might have
participated in those illegal activities.

"I didn't name names," Kylie quickly pointed out. Why,
she didn't know. However, she suddenly felt the need to defend herself and her approach to journalism.

"But along with the San Antonio Police Department,
hundreds, if not thousands, of readers figured out that you
were referring to Isaac Dupont," Lucas countered just as
quickly.

Kylie was sure she blinked. "San Antonio PD? What
do you mean?"

He shut the back door and locked it. Then with that same
quiet, almost graceful confidence, he strolled toward the
laundry room. "On the way over, I made some calls, talked
to a friend in SAPD. They might open an investigation
based on the info in your article."

The blood rushed to her head, so fast that she became
dizzy. Kylie dropped back a step and pressed her hand to
her chest. "I didn't know."

"Nothing's official." He didn't even spare her a glance. He continued his investigation by examining the garage just off the laundry room. "Besides, it might not even happen. The police are just looking into it."

She nodded and tried not to show any emotion. But inside that was an entirely different matter. Oh, mercy. She'd speculated that Isaac Dupont might be up to his lily-white neck in illegal activity, but she hadn't thought that article would cause him to try to intimidate her.

If that's what he'd indeed tried to do.

Had he hired those men to follow her? To scare her? If so, it'd worked.

She was scared.

"I'll have another look around outside," Lucas said, coming out of the laundry room. He engaged the lock on the door that blocked off the garage from the rest of the house. "If I see anything suspicious, I'll let you know."

"Thanks." She stepped back, clearing the way so he could go around her. "And thank you for coming."

It was an automatic, polite response. Something drilled into her by her upbringing. A goodbye meant to get him moving out the door.

It didn't have quite the intended effect on Lucas.

He stopped, practically in mid-step, and his gaze slid to hers. Those jaw muscles went to work again, and it seemed as if he'd changed his mind a dozen times about what to say. "This is my job."

A short, efficient, arctic comeback. His version of an automatic response. It was his way of letting her know that even though they were enemies—and sweet heaven, they *were* enemies—he wouldn't lower himself to shirking his duties because of her.

"Yes, this is your job," she acknowledged. "But I don't

think anyone in Fall Creek would have criticized you if you hadn't come."

His teeth came together, and the battle began. Not with just his jaw muscles, but with his composure. His eyes. His entire body. "I don't intend to discuss this with you."

No. But it was always there. An unspoken conversation. And it always would be, since he would never be able to forgive her for what she'd done.

But then, she wouldn't be able to forgive herself, either.

That didn't make them even.

She would always owe him. Because of the promise she'd made to a dying woman. Because of the promise she'd made to herself. Kylie would always feel the need to make things right with Lucas.

"If I could undo everything that happened," she said to him, "I would."

He turned. An agile shift of his body. His gaze rifled to hers, a little maneuver that robbed her of what breath she'd managed to recoup. There it was, in the depths of his saddle-brown eyes. The accusations.

The pain.

God, the pain.

Lucas combed his hostile gaze over her face, hardly more than a split-second glance. Then he took that methodical scrutinization lower, to her body.

Kylie trembled.

Waited.

She didn't have to wait too long. Lucas actually did a double take when he noticed her stomach.

Not that it helped, but Kylie adjusted her robe again. Seconds passed slowly, crawling by, until the silence settled uncomfortably around them.

"Are you..." But he obviously couldn't even finish the question. Instead, he swallowed hard.

Since it would be absurd to lie, Kylie had no choice but to admit the obvious. "Yes. I'm pregnant."

He fired a few more of those nervy glances around the house. "I didn't know," he finally said.

The words were void of any emotion. He'd done a better job of that than she ever could have. Because down deep, below the words, even deeper than his eerily calm demeanor, she figured this discovery had to be killing him.

Or maybe he wasn't affected at all because, perhaps, he truly didn't care. Maybe she was a nonentity to him. Nothing more than a 911 call on a frosty January night.

She shook her head, moistened her lips. "Not many people know about the pregnancy." And because she feared other questions, both those spoken aloud and left unsaid, Kylie went on the offensive. "I doubt those men are still out there. But just in case, I'll lock all the doors, keep my weapon nearby. I'll call you if I see anything else suspicious."

He nodded, turned and headed for the door. Lucas didn't even look back, which shot to heck her nonentity theory. She wasn't a nonentity to him, definitely not, because he still hated her.

However, as deep and as potent as that hatred was, Kylie knew that Lucas would hate her even more if he learned the truth—

That the baby she was carrying was *his*.

Chapter 2

Lucas couldn't get out of Kylie's house fast enough. It took every ounce of his willpower not to break into a run, and he was certainly thankful when he made it outside onto the porch.

He immediately pulled in a long, hard breath. Since it was just below freezing and the ice crystals seemed to burn his lungs, it should have cleared his head, as well.

It didn't.

But then, nothing would.

It didn't seem...fair.

There. He'd let the thought fully materialize in his head. Yeah, it was petty. Beyond petty, really. It was spiteful. But it put a rock-hard knot in his gut to know that the woman responsible for the deaths of his wife and unborn child was having a child of her own.

What's wrong with this picture? he wanted to shout to the powers that be.

"Are you okay?" he heard Kylie ask. Definitely not a shout. Practically a whisper.

Lucas laughed. But it wasn't from humor. Damn the irony of this. And damn the flashbacks and the nightmarish memories of that day when his world had come crashing down around him.

"I'm fine," he lied.

"Hmm." She paused. "You know, if I were wearing a BS meter, it'd be going nuts about right now. Because you don't look fine."

He shot her a glance over his shoulder to let her know it wasn't a good time to push this. But then, it was never a good time to push this particular subject.

What he should do was just leave. He should get the heck out of there. Off Kylie's porch. Off her property. Away from her. *Miles away.* Unfortunately, his legs wouldn't cooperate. They'd seemingly turned to dust. So he stood there and pretended to do a routine surveillance of the yard and the surrounding woods.

However, it was anything but routine.

Seeing Kylie again, especially a pregnant Kylie, was like ripping open all the old wounds. Wounds that would never heal. Even though, until tonight, he would have sworn that he was getting on with his life.

And he was.

Well, for the most part.

He would probably never be able to fully recover from the deaths of his wife and unborn baby. Lucas considered that a moment and took out the *probably.* No full recovery for him. He wasn't coming back from that.

But he had a future now. Heck, in four and a half months he'd even get to experience fatherhood. Finally.

No thanks to Kylie.

That thanks belonged to the anonymous surrogate he'd

hired through an agency in San Antonio. Only because of her would he get a second chance at having a life.

Hugging her faded blue bathrobe tightly to her body, Kylie stepped out on the frost-scabbed porch. She kept a safe distance, but somehow it still felt too close.

"You're upset because I'm pregnant," she said.

Leave it to Kylie to lay it all out there. That was one of the things he'd always admired about her—her frankness. Oh, and her honesty. Unfortunately, he wasn't in the mood for either tonight.

"How am I supposed to feel?" Lucas replied. And he actually hoped she had the answer. Because he was having a heck of a time sorting it all out.

"Confused. Hurt," she promptly supplied. Her warm breath mixed with the cold air and created a misty haze when she spoke. Against her pale ivory skin, it had an almost otherworldly effect. As if this were all just a dream. He wished to hell it was. "And you're probably mad at yourself for feeling those things since you're not a mean-spirited man."

Lucas scowled. "You're sure about that last part? Because I don't think it's my imagination that I'm feeling a little mean-spirited here."

The scowl obviously didn't put her off. The right corner of her mouth temporarily lifted before it eased back down.

"Lucas, you're stubborn, inflexible and prone to bouts of misguided stoicism. I blame that last part on your cowboy roots. You can't help yourself." Kylie shook her head, sending a lock of her honey-blond hair slipping onto her forehead. "But you don't have the heart to be mean-spirited."

Probably because it was too close to the truth and because he didn't want this weird intimacy and understanding between them, Lucas decided to end this little personality evaluation. "You have no idea what's in my heart."

"Touché." Kylie waited a moment while the wind howled around them. She shifted her feet. No shoes. Just a pair of grayed weathered socks that were sagging around her ankles. There was a tiny hole just over her right pinkie. "Still, I'm sorry. Being around me like this can't be easy for you."

No.

It never would be.

"The rumor mill in Fall Creek is pretty good," he said, testing the waters. Why, he didn't know. Her pregnancy was none of his business.

And he mentally repeated that to himself.

It didn't help.

He still wanted to know, which made him some kind of sick glutton for punishment.

Her body language changed. Gone was the semicocky demeanor that was part of Kylie's trademark personality, and her shoulders slumped. "I don't think the rumor mill knew about the baby."

It didn't, or the word would have certainly made it back to him. He wished it had, and then he wouldn't have been blindsided by this 911 call. And it was that *911* aspect of this visit that he needed to concentrate on.

Lucas swept his gaze around the woods. Like the other times, he saw nothing to indicate the hunters, trespassers, or God knows who or what were still around. Maybe he'd scared them off, and if so, that meant his job here was done.

Almost.

"Is there someone you can call to stay with you tonight?" Lucas asked. It was procedure. Something he would have asked of any woman who'd just been frightened enough to phone the sheriff's office.

"Sure," she said without hesitation.

Now, it was his turn to pause. He angled his head, stared

at her. "If I were wearing a BS meter, it'd be going nuts about right now. You don't have anyone to call, do you?"

Her chin came up, but that little display of bravado didn't quite make it to her slightly narrowed indigo-blue eyes. "If you mean my baby's father, no. He's not in the picture. But despite what you think of me, I'm not totally friendless. I have people who can come over."

However, that didn't mean she would rely on those *people*. In fact, he was about a hundred percent certain that she'd make no such calls tonight. No. Not the independent, my-way-or-no-way Kylie. Once he was gone, she'd lock the doors, turn out the lights and sit there in the darkness. Holding her gun. All night. Terrified. And completely alone.

Hell.

The image of her doing that brought out all kinds of protective instincts in him. After all, she was pregnant. Out in the middle of the woods.

Where anything could go wrong.

"This isn't your problem," Kylie informed him, as if reading his mind. "I'm a big girl. Trust me, I can take care of myself."

"And that's the reason you made the 911 call," Lucas commented.

That earned him another glare. She hiked up her chin again, and she cupped her hands around her mouth. "If anyone is stupid enough to be out there, hear this," she shouted. "I'm freezing my butt off, and I'm in a really pissy mood. I also have a loaded .357 Magnum that I know how to use. My advice? Go home now!"

With that, Kylie turned toward him, making sure that he understood that the *go home now!* suggestion applied to him, as well.

She swiped that lock of hair from her forehead. An angry, indignant swipe. With trembling fingers. Her bottom lip started to tremble, as well. That shot some holes in the steely resolve she was trying to project. It also tested yet more of his protective instincts.

Still, that was his cue to end this visit. After all, she'd practically demanded that he leave, and now that he'd checked off all the squares for this official visit, there was no reason for him to stay.

"I'll be at my house if you need to get in touch with me," Lucas advised. Not exactly standard procedure, but it was a courtesy he would have extended to anyone in his jurisdiction. "Since there's no one at the office, don't call dispatch or 911. Just ring straight through to the house. I can be here in fifteen minutes."

"Thanks." It had a definite *goodbye* kind of tone to it. She turned, her bathrobe swishing like a gunslinger's duster, and went back inside.

Only after she'd closed the door did Lucas realize that at some point he'd stopped breathing. He slowly released the air from his lungs and forced himself to get moving. No easy feat. He felt raw and drained from their encounter.

He stayed on the narrow gravel and dirt road that led from her house to the highway. Walking fast. Trying not to think.

It didn't work.

Not that he thought it would.

The cold darkness closed in around him, smothering him, and with it came the flood of memories. Because he had no choice, he stopped and leaned against a sprawling oak. Thankfully, Kylie's house was no longer in sight, and that meant she wouldn't be able to see him if he disgraced himself by completely falling apart.

And it certainly felt as if that were about to happen.

The adrenaline and the nausea crashed through him. As if the events of that day were happening now, at this moment, and not three years ago. However, three years wasn't nearly enough time to diminish all the brutal details that'd stayed with him. Heck, a million years wouldn't make him forget.

Deputy Kylie Monroe had been on patrol that day when the call came in. A robbery at the convenience store on the edge of town. She'd responded and gone in pursuit of two unidentified armed suspects who were on foot. Even though Kylie had called for backup, she hadn't waited. Instead, she'd begun a dangerous, unauthorized foot chase through the streets of Fall Creek.

That had set off a deadly chain of events.

One of the robbery suspects must have panicked because he stopped and fired at Kylie. He missed. Well, he missed Kylie, anyway. Instead, he'd hit Lucas's pregnant wife, Marissa, who at that moment had stepped out of the grocery store.

The one shot had been fatal.

In the blink of an eye, Kylie had lost her best friend. And Lucas had lost his wife and the baby she had been carrying. Marissa had been only two months pregnant, barely enough time for him to come to terms with the concept of fatherhood. And it'd been snatched away.

Everything had been snatched away.

He'd known that the moment he had rounded the corner and had seen his wife lying on the sidewalk. Kylie, kneeling next to her. Marissa, nearly lifeless and bleeding, whispering the last words she'd ever say. Not to him. But to Kylie. Marissa hadn't been able to say anything to him because she'd died before he could get to her.

Another irony.

Marissa, the woman he loved, hadn't even been able to say goodbye to him. Yet, the person responsible for her death—Kylie—had been the beneficiary of those final precious seconds of Marissa's life. Her last breath. Her final words. Lucas hadn't heard those words firsthand, but in the minutes following Marissa's death, while Kylie still had his wife's blood on her hands, Kylie had repeated them like a mantra.

Don't let my death kill Lucas, Marissa had told Kylie. *Look after him. Help him heal. Make sure he's happy.*

Make sure he's happy.

Right.

As if that could ever happen. Marissa had used her last breath to ask the impossible. Even if Kylie had ever had a desire to fulfill her best friend's dying wish, he wouldn't have let her try. There was no way he wanted Kylie Monroe to have any part in his healing.

Lucas couldn't bear the pain any longer, so he forced himself to think of his future. His baby. Being a father wasn't a cure-all. It wouldn't rid him of the gaping hole in his heart. But it would get him moving in the right direction. And he couldn't wait for that to begin. Four and a half months, and he'd be able to hold his child.

The sound snapped him out his daydream, and Lucas automatically aimed his weapon and turned in the direction of the noise he'd heard.

A soft rustle of leaves, not made by a stir of wind, either. No. This was much more substantial. As if someone were walking through the woods. But not walking in just any direction.

Directly toward Kylie's house.

That gave him another hefty shot of adrenaline. Not that he needed it. His body had already shifted into combat mode.

Lucas stepped back into the dense underbrush and trees. He started retracing his steps, following the road. Quietly, so that he wouldn't be detected and so that he could listen.

He didn't like what he heard.

Definitely footsteps.

Probably not just one set, either. At least two. Both heavy enough to belong to men. Big men.

And that brought him back to the two possible suspects that Kylie had spotted in the woods.

The trespassing duo had apparently returned for round two. But what did they want? Was this simply a case of trespassing, or was it something more?

Did it have to do with that controversial article she'd written? If so, if they'd been sent there to intimidate her, it could turn ugly. Because he knew that Kylie wouldn't intimidate easily. Even pregnant, she would make a formidable foe.

Lucas eased deeper into the woods as he approached the house. No sign of the men, but the porch light was off again. Maybe because Kylie had also heard them and wanted the shelter of the darkness. If so, that meant she was probably terrified. Worse, she didn't know he was still outside, still keeping watch.

He stopped at a clearing and tried to pick through the sounds and the scents to determine what he was up against. There was a rattle of motion, the sound of a scuffle. Not good. So, he hurried forward, still searching.

He didn't have to search long.

The side door to Kylie's garage flew open. Milky, yellow light speared into the darkness.

So did two armed men. Both were dressed from head to toe in dark clothes and were wearing ski masks.

And they weren't alone.

They were dragging Kylie out of the house.

Chapter 3

Kylie had no time to react.

The two men came at her—fast. Rushing across the kitchen straight toward her.

Her only warning had been the soft click of her laundry room door. That was it. The lone indication that the two masked armed men had somehow picked the lock and had gotten inside her house.

She turned to run to try to get her gun, which she'd left on the table in the foyer.

She didn't get far.

One of them latched onto her, using his beefy hand to stop her. He curved his arm like a vise around her neck. Her throat snapped shut, clamping off all but a shallow scream. But that didn't stop her from reacting.

Her instincts cried out for her to escape. And she tried. She *really* tried. Kylie rammed her elbow into the man's muscled stomach. He staggered back, just slightly, but not nearly enough for her to break free of his fierce grip.

Refusing to give up, she pivoted and went for his eyes using the heel of her hand.

It didn't work.

The man was huge, well over six feet tall and heavily muscled. Literally overpowering her, he grabbed her and shoved her forward into the waiting arms of the other man.

"Remember, don't hurt her or the kid," the first guy snarled. "We're to deliver her safe and sound to the boss. So they can *talk*." His gaze slashed to hers. His frosty gray eyes were the only part of him she could see because he was dressed from head to toe in black, including a ski mask. His partner wore a similar outfit. "Well, unless she gives us no choice about that safe and sound part. I'm sure the boss will understand if she doesn't cooperate."

Terror and a sickening dread quickly replaced the surge of adrenaline. Oh, God.

They might hurt her baby.

She stopped struggling. But they didn't stop. Kylie caught just a glimpse of the white cloth before one of the men shoved it against her face.

Chloroform, maybe.

They were obviously trying to knock her out. But at what cost?

She shoved the cloth away. "You said you wouldn't hurt my baby," she managed to say.

The man put the cloth right back in place, over her nose. "This stuff won't hurt you or the kid," he grumbled. But it wasn't much reassurance coming from a would-be kidnapper.

If that's what he was.

Was this a kidnapping? If so, why did they want her?

Kylie didn't like the first thought that came to mind. Mercy. Was this related to that article she'd written about illegal surrogacy? But it didn't matter if it were about that. If she didn't do something, these men would likely succeed in taking her.

Forcing her breathing to stay shallow so the drug wouldn't incapacitate her, Kylie tried to stay calm. She reminded herself that she had to stay alive and alert for the sake of the baby. It worked. Well, a little. She steadied herself enough so she could glance around the kitchen and laundry room for anything that she could use to escape.

But the men didn't give her a chance to escape. They got her moving outside into the freezing cold night. Away from her weapon. Away from the phone that she'd hoped to use to call Lucas. They hauled her through the garage and out the side door.

Kylie struggled against the drug-laced cloth and managed to bat it away again. But it was already too late. Everything was becoming hazy, slightly out of focus. It probably wouldn't be long before she completely lost consciousness.

She closed her eyes and decided to play along with that scenario. It was a long shot, but if her kidnappers thought she'd passed out, maybe they'd let down their guard long enough for her to escape.

Continuing the act, she let her legs and body go limp and would have fallen if her captor hadn't caught her. As if she weighed nothing, he scooped her up in his arms and kept on walking through the dense woods.

Seconds crawled by.

Each one pounded in cadence with the syrupy pulse drumming in her ears. Kylie fixed the image in her head of Lucas holding his baby, and she used that as motivation to stay awake. She had to stay awake, to survive.

And she would.

For Lucas. For his baby. For the life that he deserved to have and for the life that she'd promised Marissa that she would give him.

She silently cursed the stupid things she'd said to Lucas so that he'd leave. *I'm a big girl. Trust me, I can take care of myself.*

But she obviously couldn't.

Not only had she allowed two kidnappers to break into her home, she hadn't even been armed at the time. Instead, she'd been fighting back tears over Lucas's visit. Crying instead of grabbing her gun. And that was despite every primitive alarm going off in her head that something wasn't right. So much for listening to her gut. She'd be lucky to get the baby and herself out of this alive.

She lifted her left eyelid a fraction and saw where they were taking her. In the direction of the lake. Probably to the road that circled it so they could escape. Or else they planned to drown her. But Kylie pushed that frightening thought aside. If they'd wanted her dead, they probably already would have killed her. And they certainly wouldn't have come prepared to chloroform her.

Of course, she couldn't rule out that they were taking her to a secondary crime scene, a place where they could finish her off and dispose of her body without leaving any forensic evidence behind.

She added some mental groans to her mental profanity. She couldn't give in to these what-ifs and worst-case scenarios. If she did, she'd likely die.

Instead, she focused on the lake, on what she knew about it. After all, it was as familiar to her as her own home. It was where she took daily walks and did most of her writing. She figured that the men had parked off the road. If she got a break, one little distraction, she could dive into the water, and, uh…

Probably drown.

Yes. Drown.

Another mental groan. She was already so dizzy that she couldn't stay focused. Heaven only knew what would happen to her in the water.

Okay. Plan A was discarded. She moved on to Plan B. Too bad she couldn't think of one. Sweet heaven, her head was spinning and she felt on the verge of throwing up. Still, she fought through that haze and forced herself to think. She had to come up with something.

The thudding noise and the howl of pain jarred open her eyes. Not that she could see much. But she was able to determine that the other man was no longer in front of them. He was on the ground, writhing and groaning.

"What the hell?" the one holding her growled, a split second before he let go of her.

Kylie managed to protect her stomach and break the fall with her hands. She immediately got to her knees so that she could get away and scurried behind a tree. It wasn't easy but, dragging her way through the underbrush and soggy dead leaves, she somehow got there. It took her a few seconds to realize that her captor wasn't coming after her.

It took a few more to realize why.

One of the men was still on the ground. And he was the one who was moaning and holding on to his leg. However, the other guy aimed his gun at a shadowy figure that appeared between two trees.

Lucas.

He'd come back.

"Lucas!" she called out to warn him. It wasn't her best

effort. More breath than voice. She sounded drunk and, worse, felt that way, too.

Still, he reacted. Lucas darted to her side just as the guy fired at him. The shot blasted through the woods, clipping a tree and spraying splinters and bark. The sound was deafening and shook her to the core. Not just because it drilled home the danger for herself and the baby, but because Lucas was now in danger, as well.

Oh, God.

And she was responsible for him being here.

If he were hurt, or worse, it would be her fault. Kylie wasn't sure she could live with that. She'd already caused enough devastation in his life.

Frantically, she searched the ground, looking for anything she could use to defend them. The dizziness and nausea didn't help. Still, she kept searching, raking aside the leaves, and finally came up with a thick, long tree limb. It wouldn't be much protection against a semiautomatic, but if she got close enough, she could do some damage.

Well, maybe.

With her focus fading in and out, she probably wouldn't be much of a threat even if she'd had a loaded gun.

She peeked out from behind the tree. Neither of the kidnappers was anywhere in sight. Great. Just great. They could come at her and Lucas from any direction and, considering that she could only move slowly, she'd be a sitting duck.

"Shhh." The sound was barely audible, but it was the only warning she got before Kylie felt a rough hand clamp over her mouth.

She automatically struggled, trying to defend herself with the tree branch, but the man—and it was definitely a man—pulled her to him. Right against his solid, rock-hard body. Her face landed against a buckskin coat. A familiar coat.

With an equally familiar scent.

"It's me," Lucas whispered. Without making a sound, he eased forward and positioned himself in front of her, using his body as a shield to protect her.

Kylie quietly laid down the branch and checked to make sure he wasn't injured. Even with the full hunter's moon, she couldn't see much. Well, not much except the stalwart, determined expression on Lucas's face.

Lucas didn't take his vigilant gaze off their surroundings. He reached over, the fingertips of his left hand skimming over her stomach.

The baby kicked.

Right on the spot where Lucas was touching her.

If Lucas had noticed it, he didn't say anything. Instead, he readjusted her robe. Putting it back in place. Most likely so that she'd stay warm. In all the chaos, she hadn't realized that the only thing between her stomach and the cold night air was a thin white cotton gown.

"Are you okay?" he whispered.

She hadn't been injured in the fall, but every muscle in her body was already aching and stiff from the fight and the adrenaline. Then, there was the chloroform or whatever had been on that cloth. It might be hours, or days, before she knew what effect that would have on her. And the baby. Especially the baby.

"I'm okay."

And she prayed that was true.

Her reassurance didn't do a thing to ease his vigilance. He kept his Glock aimed and ready. And she knew for a fact that he had a lethal aim. She only hoped that it was enough to get them out of this alive.

Kylie pulled in her breath and waited. She listened carefully, but all she could hear was the wind rattling through the towering oak trees. Reality quickly began to sink in. Yes, Lucas was there, and he was armed. And he was good. But sometimes *good* just wasn't good enough.

Frowning, scowling really, Lucas brushed his knuckles over her lips. Barely a touch. Kylie flinched at the contact. However, she welcomed it in a weird, surreal sort of way. Human contact, even if it happened to be from Lucas, felt pretty comforting.

"You're humming," he whispered. "Out loud."

Kylie stopped, considered that. "Am I?" she whispered back.

A crisp nod. "'Jingle Bells.'"

No surprise there. Humming perky, out-of-season tunes was her way of dealing with stress. And right now, she was dealing with a lot of stress.

"Sorry," she offered, and she clamped her teeth over her lip to make sure it didn't happen again.

But her stress level soared when she heard someone moving through the woods.

Her heart began to pound even harder than before. She forced herself to breathe normally so that she wouldn't hyperventilate.

Beside her, Lucas didn't react, didn't move a muscle. Definitely no threat of hyperventilation for him. Everything in him seemed to still, like a jungle cat waiting to move in for the kill.

The sounds continued. They were closer now. Definitely footsteps. Despite the roar in her ears, she could measure the pace of whoever was walking. Slow, methodical steps. Not from the side, but from behind them.

God, from behind them.

They were about to be ambushed.

Lucas whipped around and fired a shot. "I'm Sheriff Lucas Creed," he called out, his voice even more of a warning than the bullet he'd just fired. "I know your partner's injured because he's got my knife in his leg. My advice? Surrender. He needs medical attention now."

The footsteps stopped.

And the silence returned.

Long, agonizing moments.

She waited. Trying to stay conscious and to still her body as Lucas had done his. Of course, the baby chose that moment to kick like an NFL punter. Kylie slid her hand over her stomach and rubbed gently.

Lucas's gaze came to hers. He didn't speak, but his left eyebrow slid up. It was a question. *Are you truly okay?* That unsaid question touched her.

Until she made the connection.

His concern wasn't for her per se. This was some kind of transference because of his own impending fatherhood. Of course, he had no way of knowing that the kicking baby was his *baby*.

She'd done everything within her power to keep it a secret. And she would continue to do that. Not just through the pregnancy and delivery, but forever.

The thought of that broke her heart. She could never let this child know that she was his or her mother.

Never.

Sometimes, like now, that seemed too high a price to pay, but then she'd created a huge debt because of that fatal shooting three years ago. And she'd made that promise to Marissa. This was the one way she could repay Marissa and Lucas. Her heart would be broken, but his would finally be healed.

"They're gone," she heard Lucas say.

Kylie listened and heard the sound of a vehicle on the lake road. Driving away.

Or better yet—*getting away.*

"You have to go after them," she whispered frantically.

But just saying those few words robbed her of what little energy she had left.

"No," Lucas answered. "I can't leave you. Not without backup."

Part of her greatly appreciated that. Especially since she was unarmed, barely conscious and a couple of steps past being defenseless. But another part of her, the former cop part, knew that without suspects in custody, she might never learn why they'd come after her. The two ski-mask-wearing men might simply disappear.

Which would create a real nightmare for her.

She'd always be wondering, worrying when, where and if they'd strike again. What little peace of mind she had would be a thing of the past.

With that realization, Kylie gave up the fight.

Because she had no choice, she leaned her head against the tree, and the murkiness and the winter night closed in around her.

Chapter 4

"This isn't necessary," Kylie grumbled. Again.

Lucas ignored her. Again.

Balancing the cell phone that he had sandwiched between his shoulder and his ear, he gently deposited Kylie onto the paper-covered examining table. She was still groggy, but not so groggy that it prevented her from insisting that she could have walked into the clinic on her own.

Yeah, right.

She was wearing only those flimsy socks. And the temperature had been below freezing. The ground had been hard and slick with frost. Still, if Lucas hadn't been concerned that she might fall flat on her face, he would have given in to her protests and let her test her theory concerning her walking capabilities. But a fall might have injured her baby. Or even her. Despite how he felt about Kylie, Lucas hadn't been about to risk that.

"You can wait out there, Lucas," Dr. Finn McGrath insisted. And to clarify what he meant by *out there,* Finn hitched his thumb in the direction of the empty reception area just outside the examining room.

"She'll be okay, right?" Lucas asked.

That earned him a flat look from Finn, a man he'd known all his thirty-one years of life. His best friend.

"I know, I know. Your psychic skills are a little rusty," Lucas jested.

"But you're in luck," Finn replied. "I'm not too rusty in the medical department."

Lucas appreciated his friend's attempt to settle him down, but the attempt was wasted. "They drugged her with something," he explained.

"Yeah. Figured that out." Finn put a hand on Lucas's back to get him moving. "I'll examine her. But since examining her means making sure she doesn't have any injuries beneath her gown, I don't think Kylie will want you to be in the room for that. Doubt you'll want to be there, either."

No. He didn't. And it made Lucas more than a little uncomfortable to think of Kylie and what was beneath that gown. Best to think of her only as his former deputy.

As his enemy.

As his most recent 911 call.

Unfortunately, it was impossible to leave out the part about her being pregnant and apparently in a whole boatload of danger.

"I need to bag her clothes," Lucas reminded Finn. "I can send them to the crime lab in Austin to see if they recover any trace evidence."

"Yes, I figured that out, too." Finn pressed a little harder on Lucas's back. "Don't worry. Clothes will be bagged and tagged, and I'll scrounge up something around here for her to wear."

Lucas nodded and stepped into the reception area. He hadn't really noticed it on the way in—mainly because his brain had been too occupied with Kylie and her need for medical attention—but he saw the recent changes Finn had made in the office. A wall mural of a serene pasture dotted with bluebonnets and longhorns. A children's corner stocked with all sorts of toys and books. Gone was the old loveseat, and in its place were four navy leather chairs. Nice ones. But Lucas was too antsy to make use of the chairs. And he was too tired to pace. So, he leaned against the wall and waited.

He glanced at the tiny screen on his phone to determine if he was still on hold. He was connected, which meant Sheriff Knight was no doubt trying to come up with a situation report on the crime scene, so Lucas used the downtime to try to figure out what the heck was going on.

Two men, both armed, had tried to kidnap Kylie.

Why?

They hadn't wanted to kill her, that's for sure, or she would have been dead before he could have gotten to her. Not exactly something he cared to admit. But he knew it was true. After mentally reconstructing the possible scenarios, Lucas figured the kidnappers had had more than ample opportunity to murder Kylie while she was still inside her house. But instead, they'd taken her outside. Toward the lake. Probably to some waiting vehicle.

And that's where his scenario reconstruction dropped like a sack of rocks.

Once he'd carried Kylie to his truck so he could get her to the doctor's office, he'd called Dillon Knight, the sheriff from the neighboring town, and asked him to proceed with backup to Kylie's house. Knight's initial report was that there were no signs of the kidnappers or a ransom note. Plus, Lucas knew Kylie wasn't a good candidate for a ransom demand since she wasn't wealthy.

That ruled out kidnapping for money.

It didn't rule out kidnapping for other reasons.

Revenge. Criminal intent. Perhaps even a way of silencing or punishing her. He'd need to narrow down the possible motives so he could narrow down the list of possible suspects.

"How far along are you in the pregnancy?" Finn asked Kylie.

Even though Lucas didn't hear Kylie's softly delivered answer, the question sent Lucas's blood pressure up a significant notch. He glanced into the examining room. Finn hadn't shut the door all the way—it was open just a few inches—but it gave Lucas a much clearer view than he wanted.

Kylie had her gaze fastened toward the ceiling, and her left arm was angled so that the back of her hand rested against her forehead. Finn had indeed pushed her gown up to her waist, exposing her bare legs. And her panties. Cotton. Nothing provocative.

Lucas mentally repeated that to himself.

And wondered why it didn't sink in.

Finn had a stethoscope pressed to Kylie's stomach, which was also bare, and after a couple of moments, he gave an approving nod.

Finn's gaze met Lucas's and with that brief look, Finn conveyed his concern. His empathy.

And his questions.

Finn knew the hell that Lucas and Kylie had gone through. And he also knew that Kylie had had a huge part in creating that particular hell. Now, Finn was probably wondering how Lucas was dealing with the fact that Kylie was pregnant.

Lucas wasn't dealing with it well.

"Is the baby okay?" Kylie asked.

Finally, she was speaking normally. No slurred words. No mumbling. Lucas felt relief. Then anger for feeling relief that she was apparently all right. Then guilt for feeling the anger.

Oh, man.

Much more of this, and he'd need therapy.

"The baby's got a steady, solid heartbeat," Finn relayed in a voice loud enough so that Lucas could hear. "Your heartbeat's solid as well, Kylie. No visible signs of injury other than a few bruises and scrapes."

So she wasn't seriously hurt. That was something at least.

"Lucas?" he heard the person on the other end of the phone line say. Sheriff Dillon Knight. Lucas welcomed the intrusion. Heck, at this point he'd welcome anything as long as he didn't have to think about Kylie, her baby and what was going on in that examining room.

"You found something?" Lucas asked, tuning out what Kylie was now saying to Finn.

"Nothing good. It looks as if the men made a getaway on the old lake road."

That's what Lucas had figured, too. "There will be tire tracks. And blood. I used my knife on one of them, and he probably left a trail of his DNA all the way to the lake."

"I saw that. We've got the area cordoned off so the county forensic guys can come out and have a look. Maybe they'll find a print or two. Or else they can run the blood and find a match in CODIS."

CODIS, the Combined DNA Index System. A data bank of sorts. But the only way there'd be a match would be if the wounded would-be kidnapper's DNA was already on file in the system.

Which wasn't too much of a long shot.

After all, neither man had been tentative about committing a felony. They'd probably done something criminal before. Or at least, Lucas hoped they had. Because a match in CODIS would give him a name. And with a name, he might be able to figure out why this had happened. That was vital; he needed to solve this case so there'd be no reason for him to be around Kylie.

"I'll keep you posted," Sheriff Knight told him as he ended the call.

Lucas slipped his phone into his jacket pocket, turned back to the doorway and saw Finn standing there, his hands bracketed on each side of the jamb. In physical appearance, they were practically opposites. Finn, with his moon-blond hair, blue eyes and his natural surfer-dude tan. Definitely not a typical Texas cowboy. Lucas knew the man didn't even own a pair of boots. No Stetson, either. And Finn liked to boast that he'd never been within ten feet of a horse. Even when he wore green scrubs, like now, he still managed to look as if he'd just stepped off a surfboard.

"She'll be okay," Finn let him know. He handed Lucas a clear plastic bag that contained Kylie's clothes. "I drew some blood so I can figure out what they used to sedate her. But she should have a checkup by her regular OB. She should have an ultrasound, too."

Lucas glanced over Finn's shoulder and saw Kylie. She was now wearing a set of Finn's scrubs. And yet another pair of socks.

"You can't do the ultrasound here?" Lucas asked.

"Sorry. Don't have the equipment." Finn hooked the stethoscope around his neck, yawned and rubbed his eyes. "There are a lot of advantages to living in a small town like Fall Creek, but we're Podunkville as far as that type of medical service. She'll have to go to a larger facility for it."

Lucas considered it and mentally cursed. "It was Kylie's trip into San Antonio that might have led to the kidnapping attempt. Kylie had said something about two men possibly following her home."

"Yes," Kylie verified. "They did."

"That means a trip back into the city isn't a good idea," Lucas concluded.

At least, not alone. However, it wasn't a trip Lucas intended to make with her. He'd have to turn this over to a deputy or else Sheriff Knight. This eerie proximity with Kylie Monroe was a lot more than he could handle.

"I'll drive her in the morning," Finn volunteered, probably sensing what was on Lucas's mind. "I have a colleague who manages one of those back-to-nature kind of birthing facilities just outside San Antonio. It's in the country. Very serene. Off the beaten path. And private. He'll let me use his ultrasound machine. We'll keep everything hush-hush."

Lucas nodded, conveying his thanks. Hopefully, a private facility also meant a safe one.

When there was the sound of movement in the examining room, Finn turned, angling his body so that Lucas and he had a clear view of Kylie. She tried to get up...and failed. With a groan, she eased back down onto the table.

"They used chloroform on me, didn't they?" Kylie asked. She didn't wait for an answer. "Will it hurt the baby?"

"Probably not," Finn answered. "We'll know more in a day or two when I get back the test results."

Another soft groan. But a groan wasn't her only reaction. A tear slid down her cheek, and she quickly swiped it away. "Did anyone catch the men who did this to me?"

Finn stepped aside. That was Lucas's cue to fill her in and ask a few questions so he'd have info for the report he would have to make. "They're still at large."

"Oh, that's wonderful," she mumbled.

Lucas ignored the sarcasm and got to work. "Did you get a good look at either of the men?"

Judging from the way her forehead bunched up, she considered that. "No. They were both wearing ski masks. Both dressed in all black. One was about six-one, the other about two inches taller. The taller one had light gray eyes. And he said something like, 'Don't hurt the kid or her. We're to deliver her to the boss. So they can talk.'"

"Talk?" Lucas repeated skeptically.

"I didn't believe that's what they had on their minds, either." She tried to sit up again. This time, she succeeded. Well, for the most part. Kylie wobbled, and she grasped the sides of the examining table. Her gaze came to his. "I'm sorry, Lucas. I'm so sorry."

He didn't want her apology. Nor did he want her to specify *why* she was sorry. Maybe it was for Marissa. Or maybe it was because she believed she'd placed him in danger with her 911 call. It was true that she had, but being placed in danger came with his job.

"I've got to phone a few people and take care of the arrangements for the ultrasound," Finn said, making his way out of the room.

Leaving Lucas alone with Kylie.

Lucas decided the best approach to this was the most obvious one—to continue his interview. He was the sheriff, after all, and he'd questioned many victims of many crimes. He would treat this one no differently than the others.

He stopped and admitted that it was a sad day in a man's life when he started lying to himself.

He had no choice but to treat this case differently. Because this case involved Kylie.

She shook her head. Winced. Wobbled again. Flashed him when she tried to use her leg to maintain her balance.

She probably would have fallen if Lucas hadn't reached out and snagged her shoulders.

"Thanks." She dropped her head against his right arm. Eased against him.

As if she belonged there.

And for some stupid reason, he didn't move. He let her stay.

She was shaking, and she looked up at him. Her eyes were ripe with fatigue, spent adrenaline and the aftereffects of the kidnappers' drug.

"I'm scared," she whispered. It was an admission he'd never heard Kylie make. And it was true. He could see that stark fear on her face. He could feel it in her. "They could have killed us. You, me, the baby. All three of us."

"But they didn't."

There was no indication in her body language that she believed him. "And here I was so full of myself. So cocky about how I didn't want anyone to protect me. God, Lucas." Her voice broke and became a hoarse sob. More tears came. "I was wrong, and that mistake could have cost you everything again. They could have killed your baby."

His heart actually skipped a beat.

Your baby.

Lucas opened his mouth to correct her. And might have done that if he hadn't felt Kylie freeze. She went completely stiff; that extreme reaction had him staring down at her.

She pulled back, meeting his gaze head-on. In the depths of all that blue, Lucas saw something in her eyes that he didn't understand.

He shook his head.

"It's true," Kylie said, as if that explained everything.

It took him a moment just to ask what he needed to ask. "What's true?"

"The only reason I'm telling you this is because I'm afraid I can't protect this baby by myself. Not now. Not with those men still out there."

"What are you telling me exactly?" Lucas tried to brace himself for the answer. Judging from her expression, he couldn't possibly brace himself enough.

A moment later, Kylie confirmed that.

"When you applied for a surrogate, I pulled some strings. Called in a few favors." He watched the words form on her lips, and each one stabbed through him. "Lucas, I'm your surrogate, and this baby I'm carrying is yours."

Well, that impromptu confession cleared Kylie's head.

The residual effects of the kidnappers' drug vanished, leaving her with vision and a brain that was a little too clear. That clarity allowed her to see the thunderstruck expression on Lucas's face.

"My baby?" he mumbled.

She watched that register. First, he shook his head. Stared at her. Shook his head again.

Then it sank in.

He stepped back, his chest pumping as if he were suddenly starved for air. He tried to speak. Couldn't. He looked as if he were on the verge of seriously losing it. Kylie reached for him, but he put up his hands, palms out, in a back-off gesture.

"Why?" he finally asked.

She didn't know how he had managed to speak. His teeth were practically clamped together, and his jaw muscles had seemingly turned to iron. But those responses were tame compared to that look in his eyes. There was fire mixed with all those shades of brown. Fire and brimstone.

"Why?" Kylie repeated. "I've asked myself that more than a few times."

"Is this some kind of warped punishment?" Lucas's anger chilled his voice. "Your way of torturing me?"

She'd anticipated a few of the things Lucas might say if he ever learned the truth, but that hadn't been one of them. "No. God, no. It's because of what happened to Marissa."

"Don't. I don't want to talk about her."

Kylie didn't even consider heeding his warning. Despite his glare. Despite his defensive posture. They had to get a few things straight. "I did this because of what Marissa said when she was dying. 'Don't let my death kill Lucas. Look after him. Help him heal. Make sure he's happy.' And that's what I promised her I would do. I owed her that promise. But you wouldn't let me help you."

"I didn't *want* you to do any of those things for me," Lucas protested, stabbing his accusing index finger in her direction. "I didn't want your help. I still don't. In fact, the only thing I wanted from you was never to see you again."

Now, that she'd expected him to say. Too bad she hadn't planned a perfectly worded response. Too bad that his words hurt.

"You think this was an easy decision for me to make?" she asked. "Well, it wasn't. I agonized over it. I'm twenty-nine years old, Lucas, and haven't had a relationship with a man in years. This may be the only baby I ever have, and it's not even mine. Hear that? It's not a baby I can hope that you'll share with me."

Nothing she said soothed him. In fact, it had the opposite effect. His jaw muscles jerked. And it seemed as if Lucas were about to let go of the choke hold he had on his anger and other emotions.

"And at no point during this monumental decision-making process did it occur to you to ask me if I wanted *you* for a surrogate?" he stormed. "No. That would have been too reasonable. Something a sane, normal person would have done. And you know what I would have said if you'd asked, Kylie? I would have told you that there's no way in hell I want you to be the mother of my child."

Oh, that stung.

Mercy.

And here she thought she was somewhat immune to anything Lucas could say to her. She was obviously wrong.

"I made a promise to Marissa," Kylie reminded him. Because that was the true bottom line of why she'd made her decision. Yes, her guilt had contributed to it. So had her need to somehow pay for her mistake. But if Marissa hadn't asked, Kylie wouldn't have become Lucas's surrogate. "And I always keep my promises."

"Oh, that's a good one." He took several steps toward her and got right in her face. "What about the promise to keep the citizens of Fall Creek safe? What about your sworn oath to follow regs? Regs you ignored when you went after those two men who robbed the convenience store? Was it worth it, Kylie? Was Marissa's and my baby's lives worth catching two scumbags who'd stolen a hundred and twenty-three dollars?"

Kylie had no answer for that, and she'd tried for nearly three years to find one. She'd made a fatal mistake that day. Not waiting for backup. Proceeding on foot after two armed suspects. Though waiting for backup might not have changed the outcome, it was a mistake she'd tried to live with.

So far, she hadn't been successful.

She wasn't holding out hope that she would succeed any time soon. Because of Marissa's death, she turned in her badge. Resigned. She'd quit a job she loved. But Kylie was under no illusions that her resignation would atone for what she'd done.

"Look, I know this isn't my business," she heard Finn

say. He had come back into the room, stepping between Lucas and her. "But you're both my friends, and I won't stand here and let you two rip each other apart. Besides, I'd like to get some sleep. My advice is that both of you should quit talking and instead start trying to figure out what you're going to do. Not about the baby," he quickly added. "Leave that for a day when tempers have settled a bit. I'm concerned about a more immediate problem here."

Kylie waited until Lucas turned his attention from her and aimed it at Finn before she followed suit. She also tried to let what Finn had said sink in. Yes. They did have a more immediate problem than her secret surrogacy.

Finn's hands went to his hips. "Let me insult your intelligence and summarize the situation, Lucas. Someone tried to kidnap Kylie tonight. She's possibly still in danger. And that baby she's carrying is yours. My advice—bury the hatchet. Not in her back, either. Bury it and get on with what you know you have to do."

Kylie figured it was a good time for her to sit there and shut up. Lucas must have decided the same thing because the conversation ground to a halt. Seconds ticked by, practically turning into minutes, before Finn cursed.

"All right. Be that way. Since it obviously isn't safe or prudent for Kylie to go home, and since I doubt she wants to sleep in the jail or on that examining table, you should take her to your ranch, Lucas."

"No!" Kylie and Lucas said in unison.

Finn shrugged and directed his attention to Lucas. "Well, I can't bring Kylie with me to my house. I can't defend her against kidnappers and other assorted felons. I don't even own a gun. And besides, protecting her is your job."

When Lucas didn't respond other than with a lethal glare, Finn huffed. "Since you're a good sheriff, and since

I know you're not an ass, I'm trying hard to figure out why you're hesitating. Is it public opinion? Gossip, maybe?" He stopped, as if considering that. "Please don't tell me you're concerned how your former sister-in-law would feel about Kylie staying at the ranch."

Now, it was Lucas's turn to huff. "Cordelia doesn't make decisions for me."

"That's never stopped her from trying," Finn mumbled. He grabbed Lucas's hand and plopped it against Kylie's stomach. "But whatever's causing you to hesitate, forget it. Do what you've sworn to do. Protect her. Protect your baby."

Lucas's hand was stiff. Even through the cotton scrubs, she could feel the calluses he'd earned the hard way—by working on his ranch. His touch stayed rigid, defensive. He closed his eyes for a moment. Swallowed hard.

Then, something happened.

His touch suddenly wasn't so hard. Wasn't so defensive.

Finn backed away. Lucas's hand stayed put. And his fingers moved gently over her stomach. Not far. Mere fractions of an inch. He didn't make a sound. Didn't say word.

But their gazes met.

And in that gaze, Kylie saw what was going on. Pain, yes. That was a given. But there was more. That gentleness wasn't about the pain, but rather about the life growing inside her.

"My baby," he said under his breath. "Why?" Not an accusation this time, but a plea.

She waited a moment, to clear that sudden lump in her throat. While she was at it, she prayed she wouldn't disgrace herself again by crying. "I wanted to try to give you back what I took from you."

He waited a moment, as well. Staring at her. Really staring. He pulled his hand away, and she immediately felt the loss of his body heat. Something stirred deep down within her. An ache. A longing. A…need.

Oh, great.

Kylie quickly shoved that ache, that longing, that blasted need aside. And silently cursed that feeling. She couldn't associate any of those things with Lucas. Heck, it was best not to associate anything at all with him.

But shoving it aside didn't make it so.

She felt that punch. It had to be lust. Temporary, fleeting lust brought out by hormones and adrenaline. It just had to be that, and that alone.

Because there was no other alternative.

"So, I'll send the bagged clothes to the crime lab for you," Finn interrupted. He grabbed a leather coat from the rack in the reception area and draped it over her shoulders. "And you'll take Kylie to your ranch?"

But it wasn't exactly a question. More like an impatient reminder that he couldn't go home until they'd cleared out of his clinic.

Lucas tore his gaze from hers. "She'll come with me," he confirmed to Finn.

And he didn't leave room for argument.

Not that she could argue, anyway. After all, her number one priority had to be the baby. To keep the baby safe. And to do that, *she* had to stay safe.

However, Kylie wasn't sure what she feared more—the kidnappers returning or spending what was left of the night under the same roof with Lucas. The first was downright dangerous. And the second—staying with Lucas—well, after what she'd just experienced, it was a danger of a different kind. Still, it was a risk she had to take.

She didn't protest when Lucas scooped her up in his arms and carried her outside to his truck.

Chapter 5

Lucas kept his attention fixed on the two-lane road that led from town to his ranch. It was nearly three in the morning, and there was no traffic. Not even an occasional deer or coyote to give them a diversion.

Just Kylie and him.

And within five minutes, she would be inside his house and well on her way to sleeping in one of his beds.

Nothing about that particular scenario pleased him.

Well, nothing except the part about keeping her safe. Finn was right. That was his job as sheriff, and he couldn't pick and choose his cases.

Even if that's exactly what he wanted to do.

"I would say thanks for doing this, but it'd probably just irritate you," Kylie commented.

She was right.

Lucas hoped his silence conveyed that.

"Okay, so a thank-you is off-limits," she continued a

moment later. "Ditto for Marissa. I guess we could talk about the baby—"

"The baby's off-limits, too."

For now, anyway. However, it couldn't stay that way for long. Someway, somehow, he'd have to come to terms with the bombshell that Kylie had delivered back at the clinic.

Lucas, I'm your surrogate, and this baby I'm carrying is yours.

He shook his head. Coming to terms with that would take a miracle.

For nearly three years, his thoughts of Kylie had been churning with anger and bitterness, and that was putting it mildly. Now what was he supposed to do? Put all that hurt and fury behind him and just accept what she'd done?

What she had done was deceive him.

She'd gone behind his back. *Pulled some strings,* she'd said. And she had done all of that so she could get pregnant with his child.

Oh, man.

Part of him was down-on-his-knees humbled by that. Another part was even thankful. Because he wanted this child more than anything. But what he couldn't deal with was this baby would always have a link with Kylie. Her DNA. Her biological child just as much as his.

Hell.

How was he supposed to get past that?

Kylie. The mother of his child. A person he didn't want to be linked with—for anything.

Other than their brief history of working together, they didn't have anything in common. She was a neohippy, for heaven sakes. Raised by a love-bead-wearing grandmother, Meg, whose claim to fame was that she'd once made out with Bob Dylan in some coffeehouse in New York City.

That was probably wishful thinking on her part. Meg had been into fantasy. Unlike Kylie. Yes, Kylie ate tofu and sprouts and had a Save The Wolves bumper sticker on her environmentally friendly car. But she was real. The kind of woman you could count on to tell you the truth.

Even when the truth hurt like hell.

That's why this lie stung so much. The one thing he'd always been sure of when it came to Kylie was that he'd get the truth. Yet, here for four and a half months, she'd lied by omission.

"Then can we talk about those kidnappers?" Kylie asked.

Lucas didn't veto that one. In fact, it was the only common ground he wanted with Kylie right now because it pertained to the case.

"Since the two men planned to take me to their boss *to talk*," she said, "it's my guess that this has something to do with the article I wrote about illegal surrogacy."

That was his guess, too, especially since there'd been no ransom note. "What made you decide to write that article anyway?"

"Kismet." She sighed. "Or maybe it was rotten luck. Right after I'd been inseminated…sorry. That wasn't an intentional reference to the baby."

Maybe not intentional, but it was a reference. Lucas couldn't disregard the fact that Kylie had been inseminated. With his semen. A totally impersonal act. As was the entire surrogacy procedure. Yet, it'd resulted in something that seemed to be the ultimate in intimacy.

A pregnancy.

"Anyway, I met this pregnant woman at the clinic," Kylie continued. "A girl, really. Her name is Tiffany Smith. She was in the ladies' room, and we struck up a conversation.

She was barely seventeen, Lucas. Definitely underage. She admitted that she was a homeless runaway."

"And this Tiffany was there at the clinic because she was a surrogate?"

She nodded. "She was maybe five or six months pregnant and there to pick up her monthly stipend. She said that a man who worked for a lawyer first approached her about surrogacy when she still living on the street. He offered her money and a place to live if she'd have a baby for a couple who desperately wanted a child. I called an old P.I. friend, told him about Tiffany, and he did some checking for me. He couldn't find her. Coincidence? I doubt it. I think the person who hired her didn't want anyone to find out she was underage so they hid her."

Kylie turned in the seat, angling her body to face him. It wasn't an especially unusual move.

Except the moonlight seemed to turn into a friggin' spotlight.

He could clearly see her midsection, and because the bulky black leather coat had gaped open, he could see the outline of her stomach. Specifically, the bulge created by the pregnancy. There was a baby inside that bulge. *His baby.*

Lucas forced his attention back to the road and their conversation.

"You think the lawyer Tiffany Smith spoke about is Isaac Dupont?" he asked.

She made a sound of agreement. "Tiffany said the man, the go-between, dropped by a lawyer's office over in Alamo Heights. He had her wait in the car, so she never saw the lawyer in question. Plus, she didn't know the specific street but was able to give a description. I drove over there, and Dupont's office is right there, just as she described it."

It was a start for circumstantial evidence. "But you don't have concrete proof that he was behind this illegal surrogacy?"

"I don't have any positive proof, but I discovered that Dupont handled the adoption of one other medically unfit surrogate. When I called to ask him about it, he threatened me with a lawsuit and hung up on me. That in itself doesn't mean he's guilty, and that's why I only alluded to Dupont and the clinic director in my article. I mentioned that a prominent Alamo Heights attorney had handled some questionable adoptions linked to equally questionable surrogates at a downtown clinic. *Alluded,*" she repeated. "Don't you just love that word? It's supposed to be clinical, as in a journalist can *allude* without putting the publication or herself at risk. Ha. It doesn't feel very clinical or safe now."

No. It didn't. But then to Isaac Dupont, an insinuation was probably the same as an outright accusation. Leave it to Kylie to go after one of the most ruthless attorneys and businessmen in the state. Dupont had a take-no-prisoners reputation, and even though the man had been implicated in other activities, such as suspicious adoptions, none of the rumors or speculation had ever led to a real investigation.

Until now.

Lucas figured SAPD would want to question Kylie and check out the crime scene—especially after the kidnapping attempt. Of course, it would be a real coup if SAPD could also link those two would-be kidnappers to Dupont. Unfortunately, if Dupont was behind this, all those potential questions and attempts to link him to the attempted kidnapping would put Kylie in even more danger.

First thing in the morning, he'd make some calls and see if he could arrange protective custody for her. That would solve both of their problems. Because Lucas figured she didn't want to stay with him any more than he wanted to be with her.

He made the last turn to his ranch, crossed the cattle guard and brought the truck to a stop in front of his house. He waited a moment, checking to make sure everything looked normal. It did. The only thing abnormal was the whirlwind of emotions he was experiencing.

Dreading the next few hours, Lucas exited the truck, but Kylie got out before he could make it to the passenger's side. She even took a few steps, her socks lightly crunching on the frosted ground. Not only that, she wobbled, reaching out to grab something. But all she caught was air. He picked her up so that she wouldn't fall.

"This *really* isn't necessary," she complained.

He ignored her and didn't waste any time walking through the yard and stepping onto the porch. Kylie immediately slid out of his grip. But not before he felt the soft thump. It had come from her stomach and landed against his chest.

"It's the baby," she explained. She seemed embarrassed. Or something. She quickly pulled her coat closed.

Lucas unlocked the door, and they went inside. "The baby kicks a lot?" he asked.

She nodded.

Intrigued by that little flutter of movement, Lucas looked at her. It was only after he'd done it that he realized looking at her was a truly stupid idea.

Kylie looked up at him at the same moment that he looked down at her.

The air between them changed.

Not because either of them willed it. It just happened. Their scents sort of intermingled. And he went from being intrigued by a baby's kick to being intrigued by the baby's mother. That wasn't even the worst part. The worst part was that Lucas was almost positive that Kylie was feeling the same thing.

He felt that little flicker of heat. A really bad kind of heat. The kind that could only happen with physical attraction. And he prayed that little flicker didn't turn into a full-blown flame.

"Well, crud," she mumbled. Then, she groaned. "Would it help if I told you what's going on here is a primal instinct that neither of us have any control over? Because this is your child, you feel this innate familiarity or something. And I feel this sicko kind of need to have you protect me. Probably something to do with continuation of the human race."

"Well, that certainly takes the emotion out of it," Lucas lied.

Kylie shrugged. "I didn't figure we were ready to deal with the emotion. Besides, it's just pregnancy hormones."

"Pregnancy hormones," he repeated. "They must be a lot like male hormones—brainless."

And he quickly got his *brain* on something else.

"The guest room's down there." Lucas pointed to the last room at the end of the hall. "There should be a robe hanging in the closet if you need it. Oh, and if you're hungry, you know where the fridge is."

She ran her fingers over the silver-framed photo of Marissa that was on the table next to the front door. "I know where just about everything is in this house," Kylie reminded him.

Yeah. She probably did. When Marissa was alive, Kylie was over at least a couple of times a month. Still, it seemed so off-kilter having her here.

Everything seemed off-kilter.

Especially him.

He suddenly wished he had livestock to tend, horses to feed. Anything that would give him a break from himself. But so that he'd have more time for the baby, he'd sold the livestock and all but one of his horses, which was literally out to pasture. One horse would hardly offer enough work to burn Kylie's scent from his brain.

"Lucas?" she said. "I just want you to know that this baby really is yours. I have no plans to keep it or the money that you paid for the surrogacy. I won't even be a part of your or your baby's life. Once I deliver, I'll give the child to you and then leave."

And with that, she turned and headed for the guest room.

It was a powerful declaration. One that soothed him far more than it should have. Still, Lucas latched onto it and tried to picture his future. He remembered why he'd wanted to become a father in the first place. Because he loved children. And because he wanted a son or daughter of his own. He couldn't lose another child, and if that meant protecting a woman he loathed....

But he stopped there.

That *loathed* part was starting to fade. And it couldn't. It just couldn't.

He wasn't ready for it to fade.

Too much was coming at him too fast. The kidnapping attempt. Learning the truth about Kylie's pregnancy. The intense longing caused by such a simple thing as feeling the baby kick. His brainless reaction to Kylie.

Especially that last one.

Because his reaction to Kylie hadn't had anything to do with protecting her. Hormones, indeed. What he was feeling was hot and primal, and it was already simmering to the point where it felt as if it might boil over.

Disgusted with himself and his own body, he followed Kylie down the hall so he could get a few things straight. Unfortunately, she'd already shut the door to the guest room; unfortunately, he threw open that door without thinking. She'd taken off the coat that she'd borrowed from Finn and was about to pull back the covers. In those few brief seconds, before she could put her stoic mask back on, he saw the fatigue. The worry.

The vulnerability.

It was a challenge, but Lucas didn't let that vulnerability get in the way of what he had to say. Because this had to be said. "It doesn't matter that you're carrying my baby. Nothing is ever going to happen between us," he informed her. "Got that?"

She gave a crisp nod. "Got it." She paused for a heartbeat, then snagged his gaze. "But are you trying to convince me? Or are you trying to convince yourself?"

Chapter 6

Kylie winced as she dried off from her shower. Spent adrenaline could do all sorts of nasty things to the body. Sore muscles. Aches. Fatigue. A general sense of feeling yucky. She'd been lucky in her pregnancy not to experience the "pleasures" of morning sickness, but she thought her luck might run out this morning.

She reluctantly put the scrubs and socks back on and topped the outfit with the thick terry cloth robe she'd borrowed from the closet. Obviously, it was Lucas's robe but not one that he'd worn, because it still smelled new. Then, she didn't imagine that Lucas was the bathrobe type. Or the pajama type, for that matter.

Which got her thinking things better left unthought.

"Get your mind out of the gutter, Kylie," she mumbled.

She glanced at herself in the dresser mirror and didn't care for what she saw. The scrubs and the robe weren't exactly her first choice of attire. Ditto for the lack of makeup or grooming supplies. Still, the clothes and bare face would have to do until she could get back to her place and change before going into the birthing center for the ultrasound. There were probably some of Marissa's things still in the house—she doubted that Lucas would have gotten rid of all of them—but Kylie would have gone naked rather than wear Marissa's clothes. She'd already rubbed enough proverbial salt in Lucas's wounds without adding more.

It'd been a mistake to tell him that she was his surrogate. Kylie knew that *now*. Hindsight was such an annoyingly accurate thing. She should have just stuck with the plan: give birth, let the surrogacy agency deliver the baby to Lucas and then leave.

For good.

If she'd done that, Lucas might have been able to forget all about her. He might have eventually been able to forgive her, as well. But by telling him, she'd ruined everything. Would he ever be able to look at his baby's face and not remember that she was that child's mother?

Of course, there was a flip side to this particular question. If she hadn't told Lucas, who would have helped protect her? SAPD, maybe. But no one other than Lucas would have had a vested interest in keeping the baby safe. She wasn't invincible. And pride was something she couldn't afford to indulge in.

At least, that's the rationalization that kept going through her head.

However, Kylie had to ask herself if protecting the baby was the only reason she'd told Lucas. Or was there something else? Some subconscious motivation? She wanted to believe that her motives were pure. But the doubts were right there next to the rationalization and the unwholesome thoughts she was having about him.

Are you trying to convince me? Or are you trying to convince yourself?

Those were the smart-mouthed questions she'd tossed at Lucas just hours earlier when he'd stormed into the guest room. Now she had to wonder if she'd aimed those questions at the wrong person.

Since Kylie didn't really want to know the answer to that, she decided to concentrate on a way to put a speedy end to all of this. Once Finn had done the ultrasound, she would call her cousin in Houston. He was a P.I., and he would almost certainly let her stay with him until the police could catch the guys who had tried to kidnap her. Heck, maybe she'd even stay there until she had the baby. That way, it would insure that she and Lucas wouldn't have any more contact with each other.

She opened the bathroom door and heard Lucas moving around in the kitchen. He seemed to be talking on the phone. And cooking. She immediately got a whiff of coffee and, heaven forbid, bacon. Her stomach lurched, but Kylie ignored it and tried to hold her breath while she went into the kitchen to remind him that she needed to pick up some clothes from her house.

However, something that Lucas said stopped her in her tracks.

"That sounds like the same two men who tried to kidnap Kylie. You said you saw them near the medical clinic?"

That was a temporary cure for her morning sickness. Instead of a lurch, Kylie's stomach tightened. If Lucas had sounded more urgent, then she would have started to hope and pray that the men were on the verge of being apprehended. But since Lucas was carefully forking out sizzling bacon from the black cast-iron skillet, it probably meant the caller was informing Lucas of a sighting after the fact.

A cold sighting.

Which was a misnomer. Because it was anything but cold for her.

"That was about an hour or so after Kylie and I left," Lucas said in response to the caller. "Did you see which direction they were headed in?" He paused. "If you remember anything else, give me a call."

Lucas slipped the phone back into its cradle, mounted on the wall, and glanced at her. "You heard?"

She nodded. "Who saw them?"

"The night security guard at the bank."

In other words, probably a reliable source. It told her two things—first, that the one man hadn't been so badly hurt that they'd had to flee the area to seek medical attention, and second, that the men weren't going to give up.

That knot in her stomach tightened.

"I don't have any tofu, yogurt or any of the other healthy stuff you like to eat, but there's coffee," Lucas advised her.

"No, thanks. I gave it up."

He blinked. "You quit drinking coffee?" Asked in the same tone as, *You quit breathing?*

"The caffeine isn't good for the baby."

"Oh."

It was as if she'd stomped right on a raw nerve again. Of course, any conversation about the baby would likely be painful. She figured it would take Lucas time to accept this, but Kylie had to believe he would. After all, he did want to become a father, and she was offering the baby to him with no strings attached.

She was about to remind him that she needed to drop by her house, but the knock at the kitchen door stopped her. Not just a knock, either. One brief tap, and the door flew open.

"Brr. It's freezing. The front door was locked so I decided to come around to the back."

Kylie immediately recognized the voice. And the owner of the voice.

Cordelia Landrum.

Owner of the town's only women's clothing boutique. Marissa's sister. Lucas's former sister-in-law. And a general pain in the butt whom Kylie didn't want to face. Not this morning. Not any morning.

Cordelia was still brr-ing and briskly rubbing her kid gloved hands together when she entered. Her mouth was wide with a rose-slick smile—until her attention landed on Kylie, that is.

"What are you doing here?" Cordelia demanded.

Kylie had gotten warmer greetings from perps as she was arresting them. But that was to be expected. Cordelia and Kylie had never been friends, but Marissa's death had certainly made them enemies. It was a shame, because Cordelia looked so much like her sister. From her sleek strawberry-blond ponytail to those aristocratic mist-green eyes. If Cordelia weren't, well, Cordelia, then it might have been nice to have her around just because it would be like hanging on to a little piece of Marissa.

"Someone tried to kidnap Kylie last night," Lucas explained. "She's in my temporary protective custody."

And he hastily jumped right in there with that explanation, too. Probably because he didn't want Cordelia to think anything funny was going on.

Funny as in sexual.

Which wouldn't have been a totally absurd conclusion for Cordelia to draw since Kylie was wearing Lucas's robe while standing in the middle of his kitchen. Of course, because of Lucas's and her history, probably even Cordelia wouldn't believe that Lucas and she were lovers.

His explanation prompted Cordelia to give Kylie a once-over. That cool gaze slid from Kylie's still wet hair, past her stomach, all the way to her feet.

Wait a minute.

Kylie didn't miss the fact that Cordelia's gaze hadn't even paused, much less lingered, on her pregnant stomach. It was such an odd thing to bypass that Kylie glanced down to make sure she appeared as large as she felt.

Yep. Her pregnant belly was there. Totally visible. Not hidden one iota by the scrubs or the robe that she'd left untied.

"How long will she be here?" Cordelia asked Lucas.

Lucas calmly put the skillet into the sink. "I'm not sure."

That answer surprised Kylie almost as much as Cordelia's lack of response to the pregnancy. What the heck was going on? Had that chloroform and adrenaline fried a few of her brain cells?

"I don't want her here," Cordelia concluded. "This is my sister's house."

An easy comeback would have been for Kylie to remind her that it was Lucas's house, as well. But Kylie held her tongue. In the grand scheme of things, Cordelia's annoyance just wasn't very important. Not when someone wanted to kidnap her and do God knows what to her and the baby.

Cordelia took a step toward her. Because it seemed like a challenge and because she couldn't resist that, Kylie took a step toward her, as well.

They faced each other eye to eye.

"I'll call Lucas this afternoon," Cordelia informed her. "I'll expect you to be gone by then. If not, I'll do something about it. Understand?"

Kylie shook her head. "Not really. But that sounds like some kind of threat. Is it?"

"Cordelia," Lucas warned.

But if Cordelia had heard his warning, she showed no signs of heeding it. She kept her focus on Kylie. "If you don't think I can make trouble for you, then think again."

Kylie considered just staying quiet, but her mouth didn't cooperate. "Cordelia, it really isn't necessary for you to keep reminding me just how much you hate me. You couldn't possibly hate me more than I hate myself."

"Don't bet on it." And with that chilly comeback, Cordelia turned, issued an equally chilly goodbye to Lucas from over her shoulder, and slammed the kitchen door behind her.

If Kylie hadn't been sure of what to do, she was after that exit. She had to get out of there.

Because Cordelia would cause problems for Lucas. And Lucas already had enough problems as it was. After all, the idea was to make him happy again. To heal his heart. To do what she'd promised Marissa that she would do. She couldn't very well heal anything if she was making him miserable.

"I'll call Finn to come and pick me up." Kylie walked toward the phone.

"You can't. He phoned while you were in the shower. One of the Krepner kids broke his arm in two places when he fell off his bunk bed. Finn said he needs to take care of that, and then he'll just meet us at the Brighton Medical Center around noon. He gave me directions."

Slowly, she turned back around to face him. "And you'll be taking me there," Kylie concluded. But before the last word left her mouth, she was already considering other options. *Any* other options.

"Don't even think about arguing. Those two men were near Finn's clinic. I don't think that's a coincidence, Kylie. They're looking for you. And they'll keep looking until they're caught."

She couldn't argue with that. It was the stuff nightmares were made of. Still, what she couldn't quite grasp was that Lucas didn't seem riled about spending what would no doubt be an entire morning with her.

"This new attitude of yours is because of the baby," Kylie said, more to herself than to him.

"Of course it is. What else would it be about?"

Nothing that she wanted to voice.

"I need to blow-dry my hair," she told him. "Give me fifteen minutes, and I'll be ready to leave."

Kylie walked out, intending to hurry back to the bathroom. Mainly because that whole bacon smell and the confrontation with Cordelia had sent her stomach into another tailspin. However, she stopped when she glanced out the sidelight windows that framed the front door.

The entire front yard and the driveway were covered with frost. It glistened in the morning light, making the ranch look like postcard material. What marred the pretty picture was Cordelia, who was still parked out front. Sitting in the driver's seat of her pricey red sports car. She had her head down, and she seemed to be talking to herself. Whatever she was saying obviously didn't please her because her expression was one of anger and….what? Frustration, maybe? Kylie couldn't quite make sense of it until Cordelia turned in her direction. And glared at her.

The emotion was anger. Pure, uncut anger.

A chill went through Kylie, and she didn't think it had to do with the temperature outside. That look on Cordelia's face said it all. Cordelia hated her. And that got Kylie thinking.

Had Cordelia already done something about that hatred?

After all, she hadn't even reacted to Kylie's pregnancy. Why? Why wouldn't she have shown at least some mild interest?

Because perhaps she already knew?

She considered that a moment, and then she took her musings one step further. If Cordelia had somehow learned about the baby, then what? She wouldn't be pleased, that was certain. And she wouldn't want Kylie to be a part of Lucas's life. So, just how far would Cordelia go to prevent something like that from happening?

Kylie wasn't sure, but she intended to find out.

Chapter 7

As a general rule, Lucas usually avoided hospitals and doctors' offices. The sterile smell and the white-jacketed doctors just didn't set well with him. It was a childhood trauma association thing. Too many broken bones, bruised ribs and stitches from trying to play rodeo.

Yet, here he was inside his second medical facility in less than twenty-four hours. This one, the Brighton Medical Center, was about twenty times the size of Finn's clinic, and despite its back-to-nature claim, it was crammed with lots of those white jackets, sterile smells and patients. In this case, the patients were dozens of pregnant women.

One of whom was Kylie.

"I really have to go to the bathroom," she complained to Finn. She was wearing a dull gray-blue paper hospital-type gown while reclining on an examining table, and her stomach was bare. Well, it was bare except for some clear gooey stuff that Finn had smeared all over it moments earlier.

"Sorry," Finn apologized to Kylie. "You'll have to wait a few minutes before you can go. A full bladder helps with the ultrasound."

Lucas figured there was a thorough explanation for that, but he didn't really want to hear it. All he wanted was for the test to be completed and for Kylie and the baby to get a clean bill of health.

Until they'd arrived at the medical center, Lucas hadn't realized just how concerned he was that the kidnappers' drug might have harmed the child. In the past twelve hours, he'd had the case, Kylie and even Cordelia's brief but irritating visit to take his mind off such things. But those distractions didn't work now.

He needed to know if this baby was okay.

Finn held up a small device. "This is a transducer," he explained and began to move it over Kylie's goo-slick stomach. "It'll transmit the images so we can see what the little tyke is doing in there."

Kylie began to hum. Softly. Lucas wasn't sure, but he thought it was "Peter Cottontail." With the absurdly cheerful Easter notes coming from her closed mouth, she kept her attention fastened to the small, grainy screen. He divided his focus between it and her.

She was nervous. The humming proved that. Not that Lucas needed such an obvious clue. After what had happened to her, any expectant mother would have been worried about the test results. As an expectant father, he was certainly worried.

In addition to the nervousness and the humming, Kylie looked exhausted. And probably was. The confrontation with Cordelia certainly hadn't helped, either. Why of all days had his former sister-in-law chosen this morning to drop by for a visit? It had been weeks, if not months, since

Cordelia had come out to the ranch. Lucas didn't have the answer as to why she'd shown up out of the blue, but because he didn't believe in coincidences, he had a really bad feeling in the pit of his stomach.

Was Cordelia up to something?

And why hadn't she reacted to Kylie's clothes? After all, it appeared as if Kylie had just climbed out of his bed. Even more, why hadn't Cordelia said something about the pregnancy? Cordelia knew about the surrogacy, of course. In fact, she'd even volunteered to help Lucas decorate the nursery. She couldn't have known that Kylie was that surrogate, but why wouldn't Cordelia at least have shown some interest, or even displeasure, in the fact that Kylie was pregnant? That revelation had certainly hit him like a sucker punch to the solar plexus.

"Just to let you know, I plan to send the ultrasound to your doctor in San Antonio," Finn continued, moving the transducer to the side of Kylie's stomach. "But so far, everything looks good. The placenta's attached normally and the heartbeat looks good. The baby's active, has two arms, two legs. If you want to see them, just look here."

Finn used his index finger to trace parts of the fuzzy image on the screen, but Lucas couldn't make heads or tails of it.

Apparently, Kylie was having the same problem because she glanced at Lucas and questioningly lifted her right eyebrow. They both seemed frozen in the moment.

They shared a smile. A brief one. It was laced with relief, fatigue and other emotions that probably only parents experienced. But it was still a smile. A reminder for him that Kylie and he had something in common, whether he wanted that or not. And suddenly that didn't seem as disastrous as it had the night before.

Oh, man.

He was so in trouble here.

Lucas didn't want his feelings toward Kylie to soften. He really didn't. But how the heck could he stop that from happening? And why did stopping it suddenly seem like a really stupid idea, anyway? After all, it was his baby, but she was the one carrying it. It just wasn't a good idea for them to be at odds.

Kylie flexed her eyebrows as if she understood the battle he was having. It was ironic. He now shared a camaraderie with Kylie Monroe. Worse, it wasn't simply camaraderie.

There was an attraction simmering between them.

Lucas mentally paused and waited for lightning to strike him where he stood. No lightning bolt. No cosmic rift. Just a moment of truth.

However, that moment of truth and admission didn't mean he would act on that attraction. No way. It would be a massive mistake. Because Kylie and he would never be able to get past what had happened to Marissa.

He mentally paused again.

Would they?

"How about the sex?" Finn asked, jarring Lucas out of his conflicted thoughts.

Since Lucas was staring right at Kylie, he saw the bittersweet reaction register in her eyes. Lucas knew there was emotion in his, as well.

She pulled in a slow breath, shook her head, moistened her lips. "I don't want to know, but you can tell Lucas."

She was obviously trying to distance herself from the baby. *Trying* being the operative word. And that led Lucas to yet another concern in his ever-growing list of concerns. This was his baby, yes, he didn't doubt that. But even though Kylie had said she would give him the child and leave, would she?

Would Kylie just leave?

"All right, we're finished," Finn announced.

He didn't have to tell Kylie twice. She barreled off the table as much as a pregnant woman could and headed straight for the adjoining bathroom.

"So, you want to know if you're having a little cowboy or a cowgirl?" Finn asked.

Of course, he was curious. Okay, more than curious. Since he'd found out that his surrogate was pregnant, he had formed mental pictures of both a son and a daughter. He had to adjust those images now that he knew Kylie was the mother. He'd always thought of his child as having dark hair. Like his. But there was a possibility that he or she would be blond.

With Kylie's blue eyes.

Fate and DNA certainly had a twisted sense of humor. Here he'd spent years despising those eyes, yet he might spend the rest of his life looking at them on a son or daughter whom he dearly loved.

"Well?" Finn prompted. "You want to know the gender?"

Lucas shook his head. "No." He wanted to get a few things straightened out in his life so he'd have time to savor the news.

Finn actually seemed disappointed. "Still having trouble coming to terms with all that's happened?"

Lucas sank down onto the chair tucked in the corner. "I'm having trouble with a lot of things."

"Hmm." Finn dropped down on the examining table directly across from him. "Buttin' my nose in here, but when's the last time you were with a woman? And I don't mean that in a general sense. I mean clothing removal, et cetera, et cetera."

It was sad, but it took him a while to come up with an answer. "About six months."

Finn stared at him.

"All right, almost a year." And it had been just sex. Comfort sex at that, with an old high school friend who'd been in town to visit her folks. Lucas couldn't even remember if it involved total clothing removal. Heck, he couldn't remember if it'd been marginally satisfying. What he could remember was that he'd felt guilty as hell afterward. It'd been like cheating on Marissa.

"There. You have the answer to some of those things that are troubling you," Finn concluded. "Maybe you've never noticed, but Kylie's an attractive woman—"

"I was married, not dead," Lucas pointed out. "I'm a man, not a eunuch. I noticed."

Finn opened his mouth, probably to continue to plead his case as to why Lucas should have yet another round of guilt-producing sex, but thankfully Lucas's cell phone rang. Saved by the bell.

"Lucas Creed," he answered, dodging Finn's disapproving you-won't-get-off-that-easy gaze.

"It's Sheriff Knight. I've been working on those things we discussed, and we got lucky. Well, in one way. In another way, our luck just didn't hold out."

"Start with the good," Lucas requested. Maybe by then, he'd be in the right frame of mind to hear the bad. God. He really didn't need any more bad news.

"I called the detective in SAPD that you suggested, and he managed to locate a Tiffany Smith through her cell phone records."

If this were true, they had gotten more than just lucky. They'd gotten a huge break. "You're sure she's the right one? There's probably more than one person with that name in a city of over a million people."

"She's barely eighteen, a runaway. She recently had a

baby, and she used that same surrogacy clinic you mentioned that your friend had used. With that kind of bio, I'd say she's the right one. I managed to talk to her, briefly, on her cell phone. She wouldn't tell me where she was. Fact is, she sounded a little scared. But she did agree to a meeting with you, me or both. Tomorrow afternoon, four o'clock, at Mama's Pizzeria on Broadway. You know the place?"

"I'll find it," Lucas assured him. Because this was too important a meeting to pass up. Since he didn't figure he would get the truth from Isaac Dupont, maybe Tiffany Smith had info or even evidence that could link Dupont to illegal surrogacy.

And to the kidnapping attempt on Kylie.

If that attempt had been made to silence Kylie, then Dupont was at the top of his list of suspects. He was also at the top of the list of people who riled Lucas the most. He didn't intend to let Dupont or anyone else get away with what had happened to Kylie.

"I did a little checking into the surrogacy clinic itself," Sheriff Knight continued. "It's just a suggestion, but you might want to take a hard look at the clinic's director, Kendrick Windham."

Lucas knew the name. It'd come up in his preliminary research. "I planned to do that just as soon as I'm finished here."

He'd read back through Kylie's now infamous article after she'd gone to bed, and even though she hadn't actually mentioned Kendrick Windham, it's possible that Windham thought she was referring to him. Or maybe he thought she was alluding to his highly successful clinic.

Alluding.

There was that word again. Kylie was right. All that sidestepping might have gotten her into a lot of trouble. Now, it was his job to end the trouble so she could concentrate on a safe and healthy pregnancy.

"Are you ready for that bad news now?" Sheriff Knight asked.

At the same moment the sheriff said that, Kylie came out of the bathroom. Lucas listened to what his fellow police officer had to say, and at the end of the explanation, he concurred. It was bad news.

Now he had to figure out what to do about it.

"Is everything okay?" Kylie asked.

Lucas nodded. That nod, though, was a huge lie. Things were far from being okay, but he'd save that for later. First, he wanted to try to sort through the implications of what he'd learned and then try to come up with a solution or two.

If that were possible.

She'd changed out of the paper gown and back into her maternity jeans and a loose tropical blue sweater that was almost a perfect match for her eyes. She glanced at both Finn and him, as if she were trying to figure out what they'd discussed.

"I'm outta here," Finn announced. He snagged his jacket from the chair and headed for the door. "I'll let you know as soon as I get the results from the lab work. But I wouldn't worry. Everything looks good."

Kylie nodded and thanked him. However, as soon as Finn had made his exit, she turned her gaze on Lucas.

"I didn't ask about the baby's gender," Lucas volunteered, putting on his coat.

Shoot. She looked disappointed, as well. Lucas preempted that look by telling her what he'd just learned. "Sheriff Knight over in Gold Creek made some calls for me. He found Tiffany Smith."

"You're kidding." Kylie slipped on her own coat. "How?"

"We got some help from SAPD. They checked cell phone accounts. Anyway, Tiffany's agreed to meet with me tomorrow afternoon."

She cocked her head to the side, studied him. "If you managed to put all of this together, you didn't get any sleep last night, did you?"

"Not much." But then, she probably hadn't either. He opened the door to get her moving, and she fell into step beside him as they headed down a massive, glossy tiled hall. "I also want to do some checking on the clinic director."

"Kendrick Windham," Kylie provided. "I met him briefly. You?"

"Never saw him. I dealt only with the intake coordinator for the paperwork and the lab tech who processed my, uh, collection."

Sheesh. Why he'd nearly tripped over that word, he didn't know.

"You were lucky," Kylie concluded. "Windham apparently likes to meet all of his *girls* face-to-face. He's as slick as spit, if you ask me. He has Hannibal Lecter eyes. Come to think of it, he has a Lecter smile too. Seriously creepy. Definitely the kind of person you don't want to cross paths with unless you have no choice."

Great. Lucas had used a clinic with a slick-as-spit director. And because he'd used said clinic, that meant Kylie had used it, as well.

Nothing like a little extra guilt to bear.

"Okay, spill it. Is there something wrong with the baby?" Kylie demanded. Not only did she demand. She came to a complete stop just inside the exit.

"No. The baby's fine. You heard Finn say so."

Judging from her expression, she obviously wasn't convinced.

"Then what's wrong?" Her voice softened. "And please don't tell me all is well, because I know from your body language that it isn't."

He hadn't realized he'd been that obvious. Still, he hadn't intended to keep it a secret, especially since it involved her. Lucas drew in a long breath before he started. "I requested that SAPD provide protective custody for you. Sheriff Knight checked on it, but they told him they'd turned it down."

"Yes." She nodded. "The kidnapping attempt wasn't within their jurisdiction. And let me guess—they don't have the manpower or the funds to assist. Not until they officially open the case against Dupont." She pulled in a hard breath. "But not to worry. I can make other arrangements—"

"What other arrangements?" Lucas glanced at her and then out into the massive parking lot.

She obviously noticed that parking lot glance because she looked out the double glass doors, as well. She no doubt noted the parked vehicles just as he'd just done. Once a cop, always a cop.

"I can stay with my cousin in Houston," she suggested.

"Delmon," Lucas said. He knew him. Had grown up with him. And trusted him, for the most part. But there was a problem. "Don't know if you've spoken to him recently, but he seems to be out of town. I tried to call him this morning. Got his machine. I tried again while you were getting ready for the ultrasound. Still no answer."

Kylie shrugged. "All right. So, if I can't get in touch with Delmon, I'll hire a bodyguard."

That nonchalant shrug didn't fool him one bit. "You could do that, yes. It'd take time to find someone reliable. Days, maybe. And even then, you might learn the hard way that this employee isn't so good at stopping determined kidnappers."

Her shrug turned to a huff. "This isn't your problem, Lucas. You have enough to deal with already, and believe it or not, there are some things I can do for myself."

"Why did you tell me that you were my surrogate?" He didn't wait for her to answer. "Presumably, it wasn't because you wanted to make a get-it-off-your-chest confession. And I don't think it was part of chloroform haze, either. It's because you were scared. *Are* scared," he corrected.

Her chin came up, and he saw the fight brewing in her blue eyes.

Lucas cut her off at the pass. "You did the right thing by telling me. I know that. *Now.* If you hadn't, and if something had gone wrong, I never would have forgiven myself."

"Or me."

He couldn't argue with that. After all, he'd managed to hang on to his anger, hurt and blame for a long time. He was still holding on to it. But he couldn't let that get in the way now.

His child needed him.

"This isn't about forgiveness or blame," he insisted. "For better or worse, you're carrying my baby. And that baby is the most important thing. I won't let your pride or your fear get in the way of what has to be done. Because you see, Kylie, no one wants to protect this baby more than I do. *No one.* I'm willing to put my life on the line. You think a bodyguard for hire will do that?"

She blinked. "Kevin Costner did for Whitney Houston in that movie, *The Bodyguard.*"

His first reaction was frustration because she seemed to be trying to brush him off. But the frustration quickly passed when he looked at her. And then he remembered. When she had been his deputy, Kylie had always been the one to infuse a little humor into a bad situation. Even if that humor was a smoke screen to hide her own concerns.

"So, your answer is yes?" he asked. "You'll let me provide protection?"

"No."

He tried very hard not to groan, but gave up. "No?"

"No," she repeated. "Lucas, think this through. You can barely stand to be in the same room with me. Now you're saying we should stay together, under the same roof. *Indefinitely.*"

He really didn't like it all spelled out that way, but even the bare facts wouldn't make him back down. Not on this. "Temporarily," he added.

"*Temporarily* won't lessen the discomfort you'll feel when you have to face me every morning."

It wasn't exactly the facing that concerned him most. The danger was his first concern, but he couldn't dismiss this sizzling attraction, either.

A burst of winter wind came right at them when they stepped out of the building. Because they had a long walk through the massive parking lot, Lucas pulled the sides of his jacket tighter around him. It didn't help; the cold got through anyway. Ditto for the jeans. They weren't much of a barrier against the unusually bitter weather. He suddenly wished that he'd asked Kylie to wait inside while he brought his truck around to the front.

Kylie struggled with her own tan wool coat, but no matter how she shifted it, there wasn't enough fabric to cover her stomach. Lucas finally just reached out, hauled her against him and pulled her into the cover of his buckskin jacket.

"Thanks," she mumbled. Then, she started to hum. He couldn't help it. He smiled. He wanted to tell her that the closeness made him as uncomfortable as it was obviously making her, but it wasn't necessary. Kylie no doubt knew.

The cold and the moisture in the air had scabbed the

surface of the parking lot with thin patches of ice. It was a reminder that the drive back wouldn't be easy on several counts. Still, he'd gotten her to agree to the protective custody. Now, they just somehow had to survive it.

Kylie stopped and glanced over her shoulder. Lucas turned, as well, and spotted what had captured her attention. It wasn't difficult to spot—a dark blue SUV entering the parking lot.

There were at least two dozen cars in the parking lot, and not all were stationary. Two were driving slowly toward the exit. Another was in the process of parking. However, the SUV seemed to stick out.

Lucas glanced at his own truck. It was still a good twenty feet away. He considered latching onto Kylie and running toward it for cover. But Kylie probably wasn't in the best condition for a run, and besides, there was no indication that they needed cover.

Well, no indication except for that tightening feeling in his gut.

"Is everything okay?" Kylie asked. But it didn't sound nearly so much a question as it did a concern.

Without taking his attention off the approaching vehicle, Lucas stepped to her side. He didn't stop there. He positioned himself slightly in front of Kylie and eased his right hand over his gun.

Just in case.

The SUV came around the corner just ahead of them. The driver must have stomped on the accelerator because the vehicle lurched forward and swerved. Not in the opposite direction, either.

It charged right toward them.

Chapter 8

Kylie saw the vehicle and reacted.

But not as quickly as Lucas did.

Yelling for her to get down, he hooked his arm around her waist, and he shoved her out of the path of the oncoming vehicle. He twisted his body to take the brunt of the fall, and they landed on a narrow gravel easement just in front of a parked car.

It wasn't a second too soon.

The SUV sliced across the path where they'd just been standing. The vehicle clipped the shoulder of the parking lot and narrowly missed the car directly in front of them.

Fear slammed through her. God, what was happening? First, the kidnapping attempt, and now this. It couldn't be a coincidence.

Lucas drew his weapon, turned again and angled his body over hers, sheltering her. She cursed. So did he. This day had doled out enough without adding a near-death experience to it. And there was no mistake about it—they'd just come close to dying.

Kylie frantically dug through her purse, the one she'd picked up at her house earlier, and she pulled out her snub-nosed revolver as well. She didn't make a habit of carrying a concealed weapon, but after what had happened the night before, she'd wanted to bring the weapon with her.

Just in case.

Well, *just in case* had happened.

The SUV screeched to a halt, and Lucas dragged himself off the easement. Kylie tried to get up, as well, but he merely forced her back down.

"Stay put," he warned. "You can't put yourself in danger. Think of the baby."

Until he added that last part, she'd been ready to disagree. He was right. However, it sent her adrenaline and fear levels soaring. Finn had just given her a clean bill of health, and the baby was right back in danger again.

When was this going to stop?

Because she had no choice, Kylie did as Lucas said. But while taking cover behind the parked car, she repositioned herself so she could assist and return fire if necessary.

The SUV had come to a stop at the far end of the parking lot. She couldn't see anything behind the heavily tinted windows, but Kylie had no trouble hearing the driver of the vehicle hit the accelerator. The SUV lurched forward, and the back tires fishtailed on the icy surface of the parking lot. It sped away, leaving behind a cloud of exhaust.

That speedy exit got Lucas moving away from the meager shelter of the easement. He kept his Glock ready and aimed, and he darted out into the parking lot.

"Did you get the license plate numbers?" he called out to her.

"No. You?"

He cursed again. Obviously he hadn't seen the license plate, either. Like the other vehicle that had followed her from San Antonio, this one appeared to have mud or something on the plates.

Without taking his attention off the exit path, Lucas took out his cell phone and used his thumb to stab in some numbers. Probably to SAPD. But that might not do any good. They were outside city limits. Again, out of SAPD's jurisdiction. But this latest incident might be enough to get them to open the investigation into Isaac Dupont's alleged illegal activity.

However, the question was, would that help? Or would it make things worse? She didn't think Dupont was the sort of man merely to accept an investigation without causing some waves of his own.

And that made her furious.

Because Dupont, or whoever was doing this, was putting Lucas's child at risk.

With her heart banging in her chest, Kylie stood, and her gaze whipped across the parking lot, first to one end, then the other. She didn't stop there. She studied the rural highway that fronted the clinic. No sign of the SUV. It, and its lethal driver, had simply vanished.

"Let's go after the SOB," she insisted, already storming toward Lucas's truck. "I think he turned left when he headed out of the parking lot. That means he's driving east."

Lucas did some storming of his own, and he easily caught up with her. He grabbed her arm, not delicately, either, and gently but firmly pushed her to the side of another car.

"You're not going anywhere. At least not until the

police arrive. And even then, you're not going after that SUV, understand?"

She wanted to argue. Mercy, did she want to argue. Kylie wanted to lash out. To scream. "That driver could have killed us," she pointed out.

"Yeah. Believe me, I know. And that's the reason you're not going anywhere near him or her."

The anger and the frustration nearly got the best of her. She kicked not one rock but two. It didn't help. But that was a lot to ask of mere rock kicking.

"The cops should be here soon," Lucas told her. He got her moving back toward the clinic. "I want you to wait inside."

Inside. Where it was presumably safe.

Well, *safer* anyway. Maybe there was no place where the baby and she would be truly safe. A disturbing realization. One that hit her almost as hard as the fear, the adrenaline and the anger. And it made her understand just how little control she had in all of this. But she did have some control, and it was time for her to use it.

"I'll do it," she heard herself say.

Probably because he was surveying the parking lot and because he was thinking about that SUV, he tossed her a puzzled glance. "You'll do what?"

She said the words quickly, before she could do something stupid and change her mind. "Accept your offer of protective custody."

With his breath still gusting, he nodded. "Good."

Not exactly the word she would have used. More like *excruciating.*

"That SUV helped make up your mind, huh?" Lucas asked.

"That, and you pulled a Kevin Costner. You put your life on the line. For the baby," she quickly added.

He made a sound that could have meant anything. Kylie understood that ambivalence. On the one hand, staying with Lucas would make her feel safer. As safe as she could feel under the circumstances, anyway. But on the other hand, it would make her feel...

That was it.

The end of the sentence.

Staying with Lucas, being around him, would make her *feel*. And Kylie was positive neither of them would care for the outcome of that.

Lucas tightened the last screw that held the tiny security alarm to the living room window. He immediately tested the device, nodding at the shrill, piercing noise before he turned it off and activated it. Hopefully, it would be sufficient to alert them if anyone tried to break into the house through this particular window.

He grabbed his tool box and went down the hall to tackle the last room. Along the way, he stopped to check on Kylie, who was installing the same type of security devices on the windows in the guest room.

She obviously didn't see or hear him because while she worked, she danced to the beat of the music coming through the tiny green headphones of the portable CD player she had clipped to the waist of her pants. For a pregnant woman, she certainly had some agile, almost seductive moves. Like a belly dancer.

Okay.

So, maybe that belly dancer part was his imagination—which seemed to be active lately.

Since they'd returned from the clinic, she'd changed her clothes because the others had gotten dirty in the fall onto the easement. She now wore gray pants and an emerald green shirt. Not some formless baggy outfit, either. The clothes clung to her, including her pregnant belly. Which for some men might have been a turnoff.

For him, it had the opposite effect.

It was as if his body seemed to know that her stomach carried his own precious cargo. That in turn became some kind of weird aphrodisiac.

And that made him one sick puppy.

Perhaps sensing he was there, gawking at her, she glanced over her shoulder and stopped swaying. With a screwdriver still in her hand, she pulled off her headphones.

"Success. I think," Kylie volunteered. As he'd done, she tested the security alarm when she'd finished the installation, and the sound momentarily stabbed through the room. "Yep. It works."

Though she quickly turned off the alarm, she didn't take her attention away from the window. Lucas followed her gaze. It wasn't on the window itself, but rather outside.

"Anything wrong?" Alarmed, Lucas practically dropped the toolbox, drew his gun from his shoulder holster and hurried across the room.

"Finn just dropped off his two Dobermans," Kylie informed him.

Lucas confirmed that when he spotted Finn by the barn. And, yep, there were the Dobermans, complete with what appeared to be a sack with a month's worth of premium dog food and two equally premium stainless steel food bowls. Except these bowls were more the size of radial tires.

Lending his pets was a huge sacrifice for Finn, since Lucas knew his friend treated the two canines, Sherlock and Watson, like pampered children. It would be a sacrifice for the dogs, as well, because they'd be sleeping in the barn and not inside Finn's sprawling house on the edge of town.

"I can't believe you're doing this. You don't even like those dogs," Kylie pointed out.

It was true. They snarled and growled at him any time Lucas got within ten feet of them. But hopefully they'd react the same way if an intruder approached.

"It's temporary," Lucas explained, aware that he was using that word a lot lately. Kylie's protective custody was *temporary*. The security alarms on the windows were *temporary*. Now, he only hoped his lust for his houseguest fell into that same *temporary* category.

Finn waved and climbed back into his car. Lucas reholstered his Glock and went to retrieve his toolbox. One room to go, and then the house would be secured. Well, as secure as he could make it. Now, he had to hope that it was enough.

He opened the door to what he'd once called the "spare room," and he heard Kylie padding along behind him. Padding, because she'd removed her shoes and was now wearing a pair of thick gray socks. He debated whether he should just close the door and create some kind of diversion so she wouldn't see what was inside. But he debated too long.

"Oh," Kylie said, looking over his shoulder. "This is the nursery." She made the comment sound cheery enough, but it didn't fool him. Seeing this had to be difficult for her. A reminder of what would happen after she gave birth—when she would no longer be in the picture.

"You chose a good room," she continued. She brushed past him so she could enter. "It's right next to yours so you can hear the baby when he or she cries." She pointed to the shrub-like tree just outside the window. "That mountain laurel is beautiful when it blooms. All those fragrant purple flowers. The baby will love that."

Her gaze eased over the crib that was still in its box. Ditto for the changing table. The only functional piece of furniture was his grandmother's rocking chair. She ran her fingers over the chair arm and gave it a gentle push so that it rocked slightly.

"I can install this last security alarm myself," he told her. And to prove it, and so they could hurry up and get out of there, Lucas got to work on the window.

"You still have a lot to do in this room. To get it ready, I mean."

"Yeah." He almost left it at that, but he didn't want her to get the wrong idea—that he was dreading the preparations for the baby or that the preparations weren't a priority. They were. "The intake counselor at the clinic told me that, uh, it was best if I waited until closer to the delivery date."

In case something went wrong with the pregnancy. Ironic. Because a lot was going wrong.

She sank into the chair and began to rock. "You know I want to go with you tomorrow for that meeting with Tiffany Smith."

"I know. That doesn't mean it's going to happen." He figured Kylie wouldn't let things end there.

She didn't.

"Tiffany is my informant, Lucas."

It was a good argument, but it wouldn't work. "And you think this somehow negates the fact that you'd be in danger if you go to a meeting in a public place with an informant you're not even sure you can trust?" Satisfied that he'd delivered the best argument he could, and equally satisfied that he hadn't convinced Kylie—he turned on his electric screwdriver to secure the alarm in place.

She waited until the whirring noise of the screwdriver had stopped before she continued. "I think my presence at that meeting might encourage Tiffany to talk. After all, she didn't have any trouble chatting up a storm when we met at the surrogacy clinic. She might not be so willing to tell you things that she'd tell me."

Lucas gave her a flat look. "Nice try. Not gonna work, though."

Kylie returned that look. "We could bring one of the deputies or maybe Sheriff Knight with us. For extra protection. That way, I'd be safe."

"Sheriff Knight's going with me, since he's the one who made contact with Ms. Smith." Lucas engaged the alarm and stooped down to put the screwdriver back in the toolbox. "One of the deputies is staying here with you, while the other mans the office. See? Everything's taken care of, so there's no need for you to try to work things out."

The rocking stopped, and Kylie eased up from the chair. He could see the battle brewing in her eyes. "And at no point during your planning did you think to discuss this with me?"

Lucas tapped his chin and pretended to think about it. "No. Because I never had any intention of letting you go to that meeting."

"I'm a trained law enforcement officer," she quickly pointed out.

"You're pregnant."

That earned him a glare and a really loud huff. "Last I heard, pregnancy and PMS don't affect a woman's aim."

"Oh, no. You're not going to drag me into a male-female argument. This isn't about your gender. It's about your being more vulnerable." He turned, planning to make a hasty exit, but she caught onto his arm and pulled him back around.

Not the best idea she'd ever had. Lucas would bet the ranch on it.

Because lately, anytime they touched, sparks flew. Heck,

who was he kidding? Every time they breathed, they created not just sparks but flames.

"The sooner we get to the bottom of what's happening, the sooner this case will be closed, and the sooner I'll be less vulnerable," Kylie said. There was a slight quiver in her voice, proving his theory about sparks and flames. "And the sooner this case is closed, the sooner I can leave your protective custody."

She was right on the money. But for some reason, that last part didn't sit well with him. Maybe because he was no longer anxious for her to leave. Or maybe because he was aroused beyond belief just by being this close to her.

Or maybe it was because he was just an idiot.

"Our living arrangements are getting to you already?" he asked.

"Of course. And it's not a guess that it's getting to you, as well."

He saw her pulse on her neck pick up speed. Like her voice, it was practically trembling. Strange, because Kylie usually wasn't the trembling sort, and that little tremble fascinated him. He frowned, rethought that. Lately, everything about her fascinated him.

The part of his brain that was still functioning logically knew nothing good could come of this attraction. Nothing good other than great sex, anyway. Which suddenly felt much more important than the nothing-good-could-come-of-this part.

He changed his mind a couple of times about what to say. "You look…"

"Best not to finish that," she interrupted.

Yeah. But he finished it anyway. "Interested."

"Interested?" she repeated. "That's an *interesting* word."

Lucas pushed for an answer. "Are you?"

She made a vague motion toward the door, as if she were indicating that she was about to leave. But she didn't leave. Instead, she huffed, an indication that she didn't have any more willpower than he did. "I'm human."

It was an odd response. Well, odd if he hadn't seen the underlying response in her expression. Yes, she was human. So, was he. And Lucas had never been more aware of that than he was now.

She angled her head slightly. Studied him. Her hair shifted, sliding over her neck and the top of her shoulder. If she'd looked even a little bit frightened, he would have stepped back. But that wasn't an expression of fear.

It was something much more dangerous.

"You look…" But she didn't finish.

Lucas supplied the answer that was already on the tip of his tongue. "Interested?"

She shook her head and mumbled some profanity. "Hot. Really, really hot."

He almost laughed. And he tried to force his mouth to stay closed so he wouldn't say something stupid like, "Kiss me." Or, "Have sex with me." In fact, his mouth was suddenly thinking of all kinds of inappropriate suggestions.

"You look really, really hot to me, too," he confessed.

She stiffened a little, as if surprised. "Strange."

"Why?"

"Because it's not hot in here."

He lifted an eyebrow. "Oh yes, it is."

Her mouth quivered, threatening to smile. Lucas could feel his own mouth doing the same. But while this little mouth conflict and word war were somewhat amusing, the rest of him felt anything but amused.

He felt…ready.

And she obviously sensed that readiness. Her gaze eased

to his. Eye contact. And she held his gaze for several seconds before hers slid over his body.

"I think I might be trying to figure out what to do with you," she admitted.

The blood rushed to his head. And to other parts of him. "You *think?*"

"Okay. I *know* I'm trying to figure it out. Trust me, anything we figure out together right now would be a mistake," Kylie whispered, her voice laced with frustration. "You'd regret it. *I'd* regret it."

He couldn't disagree with any of that. In addition, Lucas thought of plenty of reasons why he should back away. The danger. The uncertainty. Their past.

None of those things stopped him.

Before he could talk himself out of it, Lucas reached out and did the very thing he'd believed he would never do. He curved his hand around the back of her neck and hauled Kylie to him. Against him. Pressed her breasts against his chest.

The battle continued.

She looked up at him. Moistened her lips. Probably not a come-on, but it had that effect on him. Of course, at this point anything except a no would have been a come-on.

Breath met breath. And he caught her scent. Something warm, inviting and feminine. It fired his blood and sent his body into a claim-and-possess mode. Even then, he could have stopped.

But he didn't.

Instead, he leaned in and braced himself. Lucas soon realized he couldn't possibly have braced himself enough.

He took her mouth as if he owned it. The taste of her exploded through him. It was a taste he hadn't even known he'd craved until now. And he was certain that one taste wouldn't be nearly enough. Oh, man.

Her touch didn't help things, either. She slid her fingers along his biceps. A sensual, slow caress. And that wasn't all. Moving, she brushed her hip against the front of his pants. Yep. There it was. The striking match. It revved his body up another notch—as if he needed any such enticement. Kylie alone was all the enticement he needed.

He roughly caught her hair with one hand, kept the other on the back of her neck and drew her tightly against him. Until he could feel every silky soft inch of her. Including her stomach.

His lips pressed hard against hers. Taking. Not a soft gentle kiss of comfort, either. There was no comfort in the sensual moves of their mouths. This was all white-hot heat, fueled by raw emotion.

He suddenly wanted more. A lot more. Kylie obviously did, too. She fell into the rhythm of the kiss. And into the rhythm of their bodies as they adjusted. Fighting to get closer. Needing each other in only a way that lovers could need each other.

She slid her leg along the outside of his. Lucas upped the ante. He locked onto the back of her knee and positioned it so that it hugged his hip. It brought the centers of their bodies into as much direct contact as they could have, given that she was pregnant. She was soft in every place that he was hard. And that made them the perfect fit.

Lucas moved against her as she moved against him. The kiss didn't stop. Nothing stopped. Except maybe his breath. But he didn't care if he ever drew breath again. Suddenly, this seemed to be everything he had ever wanted.

And that was exactly why it had to stop.

He repeated that. Twice. It still took every ounce of his willpower to do what he knew he had to do. He couldn't let this lead to sex. He just couldn't.

"There," he said forcing himself away from her.

"There," she repeated. She sounded as if she'd just completed a marathon. Fast breath. Equally fast pulse. And she had a wild, unfocused—and yes, aroused—look about her.

"Does that prove I'm human, too?" he asked.

"No." She pulled in several quick breaths. "It just proves we're both *interested*. And stupid."

Man, was she ever right. That interest was testing the limits of his jeans. And with the flames still burning through him, Lucas desperately wanted to reach out and pull her back into his arms. If he pushed it, just a little, it would lead to sex.

And even through the lust haze, he knew that would be a really bad idea.

Lucas forced himself to consider the consequences. They could dismiss a kiss, but sex was a whole different matter. Sex with Kylie would change everything. As it was, they had a thin, tenuous agreement: protective custody for the sake of the baby. Sex would rock that agreement to the core and confuse and distract them at a time when they needed no more confusion, no more distractions.

She turned away from him and focused her attention on the picture of the crib that was pasted on the front of the huge box. "This pregnancy really has my hormones going crazy."

Lucas considered that a moment. "That's what you think the kiss was about—pregnancy hormones?"

"Yes." But she didn't sound as if she believed it any more than he did. "That, and I've always been a little attracted to you."

He couldn't totally suppress that idiotic sound of surprise that escaped his mouth. "*You* were attracted to *me?*"

"Definitely."

"You're kidding."

"No. In fact, one summer when Marissa and I were fifteen or so, we watched Finn and you skinny-dip at Palmer's Creek."

Lucas shook his head. "You did what?"

"Yeah, well, I'm not exactly proud of it, but it's what estrogen and other raging hormones do to a young woman's body. Don't worry. I averted my eyes before I could get a glimpse of full frontal nudity." She shrugged. "But I did get a mental glimpse of full adolescent lust."

Still not understanding this, he leaned closer to make sure there was no humor in her eyes. There wasn't. "Lust for me?" he clarified.

"For you. But when I saw how Marissa reacted—I'm talking she had the serious hots for you—I told my body to look elsewhere."

It was as if he'd just been given a rewritten version of the history of his life. For one thing, he hadn't even known Marissa had been interested in him until well after high school. And he'd never noticed Kylie looking at him with anything other than friendly interest. And all of this new information made him wonder—what would he have done if he'd known? Would Kylie and he have somehow found their way to each other? The attraction was certainly there.

The phone rang, interrupting Lucas's unwanted trip down memory lane. Because there wasn't a phone in the nursery, he went back down the hall to the kitchen.

"Lucas Creed," he answered.

"Sgt. Katelyn O'Malley, SAPD."

Lucas didn't recognize the caller, but he did recognize that tone. A cop's tone for official business. Any levity and lust he was feeling evaporated.

"Are you the officer investigating the incident in the birthing center parking lot?" Lucas asked.

"Not exactly. But I think our cases might overlap. I spoke to the detective that you and Sheriff Knight have been dealing with. I understand you're to meet with Tiffany Smith tomorrow afternoon?"

"That's the plan."

"Well, I think you'll have to change your plans. Ms. Smith was brought into the E.R. at Southeast Hospital about an hour ago."

Hell. "What happened?"

"Car accident. Or maybe not an accident. We're waiting on the tox results and some other tests. Looks like there's forced trauma. This might even have been an attempted homicide."

Why hadn't he seen this coming? *Why?* The moment Sheriff Knight had located the young woman, they should have somehow made her tell them where she was so they could provide her with protection.

"Tiffany Smith is in and out of consciousness, but she's asking to speak to you, Sheriff Creed. And she also wants to see someone I believe you know—Kylie Monroe."

That last request didn't do much to steady Lucas's nerves. Oh, man. What was going on?

"Ms. Smith says it's critical that she see you and Ms. Monroe immediately. A life-and-death matter, she says," Sgt. O'Malley continued. "My advice? Get here soon, because it's life-and-death for her, too. The doctors aren't sure she'll last through the night."

Chapter 9

Kylie listened as Lucas finished his phone call. It was the third he'd made since they'd started the forty-five minute drive from the ranch to the Southeast Hospital in San Antonio. The first call had been to his deputy, Will Trapani, who, judging from the one side of the conversation that she had overheard, was still sick with the flu, suffering from chills, fever and other assorted cruddy symptoms.

Will's description of his ailments had created some get-well, sympathetic remarks from Lucas, but he'd cursed when he'd hung up. Obviously, he'd counted on having the deputy as backup. He couldn't very well call out his other deputy, Mark Jensen, because that would essentially leave Fall Creek without any police protection.

Will's flu bug had precipitated a second call to Sheriff Knight, who apparently was planning to meet Lucas and her at the hospital. That was a security measure that Kylie understood because, after all, Knight was a lawman. What she didn't understand was Lucas's third call. To Finn. Lucas asked him to go to the hospital, as well.

"Please don't tell me you expect Finn to be able to return fire if we get into a situation while we're visiting Tiffany Smith?" she asked.

"I'd rather arm his Dobermans. I've seen Finn shoot, or rather attempt to shoot, and it wasn't a pretty sight." Lucas slipped his phone back into his pocket. "If there's medical red tape, I want Finn to cut through it for us. I don't want you in that hospital any longer than necessary."

The concern for her safety was loud and clear. And Kylie greatly appreciated it, too. It wasn't a question of bravery but rather one of survival. If she got hurt, or worse, so would the baby.

But she had to wonder if Lucas's concern had increased because of that hot kissing session?

Kylie wanted to dismiss what'd happened. Mainly, because it was easier to dismiss it than to try to figure out the consequences.

And there would be consequences.

No doubt about it. Lucas was probably already feeling massive amounts of remorse. Ditto for her. In her mind, he was still Marissa's husband. Except she darn sure hadn't been thinking about Marissa when she had been kissing him.

That didn't lessen the guilt.

In fact, it made it worse.

It was scary that something like physical attraction could temporarily cause them to push aside all those barriers that they'd spent three years erecting. Part of her wanted those barriers back. It was safer that way. But she couldn't deny that Lucas's kisses had awakened feelings inside her that she thought she would never have. Not for him. Not for any man.

Kylie pondered that a moment.

And since it seemed too overwhelming and totally un-solvable, she decided to continue to blame it on the pregnancy hormones. Those little suckers had gotten a lot of playing time lately, and she would continue to give them a little more.

"I should have insisted Tiffany Smith go into protective custody," Lucas mumbled.

It wasn't his first such mumbling, either. It was the fourth time he'd said something similar since he'd gotten the call from Sgt. O'Malley at SAPD.

"My guess is Tiffany wouldn't have told you where she was," Kylie informed him. "After what she's been through, I doubt she's the trusting type."

"I should have pressed her to tell me."

"And the pressing would have sent her straight into hiding. You said Sheriff Knight thought she sounded afraid. Well, there you go. She wouldn't have simply put her safety into the hands of strangers."

Apparently her attempt at reassurance meant nothing because Lucas only grumbled again. Kylie totally understood. Yet another form of guilt, but guilt all the same. It was becoming her forte. She didn't need to tell him that it would be a while, maybe forever, before the guilt would go away.

"Stay right next to me," Lucas instructed as he stopped his truck in the parking lot of the hospital. "And don't make me regret bringing you along."

As if he'd had a choice about that. Tiffany had apparently made it clear to Sgt. O'Malley that she wanted to speak to both Lucas and her. Kylie could only hope the young woman had information that would stop the kidnappers from coming after her again. Of course, Tiffany could have paid a very high price for simply having that information.

This might even have been an attempted homicide. Lucas had told her that's what Sgt. O'Malley had relayed to him.

Kylie hated to jump to conclusions because this could have been a botched carjacking or even a bad case of road rage. She prayed that's all there was to it. While she was at it, she added a prayer for the young woman. Tiffany didn't deserve this.

They entered through the emergency room, and after Lucas spoke briefly with the nurse at the check-in desk, they were directed to a tall, brunette doctor who was in the nearby hallway. Kylie glanced around and didn't see either Finn or Sheriff Knight. She also adjusted her purse, in case she needed to get her weapon in a hurry. The hospital appeared safe enough, but she wasn't about to risk their lives on that appearance.

When they approached the doctor, Lucas pulled back his jacket so she could see the badge clipped to his belt. "I'm Sheriff Lucas Creed. This is Kylie Monroe. We're here to see Tiffany Smith."

The doctor wore a nametag that identified her as Shelby Morgan, M.D. She motioned for them to follow her deeper into the hallway so they weren't right next to the other E.R. patients. "I'm sorry, but you might have made this trip for nothing. Ms. Smith isn't allowed visitors. She lapsed into a coma about fifteen minutes ago."

Kylie's heart sank. Mercy, it was awful news. "Do you think she'll regain consciousness soon?"

"Hard to say. She has some frontal lobe damage, along with some internal injuries from the accident. It also appears she recently had a difficult childbirth. She has some untreated complications from a botched episiotomy, among other things. She has an infection, a serious one, and that'll only impede her recovery. *If* there is a recovery."

Kylie's heart sank even further, and any glimmer of hope sank right along with it. "You don't expect her to make it?" she asked.

The doctor shook her head. "The prognosis isn't good. We're trying to locate her family now, but she didn't give us much information to go on."

"Tell me about this car accident," Lucas insisted. The emotion had cooled his voice, but Kylie knew that coolness wasn't indicative of the frustration, concern and even the anger he was feeling. "What happened?"

"The other sheriff already asked me that."

"Sheriff Knight?" Kylie questioned.

"Yes. He arrived just as Ms. Smith went into the coma. He's outside her hospital room. Standing guard, along with the other officer from SAPD." She paused, studied them with weary eyes. "I suppose the security's necessary?"

"Could be," Lucas answered. "It'd help to know what happened to cause the accident."

"We don't know much. According to the officer who brought her in, it appears that Ms. Smith was driving in her vehicle when she was run off the road. Her car nose-dived into the Basse Street basin. Ms. Smith couldn't or wouldn't say much, but she did tell us…" The doctor looked down at the sheet of notebook paper she held in her hand. "I'm more or less quoting here, 'I shouldn't have talked to Kylie Monroe. It's all a terrible mistake.'"

Because she needed it, Kylie leaned against the wall. "Someone wanted to silence her before she could say anything else to us."

"That terrible mistake part could refer to the car accident," Lucas pointed out.

Or maybe Tiffany had meant her conversation at the surrogacy clinic. Had she told someone about that conversation? Or had someone forced her to tell them after the article Kylie had written had been published?

Either way, they were back to square one.

No doubt that article had probably put Tiffany in the hospital. In the end, it might cost the young woman her life.

"I'll check on Ms. Smith's tox screens," Dr. Morgan informed them, heading down the hall toward the elevator. "I'll let you know what I find out. Oh, and I'll tell Sheriff Knight that you're here."

"Hell," Lucas said under his breath when the doctor walked away.

Kylie totally agreed with the sentiment. Tiffany's life was hanging by a thread, and there was nothing they could do about it. Worse, they didn't seem to be any closer to identifying the culprit.

"This is all my fault," Lucas grumbled. "It shouldn't have happened."

"Funny, I was thinking the same thing. That article—"

"I'm the one who didn't provide a potential informant with adequate protection. That's standard law enforcement procedure, and I blew it."

"Tiffany wouldn't have needed protection if I hadn't written that article."

He stared at her. "Are we vying for some blame championship?"

"No." Kylie blew out a long breath. "I think we're tied for that honor."

Kylie automatically reached out to him. Touched his arm with her fingertips and rubbed lightly. Subconsciously she'd probably meant it to be a comforting gesture, but it suddenly seemed too intimate.

She expected Lucas to back away, both mentally and physically. She also expected herself to back away.

But they stayed put.

Not only that, he reached and caught her shoulders. He looked straight into her eyes. "I'm not going to let them hurt this baby, understand? I'll do everything within my power to protect you."

It was a convincing promise. And it didn't seem to matter that he had no way to back it up. Kylie believed him. Maybe because she *wanted* to believe him.

She groaned softly, and she was the one to back away. Until all of this had started, she'd managed to suppress her feelings for the baby. Oh, not totally. But she'd certainly been able to make it through an hour or two not thinking about all the things she'd miss by cutting herself out of the baby's life.

Lucas's adamant, heartfelt promise melted away all that suppression.

"We should have never kissed," she told him. "It was a mistake, and it changed things that shouldn't have been changed."

He shook his head. "It didn't feel like a mistake."

"That's why it was one." She groaned. "Lucas, it's going to be hard enough for me to give up this baby. I can't—"

Kylie stopped herself, before she could say something they'd both regret. And they would regret it. Because if she were to fall hard for Lucas, then leaving both him and the baby would be next to impossible.

She *had* to leave.

Though Lucas had kissed her, held her and had just sworn to protect her at all costs, he couldn't give himself to her. And she couldn't try to make a relationship work when she knew in her heart that such a relationship would only cause him more pain.

He rolled his shoulders as if trying to work out the fatigue and frustration. "I don't want to feel this way. But I can't help myself."

Kylie nodded. "I understand. Because when you see me, you'll always think about Marissa."

His gaze came to hers. "That's the problem, Kylie. When I see you now, I see *you.* The mother of my child. A woman. And it's tearing me apart inside."

Kylie's mouth dropped open. "Are you saying—"

"I'm saying that I can't," he interrupted. With that, he walked a few steps away.

She understood that, as well. It encompassed a lot. Their past. Their present.

And, no doubt, their future, too.

"I need to concentrate on the case," she heard him say. "I can't let my personal feelings get in the way here. It'll only cause me to lose focus. And if I lose focus, the baby could be hurt."

"All right," she said tentatively.

Not because she disagreed. She didn't. But the problem was how to make themselves focus when they were going through an emotional upheaval. However, Lucas soon proved he hadn't just made the comment off the cuff. He truly intended to take action.

When he pulled his phone from his pocket, she walked closer until they were side by side. "Who are you calling?" Kylie asked, alarmed.

"SAPD. I want to make sure they keep a guard posted outside Tiffany's door. Then, I'm calling directory assistance—so I can get the number for Kendrick Windham, the director of the surrogacy clinic. I want to speak to him."

Kylie hadn't seen that last one coming. It seemed an almost desperate act. Of course, they were desperate. Lives on the line and all of that. "You think talking to Windham will actually do any good?"

"Probably not. But I want to hear his reaction when he learns that Tiffany Smith is in the hospital. And that she's still alive."

"Alive, *barely*," Kylie pointed out. "And in a coma with a serious infection."

"But Windham doesn't know that."

Kylie considered that, and didn't like where her consideration took her. "A game of cat and mouse," she mumbled as Lucas made the calls.

When she had been in law enforcement, she'd played a few of those games herself, but she had to wonder who the mouse was in this situation. Did Windham even have a part in any of this? It was a question she couldn't answer. Especially since her mind kept going back to Cordelia and the hatred she'd seen in the woman's eyes. If Cordelia had somehow found out about the secret surrogacy, then maybe she would have been desperate enough to stop it.

But that seemed a stretch, even for Cordelia.

"Windham didn't answer," Lucas explained, walking back toward her. "I left a message with his answering service."

Kylie didn't like the sound of that. "Dare I ask what you said in that message?"

"I simply told him what had happened and that I wanted answers about Tiffany Smith."

Well, that would certainly stir up a hornets' nest. Because even if Windham hadn't had anything to do with Tiffany's accident, he still had to address the questions of why he'd used an underage surrogate. And why she'd obviously received such shoddy medical care during and after delivery.

"I understand you're accusing me of a felony or two," she heard someone say.

She turned toward the man's voice. So did Lucas. She saw an imposing, dark-haired man making a beeline toward them. He was about six feet tall and wearing perfectly tailored khakis, a cream-colored pullover sweater and an expensive calf-length black cashmere coat. An eraser-size icy diamond winked in his left earlobe.

His stride was confident. Cocky, even. The stride, posture and attire of a man who was accustomed to getting everything he wanted.

"Now, would you care to make those accusations to my face?" he asked. He didn't ask it in a friendly sort of way, either. "Oh, in case you don't recognize me, I'm the lawyer you've been maligning—Isaac Dupont."

Well, this afternoon was just full of surprises.

Bad ones.

Lucas figured the man walking toward them would top the list of bad surprises.

"Sheriff Creed, I presume," Isaac Dupont said.

Since it wasn't exactly a question, Lucas didn't answer. But he did glare. He couldn't help himself. He disliked the man on sight. However, he had to admit his judgment might be clouded by the kidnapping attempt, the godawful experience in the parking lot of the birthing center and Tiffany Smith's "car accident." It was difficult to think highly of a man who might have been responsible for all those things.

Lucas stepped in front of Kylie and hoped like the devil that she stayed put so he could give her some shred of protection.

"I'll make those accusations," Lucas volunteered. "I'll add a few more if you'd like. And I have no problem doing that to your face."

Kylie tapped him on the shoulder and shot him a warning glance.

Which he ignored.

"What are you doing here?" Lucas asked Dupont.

"I heard the infamous journalist, Kylie Monroe, was in the building." It sounded as if he'd rehearsed his answer, or at least had given it plenty of thought. "I decided I'd pay her a little visit."

"Heard?" Lucas questioned.

Dupont bobbed his head. "Yes. It's a past tense verb. But I don't suppose a cowboy-cop like you from Hickville would recognize a grammatical part of speech when you hear it."

"You'd be surprised at what I know." Lucas leaned in, violating his personal space. "And I don't have any trouble recognizing a smart-ass suspect who's trying to avoid answering a simple question. In my experience, the main reason suspects do that is because they're guilty."

"So, now I'm a suspect?" If that bothered him in the least, Dupont didn't show it.

"Puh-leeeze," Kylie interjected. "You didn't know we were suspicious of you? Then, you're either an idiot or a liar. Maybe both."

Lucas looked at Kylie and made sure he put a little bad-ass spin on it. He wanted answers from Dupont, but he didn't want Kylie's antagonism to rile the man to the point of attempted murder. She must have gotten the point, finally, because she stepped back.

One battle down.

Another to go.

"Why are you really here?" Lucas demanded of Dupont.

"As I said, I came for a little visit. And a little warning. You can write your tabloid trash stories all you want, Ms. Monroe, but leave me out of them. I'm a respected attorney in this city, and I won't have my name dragged through your own personal version of mud."

Lucas shrugged. "She never mentioned your name. Guilty conscience, perhaps?"

Dupont met him eye to eye. "Let's just say I'm intuitive."

"Or maybe you're just paranoid," Lucas offered. "I hear there are medications for that."

Oh. There it was. A flash of anger that went bone-deep. The cool facade stayed in place, for the most part, but Dupont couldn't quite keep the emotion out of his gray-blue eyes.

"Why don't you explain what part you played in providing surrogates to Kendrick Windham's clinic?" Lucas demanded. "I'm especially interested in those who are underage and medically unqualified."

"I don't have to answer that. I don't even have to be polite to you." To Lucas, that sounded very much like a threat. "You have no jurisdiction here, cowboy."

"No," Lucas enunciated the single word carefully while trying to put a choke hold on his temper. While he was at it, he caught Kylie's arm and moved her back even farther away from Dupont.

It didn't stop her.

"But FYI, Sheriff Creed does have lots of friends in SAPD," Kylie pointed out. "Oh, and he also has a loaded .40-caliber Glock in the shoulder holster beneath his left arm."

Amused, or least trying to appear amused, Dupont flexed his eyebrows. "Am I being charged with something?"

"Maybe loitering," Lucas suggested. "Threatening a police officer? Being a general nuisance?"

"You could never make those charges stick."

"No. But it could land you in lockup for a few hours while SAPD takes their time processing the paperwork."

Dupont exaggerated a noisy yawn. "Bored now. Good afternoon, Sheriff Creed, Ms. Monroe. I trust this isn't the end of our *dispute*. I'll be in touch. But remember what I said—keep my name and any reference to me out of your so-called articles."

He turned, and it was then that Lucas saw the other person approaching them. Not Dr. Morgan. The guy was dressed in drab gray sweats, a hoodie and running shoes. His salt-and-pepper hair was damp, as if he'd just finished a workout.

And he wasn't alone.

He was walking side by side with Finn.

Lucas automatically drew his weapon, holding it close to his thigh so that it wouldn't be so conspicuous to the patients and staff but so he could use it if required.

"Well, well. The gang's all here," Dupont said, stopping. He looked back at Lucas and grinned from ear to ear—especially when he noticed the unholstered Glock. "In case you don't recognize your latest visitor, that's—"

"Kendrick Windham," Kylie supplied. Because her arm was against his, Lucas felt her muscles tighten.

"I finally made it here," Finn announced. "And I ran into an old acquaintance in the parking lot."

"You know each other?" Lucas asked.

"We attended the same conference a few years ago." Finn looked at her. "What's going on?"

"It's a long story."

"I don't have time for long stories," Windham interjected. "My answering service called, said you left a message. Something about a former client who's been hospitalized?"

Unlike Dupont, Windham's comment didn't seem threatening. In fact, nothing about him seemed threatening.

Well, except those eyes.

"Why don't you test the waters with him, Sheriff Creed?" Dupont suggested, adding a tsk-tsk. "An experiment of sorts. Accuse Kendrick Windham of a felony or two." Dupont paused for a heartbeat and aimed another of those oily grins at Kylie, then at Lucas. "He's not a forgiving kind of man, the way I am. It'd be interesting to see just how fast he kills you."

Chapter 10

Kylie had met Kendrick Windham for a few short moments nearly six months ago, but it'd been more than enough for her to form an unfavourable opinion of him. That opinion didn't change as he stood in front of Lucas and her, seemingly sizing them up just as they were him.

"See you later," Dupont said, still smiling. Not exactly subtle like Windham. Dupont simply didn't seem to care if anyone thought he was guilty of a crime. Probably because of his old money and business connections, he thought he was above the law. Maybe Lucas and she could use that arrogance to nail the guy.

Well, if Dupont was guilty, that is.

Suspect number two, Kendrick Windham, had just as much motive to silence her as Dupont had. Maybe more. Because, after all, she could directly link him to the clinic and to Tiffany Smith.

"How is Ms. Smith?" Windham asked.

"Alive," Lucas answered, reholstering his Glock.

Kylie watched Windham's expression. If he was afraid that Tiffany might rat him out for illegal surrogacy or even kidnapping and attempted murder, he wasn't showing it. Yep. Definitely slick. It made her think of pathological liars, serial killers and other unsavory sorts. Someone with that kind of personality could definitely try to kill anyone who threatened to expose his dirty dealings. And that's exactly what she'd done in a roundabout way with that article.

"Let me do some checking," Finn volunteered. "I'll see if I can find out how Ms. Smith is doing."

The moment Finn stepped away, Windham checked the budget-draining gold watch that glimmered on his left wrist. "I can't stay long. Appointments. And I obviously have to shower and change. I just popped by on my way home from the gym so I could wish Ms. Smith a speedy recovery."

"She's not allowed visitors," Kylie informed him.

"Too bad. I might be able to cheer her up. The few times I saw her, we got along quite well."

"Did you now?" Lucas asked skeptically.

Windham spared Lucas an inquisitive glance. "We got along well in the sense of a clinic director and a client. Definitely nothing to cross ethical boundaries. And certainly nothing personal." Another check of his watch. "When she's allowed visitors, perhaps you can give me a call. I'd like to let her know that I'm here for her."

His inflection didn't change, but that sent a chill snaking down Kylie's spine. If Tiffany did regain consciousness, there was no way Kylie would deliver what could easily be a veiled threat. In fact, Lucas and she would make sure SAPD had Tiffany's room well guarded.

"If you really want to help Tiffany, you could always

offer to pay her medical bills," Lucas suggested. "I'm sure she doesn't have insurance, and her injuries have been complicated by an infection from poor medical care during her delivery."

"I'm afraid that's out of the question, especially since her injuries resulted from a car accident. I phoned the hospital on the way over, asked a doctor friend who works here to give me an update on Ms. Smith's condition," he said in response to Kylie's suspicious look. "Imagine if I reimbursed all or even a few of my clients for services not directly related to their surrogacy agreements. I'd be bankrupt. I'm not in business to go bankrupt."

"And the bottom line for you is money?" Kylie asked.

"Of course." He drew in an impatient breath and tossed a glance Lucas's way. "Phone me if her condition changes. You obviously know the number."

With that, Kendrick Windham turned and briskly walked away.

"What was the heck was that visit all about?" Kylie mumbled.

"Marking his territory, I'd say." Lucas paused. "You think Dupont and he orchestrated this tag team visit, or was it coincidence they showed up here at the hospital at almost the same time?"

"Well, you don't believe in coincidences, so I know where you stand on the issue. Still, I'm not so sure what's going on with those two."

And that bugged her. A lot. Had they indeed arranged the simultaneous visits, or had someone else alerted both of them? After all, she hadn't gotten a good look at either kidnapper. Neither Windham nor Dupont matched the sketchy physical descriptions of the would-be kidnappers, but maybe one or both of the suspects were here at the hospital. Watching Tiffany to make sure she didn't say anything incriminating.

That theory sent her gaze rifling around the nearby waiting room and the curtained examination stations. She studied each person, letting her anxiety nearly get the best of her. She pulled back and tried to see the hospital through normal eyes. Everything seemed, well, normal.

But that didn't mean it was.

"Sheriff Knight won't let anyone into Tiffany's room who doesn't belong there," Lucas said.

Her gaze came back to his, and she saw that he was examining her with those cop's eyes. Not that she was difficult to read. Especially not for him. Lucas seemed to be very good at knowing her every emotion.

"So, which one do you suspect?" Lucas asked. "Dupont or Windham?"

"Both," she answered honestly. "But I don't think they're partners."

He made a sound of agreement. "Neither of them are partner material. Too self-obsessed. But I'm willing to bet either could really be into criminal intent—especially when there's money to be made."

Yes. But which one? Kylie hoped they learned that before the kidnappers decided to strike again.

Finn rounded the corner of the hall, fast. Before he could reach them, Kylie knew from his dour expression that something was wrong.

"What happened?" Kylie asked, dreading his answer.

"Tiffany Smith regained consciousness—"

"I need to see her," Lucas insisted.

When Lucas started to walk away, Finn caught his arm. "She was only awake a few seconds before she went into cardiac arrest."

The news sucked the breath from Kylie's lungs. She dropped back, leaning against Lucas, allowing him to support her. "She's dead?" Kylie mumbled.

"Yes. Dr. Morgan did everything she could to save her," Finn added solemnly. "But Ms. Smith's injuries were just too severe for her to survive."

Lucas cursed, scrubbed his hands over his face and cursed some more. He pounded his fist against the wall. Kylie pulled him back before he could hurt himself.

"Mind filling me in as to what this Attila the Hun reaction is all about?" Finn asked. "Because you didn't tell me much when you called and asked me to come to the hospital."

Kylie tried to answer and realized she needed breath to do that. Hers hadn't fully returned yet.

Lucas didn't answer right away either, though he seemed to be breathing. Angry, rough gusts of air came from his mouth. "Tiffany Smith was a surrogate at the same clinic that Kylie used. Kendrick Windham's clinic. Tiffany might have had information about those men who tried to kidnap Kylie."

"Wait a minute!" Finn's eyes widened, and he snapped his fingers. "She said something right before she died."

"What?" Kylie and Lucas asked in unison.

"I didn't hear. But I'm pretty sure Dr. Morgan did."

Lucas broke away from Kylie and Finn's grip and practically sprinted down the hall.

Kylie was right behind him.

Chapter 11

Lucas didn't think he'd ever felt more exhausted, confused...or frustrated. Tiffany's words kept replaying in his head. It had been relentless for nearly half an hour now, during the entire drive back to the ranch, and it just wouldn't quit.

One word at a time.

Like jabs from a switchblade.

They probably had that effect on him because they weren't just words. But a warning. Tiffany had apparently used her dying breath to make sure she didn't take that warning to the grave.

They'll do whatever it takes to stop Kylie Monroe and Sheriff Creed.

Too bad Tiffany hadn't identified who *they* were. Perhaps because she didn't know. Maybe she, too, had been threatened by the two ski-mask-wearing kidnappers. Maybe she'd eluded them, temporarily, only to have them run her off the road and into that basin.

They'll do whatever it takes...

Lucas hadn't exactly needed Tiffany's warning to tell him that. But it had been chilling to hear the doctor recount it verbatim. Because before Tiffany's deathbed warning, he'd been able to hope that the men had merely wanted to kidnap Kylie. Of course, that in itself was a serious enough crime. Serious, but not necessarily fatal. But if Tiffany was right, the stakes were much higher now.

Life and death.

The slight popping sound drew Lucas out of his mental word war, and he glanced at Kylie. Seated next to him, one foot tucked beneath her, she'd just blown a bubble from her strawberry-scented chewing gum. That cheery scent had permeated the entire cab of the truck. And Lucas actually welcomed it.

Actually, he welcomed *her* company.

As bad as all of this was, it felt good to have someone to share it with. Even if he would have given his right arm to make sure Kylie and the baby stayed safe.

He didn't understand this change of heart he'd had toward her. And he didn't want to question it either. Maybe the bone-weary fatigue was part of that. Lucas didn't want to question that, either. He simply wanted to accept this truce, temporary or not, between them.

Of course, there was the other thing that had settled between them. And it wasn't peaceful. It was fiery, turbulent and wrong. Yet, he didn't think he had a snowball's chance in hell of fighting it.

For whatever reason, his body had decided that it wanted Kylie. And his brain was going right along with that decision.

"They killed Tiffany because she learned something," Kylie said. Another bubble. Another soft pop. "Or maybe she knew nothing, but they thought she did."

Lucas had already gone down that road, and it led him to yet more guilt and frustration. If the kidnappers had somehow heard about Tiffany's plans to meet with Sheriff Knight and him, then that alone might have given the SOBs motive to kill her. It also might have given them a motive to kill Kylie and him, as well. Perhaps even Sheriff Knight, who would surely be watching his back.

"This isn't your fault," Lucas said, because he knew what Kylie was thinking.

"It is. Let's face it. I should wear some kind of warning sign around my neck so people won't get too close. I'm one of those crud magnets."

"No. You're a journalist, apparently a very good one, who wrote an article that hit some nerves."

"And got a woman killed."

"Don't go there, Kylie. You were a cop long enough to know that sometimes bad things just happen."

She glanced at him, as if she were trying to look into his heart.

Were they talking about Marissa now or Tiffany?

Lucas wasn't sure of the answer. But he was certain that all this stress and worry couldn't be good for Kylie or the baby.

She shook her head. "But something about what happened to Tiffany doesn't feel right," Kylie added. "You know what I mean?"

He was with her on that point, as well. Something just didn't fit, but Lucas couldn't quite put his finger on what that was. But then, lately a lot of things hadn't fit.

"A car accident's risky," Kylie continued. It didn't surprise Lucas that she was voicing the same concerns that were inside his head. Kylie and he had always worked well together as sheriff and deputy. "Why not just wait until she got to her destination to kill her? It didn't appear that she was driving in the direction of police headquarters. More in the direction of the interstate.

"If they'd waited until she was somewhere more private, they could have made sure she was dead. Left no loose ends. Perhaps even made it look like a real accident. After all, she was sick. How hard would it have been to incapacitate a sick woman?"

Both stayed quiet a moment. Thinking. Trying to make the pieces of the puzzle fit.

"So, where does that take us?" she asked. "This was perhaps a crime of opportunity? Maybe not even connected to the illegal surrogacy activity? In fact, this could have been some kind of grandstanding fiasco meant to make Dupont or Windham look very guilty."

He thought of Cordelia.

Lucas figured Kylie did, too.

And then he immediately thought of Kylie.

It was as if he had attention deficit disorder. Too many thoughts. Too many distractions. Too little focus. Or better yet—the wrong kind of focus. Yeah. There was definitely nothing semipeaceful about this whirlwind that had taken over his brain.

There was only one thing that should be on his mind: catching the kidnappers and their boss so he could ensure Kylie's safety. That was it. Nothing more.

But, of course, knowing that didn't make it so.

So many feelings were going through him. All the unresolved pain from Marissa's death. The need to protect Kylie. Her scent. Yes, her scent—not the bubble gum, either—but something warm and inviting. The way she moved. The way she looked at him. This was definitely a male-female thing, and it was gaining momentum at an alarming speed. After all, even Tiffany Smith's death couldn't cool him down.

"You must be exhausted," he said, almost hoping that was true. "When we can get back to the ranch, I'll fix you something to eat, and then you can turn in early for the night."

She slid her hand over her stomach and rubbed in wide, gentle circles. "I don't think food will sit well with little Lucas here. Not to worry. Nothing serious. Just some indigestion."

That drew his attention to her belly, and he thought of a way he could take her mind off things. "You never did ask why I didn't have Finn 'fess up about the baby's gender."

"Yeah. Why didn't you?"

"It probably seems weird, but I wanted to keep it a surprise. At least for a little while longer, until things settle down."

She paused, nodded. "I understand that."

There. He saw it. Some of the tension drained from her eyes. Her stomach massage slowed. Her shoulders relaxed just a bit. It was enough encouragement for Lucas to continue.

"Can you imagine me being a father?" he asked.

"Of course." She said it as if jumping to his defense. "You'll be great. And I know you've always wanted kids."

That put a lump in his throat. But he pushed it and the thoughts of Marissa and their unborn child aside. There was nothing he could do to help them now, but he sure as heck could help Kylie and this baby.

"I've heard diapering can be tricky. I've signed up for a class," he shared with her.

"A class?" Her tongue went in her cheek. "Oh, to be a

fly on the wall. The rough and rugged cowboy tackles a newborn and Huggies."

"There's a feeding and burping class, too."

Her lips quivered. "You're making that up."

"Scout's honor."

"You were never a Scout." She stared at him. "You smiled," she added.

"Did I?" But he was fully aware that he had. It seemed odd, as if it'd been so long since he'd given those particular facial muscles a workout that they actually felt stiff.

"There's hope for you yet, Lucas Creed."

He didn't know exactly what she was doing, but it was working. Here he'd been trying to cheer her up, but she was doing the same thing. Kylie was taking the weight of the world off his shoulders. And right now, there was an awful lot of weight on him.

He hadn't discussed his cases with Marissa. Though there'd been only a few serious crimes in Fall Creek, there had been a death resulting from a domestic dispute and several fatalities from car accidents. Early in their marriage, he'd brought up a detail or two of a case, but it had bothered Marissa to the point of giving her nightmares. He'd learned to leave his badge at the office.

Out of the corner of his eye, he watched as Kylie blew another bubble and then used her tongue to gather the pink gum back into her mouth. Despite the seriousness of their conversation, that caused him to do a double take. For such a simple, mundane thing, it seemed awfully erotic. It caused the blood to rush to his head. And to other parts of him.

Ah, sheesh.

Not this, not now.

She was exhausted. Had indigestion. Was just coming

down from a terrible ordeal. He needed to think with his brain and not the brainless part of him below the waist.

"You're upset," she said. She put her gum into the foil wrapper and discarded it in her purse. "Did you think of something we've missed?"

He almost asked why she thought that, but then Lucas followed her gaze to the death grip he had on his steering wheel. His knuckles were actually white.

In addition to attention deficit disorder, he was also wearing his heart on his sleeve.

Or rather, on his knuckles.

"It's nothing," he lied.

She stared at him. "You're sure?"

"I'm sure you don't want to know."

She waited a moment. "Oh."

Which meant she knew.

Another pause. "What if I confessed I feel it too?" she asked.

He mentally cursed. Great. Here they were up to their necks in danger, and he was getting an erection just thinking about her. "I'd tell you not to confess it."

"That won't make it go away."

"It's still better left unsaid."

"It could be a lot of things," Kylie said, obviously ignoring his not-to-confess response. "Self-imposed celibacy—"

"Has a short shelf life," he supplied.

She made a *hmm* sound, but it had just a tinge of amusement and frustration to it. "So, it could be just dark and primal animal urges."

He liked that term because it implied simple lust. But there was just one problem with labeling it simple lust— he'd lusted before. Plenty of times. But it hadn't felt like this. This was an overwhelming, consuming need that would probably drive him crazy.

Lucas came to a stop in front of the ranch, as close as he could to the front porch, and both of them just sat in silence for a few moments. Even though the sun was on the verge of setting, there was still plenty of light. He didn't let it give him a false sense of security. Nothing would after Tiffany's death.

He examined the perimeter of the house. Each sprawling live oak and pecan tree that dotted the landscape. Every shadow. Any place that a kidnapper might hide.

"I don't feel the compulsion to hum so I *think* all is well," Kylie mumbled. "How about you?"

He considered that. Considered that it was safer to be inside the house than sitting in his truck, where they were stationary targets. "Let's go."

The moment they stepped from the truck, the dogs came barreling out of the barn. With everything else going on, Lucas had somehow forgotten about Sherlock and Watson, Finn's prize Dobermans.

But he didn't forget them now.

Both came right at Kylie and him. Like oil-black streaks, complete with barking and snarling. The dogs skidded to a stop only a few yards away, but they didn't stop with their aggressive behavior.

Kylie moved closer to him, so that the side of her left breast brushed against his arm. She was the only spot of warmth in the chilly air.

"Sit!" Lucas ordered.

And much to his surprise, they obeyed. No tail-wagging or other friendly gestures, but the dogs didn't lunge after Kylie and Lucas when they stepped onto the porch, unlocked the door and went into the house. The newly installed security system immediately began to whine, and

Lucas punched in the numbers on the keypad to temporarily disarm it. He rearmed it the moment they shut the door.

"Those Dobermans hate me," Lucas grumbled, tossing his keys onto the table in the entry.

"They hate everyone but Finn," Kylie pointed out. "They're cut-rate security, though."

"You haven't seen the price tag on that dog food he buys for them. It'd be cheaper to buy a side of prime beef."

Kylie smiled. Or rather attempted it. She did manage a nervous laugh, but there was no humor in it. "I lied about the humming. I did want to hum. But I really wanted to get inside."

"Yeah. I know."

She paused.

Kylie didn't have to say a word, but he knew what she was thinking. Their conversation about dark and primal urges had zapped both their bodies into a frenzy.

"We can resist this," he said.

Her eyebrow arched and Lucas shrugged.

He thought of plenty of reasons why he shouldn't pull her into his arms, why he should back away. The danger. His badge. The need for him to remain professional, objective and focused. They were all good solid reasons.

And yet none of them stopped him.

She looked up at him. But not just any ordinary look. *The* look. Her eyes were ripe with need for comfort. And more. Much more.

Her breath was already thin and fast. He saw the pulse jump on her throat. And that air just kept on sizzling. Lucas ignored every warning his body was sending him and gathered her into his arms.

But that wasn't all he did.

He leaned in, and his mouth claimed hers. The sensations

slammed through him as the kiss intensified. Fast. Hard. Strong. Like a fist. Resisting wasn't possible. So he took everything she offered. *Everything.* And upped the stakes.

Grappling for position, she turned and shoved him against the door and went after his shirt. Fast and frantic. Like her breath. Like the hot, needy look in her eyes. It was a race. Against what, Lucas didn't know, but it didn't matter. All he knew was that they had to have each other now.

Kylie cursed when his coat wouldn't cooperate and when she encountered the shirt and its buttons underneath.

Lucas didn't help her. He was on his own mission. One that required the use of both hands. He seized the bottom of her sweater and shoved it up. The stretchable-waist pants went down, just beneath her belly. He found her panties. Cotton and lace. Not much of a barrier at all.

With his mouth on hers, Lucas slid his hand into that lacy barrier and found exactly what he wanted. *Her.* Hot and wet. Ready. He sank his fingers into her, sliding his thumb against the most sensitive part of her. And he went deeper. If they were going to cross these boundaries, he sure as hell intended to make it worth the ride.

He succeeded.

She made a sound. A rich, feminine moan of pleasure. Her eyelids fluttered down. She slid her leg along the outside of his. And she moved with him. Pushing against him. Sliding her hips forward. Moving in rhythm of the strokes of his fingers.

"You're going to have to do something about this," she insisted.

"I'm trying."

"The bed?" she managed. "The floor?"

It was tempting. He suddenly wanted her more than his next breath. But if he took her to bed, or to the floor, he wouldn't be able to think. And even though parts of him shouted that this wasn't a thinking kind of situation, it was. Kylie already had more than enough to deal with. In the past few days, she'd been through hell. So, while his body was yelling for him to take her right then, right there, Lucas knew that wasn't the right thing to do.

He continued the strokes of his fingers. Continued to push her to the edge.

"Why aren't we doing this together?" she asked.

But she didn't just ask. She reached for his zipper and hit pay dirt. She closed her hand over his erection and nearly had him jumping out of his jeans.

Once he got his eyes uncrossed, he caught her hand to stop her from fully unzipping him. "If you do that, I can't think."

"And that would be…bad?" She moaned and tossed her head back when his fingers went deeper inside her.

"That's it," he whispered. "That's the look I want to see."

"Really? This look?" She blinked, obviously trying to focus. "It can't be very attractive. I'm about to fall."

"No. You're beautiful, and you're about to fly. Fly for me, Kylie. Let me feel you when you fly."

She did. Lucas felt her body close around his fingers. Felt her soar until she reached a shattering climax.

And Lucas was right there to catch her.

He felt something brush against his arm and heard the crash. Even though her eyes were glazed from passion, he could see her fight through the haze to see what had happened. Lucas did the same.

His body went on full alert, and he reeled around. Searching for whatever had made that noise.

His first thought—and not a pleasant thought, either— was that there was an intruder in the house.

Chapter 12

Lucas reached for his gun, but Kylie saw him stop in mid-reach when he glanced down at the floor. She looked down, as well. There was the silver photo frame, the glass shattered.

Marissa's picture.

Kylie wanted to ask what had happened, how it'd gotten there, but she didn't have enough breath gathered to speak. So, she did a little mental detective work. She'd noticed Marissa's picture on top of the Mexican-tiled table in the foyer. Unfortunately, that table was right next to where Lucas and she had been groping each other. One of them had no doubt knocked it over.

Talk about a symbolic interruption.

Now that the wild passion had been sated and her body was returning to normal, Kylie quickly fixed her clothes so that she wouldn't be standing half-dressed in front of

Lucas. Not that he would have noticed. He had his attention nailed to that picture.

Lucas stooped down, slowly, and in the same motion, he slipped his gun back into his shoulder holster. He picked up the frame first, or rather what was left of it, since it was now disconnected. He touched it as if it were the most fragile, most precious thing on Earth.

Kylie felt the ache in her heart. Not just for Lucas and the guilt he was no doubt feeling. But the old guilt returning, as well.

Without looking at her, he reached up and put the picture itself into the table drawer and then began to retrieve the pieces. One by one. Again, slowly.

"It's just glass," he mumbled.

"Yes," she agreed because she didn't know what else to say. Glass. Something to protect the photograph. Too bad they didn't make some kind of protection for the human heart because Kylie was certain that her heart would be broken into a million pieces before this was over.

Lucas stood, disappeared into the kitchen, and she heard the sound of the glass being dumped into the garbage. She dreaded his return, dreaded what she would see in his eyes. Her blood pressure shot up when his footsteps grew closer, heralding his reentry into the foyer.

He stopped in the arched opening that divided the family-style kitchen from the living room and foyer.

"Thank you," he said.

Since her head was still fuzzy from the orgasm and the interruption, Kylie decided it was a good time to hush and let him finish. Because quite frankly, she didn't have a clue why he'd said that.

"I know how hard it was, *is,*" he corrected, "for you to have this baby. Thank you."

Kylie couldn't stand the confusion any longer. "Did I miss something? One minute we're doing the whole dark and primal sex thing against the door. The picture falls. You pick up the glass. Take it to the kitchen. And…okay, here's where things really get confusing for me—you obviously have some kind of mental breakdown in there?"

The right corner of his mouth lifted. "No breakdown. I just came to my senses. I've been rude to you. Angry. And God knows how many mixed signals I've sent. I want to be honest with you, Kylie. I care for you."

Her heart soared.

"I really do care," he continued. He shifted. Not just his body. His gaze, too. "But I'm not sure I can ever get over what happened."

Her heart crashed.

And she silently cursed for allowing herself to believe, even for a few seconds.

Against her better judgment, she went to him. "Lucas, if you're worried about me falling apart after I have this baby, then don't. I'm a survivor. Have been since sixth grade, when my mom ran off to find herself and I moved in with Grandma Meg." She waved off the sympathetic look he gave her. "Don't pretend you don't know what I'm talking about. Because of Grandma Meg, I had to be a survivor because I was considered a flake by association."

He shook his head, obviously caught himself in what would be a polite but obvious white lie, and then shrugged. "Okay, you were the only student in any rural Texas high school to bring tofu pitas to school. And you wore sandals that had soles made from recycled tires."

Yes. She remembered those sandals. Comfortable but definitely not a positive fashion statement.

"I'll let you in on a secret, Lucas. I was torn between loving the only person who really loved me—Meg—and trying to live the life of a normal kid. I couldn't wait to shake off all those things that made me different from everyone else. I wanted to fit in. I wanted respect. That's why I became a deputy. It took me over a year of therapy to realize that, by the way. That's why I was working at Energizer Bunny speed while I wore that badge. The feet ahead of the brain."

Kylie paused and drew in a slow breath. "Funny though, after everything that happened, after I resigned, Grandma Meg's house was the only place I wanted to be. It was a sanctuary."

"And your prison," he promptly pointed out. "You cut yourself off from people, Kylie, especially the people you'd known since you were a kid."

"I couldn't face them. Couldn't face you." She made the mistake of facing him now. He was standing there, very much the cowboy in his jeans and white cotton shirt.

Mercy, the man had her hormonal number.

Here she was, reacting to him as if he hadn't just minutes earlier given her the orgasm of her life. And he'd done that without even having sex with her. Leave it to Lucas to accomplish the impossible.

"So, where do we go from here?" she asked, not really expecting an answer. And she certainly didn't expect the answer that came from his sensual mouth, which she'd been admiring.

"Cold showers are out. They're useless. They just make you cold."

She laughed, until she realized there might be an underlying message there. "I have the same effect on you—I leave you cold."

"I wish."

He couldn't have shocked her more if he'd hauled her to the floor and had sex with her. "You're admitting that?"

He lifted his shoulder. "Seems pointless not to. I mean, after that whole dark and primal sex thing against the door."

Lucas was right. They'd been tiptoeing and lying to themselves. Well, at least she had. "I wish it was just lust," she mumbled.

"Me, too," he said after a moment.

All this honesty was really starting to get to her. "Sweet heaven, Lucas. What are we doing to each other? We're driving each other crazy, that's what. We really need to catch those kidnappers and their boss so all of this will end."

"And you think that will *end* it?"

Lucas reached out and pulled her to him, easing her into his warm embrace. Unlike before, this embrace wasn't fueled by passion. It probably would have been safer if it had. But while this wasn't safe, it was like coming home.

And Kylie wasn't exactly pleased about that.

Because this would end. The close quarters, the embraces, the kisses. The nonsexual orgasms. The poignant, heart-revealing moments.

It would end.

And like the broken glass from the picture, she'd be left with only the pieces. The Humpty Dumpy syndrome.

"You're thinking too much," Lucas said as he tightened his grip around her. He brushed a kiss on her forehead.

And that's how Cordelia found them when she unlocked the door, threw it open and stormed inside.

"What the hell is going on here?" Cordelia demanded. Her hands went on her hips, and Lucas could see that the muscles in her face were so rigid that she looked as if she just had a massive injection of Botox.

Because their guest had tripped the security alarm when she had barged in, Lucas crossed the room and disengaged it to stop the noise.

"I can't believe what I'm seeing here." And just in case there was any doubt at to what she meant, Cordelia aimed a glare at Kylie.

"Well, you wouldn't have seen it if you'd knocked first," Lucas reminded her. He also did something he should have done months ago. He grabbed Cordelia's key ring and extracted the key to his house.

She grabbed his arm with a fierce grip when he tossed the key ring into her open purse and started to walk away. "Why are you doing this to Marissa?"

Oh, this was going to get messy.

But then, things often got that way with Cordelia. She was a messy, complicated person.

For years, Cordelia had resented Kylie's friendship with Marissa. But she hadn't resented it enough to try to build a relationship with her own sister. Cordelia was a scratch-the-surface, superficial kind of person who wasn't really into deep meaningful interactions. However, there were times, like now, when he saw genuine concern cloud her eyes.

Too bad her concern was misplaced.

"Kylie is in my protective custody," Lucas explained. Of course, that didn't explain the embrace or the flush still on Kylie's cheeks. Still, he didn't owe Cordelia that kind of explanation.

"I know about the baby," Cordelia announced.

Because that intrigued him, and because he thought it was a good precaution, Lucas repositioned himself between the two women. "And what do you think you know?" Lucas asked.

"That she's your surrogate. That the child she's carrying is yours."

Okay. So, her announcement no longer intrigued him, but it was a little alarming.

"And just how do you know that?" Lucas asked.

Kylie took his question one step further. "Better yet— *why* would you know?"

She spared Kylie another glare but addressed Lucas. "I was concerned. I wanted to make sure the clinic you used was reputable so I had Finn make a few calls—"

That had Kylie moving closer. "Finn?"

Cordelia paused and had that deer-caught-in-the-headlights look. "Yes. Because he's a doctor, I thought he could get answers faster than I could."

"And he got those answers," Kylie concluded, not sounding any happier about it than Lucas was.

Why hadn't his best friend mentioned any of this? It wasn't as if they hadn't seen each other. In fact, over the past forty-eight hours, he'd seen more of Finn than he had in a month. Finn had had plenty of opportunity to tell him.

"I went to the surrogacy clinic," Cordelia continued. "I met with the director, Mr. Windham. He tried to assure me that Kylie was a suitable surrogate. Obviously, he didn't know she's unfit to carry your child."

Lucas decided to inform her of a few conclusions of his own. "You're wrong. But let's assume for one minute that you're right. What am I supposed to do about it? The pregnancy's a done deal. The baby will be here in four and a half months. He or she isn't a toy I can exchange at Wal-Mart."

Cordelia had to get her teeth unclenched before she could speak. "Just because she conned her way into being your surrogate, it doesn't mean she has to be part of your life. You could order her out of your house. You could have her stay with someone else."

"I don't want her to stay with anyone else. I want Kylie right here." To prove his point, he hooked his arm around Kylie's waist and pulled her closer.

Kylie's glanced at him. She had that have-you-lost-your-mind? look on her face.

Cordelia reacted as if he'd slapped her. She actually pressed her hand to her heart and started to back away. "I won't let you do this. I won't let Kylie Monroe destroy your life the way she destroyed Marissa's."

"Well, that's not up to you, now is it?" Lucas hated to be cruel, but what he hated even more was Cordelia being cruel to Kylie.

Now, Cordelia turned her venomous gaze on Kylie. "If you continue to stay here and insinuate yourself into Lucas's life, I'll pursue legal action."

"For what?" Kylie asked. "Last I heard, it wasn't illegal for a grown woman to become a surrogate."

"I'll sue the sheriff's office for the wrongful death of my sister. I'll ask for millions, and I'll keep suing until I've bankrupted both of you and the entire town if necessary."

It was an anger-laden threat, but Lucas knew that didn't mean Cordelia wouldn't go through with it. If she did, it would hurt not only the sheriff's office, but it would also hurt Kylie. Still, there was no way he could back down now. Kylie was just starting to trust him. He was starting to trust her. There was a spark of life in him that he'd believed he would never feel again.

Kylie and the baby were responsible for that.

He wasn't going back to that dark, lonely place where he'd spent the past three years.

Lucas was on the verge of telling Cordelia a less emotional version of that when her cell phone rang. Still obviously steaming, she gave him a this-isn't-over huff and yanked the phone from her purse. He was close enough to see the caller ID information as it flashed onto the lighted screen.

Oh, hell.

That information set off all kinds of alarms in Lucas's head.

Lucas watched Cordelia carefully as she, too, glanced down at the caller ID. Turning away from them, she answered the call. She kept her responses whispered, simple and brief. *It's not a good time. No. No. Yes.*

"I have to go," Cordelia said abruptly. She dropped her phone back into her purse and went to the door. "Think about what I've said."

"Do I have to?" Lucas called out.

But he was talking to the air because Cordelia was already gone, leaving just a blast of arctic chill where she'd once been standing.

Lucas went to the door, as well, closed it, locked it and reset the security alarm.

"Cordelia knows Kendrick Windham, the surrogacy clinic director," he said, turning back to Kylie.

Kylie blinked. "What?"

"That call was from him. I saw his name and number on her caller ID."

Kylie shook her head. "You think he's the one who told her that I'm your surrogate?"

"Seems reasonable that the info would come from him. What isn't reasonable is that those two would feel the need to continue to stay in phone contact. Maybe Cordelia bribed him, and now he wants more money." But then something else came to mind. "Or maybe Finn's the one who did the bribing."

"I don't understand—why would Finn help Cordelia find out anything, especially about the baby? And why wouldn't he tell you about it?"

Both were darn good questions, and Lucas grabbed the phone and punched in Finn's number. Because it was time he had some answers.

"Talk to me about Cordelia," Lucas said the moment Finn answered.

"Well, good evening to you, too."

"Cordelia," Lucas prompted, ignoring his friend's sarcasm. "She was just here and said you'd helped her find out about Kylie being my surrogate."

"Hell's bells." Finn didn't stop there. He cursed some more, and it would have done a sailor proud. "Cordelia is a pain-in-the-butt-blabbermouth."

"That might be, but did you help her?"

"Only because she was relentless. She kept calling and kept dropping by the clinic to say how worried she was about you. She'd read Kylie's article, and she said she kept thinking that maybe the surrogacy was all a scam."

"Why would she care if it was?" Lucas asked.

"She didn't want you to get hurt."

Lucas played with that explanation a few seconds. It wasn't something he could totally discard. From time to time, Cordelia had tried to mother him.

When it suited her mood and motives.

"I made a few calls to the surrogacy clinic for her," Finn continued. "That's all. And it was just to give her peace of mind."

"It didn't work. Definitely no peace of mind."

"No. But then, I didn't know that Kylie was your surrogate. And I damn sure didn't know that Cordelia would be able to finagle that kind of information out of the clinic director." He paused. "Does Cordelia plan to cause trouble for you?"

"Seems that way." In fact, he could count on it. "I want the truth, Finn. Is there more to this than what Cordelia and you are saying?"

"What are you accusing me of?" Finn demanded.

"I don't know—yet."

But Lucas hung up the phone with an unsettling feeling in the pit of his stomach that something horrible had been set in motion and there was nothing he could do to stop it.

Chapter 13

Something wasn't right.

That particular feeling had been with Kylie for nearly an hour now, and it just wouldn't go away. It was something raw and hot that churned her stomach. At first, she'd tried to dismiss it as indigestion brought on by Cordelia's visit and the homemade vegetable beef soup and buttery garlic bread that Lucas had fixed for dinner. But unfortunately, Kylie didn't think this uneasy feeling was related to food or Cordelia.

"Woman's intuition?" she mumbled under her breath. "Wild imagination?" She tried again. Grasping at straws. "Leftover orgasm adrenaline?"

Whatever it was, she obviously wasn't going to get much sleep tonight, so Kylie tossed back the log cabin quilt and reached for the pair of thick socks that she'd left next to the bed. She slipped them on, along with Lucas's bulky berry-red robe and started to pace across the hardwood floor.

However, she stopped momentarily when she got to the window and decided it was a good idea to avoid openly pacing in front of it. There was a curtain, but she didn't want to risk that her shadow would fall against that curtain and give away her exact location.

Oh, great.

Now, she was bordering on paranoia. This certainly wasn't the quiet, serene pregnancy she'd dreamed of having. Of course, that's exactly what she had managed for four and a half months. Peace and quiet. Well, quiet anyway. It'd been three years since she'd had any real peace. And now things had heated up with the kidnappers, Tiffany's death and the way Lucas and she were carrying on in the lust department. Kylie hoped she didn't have to say which of those things surprised her the most.

Who was she kidding?

Lucas was the big surprise. He cared for her, he'd admitted. Yet, he'd also quickly added that it didn't matter, that it might lead to nothing. So Kylie did her best to rein in her feelings.

Even though she knew it was already too late.

Somewhere along the way, she'd started to fall pretty hard for Lucas Creed. But the real question was, what was she going to do about it?

She heard the slight cracking sound, and her pacing came to a dead stop. She lifted her head. Listened. Even though she didn't hear anything else, she retraced the sound and realized it'd come from outside.

Not that unusual, she reminded herself.

After all, the ranch was surrounded by woods. Lots of things could make cracking sounds in the night. Tree limbs stirring in the breeze. A coyote savaging for his dinner. Even Finn's dogs.

But her stomach churned even harder.

Keeping out of the direct line of visibility, Kylie eased toward the window and fingered back the edge of the ivory-colored cotton curtain. The moon was still relatively full, and the sky was clear. She could see a portion of the backyard and the barn.

No one was lurking out there.

No bad guys in ski masks.

Nothing.

That thought barely had time to settle in her mind when the door to her bedroom flew open. Kylie reached for her gun, which she'd put on the nightstand. But it was Lucas. He stood there with the golden light from the hall haloing behind him. He looked like the answer to a few raunchy fantasies she'd recently had.

He was armed and naked.

Well, almost naked, anyway. He wore only gray boxers that dipped below his navel.

Well below it.

No shirt. No shoes. Nothing to obstruct the rather nice view she had of his rather nice body. And what a view it was. He was solid. Not overly muscled. Not overly anything. A real man's body, with a toned stomach and a sprinkling of chest hair.

"Did you see anything?" he asked.

She was certain that she looked surprised. Because her mind was on, well, having sex with Lucas, it took her a moment to realize that wasn't a sexual kind of come-on look in his eyes. Those were cautious, vigilant eyes. Only then did Kylie remember she was in the process of peeking out the window. Plus, there'd been that little cracking sound she'd heard only moments earlier.

Oh, yes.

She wasn't having trouble keeping her priorities straight.

"All seems well out there," she reported, releasing the curtain so that it closed. That didn't ease his vigilant expression. "Is it?"

He shook his head. "I don't know. I heard something. A crunching sound."

Cracking. Crunching. Both synonyms for noises they shouldn't ignore, especially after everything that'd happened. "I heard something, too."

That was the only verification Lucas needed to get moving across the room toward her. First, he eased her away from the curtain and, while avoiding the window himself, he reached for the phone on the nightstand next to the guest bed.

"Stay down," he told her.

Kylie did. She grabbed the log cabin quilt and carried it to the corner near the closet. That new position took her out of the line of fire from both the window and the doorway. Just in case.

She listened as Lucas called Mark Jensen, his healthy deputy, and requested assistance. He hung up and made his way to her in a crouching position.

"You think it's necessary to bring Mark in on this?" Kylie asked.

"We need backup so that someone will be in here with you while the grounds are being checked."

"Good point." Kylie didn't consider it cowardly that she didn't want to be left alone, either. The pregnancy had made her vulnerable. Dying wasn't nearly as much of a fear as was having something happen to the baby.

She motioned toward his snug boxers. "Just a suggestion, but you might want to put something else on before Mark gets here. Appearances and all that."

He glanced down at his lack of clothing. "I'm not that concerned about appearances. But I am a little worried about freezing my butt off when I head outside. Stay here. I'll grab something."

"Wait a minute. You're going out there?" It was a bizarre question, especially considering he was the sheriff and that the ranch was his property. It was reasonable that Lucas would be the one to check out things while Mark waited with her.

But to her heart, it didn't sound reasonable at all.

"Those kidnappers could be out there," she pointed out unnecessarily.

Lucas turned, stared at her. "Is this about what I think it's about?"

"Depends." She pulled the quilt around her. "If you think it's about me having irrational feelings for a man I care about, then yes."

He seemed to ponder that a moment and then nodded. "I'm still going out there."

She hadn't thought for a second that her asinine rationalization would stop him. But she would try to figure out a way to make it as safe as she could possibly make it. Maybe they could request additional backup from Sheriff Knight so that Lucas wouldn't be alone during surveillance.

"I'll be right back," he told her. Still crouching, he made his way out of the room and into the hall.

Kylie sat there on the floor, snuggled in the warm blanket, and listened. She could hear Lucas moving around in his room. She could hear the winter wind push against the windows.

And she heard the crunching sound again.

Lucas must have heard it as well, because he barreled back down the hall and into the guest room. While he kept a firm grip on his Glock, he pulled on a pair of jeans, a sweatshirt and his boots.

The sound came again.

Lucas and she went stock-still. And Kylie tried to figure out what was going on. Not footsteps, exactly. Well, maybe that's what it was. As if the person or persons were dragging something. Worse, the last sound had been closer than the others. As if the sound makers were right outside the house.

Sweet merciful heaven.

If the kidnappers tried to get in, the alarms wouldn't be much of a deterrent. They could still bash through a door and start shooting. If that happened, Lucas and she would be forced to return fire. It could turn into a free-for-all with bullets flying.

And the baby could be hurt.

Or worse.

Her heart was pounding so hard that it surprised her that her ribs didn't crack, and the baby was doing flips or something, which didn't help with the pressure building inside her.

"Go ahead. Hum if it helps," Lucas suggested.

So, she did. Kylie tried out a few verses of "Silent Night," but then she stopped. Listened again. And realized what she wasn't hearing.

"Why didn't the dogs bark?" she asked.

"I don't know." Lucas answered quickly enough and without any surprise, making her realize he'd already considered that. And it was troubling him.

Because the Dobermans barked at strangers. Heck, they barked at friends. They just plain barked.

At everyone except Finn.

"Finn wouldn't do this," she whispered. And Kylie prayed that was true. Kidnapping, attempted murder and homicide were bad enough even when those heinous crimes hadn't been committed by a friend.

"He has no motive," Lucas added.

But did he?

Had something happened when he made those calls for Cordelia? Had Finn gotten involved with something he shouldn't have?

Kylie shook her head. It just didn't mesh with the Finn she knew. As a teenager, he'd been a little wild. A lot weird. Somehow as much of a misfit as she'd been. But he wasn't a criminal.

"If someone gets in," Lucas instructed, "I don't want you to try to do anything heroic. I want you to hide."

"While you're getting shot at? Yeah. As if I could really do that. It's one thing to have you out doing a reconnaissance of the area, but it's totally different to stand by and watch someone shoot at you."

"I'm not giving you a choice, Kylie." He slid his left hand onto her stomach.

Her eyes narrowed. "That's dirty pool."

"I know. But it'll work. Because I know you care just as much about this baby as I do."

It was a powerful comment. One that she didn't want to admit was true. But it was. God help her, it was. Even though she'd tried to keep her feelings in check, she couldn't. She loved his baby with all her heart.

And then Lucas did something even more powerful. Even more amazing. He leaned over and brushed a kiss on her shocked, half-open mouth.

"Why do you do that?" she asked. Not as an accusation. Her tone was too dreamy.

But Lucas didn't get a chance to answer. There was another noise. Something soft. It was merely the calm before the storm.

Seconds later, a bullet ripped through the window.

Chapter 14

Lucas pushed Kylie down onto the floor. It wasn't a moment too soon. Broken glass burst across the room.

The bullet tore some of the wood from the window frame. The glass and the splinters created deadly fragments, one of which sliced across his arm.

His heart sprang to his throat. His muscles tightened. His body braced itself for a fight. A fight that some SOB had brought right to his home.

Lucas couldn't pinpoint the exact location of impact of the bullet, but it was somewhere in the general vicinity of the door—where he'd been standing just minutes earlier. For that matter, Kylie had been near there, as well. If they hadn't taken precautions, they could have been killed. And Lucas realized this wasn't over. The person firing those shots likely wouldn't stop until they were dead, so maybe all the precautions in the world wouldn't help them.

Adjusting his weapon, Lucas moved Kylie away from

the wall, in case the shooter was using armor-piercing artillery that would go through layers of wood, insulation and dry wall.

"You're bleeding," she whispered.

Lucas glanced at the cut on his left forearm, specifically at the splatters of blood around it and dismissed it. "It's nothing."

He pushed her into the closet and crawled toward the window so he could try to return fire.

The shooter beat him to it.

There was another shot. It slammed through what was left of the glass and created a deafening blast that filled the room. This time, he saw the point of impact. The bullet smashed into the wall near the door and sent bits of chalky material flying through the air.

Lucas felt the sting of the debris on his face. He felt the fear. It clawed its way through him, setting off a dozen nightmarish memories. Of his wife's shooting. A woman he hadn't been able to save.

Hell.

This had to stop. He couldn't risk a bullet ricocheting off something and hitting Kylie. Or himself. Because if anything happened to him, then that would likely leave Kylie and the baby at the mercy of people who probably hadn't come here to show much mercy.

Lucas made it to the window, took a quick look. Saw the barn. The yard.

But no shooter.

If it was only one shooter. There could be two or more. And there were a lot of places for gunmen to hide. Assessing those places one at a time, he glanced out the window for fractions of seconds before pulling back. Each time he was able to exclude a particular hiding place.

Until he got to the storage shed positioned only about ten yards or so from the guest room window.

The moonlight helped with the open areas, but it also cast shadows around that storage shed. If he were planning on an ambush, that would be his choice for a hiding place. Plenty of cover. Proximity to the house. Easy access into the pasture and the woods in case an escape route was needed.

"Lucas, stay down!" Kylie ordered.

"I think I know where the shooter is."

"That won't help if you get your head blown off. Let's wait him out."

Lucas considered that and thought of his deputy, who was probably still miles out. In one way, not good, because he could certainly use the backup, but it also meant Mark Jensen wouldn't be driving straight into the line of fire.

"Call Mark," he instructed Kylie, tossing her the phone. "Tell him what's going on. He's not to approach the house. It's too dangerous."

Lucas stayed near the window, still crouching and peering out, and he stayed in a position to fire. Which he would certainly do once he verified the location of the shooter. No use wasting ammunition or giving away his own position to whoever was out there.

Behind him, he heard Kylie make the call. Listened to her voice as she briefed Mark. She sounded calm. Lucas knew she wasn't. She was terrified, not just for herself but for the baby. Somehow, some way, he had to get her out of this.

Why hadn't the dogs barked?

That question kept repeating in his head, but Lucas figured he wouldn't have an answer until he could get outside and take a look around. That wasn't going to happen with a shooter out there. He couldn't risk leaving Kylie alone, and

Mark wouldn't proceed onto the property until he'd gotten some kind of okay from Kylie or him.

The silence returned. Lucas hated it. Because the gunman could still be moving closer to the house to get off a more accurate shot.

Lucas levered himself slightly and aimed. Rather than risk having the gunman getting an even better position, Lucas squeezed the trigger of his Glock. There was the lightning-fast recoil. A familiar feeling that he had no trouble controlling. His bullet slammed into the metal storage shed.

And then all hell broke loose.

Bullets came at the house.

Lots of them.

Not a single shot, but a barrage of deadly gunfire all pointed right at the window. However, those latest shots gave him his answer—there were two gunmen. At least. Because he could distinguish the sounds of at least two different weapons. So now he had to wonder—were they outnumbered? Outgunned? And if so, by how much?

Lucas quickly checked on Kylie. She was still on the floor of the closet, her arms covering her head, her gun gripped in her hands. She wasn't out of danger, not by a long shot, but at least she wasn't trying to help him return fire.

The hot metal from the bullets ripped through the fabric of the curtain, and the winter wind caught the shreds, snapping them like bullwhips. The temperature in the room plunged so quickly that he could suddenly see the foggy cloud left by his breath.

Each new round of gunfire gave him a punch of adrenaline. His heart rate was off the scale. Still, he didn't let his physical reactions cause him to lose focus. He listened. Observed.

Processed.

The next shot came close. Too close. It smashed into the window frame just to the left of Lucas's head. However, the close call allowed him to pinpoint one of the gunmen's locations. He or she was on the left side of the storage shed.

Finally, there was a lull in the attack. For whatever reason, the gunmen stopped. Maybe to reload. Maybe to listen. Maybe to move closer. Lucas didn't care. This was the opening he'd been waiting for.

Lucas fixed an image of the gunman's position in his mind. He came up and returned fire. He focused his shot directly at the left corner of the shed. To fire the second shot he moved just slightly to the right so it'd tear through the structure.

It did.

There were a few sparks, the sound of metal ripping through metal, which Lucas ignored. However, he didn't ignore the shadowy movement that he saw. He squeezed off another shot and kept on shooting. Aiming right for that sputter of movement.

Until he ran out of ammo.

"Here!" Kylie said. She scrambled out of the closet and slid her .357 toward him.

Lucas didn't waste any time. He tossed his Glock onto the bed, retrieved the .357 Magnum from the floor and came up ready to fire.

But there was nothing to fire at.

The shadow was gone.

Lucas held his position. Waited. And he listened. But the only sound he heard was the wind and Kylie humming.

"This isn't over," he mumbled. And then he cursed. Because he knew what this meant.

The moment his deputy arrived to stay with Kylie, nothing would stop him. Lucas was going after the person who'd just tried to kill them, and one way or another, there would be hell to pay.

"Lucas has been out there too long," Kylie complained to Deputy Mark Jensen. "And he's injured. He wouldn't even let me look at that cut on his arm. A scratch, he said. 'Nothing to be concerned about.'"

Mark made a sound. Not an agreement, by any means. Just a male grunt to indicate he'd heard her but that he intended to take no action.

Not that there was any action to take.

Before Lucas left to check the grounds, he'd ordered Mark not to let her out of his sight. For the past hour and a half, the young deputy had obeyed his boss's order to a tee. So, here Mark and she sat in the living room. No lights on. Only using minimal comments and annoying grunts to communicate with each other.

But the deputy kept his weapon ready and aimed.

Kylie understood the ready and aimed part. She, too, had her own gun gripped in her hands. And she was mentally ready if the kidnappers returned, made their way past Lucas and somehow got inside. It wasn't as if that didn't concern her. It did. But it concerned her more that Lucas was out there and they hadn't heard so much as a peep from him.

She shouldn't have let him go out there alone. After all, there were no guarantees that the shooters had left. They could be hiding, waiting....

And she was taking another trip down paranoia lane.

Of course, it was easy to do that, what with the fact that someone obviously wanted them dead.

Tiffany had been right. *They'll do whatever it takes to stop Kylie Monroe and Sheriff Creed.* In their case, *whatever it takes* had been a potentially fatal attack right in Lucas's own home. Kylie wondered how long it would be before either of them would feel safe again. Certainly not until the gunmen and their boss were caught.

She heard the key turn in the lock, and she jumped to her feet. So did Mark, and he caught her to stop her from running into the foyer. A moment later, they realized his vigilance wasn't necessary.

Lucas walked through the door.

"Are you all right?" she asked. Though it was a dumb question because he appeared to be fine. Other than signs of fatigue and ruddy cheeks from the cold weather, Lucas looked the same as when he'd walked out the door nearly an hour earlier.

"I'm okay," Lucas assured her.

He reset the alarm, holstered his Glock and walked into the living room. Kylie couldn't help herself. She went to him and pulled him into her arms. It was a brassy move because Mark was there and he probably would eventually let it slip that Lucas and she had been in too friendly an embrace. Lucas obviously didn't care about the potential gossip because he returned the hug.

"The dogs are questionable," Lucas told her, saying it loud enough so that his deputy could hear. "It appears someone drugged them. I called Finn. He's on his way over to pick them up so he can take them to the vet."

"Drugged?" Kylie repeated. She pulled back so she could face him and examine his eyes to see what he was thinking. "So the gunmen had come prepared." It also meant that Finn wasn't behind any of this. He couldn't have risked drugging his beloved pets.

Well, he wouldn't have risked it unless he knew there was no chance that they'd actually be harmed. But she already had enough to concern her without dwelling on such an outside possibility.

"I'll make sure all the doors and windows are locked," Mark volunteered.

Kylie waited until the deputy was out of earshot before she continued. She also took off Lucas's buckskin jacket so she could check that cut on his arm.

"Finn was at his house when you called him?" she whispered.

The muscles in Lucas's jaw tightened. "He said he was."

"Any doubts?"

"His calls are automatically forwarded to his cell phone."

Her stomach sank to her knees. "Oh."

"Yes, *oh*."

So their old friend wasn't totally in the clear after all. Too bad. It would help if she could be sure that someone other than fellow law enforcement officers were on their side.

Kylie draped his coat over the back of the chair and rolled up his shirt sleeve. "Could someone like Cordelia have gotten close enough to drug the dogs?"

"Maybe. I found them in the pasture. Both had been shot with tranquilizer darts."

In other words, the perpetrator wouldn't have had to get that close to the dogs. That meant almost anyone could have done it. Well, anyone with a grudge against them, and that obviously included Cordelia.

Kylie frowned when she made her way to Lucas's injured forearm. Not a precise cut but an angry gash nearly two inches long. "Come with me to the bathroom so I can clean that."

He looked at her. "You know how to treat wounds?"

"No. Actually, I don't, but I figure I can find some anti-septic or something to stop it from getting infected. I don't suppose you'd consider seeing a doctor?"

"Nope."

But he did go with her down the hall after he slipped his arm around her waist. Not a totally intimate, cozy gesture on his part. She suspected that he was eager to get her away from any of the windows.

"I talked to Sergeant O'Malley at SAPD," Lucas explained. "She might be able to arrange for us to stay at a safe house."

"How safe is safe?" Kylie questioned. She located a bottle of hydrogen peroxide and bandages and got to work.

"Safer than here," he qualified. "In the meantime, Sheriff Knight is sending over one of his deputies to do horseback patrol. The county CSI guys are on the way, as well. They'll be combing the grounds for anything forensic they can use to identify the gunmen."

She dabbed on some of the hydrogen peroxide and blew on it so it wouldn't sting. "You've been busy."

"Yes. After the fact."

Mercy, he sounded bone-tired and weary. "Lucas, you didn't do anything wrong."

He shook his head. "I didn't do anything right, either."

That brought her nursing duties to a halt so she could stare at him. "Excuse me? We're alive. So is the baby. That's a lot of *right* as far as I'm concerned."

He didn't get a chance to dispute that because Mark Jensen appeared in the doorway of the bathroom.

"Anything else you want me to do?" Mark asked.

"No." Lucas took the bandage from her, slapped it on his arm and shoved his shirtsleeve back in place. "I have to board up that window the gunmen shot out."

"I'll do it," Mark volunteered.

"Thanks. There's some plywood and a toolbox in the barn."

Mark stepped away, but then he turned back toward them. "Any chance the dogs will wake up anytime soon? Those Dobermans don't like me much."

"They're snoozing like babies. And Finn should be here any minute to get them." Lucas snared her gaze after Mark left. "Finn won't be coming in. I told him you were shaken up, that you needed to get some rest."

She nodded. Kylie didn't mind being used as an excuse, mainly because she really didn't want to face their old friend, who might not have such friendly intentions toward them.

"So we're staying here tonight?" she asked.

"The safe house won't be ready for at least twenty-four hours, but don't worry. Knight's deputy will be outside on the grounds. So will the crime scene guys. And as a precaution, I want you to stay in my room."

That got her attention. "With you?"

"With me." It had a *duh* ring to it. "You have a problem with that?"

"No."

"You're sure?" he questioned.

"Of course not. It's just that people will know. They'll talk."

"Then let them talk." He gave an exhausted-sounding huff and led her in the direction of his bedroom. "I want you to get some sleep."

"But the crime scene guys—"

"I told them that we'd lock down for the night so they could secure the perimeter of the house for their investigation. I doubt the gunmen will want to make a return visit with all the activity going on."

True. In fact, for tonight anyway, the ranch was probably the safest place for them. Unfortunately, that didn't make her feel as certain as it should have. Absolute security probably wasn't in the cards until the people responsible were behind bars.

He opened the door to his bedroom. It was the first time she'd seen it. Like the rest of the house, it was dark. But even if she hadn't known it was Lucas's room, she would have been able to tell.

It smelled like him.

Something warm, musky and masculine. Something that immediately made her feel as if this was the place she wanted to be. Ironic, what with all the bullets that'd come their way tonight.

The cover was already drawn back, but he urged her into bed, and pulled the sheet and quilt over her. The bedding smelled like him, as well.

"While I had Sgt. O'Malley on the phone," he told her, "she said tomorrow afternoon they're going to bring in both Kendrick Windham and Isaac Dupont for questioning."

Finally! "I want to be there. I want to see the looks on their weaselly little faces when the cops ask them about Tiffany Smith and about what happened here tonight."

"Figured that. I want to be there, as well. But I don't want to take any unnecessary risks."

Kylie nodded. "There are risks whether we take them or not, Lucas. Heck, just breathing is a risk with those kidnappers, aka gunmen, on the loose."

"I know. That's why I asked if we could be present during questioning. Not in the room. But we'll be able to observe through the two-way mirror."

Well, it wasn't as good as being able to question them herself, but it would have to do. Besides, this was their best shot at getting some answers.

It had to work, because the alternative was unthinkable.

They couldn't continue to live like this. All the stress wasn't good for the baby. Nor was it good for Lucas or her. Both of them needed to get on with their lives.

"What about you?" she asked. "Aren't you going to try to get some rest?"

"I'm resting." He climbed onto the bed with her. Right next to her. But he stayed on top of the covers. Boots and all. That *all* included his shoulder holster, weapon and even extra magazines of ammunition.

"You aren't going to get much sleep, are you?" she asked.

"No. But it's my guess you won't either."

He was right. Sleep, especially a peaceful sleep, wasn't a possibility. Not with the gunmen and kidnappers still at large. So Kylie snuggled closer to Lucas and let the silence settle in around them.

Chapter 15

The cold spell had finally run its course. For the first time in days, Lucas didn't feel the need to bundle up when he opened the truck door so he could step out into the afternoon winter air.

Kylie opened her door as well.

But Lucas didn't let her get far.

While still within the meager protection of the truck, he took her arm before she could make her way into the SAPD headquarters building. "Here are the rules. You don't leave my side, and you don't take any chances."

She paused, pursed her lips. "Why do you get to make the rules?"

Lucas couldn't think of a good reason, so he gave her the only one that came to mind. "Because I'm a cop and because I'm bigger than you."

She made a sound of amusement. "Size matters?" she questioned.

"You bet it does." In this case, anyway. If it came down to it, his body would make a great human shield to protect her.

"Hardly seems fair," Kylie pointed out.

"Yeah." Because the amusement in her tone was forced and meant to soothe him, Lucas went for some levity that would hopefully soothe her. "And I know it contradicts what men have been saying for years. Still, this is a rare instance. But it should help that I have your best interest at heart."

Lucas didn't make that last comment lightly, either. It was true in every sense of the word. Gone were the hurt and resentment caused by Marissa's death. Yes, there was still grief. Always would be. But the anger was no longer there.

It was a relief to be rid of it.

He'd yet to tell Kylie that he'd forgiven her, but somewhere amid all those shots being fired at them, he realized he had done exactly that. There was nothing like a near-death experience to get a little perspective and camaraderie.

Unfortunately, near-death experiences could also get them killed.

He had to make sure the kidnappers/gunmen didn't get another opportunity to attempt that.

Lucas got out of the truck and hurried to the passenger's side. He pulled Kylie into the crook of his arm, sheltering her, while he kept his shoulder holster and weapon discreetly accessible. He got them moving quickly into the building. They'd barely stepped to the entry when they came face-to-face with Kendrick Windham.

No gym clothes today. He looked very much the part of the successful surrogacy clinic director. A polished tobacco-colored business suit. Pricey shoes. Equally pricey haircut. His expression was different, as well, in that it wasn't as disinterested and detached as it had been when

Lucas had seen him at the hospital. Still, Windham might well have been nicknamed the iceman at the moment.

"Are you two the reason I was summoned here?" Windham immediately asked.

So he'd put two and two together. It was exactly what Lucas had expected him to do. Yet another reason for precautions. "*You're* the reason you're here," Lucas countered.

"Am I supposed to know what that means?"

Since Windham was looking directly at Kylie, or rather staring at her, she was the one who responded. "Tiffany Smith is dead. Someone tried to kill us. The police want answers, and they're looking to get those answers from you. Hence, the summons."

"Then both you and the police are going to be disappointed. But then you obviously must know that, or you wouldn't have requested Isaac Dupont to come here this afternoon, as well. Hedging your bets, I assume. If you can't get me to confess, you'll try to browbeat him." He turned that acid gaze on Lucas and hissed out a breath. "I didn't mind your courtesy call to tell me about Tiffany being hospitalized, but I won't tolerate you trying to frame me for crimes I didn't commit."

Lucas shrugged, trying to appear calm. But there was no way he could remain calm with this man so close to Kylie. It didn't matter that there were two armed officers less than ten feet away. It also didn't matter that they were inside a building crammed full of surveillance cameras and cops who could respond at the first sign of trouble. Lucas still felt as if Kylie were being threatened.

"If you didn't do anything wrong," Lucas informed Windham, "then you don't have anything to worry about."

"You're right, of course. But you and Ms. Monroe apparently do have something to worry about. Oh, and let's not forget Isaac Dupont. I'm sure he has a ton of worries right now, what with the allegations of his wrongdoing. Those allegations could destroy his career, and he won't care for that," he said, his tone placating. Definitely not a good sign. "I, too, have friends in law enforcement."

"And these friends told you about Dupont being called in for an interview?" Lucas asked.

"That, and I also heard about the shooting last night at your place."

Lucas didn't like the sound of that, or the implications. If Windham did have connections in SAPD, then he could possibly learn the location of the safe house that the San Antonio police were arranging. That would mean Windham or God knew who else would know where they'd be.

Sitting ducks was the term that came to mind.

When the interviews were finished, he'd have to come up with other arrangements to keep Kylie safe.

Since this conversation had already taken a bad turn, Lucas decided it was time to go for Windham's jugular. "Did you hire the people who fired those shots at us last night?"

Windham laughed. The sound was smoky and thick. Not placating. He'd moved on to blatant mockery. "I'm not in the habit of hiring hit men."

"That wasn't what I asked," Lucas pointed out.

"I know." Windham coupled that remark with one last icy glance, and turned, calmly put his trim leather briefcase on the conveyor belt and stepped through the metal detector. He breezed right through and disappeared down one of the corridors, apparently headed for the interview room.

Because Lucas was armed, it took Kylie and him longer to get through security. Then they had to wait for Sgt.

Katelyn O'Malley to come down to the lobby so she could escort them to the observation area.

"We have a glitch," Sgt. O'Malley immediately informed them. The tall, athletic-looking redhead motioned for them to follow her.

"Does it have anything to do with the info leaked to Windham?" Lucas wanted to know.

That caused the sergeant to slow a bit so she could make eye contact. "What kind of info?"

"He knew about the shooting at my ranch."

"Ah, that. Windham could have gotten it from a variety of sources. Maybe even here," she admitted. Huffing, she plowed her fingers through the side of her hair and briefly tipped her eyes to the ceiling. "People talk, and they aren't always careful about anyone who might be listening."

Well, that did it. The safe house was definitely out.

"The glitch I was referring to is Isaac Dupont," O'Malley continued. "He showed up about a half hour ago and demanded we start the interview earlier than we'd planned. Said he has an appointment that he can't reschedule."

Yet more bad news. Lucas hoped this wasn't a trend. There were already enough strikes against them without adding more.

"So we missed the interview?" Kylie asked.

"Just about." Sgt. O'Malley checked her watch. "I'm sure the detective will be wrapping things up soon. Dupont isn't exactly the poster child for patience. I suspect he'll be whining to get out of there as quickly as possible. But we're taping the session so you'll be able to see it."

Lucas knew it wasn't as good as witnessing the actual session, but it would have to do.

Sgt. O'Malley glanced over her shoulder at them again.

"Oh, and get this. Dupont didn't arrive alone. He law-yered up."

"A lawyer who lawyers up," Lucas mumbled. Maybe it was a weird kind of show of power or just a simple attempt to cover his butt. Either way, it meant Dupont likely wasn't going to say anything of any value.

Hell.

Lucas really needed a break soon. Kylie's and their child's safety depended on it.

He stopped when he realized the thought that had just passed through his head.

Their child.

Not *his*.

Theirs.

When the devil had that happened?

Was the shooting and the camaraderie responsible for that, as well? Of course, it could have been that whole making-out session against the door. That certainly had a way of breaking down old issues. He couldn't pinpoint the timing, but he couldn't deny what he felt.

"Are you okay?" he heard Kylie ask.

Lucas pulled himself away from his musings to real-ize that both women had stopped, as well, and they were staring at him.

"I'm fine," he insisted.

And he started walking again so that neither Sgt. O'Malley nor Kylie would ask any more questions. Instead, he needed to focus on the remaining interview with Isaac Dupont and then with Kendrick Windham. After all, Kylie and he were literally under the same roof as two potential killers. That had to take priority over any turmoil he was feeling about his relationship, or lack thereof, with Kylie.

The sergeant led them into the observation room, and

on the other side of the two-way mirror, Lucas saw Isaac Dupont, another guy in a navy suit who had lawyer written all over him and the officer who was doing the interview. Dupont was in the middle of what appeared to be an explanation as to his whereabouts the prior evening. Specifically, the time of the shooting at the ranch.

"My alibi will check out," Dupont declared. He said it with too much confidence for Lucas to believe it was anything other than the truth. No surprise there. If Dupont had indeed hired the gunmen, then he would have insured he had an airtight alibi so that no one could trace the crime to him.

"Talk to me about Tiffany Smith," the detective insisted.

Dupont and his lawyer exchanged glances, and it was his attorney who answered. "My client has no personal or professional connection to Ms. Smith."

"Sheesh. It took a sidebar with his lawyer to come up with that puny answer?" Kylie mumbled.

Lucas made a sound of agreement. "He didn't exclude an *illegal* connection with Tiffany, though." And that was the only one that mattered. Something that would connect Dupont to the illegal surrogacy activity and therefore to Kylie's article and the attempts on their lives.

But Dupont obviously wasn't just going to hand them that information.

Lucas watched as the detective wrapped up the interview. Dupont and his lawyer stood. They even exchanged friendly handshakes with the detective, and Dupont promised if he thought of any additional information to help the police, then he would call them right away.

Hell would freeze over first.

"You're just going to let him go?" Kylie asked Sgt. O'Malley. Because it was asked out of sheer frustration, she waved off her own question. Since Kylie was a former cop, she knew SAPD had no legal reason to hold either Dupont or even Windham. These interviews were basically fishing expeditions, and so far they hadn't caught anything. Lucas didn't think Windham would slip up either.

Kylie reached for the doorknob, but Lucas stopped her. "Going somewhere?" he asked.

"I want to talk to Dupont."

That's exactly what he thought she had in mind, and it was exactly what wasn't going to happen. "Remember our size and rules discussion?"

Her hands went on her hips. "You think Dupont will pull out a gun and try to kill me here? I wish. If he did something totally brainless like that, then Sgt. O'Malley could arrest him, and this would all be over."

Kylie didn't wait for him to agree. Ignoring the rules and Lucas's glare—which he knew was a top-notch expression—she opened the door and stepped into the hall. Sgt. O'Malley and Lucas were right behind her. The only person missing was Dupont. He was still in the interview room.

"As you requested, we're also looking into the financials on your former sister-in-law, Cordelia Landrum," Sgt. O'Malley told Lucas.

"And?" He was very much interested in what the sergeant had to say, but he also started jockeying for position with Kylie. So that he was between her and the interview room.

"I haven't found anything on Ms. Landrum so far," Sgt. O'Malley explained. "But she has a lot of money and money trails to sort through, including an off-shore account. Even a warrant won't get me into that. Don't worry, though. I'll keep at it, and something might turn up."

So Cordelia wasn't in the clear. Though she wouldn't

have gotten her hands dirty with the actual kidnapping and shooting, she could have hired someone to do those things.

Just like Dupont.

Just like Windham.

Lucas left Finn's name off that list because, thankfully, he hadn't been able to come up with a solid motive. So far, the only thing he could accuse Finn of was being badgered into helping Cordelia find out about the surrogacy. Hardly a crime. Well, maybe Finn could be disciplined for breaching a patient's confidentiality, but he likely wasn't involved in a felony.

The door of the interview room opened, and Lucas did a little sidestepping to stop Kylie from violating Dupont's personal space. Judging from the man's unpleasant expression, it wouldn't be a good time to provoke him.

"Sheriff Creed," Dupont said, smiling a smile that no one on Earth would have mistaken as genuine. "And your trusty sidekick, Kylie Monroe. Always turning up at the oddest places, aren't you?"

"I'm a cop. This is cop headquarters," Lucas pointed out. "This isn't that odd of a place for me to be. Besides, I heard you were in the building." Lucas intentionally used the same cocky phrasing Dupont had when he had made his appearance at the hospital.

"And you just couldn't wait to see me." Dupont's gaze slipped past Lucas and went to Kylie. "How is the little mom-to-be?"

"Peachy," Kylie let him know in her best sarcastic tone. "Well, except for someone shooting at us. You wouldn't know anything about that, would you?" Oh, butter wouldn't melt in that mouth.

However, Kylie's cool talking had no effect on Dupont. "No. Why don't you ask Kendrick Windham?"

"Because he would only point the finger at you."

"Yes." Now, there was a genuine smile. A smug one. "The finger-pointing creates reasonable doubt, doesn't it? A sort of he said, he said."

"Reasonable doubt can be eliminated with a little proof." Lucas put his hand on Kylie's arm to get them moving. He didn't want her near Dupont any longer.

Fortunately, Kylie cooperated, and they turned to follow Sgt. O'Malley back into the observation room so they'd be in place for Windham's interview.

"What—no Wild West threats about getting me no matter what it takes?" Dupont called out. "Personally, I think both of you are a threat of the worst kind."

That stopped Lucas. Kylie stopped, as well. But neither of them turned back to face Dupont.

"I don't like people who cause trouble for me," Isaac Dupont warned. "My advice? Think about that when you try to sleep tonight."

Chapter 16

Kylie took her prenatal vitamin and washed it down with a few gulps of milk. With that daily task finished, she sat on the sofa and listened to Lucas do one of the things he did best—be a cop.

Earlier, after they'd left SAPD headquarters, he'd called and arranged for a private security guard and a neighboring deputy sheriff to patrol the ranch. Now he was in contact with both of them and was giving instructions as to where they should set up security and surveillance.

Along with Sheriff Knight's deputy, that would give them three extra pairs of hands in case the gunmen decided to make a return visit. The extra hands were necessary because despite other phone calls, it appeared Lucas wasn't having much luck securing them a safe house.

That probably meant staying at the ranch again.

It was going to be a *long* night.

Kylie tried not to let the concern register on her face

or in her body language. Hard to suppress something like that, though, especially since they still had a boarded-up window from the previous night's attack.

The entire house was dark; the only light came from the moon, and those meager rays filtered in through the edges of the plantation blinds and curtains, which were all shut tight, as well. Neither Lucas nor she had gone near a window. And the alarms were set. All the doors were double-locked.

They hadn't stopped there. Both of them had their shoulder holsters, guns and extra magazines of ammunition lying on the coffee table just inches away. Wherever they went tonight, the guns and ammo would go with them.

Lucas ended his call and sank down on the sofa next to her. "I haven't given up. I'm still trying to arrange for a place for us to stay."

"And let me guess—you're not going through SAPD to do that?" Kylie asked.

"Not after hearing Kendrick Windham brag about the *friends* he has in law enforcement."

Yes, that had unnerved her, too. Of course, Windham hadn't brought up that point during the interview with the SAPD detective. Kylie had listened for any nuance of a threat or any shred of useful information.

Nothing.

Windham had been cordial. Polite, even. Definitely not menacing. But the damage had already been done. Well, if there could be any more damage to her peace of mind. She wasn't sure she had any peace of mind left.

"I don't want us to arrive at a safe house only to discover that it's a trap," Lucas added. "I considered a hotel."

Kylie was already shaking her head before he had finished. "Too hard to secure. Plus, we could endanger civilians if the shooter opened fire. And I have no doubt that he or she is gutsy enough to open fire regardless of the collateral damage it'd cause."

He nodded. "There's the jail," he pointed out.

The drawback was that it was literally in the center of Fall Creek, surrounded by shops, businesses and homes. "It wouldn't be any easier to secure than the ranch. Not unless you're willing to deputize the entire town."

"That's a scary thought. There are some people you just don't want to have in control of a deadly weapon."

Yes. At least a dozen came to mind.

Finn included.

Lucas blew out a weary breath. "We could just leave, drive to the airport in San Antonio or Houston and get on the first plane that's headed out of the state."

She'd thought of that, too. "What if the person responsible for this has us followed? Then, we're in Bermuda or wherever, and we have no backup. Plus, we wouldn't even be able to carry our guns on the plane. When we landed, we'd be practically defenseless." She paused, noted the additional frustration that her answer caused Lucas. "Staying here isn't exactly my first choice, either, but I think we need to stay put until we're certain we have something safer."

He met her gaze. "You're being awfully rational about this."

She laughed. "Then appearances can indeed be deceiving. Because beneath all this milk sipping and prenatal vitamin popping, I'm shaken to the core."

She'd tried to say it lightly enough, so that it didn't put more pressure on him, but he obviously saw through the flimsy pretense. He slid his hand over hers, linking their fingers together.

"I'm just worried this could go on for weeks," she admitted.

Or months.

Or forever.

Kylie didn't dare voice that. She was having a hard enough time trying to get past the next five minutes. She wasn't ready to deal with forever yet.

"I think it'll all come to a head soon." Lucas rotated his shoulder, testing it, and she realized he was actually testing the wound on his arm. Judging from the slight wince he made, it still hurt. "Neither Dupont nor Windham were pleased about being called in for interviews. Plus, Sgt. O'Malley is digging into Cordelia's financials."

"Cordelia won't be happy about that. She'll have her lawyers suing everyone in sight."

Of course, a lawsuit seemed positively benign compared to everything else going on.

Kylie finished her milk, set the glass on the coffee table and freed herself from Lucas's grip so her hands would be free to unbutton the cuff on his dark blue shirt. He'd changed clothes since they'd returned from San Antonio, and when she couldn't shove up the sleeve of this particular shirt far enough, she went after the front buttons.

He looked at her and even in the moonlight, she could see the questioning expression. "It's Florence Nightingale time?"

She nodded. "I'm going to check that wound."

"You mean that scratch," he immediately corrected.

"Men always say that. You could be gushing arterial spray, and it'd still be a scratch." The joke didn't settle well in her stomach. Neither did the sight of the *scratch* when she eased the shirt off his shoulder and gently peeled back the bandage. It was a brutal reminder of how close he'd come to being killed.

"You're frowning," Lucas pointed out.

She forced the frown away. Lucas had too much to deal with without her adding to his troubles. "I just wanted an excuse to get your clothes off."

"You don't need an excuse for that."

She smiled and pressed the bandage back in place. "That sounded like a come-on."

He waited a moment, long enough for her to bring her gaze back to his. "What if it was?" he asked.

Oh.

Kylie's throat clamped shut. Not the best time for that to happen, because her silence seemed like an unspoken invitation.

Which it was.

Yes, she had a lot on her mind, what with the danger and the baby. But even with all of that, she hadn't been able to forget how it felt to have Lucas hold her and touch her. She especially hadn't been able to forget those kisses they'd shared. She'd relived them too many times to count. The taste of them. The taste of *him*. And she'd also daydreamed about getting close like that all over again.

What she felt for him was strong, overpowering and always there. Always. A slow, gnawing hunger. It made her feel alive. And terrified. Because there were times, like now, when she wondered how she could possibly live without him. Somewhere along the line, he'd become more important than anything to her.

Lucas didn't move, but the narrow space between them suddenly seemed to vanish. Her heart instantly went into overdrive. And where was the air? There definitely wasn't enough air in the living room. Maybe it was the lack of air that was suddenly making her light-headed. Or maybe it was his mouth. That sensuous made-for-kissing mouth that was so close she could taste it. Kylie was no longer sure what to hope for. One thing was certain—she wanted him.

And he obviously knew it.

He reached out and skimmed his fingers over her cheek. "You didn't answer. What if this is a come-on?"

She had to clear her throat so she could speak. "Then I'd have to question our sanity. Because we're not even sure if we're safe."

But Kylie barely heard her own argument.

Much less believed it.

Lucas obviously didn't believe it, either, because he pulled her into his lap. Kylie wasn't sure how he had accomplished that little feat. One moment, she was sitting on the sofa; the next moment, she was sitting on him.

All in all, not a bad place to sit.

She glanced down at their new position and gave it a nod of approval. Lucas gave it his own approval, as well. He moved against her. Softly. Body against body. Everything slowed. Like a lazy hot breeze. It swirled around her until all she could see and feel was Lucas.

He didn't kiss her. He just looked at her as if trying to decide if this was a good idea.

"You're cold?" he asked, his Texas drawl heightening the words.

The warm air from the ceiling vent was washing over her. And the room definitely wasn't cool. Maybe because of her penchant for not wearing shoes around the house, Lucas had really cranked up the heat.

In more ways than one.

Still, she was shivering. Actually honest-to-goodness shivering. And not because she was scared.

Okay, maybe she was a little scared.

She was scared that this was all just a very good dream, and that she would wake up and Lucas would be gone. Worse, he would still hate her. They'd still be at the hellish impasse where they'd been for three years.

But then, he slid his hand around the back of her neck. Eased her closer. His mouth came to hers. Barely a touch. Enough to reassure her that this was no dream but a flesh-and-blood man who wanted her.

"If you're going to say no, do it now," he warned.

"Why would I say no?" Her breasts brushed against his bare chest and sent her pulse right off the chart.

"Because you might be having doubts."

She dismissed that with a soft sound of denial. "Lucas, I feel a lot about you, *for* you, but I don't have those kinds of doubts."

He cupped her chin, slid his thumb over her bottom lip. There was gentleness in his touch. Almost reverence. *Almost.* But in his eyes, she could see the heat. The fire. The need. There was nothing reverent about that. Mercy, she wanted him.

And the next kiss proved it.

Roughly grabbing handfuls of his hair, she wrenched his mouth to hers. And she kissed him, all right. There were no more preliminaries, no long doubting looks, no soft caressing breaths, no gentleness. Just them. Two people kissing each other as if this would be the last kiss either of them would ever get to experience.

It worked. Both for her libido and for the rest of her. Lucas was melting the cold that for years she had allowed to seep into her blood and into her heart. He was somehow making her feel new again. Had anything felt this good, this all-consuming, this overwhelming?

This necessary?

No, she admitted honestly. Nothing.

And that's why Kylie knew it couldn't stop.

Lucas had no intentions of stopping this time, but even if he'd had such intentions, they had gone south in a hurry. Frantically, he pulled at her stretchy top. Then he did a reversal.

And stopped.

His attention landed on her stomach, and his forehead bunched up. Along with that bunching came some doubts. Hell. His body didn't want any doubts. His body wanted to race full speed ahead and have wild, mindless sex. But that stomach was a cool reminder that his body wasn't calling the shots here.

"Pregnant women are allowed to have sex," Kylie assured him.

His forehead bunched up further. "I don't want to hurt you."

"Good." She exaggerated a breath of relief. "I'm not much into S and M anyway." She hooked her arm around his waist. "Let's just go with it, Lucas. Don't think about it."

He nodded. "Relying on extremely long-term memory here, sex isn't about thinking, anyway."

"I agree. Same long-term memory here. Same conclusion. Don't think. Just do it."

That was the invitation he'd been waiting for. And he didn't wait any longer. His mouth came to hers. Hot and hungry. His hands plowed into her hair, shoving it from her face so that nothing would be in the way.

Lucas hauled her against him, gently because of the pregnancy, but it got the job done. She fastened herself around him, her knees cradling his hips. On a strangled groan, her lips parted, and he took her mouth the way he wanted to take it.

He drew in a gulp of air through his mouth, inhaling in her taste and scent. It raced through him, stirring his blood and body in a way nothing else could. Man, he wanted her. Needed her. He had to have her now.

She moaned in response. It wasn't a soft moan, either. It was a lustful moan. A *thank-you* kind of sound that spilled from her mouth directly into his and became trapped within their kiss.

He devoured it.

Lucas went after her earlobes. First one and then the other, taking them in his mouth so his tongue could flirt with her satiny gold-star earrings. Against him, he felt her pulse race and her breath quicken.

Or was that his?

He couldn't tell any longer. They had pressed themselves together so tightly he couldn't tell where he stopped and she started.

Her hands quickly reminded him.

Yanking his shirt out of the waistband of the jeans, she delved underneath to his chest to explore. She sought out every muscle, every inch of skin, even the flat nipples buried in his chest hair, until the touching was apparently no longer enough. In a violent motion, she stripped the shirt over his head and sent it flying.

Stirring restlessly against him, Kylie kissed his neck, his collarbone, his shoulders. With her mouth, she retraced the path her hands had taken. Lucas grimaced and managed a strangled groan.

With a mutual effort, her garnet-red sweater came off. Her bra, a flimsy little swatch of ivory silk and lace, was only a few shades lighter than her pale skin. Her nipples were already tightened from arousal and peeked over the bra's lacy edges.

"Very nice," he said, though how he managed something like speech, he didn't know.

Slowly, keeping his eyes connected with hers, he lowered his mouth to one of those rosy nipples and nipped it with his teeth. Panting, from both anticipation and the fierce heat building inside her, Kylie grabbed him by the hair and pulled him to her, forcing him, until he took that nipple into his mouth. Leaving it shiny wet and pebbly hard, he gave the other one the same attention.

"I want more," Kylie insisted.

And she didn't wait. In a move that surprised him, she planted her feet on the sofa. Still straddling him, she rose to a near standing position so she could wiggle free of her loose black pants. Though she was obviously doing this to undress, Lucas took full advantage of it. He halted her in mid-descent by grasping her hips.

She looked down at him. Questioning. And trying to wriggle back onto his lap. Lucas stopped the wriggling. He pressed his mouth to her stomach, circling her navel with his tongue.

"Yes." Kylie nodded.

He went slightly lower. To her panties. There was so little to them he wondered why she'd bothered at all. Definitely not the functional ones he'd gotten a glimpse of at the clinic. The same ivory color as the bra, the piece of silk had a lacy triangle that almost perfectly outlined the triangle of dark blond curls underneath.

"Yes. Yes," she repeated.

He loved hearing those yeses from her and decided to do something to make her keep saying it.

Lucas went even lower. Right to that narrowest point of

the vee of lace. When his tongue touched her through that fragile barrier, her breath hitched, frozen in her throat. Her bottom lip trembled. She soundlessly pleaded for more.

He would definitely give her more.

"Please," she mumbled. "Yes."

It was the yes that flooded him with another jolt of fire. Lucas considered finishing her off right then, right there. He could have those panties off her in no time and put his mouth to good use. What would it be like to see her shatter? To taste her when he brought her to climax? He didn't think he could wait to find out.

He apparently thought about it too long, because Kylie dropped back down and went after his zipper. "I want you now," she announced. "Okay?"

As if he had plans to disagree.

"Lucas?" she whispered.

"Kylie," he answered.

"Watch," she demanded.

"I know who you are," he assured her. "I know *exactly* who you are. I'm glad it's you, Kylie. I want it to be you."

"Good," she mumbled, the one word sounding strangled.

With their gazes locked, his hands latched onto her hips, he entered her. Slowly. As gently and as carefully as their raging need would allow. Sliding hot and deep into her. Lucas stilled just for a second, to absorb and to understand. To savor.

A delicious little smile flickered on Kylie's mouth. And she said, "Yes."

There it was again. A jolt of fire caused by that one word. Lucas cursed, pressing his forehead against her cheek. This was madness and redemption all rolled into one. She was so wet, so snug, he figured this must be paradise. Of course, it might also be the most wicked sin hell had to offer, too. At the moment, he couldn't decide.

At the moment, he didn't think he knew his own name.

Guiding her hips with his hands, Lucas swept her against him, but Kylie soon moved into his rhythm until she took over the pace. She stunned him, pleasured him, until he thought he should beg for mercy. The only thing he knew for certain was he would want her again as soon as they finished. More frightening than that, he would want her tomorrow.

And the next day.

She moved against him until he felt her shiver. Until she was his pinpoint focus. Until all he could see was Kylie.

With her body closing around him, Lucas tossed back his head, the veins of his neck straining at the force of blood pumping through him.

And he went with her.

It was the only place he wanted to go.

Chapter 17

"We may have discovered a cure for the common cold," Lucas commented between gulps of breath.

Kylie did some breath-gulping of her own. "Well, it was a cure for something, that's for sure." Kylie didn't mind that her lungs still felt starved for air. She didn't mind the giddy feeling, because every part of her hummed with contentment and pleasure.

"Regrets?" he asked.

"No way. You?"

In those few seconds that it took him to answer, Kylie felt as if she were waiting for the most important answer she'd ever hear. "My only regret is that I didn't add more foreplay." He slid his hand between their bodies and stroked her belly.

The relief made her smile. "There was nothing wrong with your foreplay. Or the sex." She kissed him, long and hard. "Or you."

Well, nothing wrong except she was falling in love with him. There was no denying it. She was falling, and there was nothing she could do to stop it.

Should she tell him?

It was a risk either way. If she got up, stayed silent and let him think that this was just sex, she might not have another opportunity to tell him that, for her, they'd made love. And it'd changed everything.

The way she felt about him.

The way she felt about herself.

Yes, indeed. It had been a magic cure, and for the first time in three years she felt whole and healed.

And confused.

Because while making love with Lucas had been one of the most wonderful experiences of her life, she was already wondering where this would lead. And she had to admit to herself that it probably wouldn't lead where her heart was trying to take her.

Maybe this was it. All that would happen between them. A one-night stand, of sorts. Maybe in the morning, he'd realize what a mistake it had been and would tell her that he needed to back off. That old proverbial *I need space*. It wouldn't be a lie, either, since this would no doubt take him to a new level of guilt.

Lucas's cell phone rang. Both groaned when they had to break the intimate contact and pull away from each other. While Lucas located his phone in his jacket pocket, she located her pants, top and underwear. Best not to sit around naked in case one of the deputies or the guard was approaching the house.

"Sheriff Creed," she heard Lucas say to the caller. With the phone sandwiched between his shoulder and ear, he fixed his jeans and grabbed his shirt. "Finn, is that you?"

That got her attention. Not in a good way, either. And it frustrated her that it did. A call from Finn shouldn't have caused her adrenaline to kick in.

With her attention now glued to Lucas, Kylie stepped into her pants and pulled them on. She quickly did the same with her bra and top.

"The connection's bad," Lucas continued. "I didn't hear what you said." A pause. Then a few seconds later, he added. "And?"

Judging from his suddenly ramrod-straight posture and his tight jaw, whatever Finn was saying had captured Lucas's attention, as well.

"Okay. Of course, I'll tell her," Lucas said, and he pushed the End Call button. "Finn got back your test results from the blood he drew the night of the kidnapping attempt."

She certainly hadn't forgotten about that, or the drug that the kidnappers had used to try to sedate her. But with everything else going on, she'd put it in the back of her mind. It quickly moved to the forefront.

Kylie protectively slid her hand over her stomach. And waited.

"According to Finn, everything looks fine. The drug was chloroform, but it was in such small amounts that it won't harm the baby."

She released the breath that she didn't even know she'd been holding. It should have been wonderful news. A reason for celebration. But since the info had come from Finn, it automatically came under suspicion.

"You think he'd lie about something like that?" Kylie asked.

Lucas shook his head, then shrugged. "I want the tests repeated as soon as we can safely get to your doctor in San Antonio."

Heaven knew when that might be.

However, Lucas was right. Despite all the danger, the baby was their number one priority, and somehow they'd have to find a way to redo that test.

Because Lucas looked weary and frustrated, Kylie went to him and took his hand. She placed it on her stomach and adjusted it so that his palm was just over the little bumps and kicks that the baby was making.

"He or she is healthy," Kylie promised, though both knew it was a promise she had no control over. "By Father's Day, you'll be holding your child in your arms, and everything that's happening now will be just unpleasant memories."

He stared at her a moment as if considering that. "You'll be leaving when the baby's born."

It wasn't a question. More like a confirmation. It seemed as if he were waiting for her to deny it. But she couldn't. Even after making love to him only minutes earlier, she didn't have a clue if they had a future. He certainly hadn't asked her to be in his future.

Or the baby's.

Kylie opened her mouth—to say what exactly, she didn't know. Lucas opened his mouth, as well. Closed it. She closed hers too. And they stood there staring at each other. Apparently waiting for the other to make the first move.

The noise interrupted them both.

There was a loud crash. Not exactly a foreign sound, either. It was glass shattering followed by something metallic landing on the floor. The sound had come from the kitchen.

God, was someone breaking into the house? And if so, where the devil were the deputies and the guard? No one should have gotten close enough to break in.

She grabbed her gun and turned to rush toward that

noise, but Lucas caught her arm to stop her. He snatched up his own shoulder holster and weapon and practically pushed her back onto the sofa.

"Stay down," he warned.

Kylie did. Only because she didn't want to break his suddenly intense concentration. But she strapped on her shoulder holster, as he did, and drew her weapon so she'd be ready to react.

Lucas inched toward the sound, using the furniture and the wall as cover. Kylie watched as he peered around the edge of the arched entryway that led into the kitchen.

He cursed.

Then he put his hand to his mouth and coughed.

She started to ask what was wrong, but the question wasn't necessary. Kylie saw the wispy smoke and caught the scent of something pungent that immediately caused her to cough.

"It's tear gas!" Lucas shouted.

His cough-punctuated shout was muted somewhat by yet more breaking glass. Also in the kitchen. The sound was followed by another metal object landing on the clay-tiled floor. Probably another canister of tear gas because the yellow smoke seemed to double in volume.

And intensity.

Sweet heaven. The kidnappers had obviously returned, and they were trying to flush them out of the house.

She clamped her hand over her mouth, but that didn't stop the fumes from making their way into her eyes, nose and throat. Mercy, she couldn't breathe. Could barely see. And her lungs burned.

Somehow Lucas made it to her, though he was coughing, as well. He grabbed her arm and got them moving down the hall, away from the fumes. But the fumes seemed to be right on their heels, swallowing them up. Her first instinct was to head outside, to the fresh air, but that was exactly what the kidnappers wanted them to do. Once outside, Lucas and she would likely be ambushed. Of course, staying inside didn't appeal too much, either.

She needed air, and she needed it now.

Lucas shoved open the door to the nursery, and they hurried inside. Kylie gulped in a much needed breath and detected only a trace of the tear gas in the room. But it wouldn't be long before it seeped into every part of the house. Worse, there was another shattering of glass.

Another canister landed inside.

She hadn't needed that third canister to know they were in trouble, but it seemed to be the punctuation mark that sent her heart pounding.

The pounding only got worse when she detected another scent.

Smoke.

Real smoke.

Not from a tear gas canister, either.

Lucas whipped around to face her, and in the same motion, he lifted his head and sniffed. "Hell," he grumbled. "The house is on fire. Let's move."

At first, Kylie thought that Lucas might have planned for them to escape through the window, but he elbowed the door closed, locking them in. Then he grabbed the crib box and shoved it against the bottom of the door to create a barricade from the smoke and tear gas. A temporary barricade, because fire could easily eat through that.

Lucas reached for the pull cord that drew down the wooden attic flap. He unfolded the stairs and stepped on the first rung.

"Stay right behind me," Lucas insisted. "I need to make sure it's safe up here."

She glanced over her shoulders and saw that tear gas had started to ooze in around the doorframe.

Lucas paused at the top step, looked around and then motioned for her to join him. Kylie didn't waste any time because each passing second brought in more of the fumes and smoke. She'd dealt with tear gas during her training at the police academy, but she had no idea if this would harm the baby. And here she'd just received assurance from Finn that all was well as to the effects of the chloroform. That should have been reason for celebration. Or at least relief. Instead, she'd bypassed the relief stage and had been launched into a terrifying ordeal that she might not survive.

Kylie tried not to let the fear take hold of her. She didn't want to die. Not here. Not like this with her unborn child still inside her. But the adrenaline was screaming for her to run. To do something—anything—to escape. It was a powerful, overwhelming sensation.

Fight or flight.

Even if either option could get her killed.

"We're going to get out of this," she heard Lucas say. Maybe he'd sensed her thoughts. Or maybe she looked terrified. The humming was a dead giveaway, too. Kylie didn't care what'd prompted his response. She held on to it like a lifeline and followed Lucas into the attic.

The floorboards creaked beneath them as they meandered their way through the cluttered space. Cardboard boxes and trunks were crammed against the walls, but there was ample space for them to walk toward the attic vent at the far end.

Kylie forced herself to concentrate on her breathing. It wouldn't be a good time to hyperventilate. Besides, things were already in motion. If the kidnappers were out there waiting for them, there would be a shootout. She didn't want to speculate about who would win.

They had to win.

Their baby's life was at stake.

Lucas reached the far end of the attic first. There wasn't a window there, but a large porthole of sorts with vented slats. He yanked out those slats, leaving them a venue to fire at attackers or, if that failed, a means of escape.

Well, maybe.

Kylie peered out into the moonlit yard. She didn't see any gunmen or kidnappers. Nor any sign of the deputies or guard. There were just ghostly wisps of smoke and a whole lot of open space between them and the pasture. Still, if they could get out of the house and to the pasture, then they could use the surrounding woods as cover.

Lucas continued to watch the yard. And cursed. Which probably meant he didn't see their attackers, either. "I need to climb out on the roof."

Kylie shook her head, but the nonverbal disapproval was useless. Because she knew Lucas was going to go out there anyway.

He *had* to.

There was no other choice.

The house was on fire; if they stayed put, they'd be burned alive. And they couldn't just go barreling out into the yard, either or they'd be gunned down.

Lucas grabbed a portable steel chain escape ladder that was attached to the wall and unrolled it. He shoved it onto the roof and brushed a kiss on her cheek. "Stay put until I give the okay."

He didn't wait for her to agree. Lucas used one of the nearby boxes for leverage so he could hoist himself through the porthole. He landed on his belly and immediately re-positioned his gun so he'd be ready to fire.

Kylie didn't take her attention off him, but she was aware that smoke was beginning to fill the attic. She didn't think it was her imagination that it was getting hotter, too. She could hear the flames devouring the house.

So that she'd be able to breathe, she moved closer to the porthole. Closer to the fresh air. And she aimed her own weapon so that she could back up Lucas.

"Nothing," Lucas said. "Where the hell are the men who are supposed to be protecting us?"

Kylie hadn't wanted to speculate, but she did anyway. And it wasn't good, either. She didn't know the guard or the deputies, but she doubted if all three were incompetent enough to miss tear gas canisters being noisily shot into the house. That meant the three men were likely incapacitated.

Or worse.

She heard the roar and hiss behind her, and she risked a backward glance. There were no longer just wisps of smoke, but a column of the black stuff rising through the attic opening. It was also coming in through the floorboards. The fire was moving fast and was no doubt already beneath them.

"Lucas?" she whispered.

He looked back at her, and even in the moonlight, Kylie saw his eyes widen.

"Get out of there now," he insisted.

She didn't need a second invitation. The smoke was already so thick that it was cutting her breath in two. Lucas held out his hand to help her, but she waved him off. "You keep watch. I can do this."

Kylie stepped onto the box and crawled through the port-hole and onto the roof. She scrambled to position herself, not right next to Lucas, but in the opposite direction. At least this way, with two of them to return fire, they wouldn't be blindsided.

For what it was worth.

And it was worth only a few minutes at most because Kylie knew they couldn't stay on the roof.

She peered down at the front of the house and saw the orange-red flames lashing through what had once been the windows.

"How bad?" Lucas asked.

"Bad."

Lucas didn't waste any time. He used his foot to lower the chain ladder to the side of the house. The ladder clanged against the exterior. Probably alerting anyone and everyone. Not that they hadn't been alerted already. If the kidnappers had set the fire either intentionally or unintentionally with the gas canisters, they were no doubt watching and waiting for Lucas and her to attempt an escape. Hopefully, though, they wouldn't be looking in the direction of the roof.

"We go down together," Lucas instructed, "with me standing behind you so you won't be directly in the line of fire."

Despite her heartbeat pounding in her ears and the smoke clogging her lungs, she saw the flaws in that plan. Serious flaws. "Not a good idea. You'd have to hook your arms through the chain just to keep from falling. You'd have no way to defend yourself."

"But you and the baby would be protected."

Okay, there was another lump in her throat. More than a lump. It sent her heart soaring to know that he'd give up his life for the baby. But Kylie couldn't let Lucas's offer to protect her at all costs factor into this.

"If they start shooting, we both need to be able to return

fire. Lucas, it's our only chance of all of us making it out of here alive, and you know it."

Kylie could see the debate going on in his eyes, but she knew that debate couldn't last long. Beneath them, the flames were roaring, churning out yet more suffocating smoke, flames and searing heat. It wouldn't be long before the entire house collapsed.

"Let's go," Lucas finally said. And he climbed onto the ladder. So that he was facing out. He hooked his left arm around the linked chains, so he could keep his balance, but his shooting hand was free.

Kylie followed him. Not slowly either. They moved quickly, both trying to keep a vigilant eye on their surroundings. Hard to do, though, when she couldn't see. The smoke was already too thick to get a good look at the yard or much of anything else.

With each step, Kylie wondered if it'd be her last, and she prayed. Mercy, did she ever pray.

Lucas stepped onto the ground and didn't waste a second. He took hold of her arm and got them moving. Fast. Not toward the pasture and the woods, though. With a firm grip on her wrist, he barreled out from the meager cover of the house and started toward the barn. It wasn't hard to find. There was a dim light on inside, and the milky yellow illumination cut through the blanket of smoke and the darkness.

They had gone only a few steps before a bullet whistled past their heads.

Chapter 18

Lucas hooked his arm around Kylie's waist and shoved her to the ground.

And it wasn't a second too soon.

Another bullet smashed into the side of the house, in the exact spot where Kylie had just been standing. He didn't want to think of how close she'd come to being killed.

Putting himself between her and the line of fire, he dragged them to a row of shrubs and raised flower beds. It wasn't much protection against bullets, but it was better than standing out in the open.

Lucas did a quick check to make sure Kylie was all right. Her breathing was rough and fast, and there was a smear of dirt on her right cheek, but other than that, she appeared to be okay.

For now.

He knew that could change in the blink of an eye.

Lucas looked out through the shrubs and checked the

grounds. Specifically, the area from where those shots had originated. And, thanks to the light from the fire, he quickly spotted the shadows behind a corral fence that was adjacent to the barn.

There were two men armed with rifles with scopes mounted on them.

And the figures weren't stationary, either. The men moved slowly, barely an inch with each step while shielding themselves behind the wooden fence. With each step, they got closer, and Lucas's heart pounded faster and harder, until he thought it might come out of his chest.

Lucas figured he could probably get off a shot if he left cover. Of course, that would leave Kylie in a highly vulnerable spot since the remaining gunman would no doubt turn that rifle on her.

Hell.

How had things come to this? Lucas couldn't take the time to berate himself, but he'd sure do it later. He should have insisted they leave the ranch while they had a chance. He should have pressed harder to find a safe house. Now, his mistake just might cost them their lives.

A chunk of the flaming roof tumbled to the ground, bringing with it more smoke and fire. Lucas waited, praying the smoke would soon clear because he needed to move Kylie.

They were much too close to the burning house.

For that matter, they were much too close to those gunmen.

Beside him, Kylie whispered something, but Lucas wasn't able to hear what she said. A blast drowned her out. A bullet slammed into the ground right next to her head. And it hadn't come from either of the two riflemen.

No, this shot had been fired from the general area of the storage shed.

So, there were three gunmen. At least. That didn't do much to steady his heart. He couldn't see the one near the storage shed, but he still had a view of the others. Kylie's and his only chance was to turn the odds in their favor.

"I'll take the one on the right," Kylie said as if reading his mind.

It was the only thing they could do—eliminate the riflemen—but still Lucas debated it. Though a debate was useless. Both Kylie and he knew what they had to do. It was their only chance.

"Stay down as much as you can," he ordered.

"Ditto," Kylie ordered in return.

They exchanged one last glance, and in that too-brief moment, a thousand things passed between them. Lucas wished he had time to tell her things he should have said. But there was no time. Kylie moved, levering herself up slightly so she'd have a better position.

Lucas did the same.

He took aim and squeezed the trigger. Beside him, Kylie did the same. One shot each. Thick, loud blasts that tore through the smoke and moonlight. And Lucas immediately ducked back down. Thank God, Kylie did, as well.

And he waited.

Listening.

"Two down," Kylie said. "One to go."

Only then did Lucas realize she'd lifted her head to look through the shrubs. Cursing, he pushed her back down, came up and fired. Not one round. But three. Finally, he saw the rifleman in the pasture collapse onto the ground.

There wasn't a second of reprieve. Definitely not even time to take a breath.

Above them, Lucas heard the groaning sound of the wood, and he saw what was left of the attic tear away from the frame of the house. It was coming down.

Right on them.

Lucas grabbed Kylie's arm, though she had already started to move as well. They launched themselves off the ground.

"The barn," Lucas shouted.

And he let go of her so he could take aim. Even though they'd taken out all the visible shooters, that didn't mean there weren't others. He knew there was still a risk of being shot, and that the person could easily do that while they were out in the open. However, it would have been an even greater risk for Kylie and him to remain by the shrubs.

The attic and a good portion of remaining roof crashed onto the flower beds and sent sparks and flames flying. Lucas didn't look back. Instead, Kylie and he raced toward the barn and ducked inside.

No shots.

Thank God.

But that didn't mean they were safe.

They'd barely stepped inside when Lucas heard something he didn't want to hear. There were the sounds of a struggle, and there was the smell of fear.

He pushed Kylie behind him again and saw what had caused those sounds.

It was Cordelia.

Kylie blinked to make sure the smoke hadn't affected her vision. It hadn't. Cordelia was there in the barn. Standing with her back pressed against one of the stall gates.

Sweet merciful heaven, was she the person responsible for those gunmen?

If so, Kylie knew she didn't stand a chance of holding her temper because those three men had nearly gotten them killed.

"What are you doing here?" Lucas demanded, taking the question right out of Kylie's mouth.

But Cordelia didn't answer. She stood there, shivering. Trembling, actually, from head to toe. And it was only then that Kylie noticed she wasn't wearing a jacket. In fact, not even long sleeves. She stood there barefoot in only a pair of girlie pink silk lounging pajamas that were dotted with tiny flowers. Hardly the attire for a trek outside in January.

Or for an attack.

It was on the tip of Kylie's tongue to ask what had happened, but Kylie's question was delayed when Cordelia's eyes angled in the direction behind her.

Into the darkened stall.

Kylie and Lucas both aimed their weapons at the stall. And Kendrick Windham raised his head. Kylie saw Windham's hands covered with surgical gloves. And then she saw the gun. Not pointed at Lucas and her, but at Cordelia.

"He kidnapped me," Cordelia muttered, her voice ripe with fear.

"Guilty," Windham volunteered. "I'd so hoped it wouldn't come down to this." He sounded only mildly annoyed that he now had a hostage situation on his hands.

Kylie was annoyed, as well, but there was nothing *mild* about her reaction. They'd moved from one dangerous situation to another. Worse, neither Lucas nor she had a clean shot. If she fired now, she'd put Cordelia, and ultimately them, in even greater danger.

"Your hired guns are dead," Kylie gladly let him know. It also let him know that he was outnumbered. Of course, that didn't take away his advantage, not with his gun aimed at Cordelia.

"Hired guns? That's such a generous term for them. I'd prefer to call them idiots. All they had to do was kidnap you and bring you to me. But did they do that? No. They had to get Sheriff Creed here involved. The last person who should be involved in anything like this."

"Yeah. I see your point," Lucas interjected. Unlike Cordelia, there was no fear in his voice. But Kylie heard lots of determination. He wouldn't give up without a fight. "If your *idiots* hadn't botched the kidnapping, then you could have killed Kylie, and I would have never known about the illegal surrogacy activity. Or that she was carrying my baby."

"Oh, trust me, I would have come up with a reasonable substitute for a child. There's always a solution when money's involved. After all, I wouldn't have wanted to forfeit your final payment."

Money was his motive. Windham obviously wanted to silence her, and now Lucas, because they would have ultimately threatened his income.

"What did you do to the guard and the deputies?" Lucas demanded.

"They're alive. I used tranquilizer darts on them just like the ones I used on the dogs. Despite what you think of me, I don't enjoy killing. But I'll do it, if necessary. I think I proved that with Tiffany Smith."

"Among others," Lucas interjected.

"No others. Only Ms. Smith, who had a penchant for not keeping her mouth shut. Thankfully, she was one of a kind. My other surrogates are obedient and make me what I am—a very wealthy man. They'll continue to make me wealthy, too. Which is why we need to end this little encounter soon before those men you hired wake up from the sedation."

So, time was on their side. Maybe if the guard or one of the deputies came out of the sedation earlier than Windham had anticipated, they'd call for backup. However, Kylie couldn't count on that happening.

"You're holding an innocent woman hostage," Kylie pointed out. Then, she paused. Rethought that. "Cordelia *is* innocent, isn't she?"

"Of course, I am!" Cordelia snapped. Gone was some of the fear, and in its place was more than a little anger. Kylie understood that anger.

Windham had put all of them in grave danger.

"Well, she's innocent only in a legal sense," Windham explained. "But the police will think differently. It's her gun, by the way. So, her fingerprints are already on it. I need a scapegoat, and that means I'll have to set her up to take the blame for all of this."

Cordelia's mouth tightened. "You what?" But asking that unnecessary question wasn't the only thing she did.

"Don't!" Lucas shouted.

Cordelia either didn't hear him or didn't heed his warning because she turned, apparently to launch herself at Kendrick Windham.

Windham was fast. And lethal. He repositioned his gun a few inches lower and pulled the trigger.

The bullet sliced through the outer edge of Cordelia's shoulder. Cordelia screamed, a bloodcurdling sound. But she didn't fall to the ground as Kylie had hoped she would. That would have given her a clear shot at Windham. Instead, Windham hooked his left arm around Cordelia and fastened her back against his chest.

A human shield.

Except this human shield was bleeding, moaning and cursing in pain.

Windham jammed the gun to Cordelia's head and stared at Kylie and Lucas. "Now that you know I mean business, drop your weapons. And I won't ask twice. The next bullet goes in her head."

This was being caught between a proverbial rock and a hard place. If they didn't put down their guns, Kylie had no doubts that Windham would kill Cordelia and then try to kill them. Of course, they'd be attempting to kill him, as well. Which meant bullets would be flying.

Someone would die.

And Kylie couldn't be sure that the someone would be Windham.

"Don't shoot her," Kylie said to Windham. Not that a request or even begging would help at this point. But she hoped to distract him long enough for either Lucas or her to do something. "It's obviously me that you want."

"What the hell are you doing?" Lucas demanded in a gruff whisper.

Windham paused, staring at her. "You're absolutely right."

Before the last syllable left his mouth, he fired a shot at Lucas. It missed.

Barely.

Lucas scrambled to take cover against one of the empty stalls. He yelled for Kylie to do the same. But Kylie didn't have a chance. Windham shoved Cordelia straight at her. The impact rammed their bodies together, catching them off balance.

Kylie's gun clattered to the floor.

And before she could regain her balance, Windham reached for her. Kylie had one thought.

A horrible one.

She would die before she had the chance to tell Lucas that she was in love with him.

Windham moved fast.

Too fast for Lucas to get off a safe shot or for Kylie to try to escape. The man seized Kylie's arm, and in the same motion he shoved the semiautomatic against the back of her head.

Lucas immediately aimed his weapon and stepped out from the cover of the stall. "Put down your gun, Windham, and let her go."

Lucas said the words by rote after years of having been a sheriff, but there was nothing rote about the fury that rose in his throat. Or the rock-hard knot that tightened in his stomach.

The SOB had Kylie.

Lucas met her gaze. For only a second. It was all he could handle, or it'd distract him at a time when he needed no more distractions. However, he couldn't completely dismiss that look he saw in Kylie's blue eyes. Fear, yes. But not as much as he'd expected to see there. She was doing her best to keep herself together.

"This won't help," Lucas said as calmly as he could manage. He glanced at Cordelia to make sure she wasn't bleeding profusely. Thankfully, she was lying on the floor and had managed to clamp her hand over her wound. But she still needed medical attention ASAP. "Surrender your weapon, and you won't be hurt. You've got my word on that."

"Your word. And that's supposed to make me feel reassured? Well, it doesn't. The only reassurance I want is a trip away from this place, and I want Ms. Monroe to come with me."

So he could kill her.

And that's why Lucas had to figure out how to end this now.

Windham kept stepping back, moving toward the back exit of the barn. Kylie's expression didn't change, but she no doubt knew where this scum was taking her. Her life wouldn't be worth a dime if he got her outside the line of fire. He'd simply kill her when he no longer needed a hostage to escape.

And worse, Lucas wasn't sure how long Kylie could keep up that cool veneer. If she panicked, Windham would likely kill her on the spot. In his experience, criminals didn't like noisy hostages.

"Tell me what it'll take to get you to release her," Lucas offered. He hoped it'd stop Windham from moving.

It didn't.

"Trade me for her," Lucas suggested. "I'm a sheriff. The cops will be more than willing to bargain with you if you're holding me."

"You don't understand. I have no wish to bargain."

In other words, he wanted to carry out his plan of killing all of them.

That couldn't happen.

He couldn't lose Kylie and the baby. He just couldn't. And in that moment, he realized just how true that was. He only hoped he got the chance to tell her. Because he was about to do whatever it took, including sacrificing himself, to make sure she got out of this alive.

Lucas quit thinking, and he reacted out of instinct to protect Kylie and their baby. He lunged toward Windham, only to see Kylie slam her elbow into the man's stomach and tear away from him. She dove forward to the floor, grabbed her weapon and came up ready to fire.

Windham turned in her direction.

He also turned his gun on her.

Lucas's response was automatic. He aimed high and fast. For the head. Two shots. A double tap of gunfire. Shots not meant to distract or injure. Shots meant to kill.

The gun blasts ripped through the barn. Kylie didn't move. She kept her gun level, in case Lucas's shots hadn't done the job.

But they had.

Windham collapsed into a heap, his weapon dropping to the ground.

Lucas hurried to the man to make sure he was dead. He was. The shots had done exactly what they had been intended to do.

"It's over?" Cordelia asked.

Lucas nodded and turned back to Kylie. She was pale and shaky, but other than that, she was fine. He couldn't say the same for himself. It might take him a dozen years or so to get over almost having lost her.

He made his way to her and pulled her into his arms.

Chapter 19

Kylie came out of the kitchen and set the Blue Willow plate on the table. She had a fork in her hand and was ready to do some groveling.

Finn stared at the contents of the dish as if it were navel lint. "What is it?"

"Crow."

His eyebrow arched. "Crow?"

"Well, symbolically it's crow. Literally, it's blackened veggie beef with peppercorns that I've sorta shaped to look like a crow." Even Kylie had to admit it didn't look that appetizing.

"It looks more like a charcoal bunny," Lucas pointed out.

"Maybe. But let's all use our imagination and think crow." She turned to Finn. "That's why I called and asked you to drop by—so you could see me eat crow."

Finn glanced at Lucas, who just shrugged. "Hey, I just

wanted to apologize for thinking you were a criminal. The crow was Kylie's idea."

Finn stabbed some of the "crow" with his fork and had Kylie sample it.

"Yuck." She managed to swallow it, and that seemed to be all the punishment he was willing to force on her. "I'm really sorry."

"Me, too," Lucas added.

Finn nodded, trying to appear to be his old cocky self, but Kylie thought he was a little sentimental about all of this. "Apologies accepted from both of you."

Probably so they wouldn't have to look at it, Lucas put the plate on the counter behind him, and he and Finn finished off the longneck bottles of beer. Kylie settled in for her evening with a glass of milk, which she'd spiked with gobs of malted chocolate syrup, her own version of a celebratory treat. And there was no mistaking that they were celebrating. Windham was dead, the illegal operation had been shut down, and a new clinic would soon open to serve the needs of those who wanted qualified, legitimate surrogates. Even more, they were alive. All was right with the world.

Well, almost.

"How are your dogs?" Lucas asked.

"They're back to their old sweet selves. Cordelia, too."

"Sweet?" Kylie challenged. She started to sit down in the empty chair next to Lucas, but he snared her and pulled her into his lap instead.

That earned them a little *hmm* sound from Finn.

"Cordelia is on the mend and is singing your and Lucas's praises," Finn continued. "She's not using the s-word anymore. As in *sue*. She dropped the lawsuit. And she said she hoped you would forgive her for all the ugly things she said and did to you. I'm telling you—Cordelia's had a real change of heart,"

"I guess having someone save your life does that to you," Lucas concluded dryly. "Isaac Dupont doesn't seem so riled at us either."

"Probably because we cleared his name by nailing Kendrick Windham," Kylie pointed out. "According to Sgt. O'Malley, SAPD discovered that Windham had doctored all sorts of paperwork to make Dupont look guilty. I guess Windham did that to cover himself in case the clinic was investigated. If it hadn't been for that doctored paperwork, I would have never suspected Dupont, and I certainly wouldn't have *alluded* to him in the article I wrote."

Lucas circled his arm around her and put his hand on her belly.

Finn obviously didn't miss that, either. Both his eyebrows lifted. "I get the feeling I should go so you two can have some private time."

"We already had private time before you got here," Kylie teased.

But Finn got to his feet anyway and tossed his empty beer bottle in the recycling bin by the sink. He looked at them. "So, are you guys going to shack up here at Kylie's place?"

Lucas nodded. "Until I can rebuild the house."

And Kylie didn't mind if that took, oh, forever to do that. Still, she was probably looking at three months at most. In other words, Lucas would be in his new home about six weeks before he became a father.

The corner of Finn's mouth hitched. "You two really look like a couple."

"A couple of what?" Lucas joked.

"That's to be determined." Finn took his jacket from the

back of the chair, slipped it on and then extracted a folded sheet of paper from his pocket. "Okay. Here's my way of tormenting you for temporarily believing I was a depraved kidnapper and killer."

"What is it?" Kylie asked suspiciously.

"I've written down the gender of your baby. And a name suggestion to go along with it. Since both of you have said you didn't want this information, then I'll just put it here on the table, where it can stay for the next four and a half months. Because I know you won't change your mind and peek."

Kylie and Lucas exchanged glances. "Oh, that's cruel," she let Finn know.

"My form of revenge." He kissed Kylie's cheek and gave Lucas a friendly jab on the arm. "Be happy, guys, because, heaven knows, you deserve it." He added a wave. "Don't get up. I'll see myself out."

Because Lucas's embrace was far more interesting than her chocolate milk or seeing Finn out, she set the glass on the counter next to the "crow" and snuggled against him. "You won't mind the gossip about us living here together?"

"Maybe I will. A little. I'm an old-fashioned kind of guy."

She turned on his lap, repositioning herself so that she faced him. "Old-fashioned guys don't have sofa sex."

"They do. Floor sex, too."

Kylie smiled. "Add car sex while listening to Bob Dylan, and you'll get me hot enough to skip the foreplay."

He touched his mouth to hers. "What if I don't want to skip the foreplay?"

"Even better."

In fact, a lot of things were suddenly better. Especially

the alignment of their bodies. Kylie was already calculating how quickly she could undress him.

But Lucas obviously had something else on his mind.

He cupped her face in both his hands. "When Windham had that gun on you—"

Kylie pressed her fingers to his mouth. "You don't have to talk about that."

"But I do." He eased her fingers away and repeated it so it was no longer mumbled. "Because I want you to know what went through my mind, what I felt, what I realized. And what I realized was that I'd forgiven you—and me—for what happened to Marissa."

Kylie was afraid to say anything, afraid to move, afraid to breathe for fear he'd take those words back. Words that she had prayed she would hear him say.

"You've done so much for me," he continued, his voice a little thin now. "You made the sacrifices, Kylie. Huge sacrifices. You were willing to leave your home, your life and child just to make me happy. You gave me everything. *Everything.* You healed me. You saved me. And during those moments when Windham had that gun aimed at you, I knew I couldn't lose you. Ever."

"The baby—"

"Not the baby," he interrupted. "*You.* Don't get me wrong, I love this baby. But in that moment, I realized I love you, too."

She teared up immediately.

"Sheesh, I made you cry." He hurried to wipe the tears from her cheeks.

"It's the pregnancy hormones."

He laughed, low and husky. "Somehow, I knew you were going to say that."

"Then, do you also know that I'm going to say I love you, too?"

Lucas swallowed and nodded. "I'd hoped you would."

"You don't have to hope. It's as real and as strong as our baby's kicks."

Another nod. "If I weren't a cowboy, I'd cry." Judging from the quiver in his voice, he was on the verge of it.

Kylie kissed him. It wasn't a simple peck, either. It was long and French. Exactly what she thought the moment required. Because she wanted to remember this moment for the rest of her life.

Lucas loved her.

She loved him.

And they were going to have a baby. She didn't have a clue what she'd done to deserve this kind of happiness, but she was going to seize it and not let go. Ever.

That kiss left them breathless, and it left Kylie wanting more. A lot more. "So, would you like sex before or after dinner?" she asked.

"Both."

Kylie laughed. "I think I'm going to like having you for a housemate," she whispered.

"You'll like it even more having me for a husband."

And just like that, she teared up again. "Blasted hormones."

Once more, he wiped away the tears and let his fingers linger on her face. "Will you marry me, Kylie? Will you be my wife so we can raise our baby together?"

That didn't just produce tears, it took her breath away. "Absolutely. Will you marry me?"

"In a heartbeat."

The happiness flooded through her. The warmth seemed to fill all the dark, lonely places. There were also more tears. She hadn't ever remembered being happy enough to cry. So, was this what love was all about? And better yet, this was only the beginning.

Lucas stood, scooping her up in his arms, and headed toward the bedroom. But then he stopped. She soon saw what had captured his attention.

She eyed the note that Finn had left on the table. Lucas eyed it too, and then they eyed each other.

"Should we?" he asked at the same moment that she asked, "You want to?"

Kylie debated it. Lucas obviously did, as well, which was exactly the kind of sweet torture that Finn wanted them to experience. Finally, Lucas groaned, and while balancing her in his arms, he snatched up the note. He plopped it onto her belly and let her have the honor of opening it.

They read it aloud together.

"You should name him Bob Dylan Creed."

"A boy," Lucas said. "We're having a son." Now, there were tears in his eyes, proving real cowboys did cry when the situation dictated. And this situation definitely dictated. "But we're not naming him that."

"The name's negotiable," Kylie assured him. And this time she was the one to wipe the tears from his eyes. "What's not negotiable is everything else. Getting married, having this baby, living happily ever after."

"Especially that," he assured her.

And to prove it, Lucas kissed her. Long and French didn't even begin to describe this as his mouth thoroughly claimed hers. Building the fire and need inside her.

When he was done, Kylie knew she'd been kissed by a man who truly loved her.

* * * * *